A COLOURFUL DEATH

Also by *Carola Dunn*

A COLOURFUL DEATH

A Cornish Mystery

CAROLA DUNN

CONSTABLE • LONDON

CONSTABLE

First published in the US by Minotaur Books,
an imprint of St Martin's Publishing Group, New York, 2010

First published in the UK by C&R Crime,
an imprint of Constable & Robinson, 2013

Reprinted in 2016 by Constable

5 7 9 10 8 6

A CIP catalogue record for this book
is available from the British Library.

ISBN 978-1-78033-649-7

Printed and bound in Great Britain by
CPI Group (UK) Ltd, Croydon CR0 4YY

Papers used by Constable are from well-managed forests and
other responsible sources

MIX
Paper from
responsible sources
FSC® C104740

Constable
An imprint of
Little, Brown Book Group
Carmelite House
50 Victoria Embankment
London EC4Y 0DZ

An Hachette UK Company
www.hachette.co.uk

www.littlebrown.co.uk

AUTHOR'S NOTE

Port Mabyn is a fictional village in a fictional world lurking somewhere between my childhood memories of Cornwall and the present reality. Though in many cases I have used the irresistible names of real places, the reader should not expect necessarily to find them where I've put them. The topography resembles the North Coast of Cornwall in general, but not in particulars. The Constabulary of the Royal Duchy of Cornwall (CaRaDoC) has no existence outside my imagination. For information about the real Cornwall, I refer the reader to countless works of non-fiction, or, better still, I suggest a visit.

ACKNOWLEDGEMENTS

My thanks to: librarians Claire Morgan and Joanne Laing of the Cornish Studies Library in Redruth and Paula Nederpel of Padstow Library; Beth Franzese, for advice on Aikido moves; D. P. Lyle, MD, creator of http://writersforensicsblog.wordpress.com as well as several books on forensics for writers; Larry Karp, MD, author of the Ragtime Historical Mystery Trilogy; and last, but not least, to my sister Helen for her patience in driving me (I'm terrified of driving in England) to Launceston and Bodmin and waiting while I explored, and my son Joe, daughter-in-law Terri, and grandkids Maggie and Colin for taking me to Padstow and leaving me to explore the town while they went on to reconnoitre Trevone Bay for me (and for picking me up in the right place at the right time—not easy when it meant abandoning a beach on a sunny day).

A COLOURFUL DEATH

ONE

Eleanor parked the aged pea-green Morris Minor in the Launceston station car-park, next to a snazzy red Mini. Teazle, perched on top of a bag of donated clothes on the back seat, gave a questioning yip.

"Yes, you can come. Wait a minute, you need your lead. Where did I put it?"

The lead was found on the floor by the passenger seat. Eleanor clipped it onto the Westie's collar and they went into the station.

"Afternoon, Mrs Trewynn," said the porter. "Beautiful day. Off to London, are you, you and the little dog?" He chirruped at Teazle, who was sniffing the turn-ups of his uniform trousers. She gave a perfunctory wag of her perfunctory tail.

"Good afternoon, Mr Lobcot. No, I'm meeting the down train. My neighbour, Nick Gresham, has been in town."

Lobcot glanced at the station clock. "Five minutes to wait. She's on time, seemingly. Ah, they'll be shutting us down any day now and you'll have to go to Bodmin Parkway to catch a train. At least, till they close that, too."

"Well, it is a bit closer to Port Mabyn, but the train journey takes longer and the fare's more. Besides, my niece works in Launceston. When I brought Nick to catch his train to London, I met her for lunch."

"That'll be Detective Sergeant Pencarrow, I expect?"

"That's right." Having spent her working life travelling the world, Eleanor was often amazed at how country-people seemed to know everything about everyone. She didn't even live in Launceston. But then, the papers had made hay with that nasty business . . . Better not to think about it. She still shuddered at the memory of the dreadful photo that had seemed to show dear Megan arresting her. At least that one had been printed only in the *Sketch*, not the *North Cornwall Times*.

She nodded to the chatty porter and took Teazle for a stroll down the platform. It was indeed a glorious June day. A slight breeze ruffled Eleanor's white curls, flapped her cotton skirt, and gently herded puffs of cloud across the sky like a border collie with a flock of sheep. She would have liked to break into a few of her Aikido exercises, not having had time to practise today, though she had walked Teazle. How Lobcot would have stared!

As they turned at the end of the platform to head back towards the ticket office and waiting room, a whistle tooted in the distance. The train slid round the curve, pulled by a sleek diesel engine with far less noise, smell, and dirt than steam, though none of the charm.

"Nick's coming home," she said to the dog, who looked up at her expectantly with a vigorous wag. Teazle approved of Nick, a reliable source of scraps of batter from fried fish and other interesting tidbits. "I wonder how he's fared. The trouble with recommending one friend to another is that if it doesn't work out, one feels ridiculously guilty."

Quite a few people descended from the train, though nowhere near the crowds that would arrive later in the tourist season, after schools broke up. Eleanor spotted Nick's tall, lean figure as he waved to her and jumped down from the rear carriage, his long pony-tail swinging. For once his clothes appeared to be free of smears and splotches of paint. In fact he looked quite smart in his tan slacks and blue shirt, even though he wasn't wearing a tie. Eleanor wasn't sure he possessed one.

He carried his rucksack by the strap in one hand. He must have put his picture-carrier in the luggage van under the care of the guard rather than try to cram it into the rack. But he came to meet her rather than turn back to retrieve it.

Eleanor frowned. Nick was an even-tempered chap, surely not the sort to do anything drastic like destroy his best work because the gallery had turned him down. Besides, as he approached, she saw he was grinning.

He dropped the rucksack and picked her up in a hug. She yelped, and so did Teazle as the lead tightened.

"Sorry, girl!" He put Eleanor down, and stooped to ruffle Teazle's little white head. "I see Mrs Stearns gave you my message about the train. Thanks for coming. I tried to ring you from Paddington but you were always out, you gadabout."

"Probably walking Teazle. The weather's been so lovely, almost too warm for exercise in the afternoons, so we've been walking in the mornings. Nick, where are your pictures? What—"

"I didn't want Mrs Stearns to know before you did. Your friend Mr Alarian kept both of them. He's going to hang them, and if they sell reasonably quickly, he'll take a couple more. And if *they* sell reasonably quickly, he'll give me a show—"

"Nick!"

"At least a shared one. He sent his kindest regards. What did you do for him, Eleanor, that he should be so grateful?"

"Heavens, I can't remember. It was in the Sudan we met—or was it South Africa? Anyway, he wouldn't have taken your paintings just for the sake of that old story. He's far too canny a business-man."

While they talked they had walked through the ticket barrier, Eleanor giving the ticket collector a smile in lieu of a platform ticket. The machine had been broken since before her return to Cornwall, and no one wanted to be bothered collecting tuppences, though he did take Nick's return stub.

"Alarian wouldn't have accepted the pictures at your request," Nick agreed, "but without it, I doubt he'd have given the work of an unknown a second look."

"Why not? How else is he to discover up-and-coming young artists?"

"Yes, he'd give a first look, but if the appeal wasn't obvious—I took a couple of the music pictures, you know. My best, I think. *The Lark Ascending* and Brahms's second *Serenade*. Risky, I suppose. If you don't know the music, you wouldn't know what they're about, though they might appeal on other levels."

"I like them," said Eleanor staunchly, though her travelling life had given her no opportunity to become familiar with classical music, let alone to learn to appreciate abstract art.

They paused to let Teazle take advantage of the long grass growing along the base of the car-park fence. The station staff had lost heart for keeping things spruce when they found out the line was to be closed.

"Alarian obviously hadn't a clue, but he asked if he could hang them in his office for a couple of days. I think he must have got someone who knows both music and art to take a look. I wish I knew who. I wonder if the Wreckers has a bottle of Aussie cham-pagne at a price suited to my present budget rather than my great expectations." Nick's spirits were bubbling like Champagne. "Shall I drive?" he asked as they reached the car.

"Do. I left room in the boot for your rucksack."

Eleanor unlocked and opened the boot, congratulating herself on having remembered to lock it, and gave Nick the car keys. She went round to the passenger side and opened the door—Oh bother, she thought, she hadn't locked that! Teazle jumped in and scrambled between the seats onto the well-stuffed bags on the back seat. She didn't need help as Eleanor had been careful not to pile it high with donations, to allow for Nick's paintings in their carrier.

He unlocked the driver's-side door and folded himself into the little car. The starter caught on the second try. The Incorruptible ran pretty well, considering its age and its hard life up and down the hills of Cornwall, frequently heavily loaded.

"Books in that box in the back?" Nick asked.

"Yes, Major Cartwright, as usual. It's very good of him to keep giving them to LonStar when he could sell them on to the used book shop that just opened in Bodmin."

"Perhaps he doesn't know about it."

"Nick, I told him as soon as I found out."

"I was teasing. And don't worry, I'll go on buying his thrillers and detective stories from your shop and giving them back after reading."

As they drove up St Thomas Road past the castle, in ruins but still towering on its mound, Eleanor said, "Let's park and find an off-licence. I'll buy a bottle of Champagne, or at least Asti Spumante, in case the Wreckers lets you down. But I thought you'd gone back to the Trelawny Arms since Donna decided you don't look sufficiently like Ringo."

He laughed. "Thank heaven! No, let's press on. One of the pubs is bound to have something sparkling, whatever the label. I want to get home. I've got a commission I need to get going with right away."

"A commission?"

"You won't believe this. I went for a walk in St James's Park and there was a concert going on at the bandstand. The brasses were shining in the sun and they were playing Elgar, the first *Pomp and Circumstance March*. You probably know it as 'Land of Hope and Glory.'"

"Oh yes, I know that."

"Well, it gave me an idea. I started sketching and a girl who was sitting nearby asked if she could look. Turned out she was an American, on her honeymoon but her husband was busy taking photos of the Horse Guards or something. She'd walked on to listen to the band because she plays in one in the States. Alto sax, I think she said. To cut a long story short, she said she'd buy a painting of the band if I'd paint it."

"But it won't look like a brass band, will it?" Eleanor said doubtfully. "Or are you going to do something more like your landscapes?"

"No, I explained to her that I paint the images the music makes in my head. She said that's okay by her. She's sure she'll like it and it'll be a very special souvenir of England. Her family has some connection with England—supposedly an ancestor jumped into the Thames and saved Charles I's life, and they have an antique walking-stick to prove it."

"Before he had his head cut off, I take it?"

"Oh yes, before he became king, I think. Yes, must be, because she said her maiden name, Hazard, was bestowed by a grateful James I. Janice Hazard Harrison—what a mouthful! When I suggested a price she didn't even blink, just asked how much deposit I wanted. Her husband turned up and wrote a cheque on the spot."

"So now you have to paint it."

"Yes, before inspiration fades and before the Harrisons fly back to America, so I've got to get cracking. Besides, I want to get home and see what sort of mess Stella has made of my place. Her sculptures are so perfectly finished, it's hard to credit that she's such a slob in everything else."

"She dresses very nicely, dear. Except, I dare say, when she's actually sculpting. Is that the right word? It sounds rather odd."

"Yes, that's right. It can get pretty dusty, and then there's always the odd slip of the chisel and blood everywhere."

"Nick!"

"Not likely for Stella. She works in serpentine, which isn't all that hard. Though she did talk about trying something in granite, something more recherché than her usual seals and seagulls. I don't know if it's just talk, or if she's started work on it. I haven't been to her studio in ages."

"In Padstow, didn't you say?"

"Yes, just outside. Did you see much of her while I was gone?"

"No, hardly anything. When I invited her over for lunch, she said she always brought sandwiches. Perfectly politely, but I'm afraid she doesn't have much time for little old ladies, unless they're customers."

"More fool her." Nick seized his chance between two lorries and swung round the roundabout onto the A30. The Incorruptible groaned a bit as they started the long climb up onto Bodmin Moor. "How's my favourite little old lady been while I've been gone? Busy as always?"

"Busy as always. The summer people have started to arrive. So many emmets seem to forget what they already have at their 'little place in the country,' especially in the way of kitchen stuff and linens. They bring more down and then give the old to Lon-Star. Joce is tearing her hair to try to fit everything into the stockroom. She says I'd better take a few days off from collecting."

"I can't imagine Mrs Stearns tearing her hair, under any circumstances. Do you think we can pass this exceptionally slow and smelly lorry?"

"No, Nick! Don't even try. You know the Incorruptible hates going uphill."

He obeyed, or more likely saw reason. They toiled upwards between hillsides patched with still-golden gorse and the pinkish-purple of heather coming into bloom. The bracken was bright green, not yet darkened by summer. Looking south towards Rough Tor, Eleanor saw a herd of wild ponies grazing on the spring grass.

She had often dreamt of these moors during the long years of journeying, usually to the hotter parts of the globe, working for the London Committee to Save the Starving. She and Peter had always intended to retire to their home county. When he was killed, in a riot in Indonesia, she had come sadly home without him. But she couldn't abandon LonStar, not when so many had so great a need. With their savings, she had bought a cottage in the small fishing village of Port Mabyn and turned her ground floor into a charity shop. Under the efficient guidance of Jocelyn Stearns, the vicar's wife, it was flourishing. If dear Joce was sometimes just a trifle bossy, it was a small price to pay for the pleasure of sending off the pounds, shillings, and pence to LonStar's headquarters.

"Made it!" said Nick in triumph as they reached the top of the long hill at Cold Northcott. There were more hills ahead, but none so trying to the Incorruptible's old bones.

A worrisome new rattle developed as they started down the steep lane that became Port Mabyn's only street.

"Do you hear that?" Eleanor asked.

"The church clock? Five o'clock. We've made reasonable time considering. Stella will still be at the shop. Like LonStar, I don't close till half past at this time of year. Oh, by the way, though I didn't tell Mrs Stearns, I did tell Stella about Alarian's offer when I rang up to say I'd be back this afternoon."

"Of course, she's a colleague. There, listen!"

But Nick was concentrating on parking—on the wrong side of the narrow street, with two wheels on the pavement and the car's nose inches from a NO PARKING sign outside the LonStar shop. At the same time, a bustle of chattering pedestrians flocked out of the bakery opposite after their Cornish cream teas. Never mind, Eleanor thought. In the mysterious way of such things, the rattle might well disappear by tomorrow.

"Damn!" Nick exclaimed, putting on the hand-brake and turning off the ignition. "She's shut up shop early."

And indeed, the glass door of the next shop down the hill displayed a CLOSED sign and the blinds were down.

Frowning, Nick opened the car door and twisted to get out in the narrow space between the car and the LonStar shop window. Teazle jumped over the brake and sprang down after him. Luckily Nick remembered her just in time not to shut the door on her. By the time Eleanor had climbed out on the street side, Nick was unlocking the door to his gallery, the dog at his heels.

"I'll just see if she's still here," he called over his shoulder to Eleanor. "I'll be back in a minute to help you unload."

"Teazle, come!"

Eleanor's words were drowned in a burst of laughter from some happy people full of splits with strawberry jam and clotted cream. Longing for a cup of tea, she followed Nick to retrieve Teazle, who by then had gone with him into the gallery.

"Bloody hell!" Nick stood just inside the door, gazing around wildly.

For a moment Eleanor couldn't see what was wrong. Then the first thing she noticed was that all the sculptures were gone. They had occupied a shelf on the wall to the right of the door—sleek seals, seagulls, and dolphins, carved from serpentine mottled and streaked in blues and greens and browns. Still there, drawing-pinned to the shelf, was the card with the sculptor's name: Stella Maris.

Star of the sea, Eleanor thought irrelevantly. Surely a pen-name, or the sculptural equivalent.

"Bloody hell!" Nick repeated violently, striding round behind a three-panelled screen hung with pictures.

Looking after him, Eleanor realised that the paintings hanging on the outer panels of the screen had been slashed. Someone had taken a knife to the two landscapes, making three parallel diagonal cuts in each canvas. The wildflower miniatures on the centre panel had been spared, perhaps considered insignificant.

Speechless, she followed Nick. White-faced, fists clenched, he was staring in stunned silence at three of what he called his "serious" paintings. Eleanor didn't understand or properly appreciate them, but these were the sort of things Alarian had chosen to hang in his prestigious London gallery. They, too, had been sliced diagonally but cross-wise, so that a sad triangle drooped from the centre of each.

"Oh, Nick!"

"I know who did it."

"Not Stella?"

He shook his head. "There's only one possible person. And he's going to get what's coming to him!"

TWO

"Yoohoo, Mrs Trewynn!" Donna, the teenage daughter of the landlord of the Trelawny Arms, stood on the threshold, her plump form barely encased in an op-art mini-dress. Eleanor hurried to stop her coming any further into the gallery. "I saw you come in here. D'you need help unloading?"

"Yes, dear. That would be very kind. I'll be out in a minute."

"Thass all right, take your time. You left the car windows open, so I can get in okay." She raised her voice. "You coming up the Arms tonight, Mr Gresham?"

Nick achieved no more than a strangled grunt. Fortunately Donna was quite accustomed to receiving no more by way of response from him. Besides, she had confided to Eleanor a few days ago that Mr Gresham, though dishy, was really too old for her. She went off happily crooning something about love, which Eleanor assumed to be one of the Beatles' songs rather than a personal declaration.

She turned back. "Nick," she said urgently, "you mustn't do anything hasty."

"Don't worry, I wasn't going to cut his throat with his own knife, no matter how much I feel like it."

"Just going to 'pop him on the nose'? I realise I can't possibly understand how you feel, but really, my dear, that's not a good idea." She didn't want to sound goody-goody, but she had seen too much of the effects of violence ever to be complacent about it. "Please, at least come and have a cup of tea before you do anything you'll regret."

He scowled. "Tea! You'd have better luck dissuading me if you got me too sozzled to ride my bike."

"I knew we should have stopped for a bottle of Asti."

His lips quirked and he said more calmly, "It'd take more than a few glasses of wine—"

"Then it's just as well I didn't buy it. I don't want you pot-valiant. Where does he live, the man you suspect?"

"Padstow."

"I'll tell you what, if you'll come and drink a cuppa, I'll drive you down there."

"Oh lord, Eleanor," he groaned, "if you're present, I won't be able to sock him one."

"Exactly. Come on, lock up so no one can get in and see." She nearly suggested that he should go round by the back doors, but the need to seem normal to Donna would probably do him good.

Reluctantly he followed her out. Teazle scooted past them and through the open door just past the LonStar shop. She'd go and wait at the top of the stairs, outside the door to Eleanor's flat, out of the way of people tramping back and forth. Donna had already cleared out the interior of the Incorruptible, with the assistance of Ivy and Lionel, the children from Chin's Chinese. Having just opened the boot, the obliging teenager was tugging with both hands at Nick's rucksack.

"Golly, it's heavy. Whatcher got in there, Mr Gresham?"

"Among other things, books. Ever heard of them?"

She giggled. "Yeah, like we're s'posed to read at school."

"Oil paints, too. They weigh a ton. Leave it. I'll get the rest."

He went round to the back of the car and lifted out the ruck-sack, easily, with one hand. Donna didn't kid him about his muscles, as she usually would have. Eleanor had never considered her sensitive, but obviously, though he had teased her, she had seen something in his face that told her this was not a good moment for joshing.

While Nick deposited the rucksack just inside the door and returned for the box of books, Eleanor thanked Donna and the children.

"Me and Ivy put your shopping on your stairs, Mrs Trewynn, so's they wouldn't sell it with the rest of the stuff."

"Thank you, Lionel. That was very thoughtful. I'd quite forgotten I went shopping before I met the train."

"It was down on the floor behind the seats," Ivy explained kindly, "where you couldn't see it."

"That's right. I remember putting it there to leave room for Nick and his . . . luggage."

"You ought to put the frozen stuff away in the fridge right away, or it'll melt."

"Thaw," her brother corrected her.

"You're quite right," said Eleanor. "I'd better go and do it this very minute, before I forget." She escaped.

In the passage she met Nick on his way out. "I'd better take the Incorruptible down to the car-park," he said. "It'd be a pity if Bob Leacock came by and felt obliged to give you a fine. I'll drop off my rucksack." He reached for it.

Eleanor put her hand on his arm. "No, leave it here. Don't go back in there till you must. Perhaps I'd better take the car down while you make the tea."

{ 13 }

"I promise I won't hop it to Padstow without you, however great the temptation."

She followed him to the street door and watched him drive off down the hill, till he turned into the field on the far side of the stream, the only flat space in the centre of Port Mabyn. Then she went into the shop.

Jocelyn was behind the counter, ringing up a sale. She nodded and smiled at Eleanor. Having completed the business, she asked, "Good haul?"

"Not bad. I didn't fill the car, as I had to leave room for Nick and his baggage. Joce, my friend, the London art dealer, has accepted the paintings he took with him!"

"I trust Nicholas is duly grateful for the introduction. What's up next door? I noticed the gallery closed early, and Nicholas came past with a face like thunder just now."

"He's annoyed because of the early closing," Eleanor hedged. Sooner or later, Jocelyn—and indeed the entire population of Port Mabyn—would find out what had happened, but with luck not until Nick had simmered down. Though she might have told Jocelyn, another volunteer and two customers were at the back of the small shop. "His friend promised she'd be able to cover for him the whole time he was away."

"I'm not surprised he's annoyed. It may not be the height of the holiday season yet but business has been pretty brisk this afternoon. I even managed to get rid of that appalling muu-muu, the one with palm trees and Hawaiian dancers in grass skirts."

"Congratulations! It's amazing what people will buy. I must go and put on the kettle. Nick's coming to tea. He's going to tell me all about Mr Alarian," Eleanor invented hurriedly, hoping Jocelyn wouldn't wonder why Nick hadn't told her everything on the way home from Launceston.

Fond as she was of Joce, she didn't want her popping in for a cuppa while she was trying to smooth Nick's ruffled feathers. The vicar's wife wouldn't be interested in the artist's negotiations with the London gallery owner.

"Tomorrow's Mrs Davies's day for the shop," said Joce. "Come and have a cup of coffee with me at eleven."

Eleanor accepted and went upstairs to her flat.

Teazle was on the landing outside the front door, impatient to get in. She headed straight for her water bowl in the kitchen, the front part of the room that stretched from back to front of the cottage. The windows were open and the breeze blowing off the sea was beginning to feel a little chilly, so Eleanor closed the back ones. She paused for a moment to enjoy the view up the rough slope to Crookmoyle Point and down to the left to the inlet and harbour with their sheltering cliffs. How lucky she was that this cottage had been vacant just when she needed it!

Returning towards the kitchen, she stopped again, to study the painting over her mantelpiece. Nick had given it to her. It was one of the "tourist" pictures he scorned, but which provided his bread and butter. A little grey-brown donkey trotted down a steep cobbled street in Clovelly, between white-washed stone cottages splashed with the scarlet of geraniums in window-boxes. Eleanor loved it and didn't care if it wasn't high art.

She put on the kettle, and stowed away her shopping, remembering with a smile Ivy's grave warning. Her father, Mr Chin, though born in London, was an excellent Chinese chef. No doubt he'd impressed on the children the care that must be taken in storing food.

Her smile faded as she took down a plate for the chocolate digestive biscuits she had bought to welcome Nick home. His favourites—but the present circumstances were not conducive to the enjoyment of simple pleasures.

Who was the man he was so sure had wrecked his work? Why

had he done it? Could Nick find proof of his being responsible, so as to be able to demand restitution? Was the damage repairable, or would all those beautiful paintings have to be thrown away?

More important, who could possibly dislike Nick so much, and why?

Surely such destruction must be a crime. Vandalism, perhaps? As soon as he came in, Nick ought to report the damage to Bob Leacock.

She looked out of the window into the street. Nick was just crossing, from directly opposite the passage door below, thus avoiding having to walk past his desecrated gallery. He didn't even glance that way, his gaze fixed directly ahead, his face set. Several people in the street, a couple of them local, gave him curious looks.

"*Wuff?*"

"Do you want your dinner, girl? It's a bit early, but we've had a busy day." She was opening a tin of Chum when Nick came in.

The kettle began to whistle, a wavering, rising note that would quickly become a shriek. Nick turned down the gas. "I'll make the tea."

"Thank you, dear. I must just grate a bit of carrot for Teazle's dinner, and reach me down the rolled oats, would you?"

"Nauseating mess," he said, "but she seems to thrive on it. Eleanor, what am I going to do?"

"Concentrate on making the tea," she said sharply. "Scalding your hand won't help matters." Or perhaps it would, preventing serious mayhem.

"No. Sorry. I must sound very self-indulgent. When I think of the people LonStar is trying to help—"

"Nick, it was a beastly thing for anyone to do. Who is it you suspect? And why?"

Without replying, he set the teapot on a mat on the table between kitchen and sitting room. He added mugs, milk jug, sugar basin, and the plate of biscuits, and pulled out a chair for Eleanor. Too well-mannered to sit down before she did, he waited for her to finish preparing the dog's dinner. However, he absently took a biscuit and crunched, too accustomed to the casual ways of the times to be conscious of the lapse from old-fashioned etiquette.

Since Eleanor had spent a good deal of time in cultures where no mere female would dream of touching a morsel before every male had eaten his fill, she paid no heed.

She sat down and poured. "Is it someone I know?" she asked, passing over his tea.

He stared into his mug. "I think you've met him. I'm pretty sure it must have been Geoff, Stella's boyfriend."

"The rather greenery yallery young man?"

Startled, Nick looked up with a laugh. "That's him. 'Greenery yallery, Grosvenor Gallery.' A would-be Pre-Raphaelite, born a century too late. Corduroys, flowing cravats, and a velvet beret, and he spells his name the mediaeval way, G-e-o-double f-r-o-i-e, though to my certain knowledge it's r-e-y in his passport. His real surname isn't Monmouth, either."

"Why him?"

"He's always been—I suppose you'd have to call it envious. He makes a lot more money than I do but it's from commercial art, paintings for adverts. His other work just doesn't sell. He has an inferiority complex or something because I can actually live on the proceeds of my work, even if most of it comes from tourist stuff. He's always making snide comments, supposed to be joking but . . . You know?"

"With an edge?"

"Exactly. I don't think I'm being oversensitive . . ."

"I shouldn't think so, dear. I really didn't take to him."

"Of course that's not enough to make me suspect him, but if

you add that Stella's the only person I'd told about Alarian and that Geoff's quite likely to have popped in to see her in the gallery. On his way to Tintagel, perhaps. It's a favourite haunt. If he came, she'd have told him."

"And you're afraid your prospective success in London would be enough to incite him to violence?" Eleanor asked doubtfully. She took a comforting gulp of tea.

"Violence! I'm not saying he'd have slugged me if I'd been there, but attacking my work . . . Well, I can't read his mind. Who can tell what will be the tipping point for someone else?"

"Surely Stella wouldn't stand by and let him do it?"

"No, of course not. We've always been on reasonably friendly terms and she's done quite well by selling her things in my shop. Perhaps she went upstairs to the loo, or to get a cuppa or something, leaving that stupid nit in charge. In any case, I wouldn't expect her to shield my stuff with her body against a knife-wielding maniac."

"Good heavens no! But don't you think it's odd that she just walked out, without a word to you? And taking her sculptures, too."

"He may have made her. She may have left a note, in the cash register or the studio. I didn't look."

Eleanor felt herself pale. "We didn't look in the studio. Oh, Nick, what if—?"

"For pity's sake, don't start imagining horrors," Nick said irritably, taking another biscuit, his fourth. "He's crazy about her."

"It was you who talked about a knife-wielding maniac."

"True. I was exaggerating. I can't really see Geoff running amok. Slashing pictures, yes. Slashing throats, no." He didn't sound entirely convinced by his own argument. He stood up, half the biscuit in his hand. "All the same, before I go to Padstow to confront him I'd better look around—just in case Stella left a note."

"Nick, you ought to report the damage to Bob Leacock."

"The police? Later." Suddenly he was in a hurry. "I'll be right back."

His haste suggested to Eleanor a possibility much more disturbing even than Stella lying dead on the studio floor. Suppose she was injured, quietly bleeding to death while Nick and Eleanor indulged in tea and biscuits?

She decided she had better go, too, in case her help was needed.

THREE

Nick had picked up his rucksack from the landing and was at the bottom of the stairs before Eleanor shut her front door behind her. She was too flurried to make Teazle stay behind, so the dog was at her heels as she rushed down. Her regular practice of Aikido kept her fit enough to take the stairs at speed, but Nick had much longer legs. When she reached the street door, he was already unlocking his shop door. The bell jangled as he opened it.

Turning to lock it behind him, he found Eleanor right behind him. He was pale.

"You shouldn't have come."

"If she needs help . . ."

His face turned—as Eleanor had once heard Donna singing—a whiter shade of pale. "I wish you hadn't said that! I was thinking of my stuff in the studio. I hadn't thought—Stay here. Keep Teazle here."

She picked up the dog, only too glad to comply.

He strode straight past the cash register without pausing to glance at his desecrated work, let alone to check for a note. The door to the studio, behind the gallery, was locked.

Could Stella have run through, locked it against the marauder, and escaped by the back door onto the path that ran up and down the hill behind the row of shops? Yes, thought Eleanor in relief, that must be what happened. When Nick returned, looking equally relieved, she presented this suggestion.

"Possible," he conceded. "But when would she have taken her sculptures? I'm inclined to think she just went off with him. Failing a body, let's see if she left me an explanation."

The cash register pinged as he opened it. He took out a couple of cheques, muttering gloomily, "I hope these don't bounce. I'm going to have precious little coming in while I replace what's done for. I've just lost four days' painting running after vain hopes in London, too. Ah, here. Written on the back of a blank receipt. Typical! That's going to muck up the numbers in my records. Ah well, let's see what she's got to say for herself." He read it and passed it to Eleanor.

Nick, I'm dead sorry!!! G. drove me here—went on to Tintagel—came back for lunch. Should've known better than to tell him your news. He was livid—'Not fair!' I was gone 5 min. getting pasties across the street—the damage was done. What a drag!! Know you won't take it out on my stuff, but just in case . . . !!! Gotta run or I'll hafta walk. S.

" 'Not fair!' " Nick said bitterly. "What the hell does he expect? I knew it was him."

"Did he . . ." Eleanor hesitated, hardly daring to ask. "Your studio?"

"No, she seems to have managed to keep him out of there, thank heaven! I'm going to have it out with him right now. Come on, if you're still willing to drive me, or I'll get my bike."

"I'll take you. And I'll drive. I wouldn't trust you behind the wheel just now."

He managed a crooked smile. "You're probably right."

Too impatient to wait for Eleanor to fetch Teazle's lead, he provided a bit of parcel string. Teazle sniffed at it suspiciously, but did not seriously object to the ignominy. They walked down the hill. Nick, after moving ahead, tempered his long stride to Eleanor's shorter pace.

Few people were about in the street. The shops were closed and Nick and Eleanor didn't pass either of the pubs. As they came to the bottom of the hill and the narrow stone bridge over the stream, Eleanor saw a couple of smacks preparing to set out for a night's fishing when the tide turned. Two seamen were stacking lobster pots to one side of the life-boat slipway. The air smelled of tar, fish, and seaweed, and herring gulls screamed overhead. One of the big grey-and-white birds perched on the wall of the bridge, watching Nick and Eleanor with an impudent, sceptical stare.

Out on the jetty that protected the small harbour, several figures in bright holiday clothes were strolling, watching the swells break booming against the rocky sides of the inlet. Others, more hardy, hiked the path on the south side, leading at first gradually then steeply up to Crookmoyle Point, saved from builders by the National Trust. Darkness would not fall for hours on this June evening.

Nick and Eleanor crossed the bridge and turned into the car-park. Eleanor rented a ramshackle shed on the far side for the Incorruptible, but Nick hadn't garaged the car, proof of his determination to go to Padstow. Further proof was that he had the keys in his pocket, having kept them when he came up to the flat after parking, instead of hanging them on the key hook by the door.

With a sigh, Eleanor gave up hope of deterring him. She drove up the hill, past the Wreckers Inn, and out of the town. The lane was bounded by high banks overgrown with cow parsley, red and white campion, toadflax, foxgloves, and nettles. A resplendent cock pheasant dashed out from a gateway and scurried along in front of them, then ducked aside into the undergrowth. The Incorruptible reached the top of the hill and found its second wind.

They turned south on the B road. To their right, rough grassland criss-crossed by drystone walls sloped down to the invisible cliffs and glimpses of the boundless sea beyond, ruffled with whitecaps. The gentle breeze had turned into a steady blow from the southwest. A dark line on the far horizon suggested rain before morning.

They hadn't spoken since leaving the car-park. Now Eleanor asked, "Can you repair them?"

"Possibly. It's a lot of work. Hardly worth it with the tourist stuff. Most people won't buy if they see a repair on the back, even if it's invisible on the front. The good pictures, I'll have to give it a try. They're not something I can paint again from scratch. You can't duplicate inspiration, only hope it'll strike again."

"It will. I know it will. Nick, I can't see much I can do to help, but if you'd like me to work in the shop to allow you more time for painting and repairing—"

He gave a shout of laughter. "My dear Eleanor, that's very sweet of you, but I've heard what Mrs Stearns has to say about your fatal effects on the LonStar cash register!"

"I'm sure I could manage with a bit of practice," Eleanor said with dignity. "Or I could simply call you if I made a sale." At least she had cheered him up a bit.

"You know, that just might work." Gloom enveloped him again. "Once I've produced something to sell."

Coming down from the moor they drove through farmland, wheat fields edged with blood-red poppies, and buttercup-gilded meadows grazed by heavy-uddered cows. The hamlets of

{ 23 }

St Endellion, St Minver, Tredrizzick, and Pityme were deserted at this hour. They came to Rock and Eleanor parked in the old quarry. Thence they walked to the ferry, with Teazle on her demeaning length of string.

"Nick, what are you going to do?"

He shrugged. "I don't know. I expect I'll find out when I see what his attitude is."

He fished in his pocket for a shilling for tickets as the motor launch approached the jetty, all too quickly for Eleanor's liking.

Several other passengers made the fifteen-minute crossing of the Camel estuary with them, so it was impossible for her to seek further elucidation. Teazle sat at her feet, her gaze glued to a large boxer whose owner kept it as far away as possible on the small boat. With dismay, Eleanor watched Padstow's ancient quays grow nearer. Perhaps she should have let Nick bicycle. The exertion might have dispelled his spleen, or at least tired him enough to make violence unattractive. Surely he retained enough of the old-fashioned gentlemanly virtues not to start a dust-up in her presence!

Once ashore, they walked along the North Quay and crossed into the network of narrow streets behind the harbour.

"There it is." Nick pointed to a narrow shop front opposite the Gold Bezant Inn.

It took Eleanor a moment to decipher the sign above the shop window, as it was written in Old English script. KING ARTHUR'S GALLERY, it said.

"King Arthur? Shouldn't that be in Tintagel?"

"He couldn't find a suitable place in Tintagel, but he's obsessed with King Arthur. Come and look."

In the window was a display of three paintings. At first glance, they seemed to Eleanor to be quite pretty but rather depressing. She could understand why holiday-makers didn't choose to buy pictures of slender mediaeval maidens with flowing hair and tragic mouths drooping over dead or dying knights, however meticulously portrayed. She wouldn't want one on her wall, breathing gloom every time she looked at it. They were flamboyantly signed: Geoffroie Monmouth.

But she didn't have time to study them. Nick had pressed the electric bell button. No one came. Heedless of the CLOSED sign, he pushed the door. Opening, it set off a jangle, just like his own shop door. The fact that it was not locked suggested to Eleanor that the artist was still within, probably in the throes of producing another grim *memento mori*. She tied Teazle's string to an ancient, worn boot-scraper to one side of the door and hurried after Nick.

The blind at the rear of the display window was pulled down, so the interior of the shop was dim. Facing the door, a life-size and remarkably lifelike King Arthur stood, barring the way. Grey-bearded, he wore a crown encircling his helmet, and his visible arm and his legs were clad in gleaming armour, the rest covered by a crimson tabard embroidered with flowers. In his right hand he wielded Excalibur. His other arm was hidden by a blue shield with a device of three crowns. Exquisitely detailed flowers surrounded his mailed feet.

Though Eleanor was sure she had never seen the picture before, it was vaguely familiar.

The jangle failed to bring any response. Nick looked around. "Damn," he swore under his breath. "If he's not in the back room, I'll have to trek up to his bungalow."

"Not a bungalow, surely! He ought to live in an ancient cottage overgrown with rambling roses, if he can't manage a crumbling castle."

"A 1950s bungalow," Nick said firmly, striding round behind King Arthur. "And any interest he has in flowers he devotes to his painting, not his garden."

Reluctantly Eleanor followed. He flung open a door in the back wall and stepped through into a room lit by a window facing north, high in the far wall.

"Ye gods! Eleanor, don't come in!"

But Eleanor was already on the threshold. She saw a figure sprawled face down on the bare boards. His beige smock was drenched with crimson, and a crimson pool had spread across the floor around him.

Someone pushed past her and cried in an anguished voice, "My God, Nick, what have you done? You've stabbed him!"

FOUR

Eleanor was icy cold. She tried to speak, to say, "That's nonsense!" but only a squeak emerged. Shock, she diagnosed woozily. She was all too familiar with death from endemic disease, starvation, and violence, though never reconciled to it, but one didn't expect to walk into an artist's studio in peaceful Cornwall and find . . .

In the commotion surrounding her, no one heard her feeble bleat.

Stella, having accused Nick, called out, "Doug, ring the police." She dropped to her knees beside the body.

Nick was kneeling on the other side, though Eleanor hadn't seen him move.

Behind her, a bewildered, rather plaintive, and slightly slurred male voice with a bit of a local accent asked, "The police? What does she want the police for?"

"Geoff appears to be dead," said a woman very close to Eleanor, grasping her arm, "and there's blood everywhere. Ring 999. You'd better ask for an ambulance, too, just in case." She sounded very cool, calm, and collected. "Come and sit down, dear. You're white as a sheet, and no flipping wonder."

Eleanor would have preferred to retreat into the shop, but the woman led her to a sort of divan, a model's couch, perhaps, in the studio. It was draped with crimson cloth. Sitting down with the utmost reluctance, Eleanor had her head pressed forward onto her knees.

"I'm all right, really," she protested weakly.

The hand on the back of her neck eased up. "You'd better lie down, so you don't have to look at that unholy mess."

"Really, I don't—"

"He's dead, Marge!" Stella wailed.

"I can't believe it! But you're a nurse, I suppose you must know . . . Nick, how could you do such a dreadful thing?"

"He didn't!" Eleanor insisted.

"That's fresh blood, not dry."

"It's not blood," said Nick loudly, standing up.

"It's no use denying it, you murdering bastard!" Stella screeched. "You stuck a dagger in his back and he's dead." She reached for the haft protruding from the dead man's back.

"Don't touch it!" Nick's exclamation came too late. Stella had already grasped the dagger.

She let go as if it were red-hot. "Why not?" she asked suspiciously. "It's indecent to leave him lying here on his face with that sticking into him."

"Fingerprints. I didn't kill him. Now you've mucked up the fingerprints, the police may never find out who did."

Stella stared at him. "Wouldn't that be convenient for you. I wonder why you didn't warn me in time?"

"Because I hadn't realised you were quite such an—"

"Nick!" Eleanor just wanted to stop them squabbling over the body.

He came towards her, but turned his head to say, "Do not pull out the dagger. Do not move him." He took Eleanor's hands. "Are you all right?"

"Yes, it was just the shock. All that . . . Is it oil paint? It really looks like blood."

"Not oil paint, no. Let me get you out of here."

"No, you don't!" Stella cried. "Doug, don't let him get away."

The hitherto invisible Doug had appeared in the doorway. He was a sturdy man with a fluffy aureole of greying hair surrounding a weathered pate, in flannels and a well-worn tweed jacket. "Jerry Roscoe is on his way," he announced. "I rang him instead of 999." He flinched as he caught sight of the body, with Stella still kneeling beside it.

Eleanor looked that way, for the first time deliberately. The tableau reminded her forcefully of the paintings in the window, except that all the dead knights had been face up, the better to display their chiselled profiles. In fact, Stella's features and long hair, a rich copper colour, strongly resembled those of the mediaeval damsels. Presumably she had been Geoff's model as well as his girlfriend.

Geoff wasn't lying flat. He seemed to be sprawled over—Was that his easel flattened beneath him?

"Would someone kindly explain what's going on?" Doug demanded, appalled.

"Isn't it obvious?" Stella said scornfully. "I told you what Geoff did to Nick's pictures. Nick's gone crazy and stabbed him."

Eleanor nearly protested again, but decided the girl was too distraught to listen. She'd do better to save her breath for the police.

Nick apparently came to the same decision. "We'd all better move into the other room," he said, quite calmly. "The coppers don't take kindly to people who breathe on their evidence."

"Heavens, yes." Eleanor quickly stood up. She looked back at the couch, hoping she hadn't inadvertently obliterated some essential clue.

"What do you mean?" Marge—Margery?—also stood up in a hurry. She looked uneasy.

Until then, Eleanor hadn't noticed anything but her voice, kind, firm, with no hint of Cornish. She was a tallish woman, apparently about forty, round-faced and comfortably plump, with corn-gold hair plaited and wound into a coronet on top of her head in a very old-fashioned style. Unless it was the latest thing? Eleanor wondered. Her ankle-length skirt, though it looked very old-fashioned to Eleanor, was undoubtedly up-to-date. Maxis, they were called. Unless, of course, it was some sort of protest. It was so difficult to be sure these days, especially with artists. The Bohemian life, she thought vaguely.

Stella's skirt was similar, bright-coloured cotton swirling as she sprang to her feet. "Yes, what do you mean? About breathing on evidence?"

"It's true," said Doug apprehensively. "Touching stuff, anyway. I've seen it on *Softly, Softly*."

"Oh, the telly," Stella jeered. "You don't want to believe everything you see on telly."

All the same, she followed the others through to the gallery. She went to the door and stood looking out.

Marge and Doug stuck together, talking in low voices. Eleanor didn't want to appear to eavesdrop. She moved away, behind a folding screen like those in Nick's shop. He followed her.

"The cop-shop's just round the corner," he said. "In New Street. Jerry Roscoe's a sergeant. He'll be here any moment."

"Thank heaven! And thank heaven I came with you."

"Yes, I'd be in a pretty mess if you hadn't insisted."

"What are you talking about?" Stella came round the screen. "I suppose she's ready to lie her head off for you."

"I don't need to lie because—"

Ignoring her, Stella stormed on. "It won't do you any good. I saw you! Geoff didn't deserve to die. Just when—"

"Hush, love." Marge appeared. "You're going to make yourself ill."

Stella collapsed, weeping, against her friend's shoulder.

When Nick and Eleanor moved away, however, she wasn't too overcome to raise her head and call to Doug to guard the door.

"I wish she'd stop harping on that," Nick said irritably.

"It's only natural, dear, as she's managed to convince herself that she saw you stab her . . . I take it 'boyfriend' was a euphemism?"

"You take it correctly. They pretty much lived together, except that she's kept a studio of her own at the farm."

"Farm?" Eleanor asked uncertainly.

Her question was not answered. The street door opened with the usual jangle of the bell, and a gruff, slightly out-of-breath voice demanded, "Well now, what's all this about a body?"

A uniformed sergeant came in, followed by a large, very young, and gormless-looking constable, with carroty hair and lots of freckles. Doubtless he had been sent to learn the ropes in this quiet backwater where nothing ever happened.

"He did it!" Stella cried, pointing at Nick. Eleanor, while recognising that she had ample reason for her distress, was getting fed up with the histrionics, even fearing that they might turn into hysterics. Not that Eleanor had ever been a particular advocate of the stiff upper lip, taken to excess, but in its absence she recognised its virtues. In the current idiom she was—if she'd got it right—a square, no doubt, and very likely "uptight," too.

"Did what?" Sergeant Roscoe asked stolidly.

"Stabbed Geoff. I saw it."

"That's torn it," Nick said softly as the sergeant frowned at him.

But Roscoe said to the constable, "For Pete's sake, switch on the light, Arnie." Then he turned to Doug. "So what's up, Doug? You really got a body? You're not having me on?"

"In the back room." Doug hoicked a thumb. "The studio. It's the artist, Geoffrey Monmouth. Stabbed."

"And you saw this chap do it?" The light came on. "That's better. Oh, it's Nick Gresham, isn't it. You're on the Trelawny Arms darts team, Port Mabyn, right? Wotcha do, throw a dart at him and hit a bull's-eye by mistake?"

"Come off it! I—"

"How can you joke about it?" Stella interrupted passionately. For once, Eleanor agreed with her.

"Not joking, miss. Just trying to find out what's going on. Don't want to call in Bodmin for nothing, do I."

"Nick stabbed Geoff with a dagger."

"I did not—"

Roscoe ignored him. "Doug, you saw this?"

"Not me! Stella did. She said to phone the police, so I did. I didn't go in there till after."

"Hadn't you better go and take a look, Sergeant?" said Marge.

"S'pose so, Mrs Rosevear," Roscoe said with obvious reluctance. He looked at his constable as if debating the wisdom of sending him instead to view the body. With a gloomy shake of the head, he said, "You stay there by the door, Arnie, and don't let a soul through."

Which was, Eleanor thought, a surprisingly tactful way of telling them all to stay put. But a face peered in through the door glass as if to prove the precaution was aimed in both directions.

Her start when she saw it alerted PC Arnie. He drew down the blind. Not quite so gormless as he looked.

Meanwhile, heavy police boots tramped across the stone floor. The last person out of the studio had left the door open. Roscoe stopped on the threshold, looking in.

"Bloody 'orrible!" he exclaimed with a shudder, and turned away quickly, his face pale.

"Bloody's the word," Nick murmured, "at least at first glance."

Eleanor gave him an old-fashioned look. "Really, Nick, being facetious is not helpful."

"It's helpful to my nerves."

"Miss Maris," the sergeant said hopefully, "you're a nurse, I've heard? You're quite certain he's dead?"

"Quite certain."

So Sergeant Roscoe wouldn't have to check the body close up. He gave a sigh of relief, then tried to turn it into a cough. "I rang Dr Wenlow—our local GP—before I came over, but he's gone out to a confinement." He took out an enormous handkerchief and used it to hold the doorknob, gingerly, as he closed it. "You'd all best come up to the station—"

"Nick's the one you want," objected Stella.

"I've got to take statements from all of you, miss. 'Specially you, that saw what happened. And Bodmin'll want you to wait till the detectives get here, I don't doubt. I must call them in right away."

"Phone's over there," said Doug, pointing to a shelf behind the cash register. As the gigantic handkerchief once more emerged, he added, "I used it to ring you."

"You never know," Roscoe observed weightily, dropping the handkerchief over the receiver before he picked it up and dialled. His beefy forefinger barely fitted into the holes.

Of his end of the ensuing muttered conversation, Eleanor heard little: ". . . blood everywhere . . ." made her look at Nick.

He shrugged, resigned. "I assume the CaRaDoC CID is capable of telling the difference," he said in a low voice.

"Of course!" After all, Eleanor's niece was a detective in the Constabulary of the Royal Duchy of Cornwall. "Sergeant Roscoe didn't even look properly."

"No point arguing with the locals. Besides, I'm not sure what exactly it is."

Most of the rest of what she heard was "Yes, sir," "No, sir." There was an interruption when Teazle barked outside.

"My dog! She sounds upset. I must bring her in, officer."

The constable blushed and looked at the sergeant. "Sarge . . . ?"

Roscoe gave him a ferocious scowl, then shrugged, nodded, and returned his attention to the telephone. "Yes, sir."

"You're not supposed to go out, madam," PC Arnie whispered. "I'd better get it. Will it bite?"

"Certainly not."

Arnie—Arney? Christian name or surname? Eleanor wondered—opened the door to admit a babble of voices. "Move along there," he said officiously. It was probably about the only thing he ever did have to say in the normal course of his duties.

A moment later Teazle pulled the string out of his hand and bounced to a halt in front of Eleanor. "*Woof?*" she asked.

"Yes, we'll be leaving soon," said Eleanor. "I hope." She stuck her hand in the pocket of her skirt, but she'd come away in such a hurry she hadn't brought any dog bics.

Blushing furiously, Arnie dug a small-size Bonio out of the depths of his uniform tunic and, with a sidelong glance at his superior, bent down to offer it to Teazle. Delicately she took it from his fingers. He smiled and patted her head.

If they were to be stuck in the police station for several hours, as seemed probable, Eleanor hoped he had plenty more.

With a final "Yes, sir, PC Bennett's with me," Roscoe hung up and turned to face them. "Well, they're on their way, Scene of Crime team and all. Nothing like this has ever happened in all my years here in Padstow, and I'm bound to say, I don't like it."

Looking round those present, Eleanor felt she could safely say none of them liked the situation, except possibly Teazle, who was advancing hopefully, stumpy tail wagging, on PC Arnie Bennett. On the other hand, no one, not even Stella, looked exactly dev-astated by Geoff Monmouth's death.

Stella did look overwrought, keyed up to a pitch that might very well result in hysteria. She could hardly be blamed in the circumstances. Eleanor hoped the police station would provide a nice, soothing cup of tea. She could do with one herself, come to that.

Contrariwise, Marge and Doug seemed uncomfortable but re-markably calm. Where did they come into the picture? They were obviously friends of Stella's, and Nick knew them, if only through the darts team. They must have been acquainted with the dead man. Doug, at least, knew Sergeant Roscoe well enough to be on christian-name terms, so he must be a local. Marge was Mrs. Were she and Doug married?

"Let's get going," Roscoe said without enthusiasm. "You'll have to walk beside me, Nick—Mr Gresham. It's that or handcuffs, the detective inspector says, and I don't want to . . . If it wasn't for what *she* says, and what I saw with my own eyes . . ." His voice trailed off.

Suddenly Eleanor was worried. The sergeant seemed to be un-willingly convinced that Nick had killed Geoff. What if her faith in CaRaDoC's detectives proved misplaced?

Nick would be in desperate trouble.

FIVE

The march through the streets to the police station was embarrassing, but not as embarrassing as Eleanor's previous similar experience. For one thing, unlike in Port Mabyn, she wasn't known to everyone here in Padstow, nor were many people out and about. For another, she didn't have a police officer holding her by the arm, just the sergeant in front and Constable Bennett bringing up the rear. She wasn't alone, she was one of five, not counting Teazle; and best of all, the press hadn't arrived yet.

On the other hand, last time she had been escorted to her own home. This time they were heading for the police station.

It might be just around the corner, but it was up a steep hill. Trudging upwards, Eleanor was growing tired. It had been a long day, and it wasn't over yet, not by a long chalk.

Whereas the Port Mabyn police station consisted of Bob Leacock's front room, Padstow's occupied one half of a double, two-story cottage. Over the entrance a POLICE sign glowed blue. Painted on the glass of the door was CRDC, with the Duchy's arms beneath, and then in smaller letters: Police Station.

Roscoe unlocked and opened the door and ushered in his

flock. He sent PC Arnie Bennett back to guard King Arthur's Gallery.

It was gloomy inside. Clouds had hidden the sun, now low in the sky, and dingy paint and battered furniture failed to brighten the room. Roscoe turned on the light. It glared down shadeless from the centre of the ceiling, pitilessly illuminating the scratches and worn patches in the grey linoleum. There was a wooden counter with a stool and a couple of brownish-grey metal filing cabinets behind it. An extremely unhappy aspidistra wilted on top of one of the cabinets. Against one wall a bench offered an unpadded seat to no more than three people at a time.

"Sit down, Eleanor," Nick urged. He was too polite to say she looked like death, but she was sure she must. She took a seat on the bench and Teazle hid behind her legs. To the sergeant Nick proposed, "Jerry, how about rustling up a cuppa all round?"

Jerry Roscoe looked disconcerted. Eleanor sympathised. It must be difficult for him to hold his darts opponent in what amounted almost to arrest. "I'll see what I can do," he muttered.

"I'll do it," Marge offered. "Just tell me where."

"There's a kettle and the makings upstairs in the office, Mrs Rosevear, thank you kindly."

Marge went up the stairs against the wall on the other side of the room. Next to them was an alarming steel door with a small barred opening high up.

Nick noticed Eleanor regarding it with dismay. "Yes, the lock-up," he said, sitting down beside her. "I'd be in it, no doubt, if I hadn't been playing darts with Jerry for years."

Sergeant Roscoe caught his name and looked up. He had moved behind the counter, taken off his cap, put on a pair of wire-rimmed spectacles, and was laboriously writing something in his notebook. "Sorry, Nick," he said, obviously deeply embarrassed. "They said I'm not to let you talk together. Not none of you," he added severely to Doug and Stella, who were conferring in low tones at the far side of the room.

"They can't have meant me," Stella protested. "I'm the one who—"

"Not *nobody*. Now, what I've got to do is, I've got to get all your names and addresses. Miss Maris, from what I've heard, that's not your right name. More like a pen-name, is it?"

"More or less," she said ungraciously.

Pencil poised, he waited. And waited. "Miss Maris? Your real name?"

"It's a free country. I can call myself whatever I want."

"Very true, miss. But there's times, like this here, when what's needed is your true legal name. So, unless you changed it by deed-poll, the which I take it you haven't or you'd've said by now—"

"Oh, if you must know, it's Weller. How would you like to be called Stella Weller?"

Nick hummed a tune. "Mellow yellow"; the words, in a vaguely American accent, floated into Eleanor's mind. More like "mella yella"; pop music, she guessed, not his usual classical. She must have heard Donna singing it, she supposed.

Mella yella. Stella Weller. What could her parents have been thinking of?

"Thank you, Miss Weller."

"You can call me Miss Maris, can't you, whatever you have to write down? Or just Stella."

Roscoe nodded. "I reckon so, seeing I've got you down as 'known as Maris.' Address?"

"Upper Trewithen Farm."

"One of your lot, Doug. Thought so. Douglas Rosevear. Now spell that for me, would you? I never was certain just how it's written."

"Old Cornish name," Doug said complacently.

As he spelt it, Nick whispered to Eleanor, "Turned his family farm into an artists' colony. Sort of half-baked commune. His forebears must be spinning in their graves."

The sergeant gave him a severe look and he shut up.

"And your missus, Doug? Would that be Margery with a *g-e* or a *j-o*?"

"*G-e*, and a *y* on the end, not *i-e*."

"Doug, give me a hand with the tray!" Margery with a *g-e* and a *y* called from above.

Obediently, Doug arose.

"No comparing notes," Roscoe reminded him. "You come right on down again. Now, madam." He turned to Eleanor.

"Eleanor Trewynn, Mrs." She spelt it, and couldn't resist adding, "An old Cornish name. I live in Port Mabyn, next door to Nick. Number 21a, Harbour Street, above the LonStar shop."

Roscoe stopped writing and stared at her. "Not *that* Mrs Trewynn?"

"What exactly do you mean by that?" Nick demanded, starting up.

Eleanor put her hand on his arm, but said a trifle tartly, "Yes, though the LonStar affair's got nothing whatsoever to do with this imbroglio."

"Are you Nick's aunt or something?" Stella asked.

"No relative, just a friend and neighbour."

The sergeant's lips ceased moving silently in what seemed to be a puzzled rehearsal of *imbroglio*. "No talking, *if* you please! Nick—Mr Gresham, is that your legal name or some la-di-da invention?"

"What's la-di-da about Nicholas Gresham, for heaven's sake? It's on my birth certificate. I don't happen to have a copy in my pocket."

"You're another artist. And you live next door to Mrs Trewynn, in Harbour Street, Port Mabyn?"

"Guilty as charged, officer. Number 22."

"Nick," Eleanor said crossly, "stop being so stroppy. Sergeant Roscoe has to ask these questions for the record, as you know perfectly well."

This time the look Roscoe cast at her was grateful. "That's right, madam. Have my hide, they will, if I don't get all these details down right."

"Sorry. This is getting on my nerves, I suppose. And you don't need to write that down, Jerry."

"Only natural," said the sergeant non-committally, "considering the sticky spot you've been and gone and got yourself into."

"Oh lord," Nick groaned, but to Eleanor's relief he said no more. Nothing was to be gained by antagonising the local man, and it would all get sorted out as soon as the detectives arrived.

Doug brought down a tin tray of tea, a large brown earthenware teapot, thick white china mugs, a half-empty bottle of milk, and an opened packet of sugar. He put it on the scratched counter, beside the sergeant.

At least, Eleanor thought, there was a pot, rather than a soggy tea-bag lurking in each mug. And Margery had thought to find and fill a bowl with water for Teazle. Eleanor thanked her as the dog lapped thirstily.

"Shall I pour, Jerry?" Margery asked.

"If you'd be so kind, Mrs Rosevear." Roscoe glanced around the room in a dissatisfied way. "Doug, would you mind bringing down a couple of chairs? There's no knowing when they'll get here from Bodmin."

"I'll give you a hand," Nick offered, "unless you're afraid I'll shove you down the stairs."

"Don't be an idiot," said Doug. "Come on."

Stella came over to sit on the bench.

The men returned with two folding metal chairs, the kind

designed by someone who never expected to sit on them. Nick set his near the window and subsided onto it.

The only words exchanged for the next quarter of an hour concerned milk, sugar, and refills. Sergeant Roscoe continued to write industriously as he drank. Presumably he was producing a report. In moments of disillusionment, Megan claimed that the chief purpose of the police force was not the reduction of crime but the production of reports, most of which were filed unread.

The tea made Eleanor want to go to the loo. She had noticed a door under the stairs with a wc sign, but she wasn't sure if she should just get up and go, or would that lead to Roscoe's demanding to know where she thought she was off to? She felt like a small child wondering whether she dared raise her hand and tell the teacher she needed to spend a penny. She reminded herself of the many and varied parts of the world where, as LonStar's roving ambassador, she had met similar circumstances with dignity, in Bedouin tents and Mongolian yurts alike.

As an American friend had once said to her, "When you gotta go, you gotta go."

"Stay," she told Teazle, and she got up and went. Glancing up, Roscoe nodded as she passed the desk.

When she came out, Nick stood up, gestured at the window, and said, "Here come our interrogators. I'll follow your example while I have the chance."

Eleanor looked out into the dusk. It was darker than she expected. She glanced back at the clock over the counter. Nearly ten o'clock. No wonder she was hungry, and Teazle must be starving! She was sniffing at the water bowl in a discouraged way.

A dark grey saloon had stopped directly outside the station. Headlights blazing, two police cars pulled up to the kerb behind it, and a large van with police markings passed them all and parked just ahead. Doors opened. Large men, some in suits, some in uniform, climbed out of the vehicles to gather on the pavement around one of the plainclothes officers. He must be a detective inspector, Eleanor assumed. He had his back to the window so all she could see was that he was balding, taller than many of the others and comparatively slender.

She suddenly pictured all those giants tramping into the room and the dog getting lost underfoot. "Teazle, come!" she called.

Teazle whined and went to the door.

"Sergeant, the dog needs to go out."

"*Now?*" Roscoe had just thumped down from his stool and was lumbering around the counter. "Just when the brass has arrived?"

"Yes, now. She's been terribly good but you can't expect her to hold on forever."

"Not *now*!"

"Well, if you want to risk a puddle—"

"All right, all right, take her out. Under proper control," he added sternly.

Eleanor couldn't find the length of string. She searched her pockets and her handbag with increasing urgency as Teazle's whine took on increasing desperation.

Nick, returning, took in the scene at a glance. "The string's still attached to her collar, Eleanor. Here."

As he stooped to pick up the end and hand it to her, she whispered, "Nick, for pity's sake don't argue or play the fool with the detectives."

"Don't worry, I won't. It's hard to resist taking the mickey, but I'll behave myself."

The sergeant reached them just in time to hear his last words. "You'd better, Nick," he warned. "You're in big trouble, and these blokes don't mess about."

Nick opened his mouth, caught Eleanor's eye, and closed it again.

"Here you go, madam." Roscoe opened the door.

Teazle shot out, and Eleanor lost the end of the string.

The pavement, the Westie had been taught, was not a suitable place for relieving oneself. From a patch of lawn diagonally across the street, the sweet scent of greenery reached her quivering nostrils. She had also been taught to cross streets with caution, but desperate times call for desperate measures. Circling the group of detectives, she dashed between the grey saloon and the rear police car with Eleanor in hot pursuit.

"Stop!" someone shouted. Heavy footsteps pounded after her.

As soon as Teazle felt grass beneath her paws, she squatted. Half a dozen large policemen found themselves surrounding a small white dog and a small white-haired old lady.

The tall, thin, balding man stepped into the circle. "What's going on here?" he demanded.

Eleanor had had enough. Irritably she cut through a babble of bass voices explaining that they had taken her for a murderer on the run.

"My dog is answering a call of nature. These gentlemen seem to be extraordinarily interested in her bodily functions."

"Extraordinary, perhaps, madam," he said gently, "but hardly unnatural. You came rushing out from a police station where a murderer is being held under arrest."

"He's not under arrest. And he's not a murderer." Eleanor found herself in just the sort of argument she had advised Nick against.

"Oh?" He had his back to what little light there was, so she couldn't make out his expression, but she could hear his raised eyebrows. "You know more about the matter than I do?"

"Yes."

"Excellent. Then let's go inside and you can tell me all about it." He bent down to scratch behind Teazle's ears as she sniffed at his shoes. "What's her name?"

"Teazle."

"Come along, then, Teazle." He took the end of the string from Eleanor. Teazle gave a short, sharp bark of protest. "What's up? Don't you want to come with me? But your owner's coming, too."

"She's hungry. She hasn't had her dinner. And all the shops are long shut."

"You don't live in Padstow? Ah, well, we'll manage something. Pearce," he said to the one remaining detective who hadn't melted away, "doesn't DC Wilkes generally have something edible in his pocket? A former Boy Scout, I believe."

"Yes, sir. I think I heard mention of a ham sandwich."

"That will do very well, won't it, Teazle? I'm sure Wilkes will be happy to come to the rescue."

And so he should, Eleanor thought, considering how many meals she had fed the detective constable. She decided against informing this soft-voiced yet somehow alarming man that she was acquainted with Wilkes, though no doubt he'd find out sooner or later.

As they went back across the street, he said, "I haven't introduced myself. How very remiss of me. Detective Chief Inspector Bixby."

"Mrs Trewynn." Eleanor would have preferred him to remain ignorant of her name. But after all, Trewynn—variously spelt— was quite a common Cornish name. He wouldn't necessarily associate her with the LonStar affair. At least, not at once. Not until Sergeant Roscoe told him, she remembered gloomily.

Why had she ever presumed that her retirement would be peaceful?

SIX

Roscoe stood at attention by the door of his station. He saluted as DCI Bixby approached with Teazle on her string and Eleanor at his side.

"Sergeant Roscoe, sir. I hope it's all right, sir, letting the lady take the little dog out for a minute."

"Unavoidable, I suppose, considering the alternative," drawled Bixby. "Go and direct the lads in the van to the scene, would you, Sergeant? And that looks like Dr Prthnavi pulling up behind them."

Rajendra Prthnavi! The police surgeon was a friend of Eleanor's, but she had forgotten he was bound to be called in to examine the body. Rajendra wouldn't be fooled even for a moment by the red paint.

"Yes, sir, right away. My report's on the desk, sir."

"Excellent." He gestured to Eleanor to precede him inside.

The Rosevears and Stella were sitting on the bench. Nick stood apart, by the window, turning away from it to face Eleanor and her escort as they entered.

"Detective Chief Inspector Bixby," the thin man introduced

himself. "And this is Detective Inspector Pearce, who will be in charge of the case, under my direction. I've already made the acquaintance of Mrs Trewynn and the delightful Teazle." He handed the end of the string to Eleanor. "So I'd be grateful if the rest of you would be so kind as to give us your names?"

Having spoken, Bixby crossed to the counter, sat down on the stool, and proceeded to read Roscoe's report.

While DI Pearce, a pale, plump man in heavy black-rimmed glasses, took down Margery's name and address, Eleanor went to sit on the chair by the window, close to Nick. He put his hand on her shoulder and gave a slight squeeze, whether for comfort or warning she couldn't tell. Teazle sat in front of her looking up hopefully.

DC Wilkes separated from the group of large men—a mixture of detectives and uniformed officers—who had entered after Pearce. He came over, and Teazle immediately transferred her hopes to him. When he squatted down, she put her forefeet on his massive thigh so that she could reach to nose at his jacket pocket.

He laughed. "Hungry, eh? Well, you're in luck." He took out a square package wrapped in wax-paper. "Ham and cheese do you? I better take out the pickle." He looked up at Eleanor and whispered, "In hot water again, eh, Mrs Trewynn? That's lah vee for you, as the Frogs say."

"Please, don't tell Mr Bixby it's 'again'," she whispered back.

He winked. Grateful for his sympathy as well as his sandwich, she persuaded him to give the little dog no more than a quarter of the latter. "And perhaps you'd better take the top bit of bread off. I'd hate her to be sick on Sergeant Roscoe's floor after he so kindly let us go out."

Wilkes took out a pocket knife. With the aid of the window-ledge and Nick, he managed to cut one half of the sandwich in half, rather messily. While they were at it, Eleanor listened to

Stella arguing with DI Pearce about whether she should be addressed as Miss Weller or Miss Maris.

"Honestly, Stella," said Margery, exasperated, "how can you make a fuss about your name when Geoff's lying murdered?"

Stella buried her face in her hands and said in a muffled voice, "I just can't believe it."

Margery put a comforting arm around her shoulders.

Doug said plaintively, "What I can't believe is that they're getting fed while we're starving." He was staring towards Eleanor.

"It's just the little dog," Wilkes told him, and hastily rewrapped the rest of his sandwich while Nick fed the mangled quarter to Teazle.

Eleanor glanced at DCI Bixby, who looked as if he wished he had never suggested offering Wilkes's sandwich to the dog. He called Sergeant Roscoe over to explain something in the report.

Pearce had overruled Miss Stella Weller, on the grounds that the police couldn't be expected to address her by her pseudonym while using her legal name in their reports, as required by regulations. He was aided by the fact that she was now weeping copiously into his handkerchief. He wrote down Douglas Rosevear's name and came over to Eleanor and Nick. Wilkes hastily rejoined the group of officers at the door.

"Your name, if you please, madam?" Pearce asked. He seemed to favour his boss's soft-spoken approach.

"Eleanor Trewynn, Mrs."

"Would you mind spelling that for me?"

Eleanor complied. He wrote it down, then stared at what he had written.

"Not . . . Where do you live, Mrs Trewynn?"

"In Port Mabyn."

"Not, by any chance, at the LonStar shop?"

"I'm afraid so," she admitted.

"Now look here!" said Nick angrily. "Just because—"

"Hush, Nick. It's not as though I have a police record or anything I desperately want to keep quiet."

Pearce had turned to Nick. "And according to what Sergeant Roscoe told us on the phone, you must be the person Miss Weller says stabbed the victim."

Nick bowed. "Nicholas Gresham at your service. Port Mabyn. Gresham's Gallery, next door to the LonStar shop."

Frowning, the inspector gave them both a slow, thorough scrutiny. Eleanor had to resist an urge to poke at her hair, sure she must look as if she'd been dragged through a bush backwards. Usually her white curls stayed reasonably tidy through thick and thin—in her opinion if not in Joce's—and she'd been in too much of a hurry to bother to check in the mirror in the loo.

"Thank you." With a nod, Pearce left them and went over to DCI Bixby. They spoke in low voices, with frequent glances at Nick and Eleanor.

Just then, a uniformed constable came in and joined them. "Message from Superintendent Egerton, sir. Will you please call in at once."

Bixby reached for the telephone, then looked around the crowded room and drew back his hand. "Suppose I'd better take it on the car radio. You hold on here till I see what's what, Pearce. Take a dekko at Roscoe's report."

He and the constable went out. For a few minutes, the only sounds were the rustle of Pearce turning pages, the shuffle of feet, Stella's sniffs, and Teazle's nails scrabbling on the lino in a dream. She had fallen asleep after eating and was probably chasing rabbits on the cliffs. Eleanor wished she could follow her.

Bixby came back. "Something's come up," he told Pearce. "I've got to go back to Bodmin right away. You can cope with this business. It looks pretty straightforward."

"With respect, sir, I should like at least to consult DI . . . you know."

"You really like to complicate your own life, don't you," Bixby said impatiently, moving towards the door as he spoke, with Pearce at his heels. "Have it your own way. Ring him in the morning. I must go. Tonight you'd better take statements from—" The door closed behind them.

"That's a good sign," Eleanor said.

"A good sign?" Nick asked with the gloom attendant upon an empty stomach with no prospect of food. "I haven't noticed any. What is?"

"That Inspector Pearce doesn't agree that it's straighforward. Bixby seems to assume you're guilty."

"Oh, that. He'll have to change his mind as soon as he gets reports from the forensics men and the pathologist."

"I suppose so. But first impressions are so important. Once someone's made up his mind, it's much more difficult to make him change it than to make him see reason in the first place, no matter what the evidence."

"True." He smiled at her. "We'll regard DI Pearce's open mind as a good sign. I don't particularly want to spend a night in the lock-up."

"Nick, surely not!"

"If they believe I'm a murderer, they can hardly let me run loose. I might bump off the supposed eyewitness to my crime."

"Don't joke about it."

"It's not really a joke. The woman's a menace to society. I could kill her. Metaphorically, of course," he added hastily as DI Pearce returned at precisely the wrong moment and gave him a hard stare. "Damn, that's torn it."

"Do you think he heard? You really shouldn't talk any more without a lawyer present."

"I don't seem to be able to stop putting my foot in it tonight," Nick admitted ruefully. "I'm dog-tired."

They both looked down at Teazle, snoring peacefully in the sleep of the exhausted. They were both taken by surprise when Pearce said, close by, "It is my duty, Mr Gresham, to advise you that you need not say anything, but that anything you choose to say will be taken down and may be used in evidence."

"Oh hell!"

Wilkes, at Pearce's elbow, solemnly wrote it in his notebook. Nick was not amused.

"I want to go home!" Stella wailed.

"Inspector," Margery appealed, "can't I take her home? She's just about had enough."

Pearce swung round. "I can't let you go quite yet, I'm afraid. I'll make it as short as I can. I must read the sergeant's report, and then there'll be just a few questions."

"We've already told Jerry Roscoe everything."

"Regulations, madam. It's my duty to get the information first-hand. It will be taken down and used to prepare statements which you'll be asked to sign. The signing can wait till tomorrow."

"I should hope so. We're first in line, I hope."

"Inspector," Nick intervened, "Mrs Trewynn should be first, on grounds of age and—"

"*Not* infirmity, Nick. Besides, it doesn't really matter, because I don't see how I can get home tonight. The car's on the other side of the river, the ferry must have stopped long since, and all the hotels will be closed. Not that I have any money with me. So I might as well stay here, where at least it's warm. If Sergeant Roscoe will have me, that is."

"Happy to, ma'am. The missus'll make you up a cosy bed on the sofa in our parlour next door."

"No need for that," said Marge. "You must come up to the farm, Mrs Trewynn. There's no one in the spare room at present."

"That's very kind of you," said Eleanor, with a doubtful look at Nick. She didn't want to appear disloyal. "But I'm not sure—"

"Don't look a gift horse in the mouth, Eleanor," he advised. When she had accepted the invitation and thanked the Rosevears, he added in an undertone, "You can do a bit of snooping around up there. After all, that's where he spent his time when he wasn't in his shop and studio. His bungalow's on farm land. You might get a lead on who could have done the fell deed."

"How many people live there?" she asked, surprised.

"I told you, it's a sort of commune, an artists' colony. There's a certain amount of coming and going, but I should think there's at least half a dozen or so in residence at any time."

"Mr Gresham!" Pearce, at the counter, looked up from Roscoe's report. "If you won't stop talking to Mrs Trewynn, you'd better come over here."

Meekly, Nick obeyed.

Pearce quickly finished reading the report. He asked Roscoe about facilities in the office upstairs, then sent him home to his cottage next door, not to mention his wife and his dinner. Of the men still waiting, with varying degrees of patience, by the door— Bixby had taken a couple of them with him—Pearce sent one detective to King Arthur's Gallery, to find out how the Scene of Crime team was getting on. Leaving a detective and a uniformed officer on guard, he ushered Stella up the stairs, followed by DC Wilkes, notebook at the ready.

Eleanor was disappointed. She had hoped to hear what everyone said. She knew, though, that she was getting close to the point of exhaustion where she couldn't concentrate anyway. It was very fortunate that she didn't have to lie for Nick, because she'd never have been able to remember what she was supposed to say.

Would she lie for him if she had any doubt about his innocence? He was a dear friend, but murder was murder. It would depend, she supposed, on the circumstances. She couldn't imagine . . . any . . . possible . . . She jerked awake just in time to save herself from falling off the chair.

"Eleanor!" Nick was there, on his knees, supporting her.

He was a good friend. She had been thinking so when she nodded off. There was something else . . . but it was gone.

"I'm all right, dear. Just closed my eyes for a moment."

Letting go of her, he stood up. "Officer—I don't know which of you is in charge—Mrs Trewynn can't go on sitting on this grotty chair all night. She'll drop off and break her neck."

"I'd be all right if I was just allowed to talk to someone. Just something to keep me awake . . . A cup of tea, perhaps?"

"I could do with one, too," Doug observed querulously. "I'm a farmer, up with the sun, and that's early this time of year. And I just finished the haymaking this afternoon. I haven't had my supper yet."

"I'll go up and make another pot," Marge offered.

The plainclothesman shook his head. "Mustn't interrupt DI Pearce. I daresay he'll be calling for you, Mrs Rosevear, any moment. Mrs Trewynn, suppose I come and sit beside you and we have a nice chat."

He brought over the other metal chair and dropped into it with a sigh of relief as Nick moved back to lean against the counter. Teazle woke up and raised her head to inspect him.

"I'm Detective Sergeant Weddell, ma'am."

"Have you been on your feet all day, Mr Weddell?"

"Not to say all day, but a good bit of it." He leant down to scratch behind Teazle's ears and she rolled onto her back to allow him to rub her tummy. "You've been busy yourself, I dare say. This little girl, now, I bet she likes her daily walkies."

Teazle sprang to her feet with a short, sharp bark, bright-eyed and ready to go.

"She does," Eleanor agreed. "Not now, girl. False alarm. Lie down."

"Oops, should know better than to say that word," DS Weddell apologised. "Me and the wife, we've got a spaniel, Welsh springer. Loves to swim in the river, he does. You can give him his exercise just standing on the bank throwing sticks. Not that he brings 'em back, half the time."

They talked dogs for several minutes. Then Stella came down the stairs, her eyes red and swollen. She ran across to Margery, who met her with open arms.

DC Wilkes followed her down. Weddell went over to have a word with him.

He looked at Eleanor and nodded. She hoped she was about to be summoned, but he said, "I'll tell him, Sarge. Mr Rosevear, the inspector will see you now."

Doug tramped up after him.

Eleanor no longer felt somnolent. Now, twitchy would be nearer the mark. She was anxious about what Doug was going to say to the inspector. Apparently, Stella had managed to convince herself that she had actually seen Nick stab Geoff. The question was, had she convinced Margery and Doug that they had witnessed it, too? Sergeant Roscoe had taken one look and backed out, sure he'd seen a lake of fresh blood. What evidence could the scientific people provide to refute such preconceptions?

Even if they did, plenty of people would listen to rumours and believe Nick was guilty, as long as the real murderer was at large. How lucky that Margery had invited Eleanor to the farm. If only she had some notion what she should be looking for in the way of clues!

Surely nothing so easy to find as the weapon, which had been left in the body. With fingerprints all over the haft, Eleanor remembered. Had Stella mentioned to DI Pearce that she had grabbed it? Or had she left the police to find out for themselves, and if so, how was she hoping to explain it?

Naturally one wouldn't want her to get into trouble for such a mistake, especially when she was so upset by the death of her boyfriend, but if it served to divert suspicion from Nick—

"Are you okay, Mrs Trewynn? Not falling asleep again?"

"Oh!" Eleanor was startled. "No, thank you, Sergeant, I'm fine. Just thinking."

Doug came down and Margery went up. Eleanor wondered whether she or Nick would be next. She tried to prepare herself, sorting out in her mind what were her own impressions, which needn't be passed on unless they were helpful to Nick, and what were facts that must be told to the police, however detrimental. It was no good trying to suppress facts. They'd winkle them out, and then their having been suppressed would make them look worse than they really were.

They were bad enough. Eleanor shuddered as she recalled the viciously slashed pictures, those that were his livelihood and those irreplaceable few that expressed his dreams. In someone less well-balanced than Nick, they might indeed appear to provide sufficient motive for murder.

And, unfortunately, he had been quite sure Geoff was the destroyer.

She needn't tell the police so, need she? It wasn't exactly fact, just an expressed belief. No one but Eleanor herself had heard him. She wished she could consult him, to make sure they agreed on exactly what must be reported.

But that, of course, was why the police didn't allow them to talk.

Suddenly she remembered Stella's note. That was an indubitable fact she could hardly suppress, so she'd have to tell them Nick knew who had wrecked his work.

Margery came down, followed by DI Pearce and DC Wilkes. Wilkes looked over at Eleanor with a grin and a wink.

What on earth did he mean to convey?

She soon found out. Pearce announced, "That'll be all for tonight. We can't have Mrs Trewynn complaining that she was questioned when half-asleep. You'll be spending the night at the Rosevears', madam?"

"Yes, I think . . . You're sure that's all right, Mrs Rosevear?"

"Of course, dear."

"Then please remain there in the morning until someone has come to take your statement." The inspector turned to Nick. "As for you, Mr Gresham, I'll have to ask you to accompany us to Bodmin."

"Under arrest?" Nick demanded.

"Oh no, sir, merely helping the police with their enquiries. Not under arrest. Not yet."

SEVEN

The Rosevears' vehicle was a mini-bus. Judging by the effluvium, it had recently been used to transport pigs. At the best of times, Eleanor did not travel happily in a mini-bus. She just hoped she could hold out until they reached Upper Trewithen Farm. It was just as well her stomach was empty.

Luckily, even the worst Cornish lanes were an improvement on many she had been driven over in the Third World, and English drivers were less inclined to leave their own and their passengers' fates in the hands of Allah. Still more luckily, the farm was just a couple of miles outside Padstow. The last few hundred yards, though, were over a rutted, potholed track that tried Eleanor severely.

As Doug helped her down, she swallowed a last attempt of her stomach to rebel and thanked him.

There was just enough light left in the west to see that they had stopped in a cobbled yard in front of a two-storied house. On either side ranged outbuildings of various sizes and shapes, three or four of them with squares of light, some curtained, some bare.

"Soup and cocoa," Margery said decisively.

Her offer nearly undid the good effect on Eleanor of cessation of motion and escape from the smell of swine. She was firm with herself. She had eaten nothing but a couple of biscuits since lunchtime. If she was to do Nick any good, she must keep up her strength. She accepted.

Then she wondered whether so much liquid so near to bedtime was a good idea. Did the farm have indoor plumbing? Stumbling about in a strange place in the dark was not an attractive prospect, no matter how often she had done it in deserts and jungles. She had been younger then.

Margery opened the front door of the house and flipped on an electric light switch. She led the way into into a wide, slate-floored, dark-beamed kitchen-living room, with a huge Aga on one side, old wooden settles, and a couple of comfortable, overstuffed chairs on the other.

Following her, Eleanor said, "Mrs Rosevear, I must wash my hands before supper. And—oh dear! I haven't any night things."

"We'll rustle something up. The bathroom and loo are through that door there. Light switch on the left. You'll find a clean towel in the airing cupboard and there should be a new toothbrush in the drawer. Stella, dig up a pair of pyjamas for Mrs Trewynn. You're nearer her size."

Stella, drooping gracefully in the doorway, pouted. "I don't see why I should be expected—"

Eleanor closed the door on Margery's sharp retort. Teazle sticking close to her heels, she found herself in a white-washed corridor with two doors on either side and one at the far end. The farther door on her right stood open. At a peek, it appeared to be the farm office. On the left were a fully modernised bathroom, created, she suspected, from a scullery, and a loo that had probably once been a pantry. The latter was windowless but had a circular ventilator, the kind with a fan that revolves at the slightest breath of wind, high in the thick stone wall.

All electrically lit, thank heaven. Eleanor remembered well the pre-war days of paraffin lamps and even candles to light one to bed in the country.

Here is a candle to light you to bed,
And here comes a chopper to chop off your head . . .

The sinister old rhyme focussed a sense of unease she hadn't recognised, being preoccupied with her uneasy stomach. It dawned on her suddenly that she might conceivably be in danger at the farm. Margery Rosevear's invitation had seemed an unmixed blessing. Yet here, in the community where Geoffrey had lived, was surely the most likely place to find someone who had hated him enough to kill him.

Suppose the murderer were to realise that Eleanor was the only person who could give Nick an alibi and thus force the police to look elsewhere? Too late, Eleanor wished she had insisted on giving her statement that evening.

With her Aikido experience, she was reasonably confident of foiling most attacks from in front, barring firearms, and unarmed attacks from behind, but a silent knife in the back was another matter.

Apart from vigilance, the best course of action was to find out as much as she could about the residents at the farm. With any luck she might work out who, if anyone, posed a danger to her. Since only Geoffrey's killer had any cause to silence her, identifying him would also serve her primary aim: to convince the world of Nick's innocence.

Her course of action settled, Eleanor looked around the bathroom as she combed her hair. It seemed surprisingly clean and neat for a communal situation. She had never come into contact with an English commune before, though she had seen similar living arrangements in other countries. The Bushmen of the Kalahari, for instance, survived in rigorous conditions without much of a hierarchy, at least until they came into contact with agricultural communities.

However, in individualistic Britain, she would have expected everyone to leave uncongenial tasks to someone else. Perhaps one of the residents actually enjoyed housework.

Or perhaps the commune wasn't any more truly communistic than the ones in the Soviet Union. Nick had called it "half-baked," she recalled, and had also referred to it as a colony. Doug Rosevear owned the farm so perhaps, as well as keeping pigs and making hay, he ran the colony and kept its artistic members up to the mark. He hadn't struck Eleanor as a very forceful personality, though.

More likely she was thinking up unnecessary complications and the others simply had their own washing facilities.

Through the window, left a couple of inches open for ventilation, came a chilly draught and the sound of rain. Eleanor glanced at herself in the medicine-cupboard mirror and decided lipstick would be superfluous in view of the promised soup and cocoa. She never had been able to keep lipstick on while eating. Come to think of it, she didn't have one with her anyway.

Closing the bathroom door behind her, she returned to the kitchen. Here any draughts were kept at bay by the cosy warmth of the big iron range. Margery stood before it, stirring something steaming in a saucepan.

"That smells delicious," said Eleanor. Her roving life had never allowed her any opportunity to master the culinary arts and she greatly appreciated other people's abilities.

"I hope you like lentils."

"Oh yes." She had once, after an extended sojourn in India, vowed never to eat another lentil, but that was long ago. "So versatile."

"So cheap and filling," Margery retorted, "and easy to reheat. When you have as many mouths to feed as I do, and most of them extremely erratic as to keeping an eye on the time, you don't waste a roast on them. At least, not often. The idea is I have a meal on the table at seven every evening, but I always have stuff available so that they can make a sandwich or, as in this case, heat up some soup. This is so thick it's more like a stew, really, and full of vegetables."

Eleanor couldn't have asked for a better opening. "How many do you cook for?"

"It varies. Not that they usually bother to let me know when they'll be out. Sorry, I'm being grouchy. Doug was up at four to get the hay in, and then Geoff . . . It's been a long day. Do sit down. We won't bother with a tablecloth at this time of night. It'll be ready in just a minute. You'd like bread and butter, I expect, and some cheese."

"I'll get them."

"Thanks." Margery pointed out the bread-bin, an old-fashioned wooden one with a roll-up lid. "And that's the larder, there."

Eleanor took a bread-board from behind the bin and put it on the long, well-scrubbed table. In the bin she found a bread-knife and an unsliced wholemeal loaf of somewhat irregular shape. "You make your own bread, Mrs Rosevear?"

"Marge. Yes, I like baking. I don't really mind cooking for a crowd, you know, though there are times . . . But Doug couldn't have kept the farm without doing something on the side, and taking in boarders was the obvious solution in this part of the world. It was my idea to collect a flock of artists who'd stay year-round, instead of summer visitors. I had artistic leanings in my youth." The ironic tone of her last words had a tinge of wistfulness.

In the larder, Eleanor found a wedge of cheddar, and the butter in a small crock of unglazed earthenware, covered with cheesecloth and standing in water to keep it cool. Also home-made, she thought, but she didn't ask. She didn't want to distract Marge from the subject of her paying guests.

"A group of artists must be more interesting than the general run of summer visitors," she observed, emerging from the larder with the butter as Marge set out a variety of unmatched pottery bowls and plates on the table. "Less work, too, as they don't keep coming and going."

"Yes, and we get all their rejects, too," said Marge, adding a particularly lopsided greenish-blue plate to the collection.

They looked at each other and laughed.

"How can you laugh?" Stella stood in the doorway, glaring at them accusingly. Swathed in a scarlet hooded cape, she was a figure of wrath straight from some bloody myth. "Have you forgotten already that Geoff is dead?"

Margery was guilt-stricken. "Of course not, dear. I'm sorry. Come and sit down. You'll feel better when you've had something to eat."

"I'm not hungry." She turned, the cape swirling about her ankles, and disappeared into the night.

"Oh dear." Margery sighed. "She's right, I shouldn't have laughed."

"It's a pity she heard us," Eleanor agreed, "though I think she would have been angry regardless. Grief takes some people that way. They're looking for someone to blame, and failing that, they'll turn their hostility on anyone within reach."

"But Stella knows who's to blame."

"Nick did not—"

"All right, sorry, I spoke out of turn," Margery said wearily. "I'm too tired to think straight. The police will sort it out. As Stella isn't going to grace us with her presence, let's just not talk about it over supper, right?"

"All right," Eleanor conceded. Nick's vindication would take more than her protests of his innocence and the inevitable decision of the police not to charge him. "Tell me about your artists. How many are there living here?"

"Seven at present, not counting the bungalow we built to rent out ten or twelve years ago. Geoff has—had—that. Then we converted the barn and stables and byres into six bedsitters and a flat, all with studios attached, of course. They're the old farm buildings, good, solid stone. It meant we had to put up those ugly modern metal outbuildings behind the house, but . . ." She shrugged. "You cut your coat according to the cloth. Doug says they're easier to keep clean."

"The silver lining. Are they all painters? No, Stella's a sculptor, and you've got a potter."

"Jeanette paints. Wildly abstract, things with titles like *Green Diagonal* and *Blue on Blue*. She does sell them occasionally, but her bread and butter is illustrating books for children. She specialises in rolypoly puppies and kittens with enormous eyes, often playing musical instruments."

"Good heavens! Each must come as something of a relief after the other."

"I never thought of it like that, but I daresay you're right. You're just in time, dear," she said as Doug came in through the door to the bathroom and office. "Soup's ready."

"Soup! A working man needs something solider than soup."

"There's cheese. And I forgot, there's the last of the ham off the bone. I put it on the top shelf. As long as no one's found it . . ." She disappeared into the larder and returned with a plate. The scraps of meat were abundant, if inelegant—as inelegant as the plate, another reject. "Mrs Trewynn, please help yourself while I dish up the soup. Oh, what about the dog?"

"Thanks, but I don't think she'd better have anything else on top of that sandwich."

While Margery ladled soup into the bowls, Eleanor passed the plate of ham to Doug and cut some slices of bread.

"Who is your potter?" she asked.

"Tom," said Margery. "You mustn't judge his work by these. He makes beautiful stuff and it sells very well."

"Must have a packet put away," Doug grunted. "More like a businessman than an artist. Never late with the rent. I've got no patience with some of 'em, always coming whining with excuses for paying a few days—or weeks—late. Stella's all right, and to give the devil his due, Geoff was usually on time."

Eleanor pricked up her ears at this evidence that Geoff had not been universally popular.

Margery said hastily, "Oswald's another painter. Cornish land-scapes, like Nick, but I have to admit not as good. Then there's Quentin. He sculpts, but on a massive scale. He's been working on the same hunk of granite for three or four years now. Luckily he has a rich aunt who thinks he's going to be the next Henry Moore."

Doug snorted. "Some hope!"

"Leila does the most beautiful shell-work. I'm sure you know the sort of thing. Ladies in hooped gowns and jewelry boxes en-crusted with shells, but also hangings and necklaces and so on based on African and Asian designs. Beautiful mobiles. Some silverwork, too, set with local stones. More craft than art, strictly speaking, and so is Bert."

"Who cares, as long as the rent's paid."

"What does Bert do?" Eleanor asked.

"He knits." Margery threw a warning glance at Doug, who was grinning. "Don't say it! He pays on time, doesn't he? And by your own words, that's what counts. He creates his own patterns, Mrs Trewynn, really gorgeous things. Used to design for a big knitwear manufacturer up north. He sells both designs and one-of-a-kind jumpers. You have to admit, Doug, the one he made for me is simply smashing. I'll show it to you tomorrow, Mrs Trewynn."

"I'd love to see it. And everyone else's work, too, if they won't mind showing me."

"That's one thing you needn't worry about," said Doug. "They're all keen as mustard to show off their stuff."

Perfect, thought Eleanor. She wouldn't have to think up excuses to call on all her prospective suspects. If she couldn't get them talking about Geoffrey Monmouth, or whatever his real name was, then she had somehow managed to lose all the skills that had taken her round the world as LonStar's roving ambassador.

What was more, even artists were human, and it would be only human to be eager to discuss the murder of one of their company.

She hoped they wouldn't be too eager, to the point of being ghoulish. Were they even now talking to Stella, hearing her description of the scene of the crime, absorbing the supposedly gory details? Would Stella already have prejudiced them against Nick, before Eleanor had a chance to explain what had really happened?

The poor girl had had a frightful shock. It was not surprising she'd been making wild accusations. Also, considering her partial responsibility for the damage to Nick's paintings, there might be a bit of "attack is the best method of defence" in her ranting. All in all, she must be in a thoroughly confused emotional state.

"Do you think Stella is all right?" Eleanor asked.

"I'll pop over to see her before I go to bed. But let's go up and make up a bed for you first. You look all in."

"To tell the truth," she confessed, "I'm feeling my age."

EIGHT

"It's all your fault, Pencarrow!"

Megan held the receiver several inches from her ear, a precaution always advisable when her boss, Detective Inspector Scumble, was in a state. At least it gave her time to wake up. She'd gone to bed early after too little sleep the night before.

As soon as Scumble paused for breath, she asked cautiously, "What's my fault, sir?"

"That snake Pearce has got DCI Bixby to dump a case on us. You know what that means."

Megan had been with CaRaDoC long enough to have a fair grasp of the personalities and politics concerned. "Either it's so simple there's no kudos in solving it, or it's so complicated he doesn't think the kudos is worth the effort, or he thinks it's unsolvable."

"Give the little lady a prize! Whichever, it's no kudos."

"But I still don't see why it's my fault, sir."

"Because," he snarled, "their excuse for foisting it on us is that your bloody aunt is involved."

"Aunt Nell?" Megan's heart skipped a beat. "Is she all right? I must phone her."

"Perfectly all right. She's spending the night at some commune near Padstow."

"A *commune*? Why on earth?"

"How the bloody hell am I supposed to know? Padstow's the scene of the crime. Another pal of yours, that artist fellow, Gresham, is spending the night at Bodmin nick. Helping police with their enquiries, officially, but the Super says Bixby told him they're just waiting for a magistrate to wake up in the morning and sign a warrant. They have an eyewitness."

"Then what do they need us for?"

"You think I know? I've no idea what the silly buggers are playing at. The sooner we find out the better. Pick me up at home at half six. I want to be in Bodmin by seven."

"Yes, sir. Er, sir, eyewitness to what?"

"Murder, Sergeant. Eyewitness to murder." He hung up.

Megan reached out her arm to replace the receiver on the phone on her bedside table. She reset her alarm.

A few minutes ago she had been warm and cosy and asleep. Now she was wide-awake with cold shivers running up her spine.

She didn't have enough information to make any guesses as to what was going on. Was Aunt Nell the eyewitness? If she had seen Nick Gresham kill someone, she must be shattered. He was more like a son to her than a next-door neighbour. What was she doing in a commune, near Padstow or anywhere else? Why did the Bodmin CID want Launceston to take over, if they had a cut-and-dried case? Just so as to avoid the drudgery of taking statements and writing reports? It didn't seem sufficient reason for the top brass to go along with the transfer.

In vain Megan told herself to stop worrying; she'd find out in the morning. She was too concerned about her aunt to fall asleep. She reminded herself that, far from the sheltered existence one associated with old ladies, Aunt Nell had led an unusually adventurous life. That enabled her to drift off, only to find herself suddenly wide-awake again and worrying about Nick Gresham.

She had met Nick now and then at Aunt Nell's, and liked him, though he was not her type and sometimes irritated her almost beyond bearing. The artist had always struck her as extremely easygoing. In fact, it was his casual attitude to life that irritated her. What provocation could have made him blow his cool to the point of murder?

When at last she slept, she had horrible dreams in which Duty, in the form of DI Scumble, obliged her to testify in court against Nick Gresham, and Aunt Nell swore never to speak to her again.

The alarm awoke her all too soon. She felt as tired as last night, but she had retained one certainty from her dreams: Given that Pearce was keen to hand over a case to his arch-rival Scumble, it was by no means cut-and-dried. For some reason he didn't like the look of it. And the reason more than likely had something to do with Mrs Eleanor Trewynn.

A light rain was falling. "Rain before seven, fine by eleven," Megan told herself.

After a quick wash, followed by toast and coffee, she rode her bike down the hill to the fenced-off police section of the public car-park behind St Mary Magdalene church. She stowed it in the bike-shed and went to ask the uniformed sergeant in charge for the keys of an unmarked car.

"DI Scumble?" he said. "I'll give you an 1100. He's hard on the springs of my Minis. Maybe it's not his fault, though."

"There are plenty of outsize coppers around here," Megan agreed.

"Wasn't thinking of that so much. Just wondering if the problem is him so often taking a woman driver." He chortled.

Megan, furious with herself for not seeing he was setting her up—as usual—rolled her eyes. "I'm surprised you trust me with an 1100," she said dryly.

"We can't have them in Bodmin thinking we haven't got any decent cars for our CID. What's taking you down there, then?"

"I don't know the details."

"What I heard is, your auntie's in trouble again and they need you and Mr Scumble to help 'em cope with her. These old ladies, they get a bit funny in the head, don't they."

She had had enough. Taking her notebook from her shoulder-bag, she said coldly, "Who told you that? You know how the Super feels about gossip."

"Hey, keep your hair on! I was just kidding, see? I don't know nothing. Nobody ever tells me anything. Here." He thrust a set of car keys at her. "That dark blue one over there. Just been serviced and rarin' to go."

"Thanks." She started towards the car, knowing she'd overreacted.

"You're not gonna report—"

"Just kidding," Megan tossed over her shoulder.

Whatever his faults, he and his assistant had done a good job on the car. The engine ran smooth as silk as Megan negotiated the one-way streets of the town centre, still empty at this all-too-early hour, and zipped along Western Road to the new roundabout. The A30 was clear, too, apart from a few lorries. In a couple of minutes she reached the turn-off to the village where Scumble lived.

Tregadillet was a typical Cornish hamlet, built mostly of moorland granite with roofs of Delabole slate. A few of the cottages had been white-washed, but the majority were the natural grey of the stone, patched with yellow lichen. Here on the north edge of Bodmin Moor, it was too far from the coast to have attracted the rash of holiday bungalows and caravan parks that disfigured so many seaside villages.

The sun broke through the clouds, illuminating Scumble's small front garden. It was bright with columbines and Canterbury bells, with tall hollyhocks against the wall of the house. Megan was always slightly surprised by her boss's love of gardening. In fact, she suspected he took credit for his wife's green thumb. He seemed too belligerent by nature to grow anything so delicate and fanciful as columbines.

On the other hand, perhaps he worked off his aggressive instincts on slugs and snails and greenfly.

She had only ever met Mrs Scumble to say "good morning" on the doorstep, and today was no exception. Though she was ten minutes early, Scumble was waiting for her. He popped out of the glossy green front door before she had time to turn off the ignition.

"What took you, Pencarrow?" he demanded accusingly. "Well, now you're here, let's get going. I know those tricky bastards have something up their sleeves, and they're not going to catch me with my trousers down."

The image this conjured up was too appalling to contemplate. Megan said without sufficient forethought, "You don't suppose it's only because Aunt Nell is mixed up in it, sir?"

"Don't suppose . . . ! Of course it's because your aunt's mixed up in it. They hope because I've survived one encounter with Mrs Trewynn more or less intact, I may conceivably do so again. They may even be cretins enough to imagine having you with me will be more help than hindrance."

Megan held her tongue. Scumble held his breath while she did a three-point turn in the narrow lane. Then he resumed, his voice taking on a ruminative note.

"That's how the brass see it, I bet. If her part in it can be swept under the carpet, so much the better. A sweet little white-haired old lady who runs a charity—there'd be hell to pay if we came down too hard. But that's not why Pearce'd hand over a nice, simple murder case. After all, he's much better at the kid-gloves stuff than I am. Wouldn't you agree, Sergeant?"

The sod! Reaching the end of the lane, Megan leant forwards over the steering wheel and glanced from side to side, pretending she had to concentrate on oncoming traffic in order to turn right, back onto the A30.

Luckily he was always a bit twitchy when being driven. He waited until she'd made the turn before he jeered, "Cat got your tongue? All right, no need to incriminate yourself. We both know diplomacy isn't my strong point. So something's making Pearce think that sweet-talking witnesses isn't going to be enough to pull him through on this one. Right?"

"It makes sense, sir. You did say Bodmin, sir? Isn't the crime scene in Padstow?"

"The SOC team have done it over and the body's gone to the mortuary. We'll go over there later, but I want to read the reports first, take a look at the photos, and talk to Gresham."

So Megan stayed on the A30 instead of branching off towards Wadebridge and thence to Padstow. They were climbing up onto the moors now. On either side stretched slopes of pinkish-purple ling heather; the grey-green of gorse thickets, still in vivid yellow bloom here and there; short, wiry grass, with an occasional emerald patch of bog; lichened slabs of granite—the Earth's skeleton exposed to view.

A particularly noisy lorry scared a group of wild ponies into galloping off, tossing their shaggy manes, westward towards Brown Willy. Sun shone on the great boulders atop the rugged tor, but in the far west a line of cloud on the horizon warned of more rain on the way.

Megan overtook the lorry. The road was clear ahead. The Morris 1100 leapt forwards and Scumble studiously kept his gaze turned away from the speedometer.

"Something's fishy," he said, "and I want to get there early to see if we can't find out what smells before the others come in. Step on it, Pencarrow."

Megan obeyed.

The Bodmin police station, set on a hillside by the church, was an ugly modern concrete building with big windows, very different from the ancient, cramped Launceston nick. Several panda cars were parked underneath, in a sort of open semi-basement, but as a visitor Megan drove round behind. They climbed the steps to the entrance. The duty sergeant, obviously surprised to see them so early, took one look at Scumble's stormy expression and directed them to an office set aside for them.

The décor seemed to have been imported wholesale from the old place. Dingy green and sickly pale yellow walls surrounded a battered metal desk with a swivel chair behind it and two wooden chairs in front. On the desk were a telephone, an old biscuit tin—so scratched that the words PEEK FREAN'S TEA TIME AS-SORTMENT were barely legible—half full of jumbled biros and varicoloured pencils, a memorandum form addressed to DI Scumble, and several manila file folders.

Ignoring the memo, Scumble pounced on the pile of folders.

"This is something like!" He read the name on the label of the top one: "Rosevear, Douglas." Flipping it open, he remarked, "Someone was up late typing. Sit down, Pencarrow, and have a gander at this." He dropped into the swivel chair and pushed a smudged carbon copy across the desk.

Megan picked it up, looking forward to the day when she'd have enough seniority not to get the carbon every time.

Douglas Rosevear was a farmer, aged forty-two. Yesterday afternoon he had finished the hay-cutting, so he had been able to take the time off to go to the pub for a pint before supper. He had driven into Padstow to the Gold Bezant Inn—

"What the hell's a bezant when it's at home?" demanded Scumble.

"A Byzantine coin," said Megan. "There's several on the coat of arms of the Duke of Cornwall."

"Hmph."

—with his wife and Miss Stella Maris. Yes, he knew that was not her real name; he had been told she used it for artistic reasons. He didn't understand that sort of stuff. It was none of his business what she chose to call herself.

"Stella Maris!" Megan exclaimed. "Flying high!"

Scumble looked up with a scowl for the interruption, since he wasn't doing the interrupting. "Flying high? What's that supposed to mean?"

"It means 'Star of the Sea.' *Stella maris* does, I mean. In Latin. It's one of the titles Catholics give to the Virgin Mary. The only reason I know is that it was in a piece we sang in my school choir."

Somewhat to her surprise, Scumble was interested. "Star of the Sea, eh? Fancies herself, doesn't she!"

"Either that," Megan said cautiously, "or she's got so little self-confidence, she thinks she can boost it by giving herself a fancy name."

"You reckon?" He didn't slam her down, as she half expected. "Well, now, we'll find out when we meet her, I expect. Or when we read her statement." He shuffled through the folders. "Here, third down. Might as well take 'em in the order Pearce left 'em."

Megan returned to Rosevear's statement. At the Gold Bezant, he had reported, Miss Maris, alias Miss Weller, insisted on sitting in the window although it meant waiting for seats. She wanted to be able to see people in the street, because she was anxious about the safety of the deceased, Geoffrey (alias Geoffroie Monmouth) Clark.

Geoffroie indeed! thought Megan. *Talk about the artistic temperament!*

Stella Whatever—the detective constable taking notes had conscientiously written both names every time—told the Rosevears that Clark, in a fit of envy at Nicholas Gresham's good fortune in placing pictures with a swish London art dealer, had damaged several of Gresham's paintings. Stella was afraid Gresham might physically attack Clark.

"Bash him on the nose," Scumble said doubtfully, obviously reaching the same place in the statement, "but would you call that a motive for murder?"

Douglas Rosevear, himself, couldn't see what all the fuss was about. You could always paint more pictures. It wasn't like burning a hayrick or leaving a gate open so the cows could wander off and get hit by cars.

"Depends how bad the damage is, I suppose," said Megan, equally doubtful, "and which paintings. What if it was the ones—or the kind—the London dealer was keen on?"

"That's a thought. There's been murder done for less."

"But why hang about in the pub watching? Why not go and guard Clark at close quarters?'"

Scumble shrugged. "Who knows? Maybe Rosevear turned bolshie and insisted on drinking his pint in peace. Read on for the next exciting installment."

He was getting impatient, though this latest interruption had been his own. Megan took out her notebook so that she could write down questions. She read on quickly and kept her comments to herself.

According to Rosevear, he had proposed the obvious step of going to the nearby gallery. Stella said Clark was in such a foul mood, he'd probably walk out the moment they appeared, and then they'd have to try and follow him.

So they stayed in the Gold Bezant, Rosevear getting hungrier and hungrier for his supper and Stella refusing to leave. He'd have left her to walk home—it was only a couple of miles, after all— well, maybe three—but Mrs Rosevear wouldn't hear of it, considering the state Stella was in. He'd had a few pints. Dusty work, haying, and say what you would, a packet of crisps and a pickled egg wasn't a decent supper for a farmer who'd been at it all day and he didn't much like pickled eggs anyhow.

DI Pearce must have told his note-taker to write down every detail, if not exactly in Rosevear's own words. What on earth could potato crisps and pickled eggs have to do with the murder?

At last, Stella had announced that Gresham was coming up the street.

No, Rosevear didn't know what time it was. Clock-watchers were no use on a farm. You couldn't tell a cow in need of milking that the government had decided the sun was going to rise an hour later on a certain day in April. Time enough to have drunk enough to need to visit the WC . . .

Officialese, Megan thought, not the term Rosevear would have used.

. . . before tramping off to confront an angry artist. Yes, he'd known Nicholas Gresham for years. An easygoing chap, never got in a fuss over a game of darts. But what Clark had done was a bit thick. Rosevear considered Gresham had a right to be narked.

Megan glanced back through the statement—yes, the opposite of what he'd said before, but probably the man had mixed feelings on the subject.

Whatever Stella said, Rosevear wasn't going to stop Gresham taking a pop at Clark. He agreed to go along more to make sure the women kept out of it, really. But by the time he returned to the bar, they were already halfway across the street.

He had hurried to follow and arrived at Clark's gallery feeling a little dizzy. No, of course he wasn't drunk. Lack of food was what it was, after a day slaving in the sun.

The door to the gallery wasn't locked. He was close enough to see Stella push it open and to hear the tinkle of the bell. The door swung closed behind the women, so he had to open it again to go in. His fingerprints would be on it, but they already knew he'd been inside.

As he stepped in, he heard Stella cry out in the inner room, Clark's studio, accusing Gresham of killing Clark. He hadn't gone to see for himself because his wife had told him to ring the police.

He had done so, using the telephone behind the shop counter.

And there the statement ended. Megan turned over the paper in a futile attempt to find more, though it was obviously complete as it stopped in the middle of a page.

"Part of my copy seems to be missing, sir."

"I don't think so, Pencarrow. The lazy sod was so sure he knew the answers he didn't bother to ask half the obvious questions." Scumble sounded oddly pleased. "Hell, he didn't even bother to think! Didn't want to risk being confused by the facts, maybe. Too happy to use Auntie as an excuse to pass off the drudgery to us. If he'd done a more thorough job, I'd be worried."

"Uh, worried, sir?"

"That he might be right. We'll look at the rest of this stuff before we count our chickens, but the way it looks, it's worth doing my damnedest to prove Pearce wrong."

NINE

"Wuff?"

Eleanor opened her eyes to see Teazle's bright brown ones under their white fringe, peering anxiously at her from a few inches away. The dog had slept on the bed as usual, with Margery's permission.

Margery. Yesterday's events, never far from Eleanor's dreams, flooded back to her consciousness. She felt as if only an hour or two of sleep had intervened, though it was broad daylight outside the open window.

The feeling was probably perfectly accurate, she thought. She had gone to bed very late, and June nights were short.

From below came the sound of movement, doubtless what had roused Teazle.

"Wuff?"

"It's all right, girl. I expect they have to milk the cows or something. No need for us to get up yet." Except that, now she was awake, she was going to have to make the trek downstairs and through the kitchen to the loo.

She sat up, pushed back the covers and felt with her feet for the slippers Margery had lent her, reached for the blue candle-wick dressing-gown. How kind the Rosevears had been. They were friends of Nick's, of course. Or had been. Could the friendship survive the suspicion that now hung over him? They also had been friends of the murdered man. When the police let Nick go, as they were bound to once they bothered to listen to her, would anyone truly believe he wasn't guilty? Once the police had someone in their clutches, if he was let go and no one else was arrested, people always assumed he must have been released for lack of evidence, not because he was innocent.

No doubt it would all get into the newspapers, too. What if it spoilt Nick's chances of selling his pictures in London?

Yesterday's sense of urgency returned full force. Here she was in the heart of Geoff's territory. Margery seemed to think all her lodgers would be eager to show off their arts and crafts, regardless of the sudden demise of one of their number. Eleanor had the perfect opportunity to find out whether any of the inhabitants of Upper Trewithen Farm had a motive to kill him.

She wondered whether she ought to wait until she had spoken to the police. Once she had provided Nick's alibi, she would be no threat to the murderer. However, they didn't seem to be in any hurry to see her. If she delayed, her opportunity might evaporate.

Besides, now she thought about it, it seemed unlikely that any of them—even Stella and the Rosevears—had any idea as yet of Eleanor's part in the business. She tried to remember exactly what she had said last night. Surely only that Nick hadn't done it, no more than what she might be expected to say in his support regardless of whether she actually knew anything about it. Anyway, she wasn't going to be in any danger in broad daylight. Everyone else would know where she was and who was with her.

Opening the door at the foot of the stairs, she found Margery already busy in the kitchen. She looked frazzled, as if she hadn't slept much. Eleanor asked her whether she should let the dog out the back door or the front.

"The back is better, unless she's afraid of other dogs."

"She doesn't usually pay them much heed."

"She'll be fine, then. If Doug's farm dogs are there they'll want to investigate, but they won't harm her."

The door at the end of the passage opened onto a kitchen garden bright with the scarlet blossom of runner beans. To the left was a row of fruit trees; to the right, washing lines, with a view of moorland rising beyond. A flagged path led back to a gap in a hedge of red and purple fuchsias, giving a glimpse of a muddy yard surrounded by the metal buildings Margery had mentioned.

Teazle ventured out of the house. Alerted by canine radar, two black and white collies dashed over from the yard, barking.

Teazle met them with unconcern. They stopped barking to sniff. Since there was no growling, snapping, or snarling, Eleanor left them to it. As she closed the door, she heard a whistle and someone shouted for the farm dogs.

Since Margery was up and about, Eleanor decided she might as well have a quick wash and go and get dressed. But when she returned to the kitchen, Teazle once more at her heels, Margery had just made tea.

"Here's some bits and pieces for the dog, and I thought you might like a cuppa. Take it back to bed with you if you're not ready to face the world."

"Thanks, that's just what I need. I'll drink it here, if I won't be in your way."

"Not at all. I'll join you." For a few minutes they sat sipping in silence, while Teazle polished off a bowl of ham scraps. Then Margery said in a low voice, "I didn't sleep a wink. I couldn't stop thinking about it. It was horrible! All that blood . . . I understand why Nick was upset. Geoff was a bastard, but you don't go round killing people because they're a pain in the neck. Nick's always seemed so laid-back. I wouldn't believe it if I hadn't seen it with my own eyes."

"You didn't."

"What do you mean? Are you feeling all right? I was right there."

"Come on, you can't leave it at that. What did you actually see, with your own eyes?"

"Nicholas Gresham standing over the bloody body of Geoff Clark."

"If you walked into a room where someone was apparently lying on the floor in a pool of blood, what would you do?"

"Faint."

"I don't think so, Mrs Rosevear. Margery. I almost fainted, and you dealt with the situation calmly and competently. And kindly, I might add."

"I suppose I'd check his pulse."

"So what would the next person coming in see?"

"Me, standing over the body," she said slowly. "But Stella said she saw Nick kill him."

"Would you consider her to be totally *compos mentis* at the time?"

Margery frowned. "No. That's hardly likely, when her . . . boyfriend was weltering in his own blood—"

"It wasn't blood."

"What do you mean? That much I did see with my own eyes. Bright red, not the colour of dried blood, and glistening. A great pool of blood."

"On the contrary," said Eleanor, shaking her head. "If anything's certain, it's that the red wasn't blood." Not that she had checked for herself. In fact, on seeing it she, too, had taken it for blood, but she wasn't going to admit that. She trusted Nick, though it was a pity he hadn't been able to identify the substance. "The police won't have any trouble telling the difference."

"Then why did they arrest him?" Margery's tone suggested she was now just humouring Eleanor.

"They didn't. He's helping them with their enquiries."

"Everyone knows that's the same thing. Look, Mrs Trewynn, I don't want to believe Nick's guilty any more than you do, but you have to face facts."

Eleanor had thought she was doing brilliantly at leading Margery to grasp the truth. Discouraged, she realised they had just gone round in a circle. She made one more attempt.

"It's not a matter of belief. I *know* Nick didn't kill Geoffrey."

"Why didn't you tell the police?"

"I was waiting for my turn to answer their questions, but they packed it in for the night before they got to me. It's the little-old-lady syndrome. You just wait till you're white-haired and over sixty and you'll discover lots of people—men in particular—assume you have nothing to contribute that can possibly be worth their time. I didn't kick up a fuss, because as soon as Inspector Pearce consulted the policemen who actually went to the gallery he was bound to find out Stella was talking through her hat."

"Jerry Roscoe, our local sergeant, was at the gallery."

"But he barely glanced into the studio. I noticed."

"Well," said Margery doubtfully, "we'll see." She turned with obvious relief to the two women who came in through the front door at that moment. "You're up with the lark this morning."

"Is it true what Quentin told us?" demanded one of the two, a short, thin woman with very short dark hair, wearing trousers and a man's striped shirt.

"This is Mrs Trewynn," Margery said in a tone of slight re-proof. "Leila and Jeanette."

As they exchanged greetings, Eleanor tried to recall what her hostess had told her about these two yesterday evening. The second, Jeanette, was tall, sturdy, and rather pale, with fair, flyaway hair cut in a pageboy, the refusal of which to lie sleek probably caused her much anguish. Shell-work, Eleanor thought. And Leila must be the one who painted abstracts to compensate for the sentimental puppies that paid her bills.

Leila returned to her question. "Well, is it true?" Away from the back-lighting of the doorway, she was obviously older than she had first seemed, in her forties, at least, though it was difficult to tell, as she appeared to have spent a lot of time in the sun.

Eleanor hoped no one could call her vain, but she was glad she had grown up before sun-bathing became fashionable. Spending so much time in the tropics, she had always worn a hat. Crinkles at the corners of her eyes from squinting against the glare were the worst damage the sun had inflicted on her.

"Is what true?" Margery temporised.

"Quentin says Stella told him Geoff is dead and she saw Nick Gresham stab him."

Margery glanced at Eleanor. "It's true that Geoff is dead, and Stella says she saw that happen."

"I don't believe it!" Jeanette was obviously upset. She was considerably younger than the other two, in her late twenties, perhaps thirty.

"It's true that that's what Stella's been saying."

"I can easily believe that. What I can't believe is that Nick killed Geoff. He wouldn't! Even though Geoff mucked about with Nick's pictures, he just wouldn't."

"Come off it, Jeanette," Leila sneered. "Everyone knows you've had a lech for Nick forever."

"Leila, must you be so vulgar? Honestly, sometimes I wonder if I'm running a home for deliquent adolescents!"

Jeanette was scarlet. "What about you and Geoff, then, Leila?"

she retorted. "At least Nick's a nice person. I'd like to hear either of you two say as much of Geoff."

The other two looked at each other sideways, not quite meeting each other's eyes. Eleanor watched with interest. What did it mean?

Neither answered directly. Leila muttered, "Nice?" though whether she wondered if the word could be applied to Geoff or merely scorned its feebleness was not apparent.

"I suppose you want breakfast," said Margery. "What about you, Mrs Trewynn?"

Eleanor realised she was still draped in the borrowed dressing-gown, several sizes too large. "I'd better get dressed," she said hastily.

No doubt she was old-fashioned—and certainly she had been in many parts of the world where women wore a great deal less— but the men would be coming in soon, she assumed. She'd feel more comfortable asking them about Geoff if she were fully dressed, though she risked missing whatever else Margery, Leila, and Jeanette had to say about him.

As she went out, she heard Leila say, "I've got to get down to the cove while the tide's low, Marge. Any hope of a lift?"

Which suggested that Leila, not Jeanette, was the shell artist. So much for appearances, though it would explain her tanned face.

Teazle scampered up the stairs ahead of Eleanor, already quite at home. Eleanor had hung up her blouse and skirt to air, and in the hope of getting rid of some of the wrinkles. The results were not entirely successful. She really ought to try to get over her prejudice against dacron and terylene. Everyone said they were so easy to care for, and she wasn't one of those people like Jocelyn Stearns who could wear a linen suit all day and emerge uncreased.

On the other hand, slightly crumpled cotton was less likely to arouse mistrust in a colony of artistic types than Joce's immaculate smartness. No one could guess from her appearance that the vicar's wife clothed herself almost exclusively from the LonStar shop.

Eleanor dressed and went down, again preceded by Teazle. At the bottom, Teazle waited at the closed door. A babble of voices came from the kitchen, both male and female. Pausing with her hand on the doorknob, Eleanor heard Nick's and Geoff's names, and once her own, but she couldn't make out much else. She opened the door and went in.

For a moment no one noticed. Then, abruptly, silence fell. The only sound was the spitting of frying bacon on the range and the click of Teazle's nails on the stone floor as she headed straight for the heavenly aroma.

"Gosh," said Eleanor, "I do adore the smell of bacon. It always makes me ravenous."

Someone laughed, uncomfortably.

A tall, muscular man—the large-scale sculptor with the rich aunt?—stood up from the table, pulled out the chair next to him, and said, "Mrs Trewynn, I presume. Do come and sit down. I'm Quentin. These chaps are Tom, Albert, and Oswald. You've met Jeanette and Leila, haven't you? And Margery, of course. That's the lot of us, except Stella . . . and Geoff."

"Good morning," said Eleanor and wondered how on earth she was going to keep them all straight. "I'm sorry you've lost . . . one of your number."

Amid a general murmur, one voice—male—emerged: "No great loss." It was the oldest person present, other than Eleanor. He looked about her age, on the small side, balding, with a face like an intelligent monkey. His clothes were the most conventional present, a suit of pale grey, lightweight summer worsted, with a pale blue shirt open at the neck. "I won't miss him."

"Really, Albert," said Margery, "that's not very nice."

"But true. It's a loss to you, of course, Mrs Rosevear. You'll have to find another tenant for the bungalow. But, to call a spade a spade, Geoff had a nasty tongue on him and I defy anyone here to claim otherwise." Albert had a trace of an accent that was not Cornish. North of England, Eleanor thought; Yorkshire, perhaps.

No one contradicted him.

Leila stood up and leant with both fists on the table. "He was an arrogant pig. Albert's right. Now, is anyone going to drive me down to Trevone Bay while the tide is low?"

"I will," Albert offered, "assuming the bus is available."

"Doug doesn't need it till this afternoon," said Marge.

"You can drop me off at the shop," said Quentin, Eleanor's neighbour at the table. "It's my day and I don't mind getting there early."

"Shouldn't we stay closed today?" proposed Jeanette tentatively. "Out of respect, I mean."

"No!" There was nothing tentative about red-bearded Oswald's outburst. "He chose not to belong to the co-op. Even Quent does his day in the shop, though he doesn't have anything to sell. I don't see why we should lose sales because Nick Gresham did us all a favour and did away with Geoff."

Eleanor was going to suggest that everyone should stay at the farm until the police had come to question them. However, DI Pearce had said nothing last night about wanting to see Geoffrey's colleagues, if that was the right term. As soon as he found out Nick was not the killer, he would certainly need to check where they had all been at the time of the murder, especially once Eleanor told him how unpopular the victim had been.

Before she decided whether to speak up, Marge placed in front of her a misshapen plate of bacon, fried egg, fried bread, sausages, and baked beans. "Help yourself to toast," she said. "There'll be fresh coming up in a minute. Leila, get Mrs Trewynn coffee or tea, will you?"

"Coffee, please." She would need her wits about her this morning. "Milk, no sugar."

Leila presented her with a huge mugful. Quentin, standing up to leave for his stint at their co-op shop, passed her a toast-rack, butter and home-made marmalade, all in various pieces of peculiar pottery.

In the face of this overwhelming hospitality, Eleanor felt a bit guilty for her intention of reporting the general dislike of Geoff to the police. She hoped she wouldn't have to open the subject, but if she was asked, she couldn't lie about it. Not that Pearce seemed very interested in what she had to say, but once she'd provided Nick's alibi, perhaps he would change his mind. She wished she could explain everything to Megan—if it weren't that Megan came with DI Scumble attached.

Quentin, Leila, and Albert departed.

The potter, Tom, hitherto had been silent as he ate his way through an even larger plateful of breakfast than the one Eleanor was bracing herself to tackle. Now, his fingers permanently stained with clay, he wiped up the last of the egg yolk with a final piece of toast and asked, "Where's Stella?"

"She was asleep when I went down earlier to check." Margery at last sat down with her own breakfast. "She was in such a state last night, I gave her . . . something to help her sleep."

Something illegal? Eleanor wondered. It was none of her business. Anyway, in many parts of the world, marijuana was regarded as a useful medication.

"I was just thinking," Tom went on, "will she be fit to work this weekend? Because if not, maybe someone ought to phone. She's always on about how the place couldn't function without her."

"By someone, I suppose you mean me," said Margery resignedly. "You have a point, though. I wouldn't want all those convalescents to be without proper care. But I don't want to get the doctor in a fuss over nothing, either. I'll go over a bit later and ask Stella if she feels up to it."

"Stella works in a convalescent home?" Eleanor asked. "I remember you said something about her being a nurse."

"She's not a Registered Nurse," Jeanette said. "She got bored with the training before she qualified. She made quite a habit of dropping out of various courses, I think. But she got a job at the Riverview Convalescent Home, near Wadebridge. They have a hard time getting staff for the weekends. The people aren't that ill. I mean, obviously, they're supposed to be getting better or they wouldn't be there."

"Riverview? It sounds familiar. It has a good reputation, doesn't it?"

Margery snorted. "Dr Fenwick—he's the owner—spends his weekends there, too. With him in charge, I dare say even Stella can't do much harm. I can't remember why on earth I mentioned to you that she's a nurse."

"When was that?" Oswald asked. "Not to be nosy, but didn't you say you just met Mrs Trewynn at Geoff's gallery last night?"

Eleanor had a sudden flash of memory, so clear she could almost hear the tones of voice. "It was when I was so stupidly faint," she recalled. "You were helping me, Margery. Stella told you Geoffrey was dead. You said you couldn't believe it, but that she was a nurse so she must know." Margery had sounded more preoccupied than shocked, as if Geoff's death came as no surprise. Of course, she had been concerned about Eleanor's condition, but all the same . . .

And while considering odd reactions, what about Doug, who hadn't even taken the trouble to come and see what was going on before calling the police to report a murder?

Stella, on the other hand, had sounded melodramatic, as if determined to wring the last ounce of histrionics out of the situation. Still, to be fair, was there or could there be such a thing as a "normal" reaction to finding one's lover's body sprawled on the floor with a dagger in his back?

TEN

"Hysterical," said DI Scumble in disgust. "If there's anything I can't abide it's a hysterical witness."

"Difficult to deal with," Megan agreed.

"That's the least of it. With any luck, she'll have calmed down by today. The thing is, you can't trust a word they say. What we'll get is what she believes she saw, which may or may not have much relation to reality. And there's no way of knowing, because she's sure she's telling the truth. They can be damnably convincing."

"We've got the other witnesses." Megan didn't want to believe Nick Gresham was a murderer, but the evidence seemed plain.

"Pah! The Rosevears? Not worth the paper it's written on. Rosevear doesn't even claim to have seen the stabbing. And I'll bet when we take his missus through it carefully, all she saw was the body and the blood. She heard this Maris woman shrieking that she saw Gresham kill Clark, but she also says she was concentrating on getting your auntie sat down before she fainted."

"So even though she doesn't seem to have been hysterical, her evidence isn't worth—"

"Evidence! I haven't seen any evidence yet." Scumble stuck Stella's statement back in its folder and, pushing it aside, read the name on the last in the pile. "Jerry Roscoe, Sergeant. Ah, here we are. The local copper. Last but let's hope not least. We ought to be able to believe the evidence of *his* eyes."

Sergeant Roscoe's report was that of a man to whom the written word does not come easily. It relied heavily on police jargon and tended to get bogged down in lengthy clauses.

For all its weightiness, however, it did not actually say much. Scumble skimmed it in less than a minute and threw it down on the desk with a snort.

"He didn't even go into the studio. Afraid of disturbing the scene of the crime! Glanced in and closed the door. For all he knew, the chap could have been lying there slowly bleeding to death."

Megan, struggling with a copy from a carbon paper on its last legs, took a little longer to finish. "Mr Gresham went quietly. You think Nick—Mr Gresham can explain what he was doing there, sir?"

"Oh, I think the Rosevears and the Weller woman are probably right that he went to the gallery to have it out with Clark about the damage he'd done. What came next we might have some idea of if that idiot Pearce had taken the trouble to ask instead of going along with a load of hysterical rubbish."

"Was DI Pearce trying to soften Gresham up, letting him stew for the night in the cells?"

"There's nothing to say Gresham wasn't willing to talk. Let alone Mrs Trewynn, who was doubtless dying to have her say, though on past form she would probably have left out the important bits. Pearce was just too bloody lazy to talk to them when he hoped to pass this mess off to me. What's harder to credit is that he doesn't seem to have gone himself to the gallery. Or if he did, he didn't bother to give us a report of what he saw."

"It's odd, isn't it, that Gresham didn't explain his side of the story in the car on the way over from Padstow?"

"For all we know he did, and no one bothered to write it down."

"Shall I bring him in here, then, sir?"

"Hmm. I'd really like to hear what Forensics have to say before I talk to him. Dr Prthnavi, too. I need something concrete to go on. I wonder if it's too early to get hold of them?" He frowned at the wall clock. "I doubt they'll have written up their reports yet, but anything they can tell us will be more than we know. You might as well give 'em a try."

Megan dialled the switchboard and asked for Forensics. The girl put her through.

"Jenkins."

"DS Pencarrow here. DI Scumble would like to know what you've got on the Padstow murder."

Jenkins snickered. His voice came to Megan slightly muffled, as though he had turned away from the phone: "Padstow."

The single word was sufficient to provoke gales of mirth from someone in the background. Megan held out the receiver towards Scumble. She expected fireworks, but after a momentary tightening of the lips, he looked smug and waved to her to continue.

"Well?" she said. "You have something to tell us?"

"Scumble, you said? DI Pearce was in charge."

"He handed over to Mr Scumble. What's up?"

"Not what we were told to expect, at any rate. Bloke swimming in his own blood, I don't think. Course, time of death's not our business, but I was the SOC man on duty last night and you can take it from me, when we got there the victim had been dead for several hours, and he had hardly bled at all. As DI Pearce would've known if he'd bothered to take a look. Or condescended to ask us. Cold as charity, he was, with a lot of red ink splashed about, dry as a bone."

"Red ink?" Megan repeated, astounded.

Sounds of merriment assailed her ear.

"Give it here." Scumble reached for the receiver. "All right," he bellowed, "you've had your fun. What's this about red ink? You'd better not be cackling about the plonk you swilled last night!"

As he listened, Scumble reached for a biro from the biscuit tin and started scribbling notes on one of the folders. As he wrote, a smile started to spread across his face, a sight that astonished Megan almost as much as the transmutation of blood into red ink.

"You're dead certain?" he said at last. "Right, thanks. I owe you one." He hung up. "Pearce really buggered up this one," he told Megan with immense satisfaction. "Jenkins swears the artist'd been dead at least several hours, and I'd trust his judgement over a hysterical woman any day. We needn't bother Dr Prthnavi yet. Also, there are fingerprints on the hilt of the dagger. Not Gresham's. Probably a woman's."

"A lovers' tiff?"

"Could be. You can go fetch Gresham now. And be polite."

"Should I tell him he's off the hook?"

"Off Pearce's hook, at any rate. But no, don't tell him. For all we know, we may have to hook him again ourselves, who knows? With any luck his story will give us a clearer picture. If I ever get to hear it . . ."

"I'm on my way, sir!"

"Good." The inspector was back to his sarcastic self. "On your way back, no chitchat and kindly do not inform the suspect that his custody was a mistake. Even though," his triumphant words followed her out of the room, "it was not *my* mistake!"

When Nick was brought out from the cells, the first words he said to Megan were, "I've worked out what it was. Obvious, really, but I suppose I wasn't thinking very clearly last night." Then he did a double-take. "Megan? Though, in the circumstances, I expect you'd prefer Sergeant Pencarrow. Have you been transferred to Bodmin? I hope you're not having to work with that cretin Pearce."

"No, sir," Megan said as stolidly as she could manage. "DI Scumble has taken over the case."

"'Sir!' Well, tit for tat, I suppose. So Scumble's in charge now? He's a bloody-minded so-and-so, but at least he's not stupid. He must have realised by now that—"

"Save it for him, will you?"

He grinned. "I was only going to say, all that glitters is not gold."

Megan was reminded just how infuriating he could be. Here she was brimming with sympathy for his plight, while he loped along the corridor ahead of her with a jaunty insouciance that failed to recognise any need for sympathy.

On the other hand, if he expected sympathy it would be because he felt badly treated, in which case she'd now be dealing with an angry man. She should be grateful, not irritated. Which conclusion didn't make her any less resentful. He ought to be angry.

Could anyone who took a night's false imprisonment with such calm conceivably work himself up to murder?

He paused at a cross-passage to wait for her. She ushered him into the room where Scumble sat waiting, spiderlike, weaving a web not for Nick but for DI Pearce.

"Hello, Inspector," Nick greeted him cheerfully. "We meet again."

"Good morning, Mr Gresham. Have a seat and tell me how you got yourself into this mess."

"It's not my mess." He moved to the chair facing the desk, then glanced around and saw Megan still standing. "We need another chair."

"I can stand."

"I dare say, but I can't sit if you don't. I were brought up proper, I were."

"Sergeant Pencarrow's a police officer," snapped Scumble. "She's accustomed to standing."

"But Miss Pencarrow is also a . . . female—I expect she'd be insulted if I called her a lady. *O tempora, o mores!* Come on, I don't want to be here forever. I have an urgent commission I need to get going with. I don't mind standing. Or better, *I'll* fetch a chair."

"You stay here! Pencarrow, go find yourself a bloody chair."

Hastily, Megan went. It was lucky for Nick, she thought, that Scumble was after other game and willing to conciliate him. On the other hand, Nick was virtually uncrushable so perhaps it didn't make much difference. The trouble was, you could never be sure whether he was deliberately being difficult with intent to annoy, or just being his maddeningly flippant self.

When she returned with a chair from the office next door, Nick was lounging on the corner of the desk, whistling "Land of Hope and Glory." Scumble was tight-lipped, fingers tapping impatiently on the desktop.

"Where the hell you been, Pencarrow?"

"I made a quick telephone call, sir."

"Not to your auntie, I hope! She's a witness, remember."

"No, sir, I didn't speak to any of the witnesses." Megan sat down quickly and took out her notebook. Nick took the other chair.

"May we now proceed?" Scumble asked acidly.

"Certainly. I didn't want DS Pencarrow to miss any of my enthralling story. As I'm sure you've worked out by now, it's all about red ink. Ironic, really, considering Eleanor and I never even acquired the bottle of bubbly I'd been looking forward to."

Scumble gave Megan an I-told-you-so look. As he'd said, Aunt Nell had somehow got herself mixed up in the case.

To Nick he said in a heavily patient voice, "Perhaps we could begin at the beginning, Mr Gresham? Don't worry about what we already know or don't know. Just tell us what led to you being found yesterday evening in a picture gallery in Padstow with a dead body at your feet."

Nick reflected. For a moment, Megan was afraid he was going to be stroppy, but apparently he decided the moment had come to tell his side of the story.

"Since, presumably, you're by now aware that Geoff must have died hours before Jerry Roscoe arrived—Sergeant Roscoe, if you prefer—I suppose yesterday morning would be the place to start. I was in London, had been there for a few days. I had a business appointment in the morning—"

"Who with?"

"Mr Alarian, of Alarian Galleries, in Albemarle Street."

"Time?"

"Half ten. I got there a bit early, actually, but the place didn't open till then so I hung about outside. You see, he—"

"I don't need to know your business, Mr Gresham. Not at present, at least. How long were you with Mr Alarian?"

"An hour? About that. It was about noon when I phoned from Paddington."

"Phoned who?"

"I tried Eleanor's number—Mrs Trewynn—but she wasn't at home."

"Pity! Not that there'd be much hope of Mrs Trewynn knowing what time she talked to you, if she had."

"Ah, but then I rang up Mrs Stearns. I shouldn't think you could ask for a better witness than Mrs Stearns."

"True," Scumble admitted grudgingly.

"I told her the time my train was supposed to arrive at Launceston, just in case Eleanor might be collecting in that direction that afternoon."

In the sure and certain belief, Megan translated to herself, that Aunt Nell would pick him up at the station.

"And I also rang Stella—Stella Maris, or Weller, whichever you prefer. She was taking care of my place. I sell her stuff for her in exchange for her taking over now and then, giving me a break."

"So your relationship with Miss . . . Maris was a business one."

"Yes. Well . . . yes."

Scumble pounced. "Well?"

"She was a friend of mine. I did once think—Oh lord, there's no way to say this without sounding a complete creep." Nick glanced at Megan, who pretended she didn't notice and kept her eyes on her notebook.

"Get on with it," the inspector said impatiently. "Pencarrow's a police officer, not a little old lady."

"I wouldn't tell you if it weren't that Stella's gone and landed me in the sh—in this mess. She did once gave me the come-on—what they used to call a come-hither look, but considerably more explicit. After I made it clear I wasn't interested, she was a bit snotty for a while, and things were never quite comfortable between us after that. On my side, at least."

"Are you a homosexual, Mr Gresham?"

"I can't see what that has to do with anything, but no, as it happens, I'm not." Nick's tone of mockery returned. "I'm just saving myself for the right girl. Besides, being propositioned by Stella is not particularly flattering."

"Oh?"

"I don't care if Miss Pencarrow is a police officer or the man in the moon, I'm not going to elaborate. I shouldn't have said that. Spiteful, and irrelevant."

"All right, we'll leave it at that. For the moment. When you phoned Miss Maris yesterday, what did you say to her?"

"I told her I'd be home that day, probably before closing time, possibly later."

"So you didn't tell her exactly what time?"

"I probably gave her the time the train reached Launceston. I expect I did, but I couldn't swear to it. I couldn't say when I'd reach Port Mabyn because I didn't know whether Mrs Trewynn would pick me up or if I'd have to hitchhike or bus it."

"Anything else?"

To Megan's surprise, a slight flush tinged Nick's cheeks. She wouldn't have thought him capable of blushing, in spite of his reluctance to state outright that Stella Maris was promiscuous.

"As a matter of fact," he said self-consciously, "I passed on some good news about my business with Mr Alarian."

"Good news? Elaborate, Mr Gresham, if you will."

"I'm sure Stella told your colleagues, and I can't believe they didn't pass on to you something so material to their imaginary case against me."

Scumble's comparative mildness vanished. "In this case," he snarled, "you can take it from me that I do not have all the information I ought to have. What's more, you should be damn glad I'm not swallowing what little I've been given. What good news?"

Nick's blush deepened. "That Alarian's interested in my work. He's actually going to hang a couple of paintings. It's rather a prestigious gallery. Of course, he's a friend of Eleanor's . . ."

He really had been "brought up proper," Megan thought, if he was bashful about touting his own accomplishments. Rather old-fashioned, in spite of his pony-tail and sandals.

"Mrs Trewynn again! Popping up everywhere. It beats me how Pearce managed to overlook her."

Nick looked amused. Megan couldn't help wondering exactly what Aunt Nell had said or done to make DI Pearce assume that taking her statement would be a waste of his precious time.

ELEVEN

Scumble sighed heavily. "I suppose Mrs Trewynn did in fact pick you up at the station in Launceston?"

"She did, Inspector," Nick confirmed with a grin. "The train got in pretty much on time, at five past four, and she was waiting."

"And she's your alibi."

"Well, yes. The Incorruptible can't make it over the moors from Launceston to Port Mabyn in much less than an hour."

"The incorr—Oh, her Morris Minor. Something about the French Revolution, I seem to remember."

"Robespierre, Inspector, whom Carlyle called the 'sea-green incorruptible.' And the pea-green car."

"Load of bollocks. We may have to test that time with a police driver. PC Dixon, I should think, would—"

"Sir!" Megan protested, with memories of a terrifying dash through the narrow, winding lanes with PC Dixon at the wheel, "I doubt Aunt Nell's car could survive Dixon's driving."

"Maybe not. But you needn't think I'll let *you* do it. Mr Gresham, can anyone other than Mrs Trewynn confirm your whereabouts yesterday afternoon?"

"I don't know. The ticket collector took my ticket at Launceston, but of course it didn't have my name on it. No reason he should remember me. Donna from the pub helped to unload the Incorruptible in Port Mabyn, and the little Chins, too—"

"The little—? Ah yes, the children from the Chinese restaurant."

"You have a good memory, Inspector. However, I suppose I could just as well have been doing that after returning from committing murder in Padstow. It must have been about five o'clock. What time did Geoff die?"

"We haven't received the doctor's report as yet," Scumble said warily.

"So it was a policeman who actually took the trouble to examine the scene who decided I couldn't have killed him just as the others arrived?"

"That's as may be. I'm the one asking questions. *Were* you unloading Mrs Trewynn's car in Port Mabyn at five after returning from Padstow?"

"Hardly! You can easily find out from Mr Alarian what time I left him, if you really must. I'd rather he didn't know anything about this business, of course. But, short of hiring a helicopter, I couldn't possibly have reached Port Mabyn—or Padstow, come to that—earlier than half past four. Someone would surely have noticed a helicopter, not that I have the funds to hire one. Nor any reason to do so, considering I didn't know till I got to my shop what that bastard had done."

Scumble sat up straighter. "What he'd done. You're referring to Geoffrey Clark."

"Of course I'm referring to Geoffrey bloody Monmouth Clark!" Nick exploded. Then he calmed down. "Sorry, bad choice of adjectives in the circs."

"That part of the story's true, is it?"

"What do you mean? What story?"

"Miss Maris's. Consider our position for a moment, Mr Gresham. When a statement is made by a hysterical woman—"

Megan coughed. For a wonder, he noticed and correctly interpreted the cough. He glared at her.

"Let me rephrase that," he responded, however, thanks no doubt to a recent memo from Superintendent Bentinck. While decrying the demands of women's lib, the Super had reluctantly ordered his subordinates to attempt to avoid stereotyping. "When a statement is made by an overwrought person, unsupported by other evidence, it is normally regarded with a degree of scepticism. When part of it is more or less disproved, the rest can't be taken very seriously."

"What did Stella say?" Nick demanded.

Scumble brushed this aside. "She has very little credibility just now. Or rather, what she said while in the throes of hyst— overexcitement has very little credibility. When she's calmed down, she'll get another chance. Why don't you tell me what happened?"

Nick frowned. "She had every excuse for being distraught," he said. "She'd been living with Geoff for a couple of years, two or three, and someone murdered him. I just happened to be there when she found him."

"We'll get to that later. Will you kindly tell me what happened when you reached Port Mabyn, or I'll start thinking you're stalling for time to invent your story."

"Sorry." Nick passed a weary hand over his face. "It's . . . It's something I'd just as soon forget. I drove back from Launceston. As I parked the car outside the LonStar shop, I noticed the CLOSED sign hanging in the door of my place—it's next door, you may remember. It wasn't my summer closing time yet by half an hour or so, so I was a bit annoyed with Stella. I went straight away to see if she was still there."

"You went into your shop? Was the door locked?"

"Yes. I think so. What does it matter? You people are always harping on locking doors."

"If it was unlocked, anyone could have got in and . . . But I'm getting ahead of you. Go on. You unlocked the door and—"

"Yes, I'm sure I did. It was locked. I went into the gallery. I could see right away that . . ." He swallowed. His face was very pale and Megan wondered if she should offer to fetch a glass of water, or strong tea, or something stronger, to counteract shock. Remembered shock, though, not immediate. He'd survive. "That several of my paintings had been wrecked."

"Wrecked?"

"Slashed, with a knife. Or perhaps a dagger. There would be a kind of poetic justice in that, if I'd stabbed Geoff. I knew at once that he must have done it."

"Wasn't that rather jumping to conclusions? Why should he do such a thing?"

"Envy. Jealousy."

"Which? Did he find out about and object to his—uh—girl-friend making a pass at you? Were you a much more successful artist?"

"Nothing to do with Stella. At least, I doubt it. And he made much money than I do. But—I don't know if you'll understand this—being an artist is as much a matter of passion as any love affair. What he hated was that I make a living of sorts solely by selling my paintings to people who appreciate them as art." He frowned, reflecting, then nodded. "Yes, I think you can say that even of the tourist landscapes. Geoff's money came from his commercial work. I'm sure you must have seen his adverts for Tintagel Brewery's King Arthur's Stout?"

"He painted those?" Megan asked, forgetting her place. "The one with King Arthur standing there with his sword drawn? And it quotes, 'A stout heart and a trusty hand . . .' That one?"

Scumble scowled at her.

"That's one of them," Nick confirmed. "Lots of people notice and remember it, but not one in a hundred knows who painted it, or cares. The trouble is, he's obsessed with the Pre-Raphaelites, and no one really cares for them these days, neither the general public nor connoisseurs."

"Wait a bit! What are these Pre-Whoosis when they're at home?"

"You've heard of the Arts and Crafts movement? No. William Morris? Burne-Jones? Dante Gabriel Rossetti?"

Scumble stared at him stolidly. Megan, anticipating a lecture, wondered how much to write down and how much to leave out of her report.

"All right. To keep it simple, they were a group of Victorians who rejected modern mass-production and advocated a return to individual craftsmanship. They also developed a style of painting based on mediaeval themes. Geoff works in—worked in that style, which has been very much out of fashion for decades, like everything Victorian. It sells beer, apparently, but people don't actually want it hanging on their walls. There's a revival of interest in the fantasy-mediaeval genre, though, since *Lord of the Rings* has become so popular. If he'd been patient—"

"Geoffrey Clark didn't choose to die just as his work was about to stage a come-back, Mr Gresham."

"That's not what I meant. I was just speculating, selfishly, I suppose, that—But you don't want to hear my speculations."

"On the contrary. Go ahead."

"Oh, it's just that if Geoff had expected success in the near future, he wouldn't have been jealous enough to damage my work.

Then perhaps he would have spent the afternoon peacefully at my place with Stella and wouldn't have scarpered to his own gallery to be murdered, saving us all a lot of trouble."

"You seem to think the two things are connected, the murder and the vandalising of your paintings."

"We'd get on faster, Inspector, if you'd just rid yourself of the notion that I've discovered some miraculous means of being in two places at once. The two are obviously linked in time, in sequence. I'm damned if I can see any cause for the sequence."

"Let's go back to your discovery of the vandalism. Did you find any evidence, beyond guesswork, of who was responsible?"

"Not right away. I didn't look very far because Donna appeared on the threshold, wanting to know if she should start to unload the car. I didn't want her to see and start asking questions, so we—"

"We?"

"Eleanor—Mrs Trewynn had followed me in. We went out. I locked the door behind me. I unloaded the car—"

"Aided by Donna and the little Chins," said Scumble, rolling his eyes.

"Exactly. Mrs Trewynn went up to her flat to make tea."

"Tea!"

"Tea. We had, after all, found damaged paintings, not, at that point, a body. Though come to think of it, we were also dosed with tea at the police station after finding the body. Eleanor hoped it would calm me down before I dashed down to Padstow and did something I might regret."

"Like killing Clark."

"Like giving him a bloody nose. Which reminds me, in the middle of tea I suddenly wondered whether Stella might have tried to protect my stuff and been attacked by Geoff, who was, you will recall, in a fury and wielding a knife. I had a horrid vision of her lying bleeding behind the counter, or in the studio, somewhere I hadn't looked. So I rushed off to check, and that's when I found her note."

"Aha! Did you keep it?"

"I can't remember. If I did, it's probably in one of my pockets, as I slept in my clothes last night." Nick felt in the pocket anorak, then snapped his fingers. "No, wait a bit, they took everything off me last night. I had to sign a list. I'm sure it wasn't there. I must have chucked it in the bin."

"Pity. What did it say?"

"I can't quote it. It was obviously written in a hurry, a mess of phrases, not a carefully thought-out screed. But she informed me that she'd told Geoff about my luck in London, he'd got into a tiswas and attacked my pictures, and she'd cleared out with him. If I'm not mistaken," he added sardonically, "she did say she was sorry it had happened."

"I'd like to get my hands on that note. I hope it's safe at home in your waste paper basket. What did you do next?"

"Eleanor insisted on driving me to Padstow, feeling that in her presence I was unlikely to resort to violence. We parked in Rock and crossed by the ferry. The door of King Arthur's Gallery wasn't locked, so we went in. And I found Geoff in the back room, lying on his face with a dagger sticking out of his back. I knelt down to feel his pulse, just in case he was still alive, though he didn't look it. No sign of a pulse."

"You're quite certain of that?"

"Absolutely. In fact, in spite of the warm day, he was already colder than I thought could be possible for a living person. I'd like to point out that I'm still wearing the same trousers, which are *not* bloody about the knees. At the time I presumed the colour I knelt on must be oil-paint, but that wouldn't have dried enough in a few hours not to stain my trousers. I remembered later that he used coloured inks for his commercial work—it reproduces better. It also dries quite fast and keeps a sheen when dry."

"Red ink."

"Red ink."

TWELVE

Margery Rosevear had declined Eleanor's help with the washing-up.

"Why don't you go and look round the studios," she suggested. "Jeanette, dear, I'm sure Mrs Trewynn would love to see your work."

Looking rather sulky, Jeanette added her own tepid invitation. As soon as they were out in the cobbled courtyard, she said, "Margery can be a bit bossy. You don't have to look at my stuff. I hate showing it to people who feel obliged."

"I'd like to see it, unless you'd rather I didn't. I don't want to disturb you if you're about to get to work."

"Oh, that's okay. I don't expect I'll get anything done today, not after what happened." She hesitated, then said fiercely, "I don't believe Nick Gresham killed Geoff. It was awful, what Geoff did, but Nick's just not that sort of person."

"He didn't do it."

"You don't think so, either?"

"I know. I was with him the whole time."

"You were?" Stopping with her hand on the knob of the middle door in the row of converted stables on the south side, Jeanette turned a hostile gaze on Eleanor. "Who are you? What are you doing here? I don't understand."

"I'll explain. Shall we go in?"

"I suppose so."

"Do you mind if Teazle comes, too? She'll stay outside if I tell her."

"She can come." Jeanette opened the door and stood back while Eleanor entered.

Following, she left the door open, though the morning air was still cool. Eleanor was quite glad to have an escape route easily available. Though she was not a suspicious person, and she was quite certain Jeanette was sincere, it did occur to her that someone more suspicious than herself might think the lady did protest too much. Her defence of Nick could conceivably be a smoke screen, though a rather complicated one, the ramifications of which Eleanor didn't have time to sort out just now.

Her immediate impression of the studio was an almost obsessive neatness. Crammed into the small space were a painter's easel, a draughtsman's table, canvases tidily stacked against the walls, a sink, shelves, and all the other paraphernalia of artistic endeavour, including a faint smell of turpentine.

Jeanette said belligerently, "Well?"

"I'm Nick's friend and next-door neighbour. I fetched him from the station in Launceston when he came home from London. I was with him all the time until we found Geoff's body. He can't possibly have stabbed him."

"Oh, thank heaven! Then why haven't you told the police? Or didn't they believe you?"

"They were busy talking to everyone else. I was waiting for my turn and it never came. That's why I'm here. Inspector Pearce told me they'd come and see me here this morning."

"Oh, I see." Jeanette sounded doubtful. "But I don't understand why they didn't question you last night. Then Nick needn't have spent the night at the police station."

"I don't understand it myself, my dear. If I hadn't been so very tired, I expect I would have made a fuss, but by the time I realised what was going on, it was too late. Margery offered to put me up for the night, and off we went."

"Margery did?" She frowned. "Don't you think that's fishy?"

"Fishy?" Eleanor asked in surprise. "I thought it was extremely kind of her."

"She complains about how much work we make for her. Why should she add another person to take care of, unless she has an ulterior motive?"

"Just for one night!"

"Suppose she killed Geoff. She wouldn't want you to have a chance to persuade the police Nick didn't do it."

"Why on earth should Margery want to kill Geoff?"

"They had an affair, when Geoff first came here. I'm not sure exactly what happened, but I think Doug found out and they had a row. I mean, no one cares about that stuff nowadays, only Marge wanted to go off with Geoff—she was really in love with him— but he said it wasn't serious. You can imagine how that hurt."

"But he's still living here? I'd have thought Doug would throw him out."

"Marge had given him a two-year lease. Of course Doug had signed without reading it. It's very difficult to break a lease, I gather. Over time, naturally, everything simmered down. Besides, apparently Geoff's one virtue is that he pays his rent on time, and it's not so easy to find someone who'll take a whole bungalow in the middle of an artists' colony. Most of us can't afford more than our two rooms."

"It simmered down, you say. Is there a reason why it should suddenly boil up again just now?"

"Oh, I dunno. I'm not saying it *was* Marge who stabbed Geoff, but if it wasn't Nick, it's got to be someone else, right? Doug perhaps. Or one of the others. No one could stand him—except Stella, of course. I just said Marge because of her inviting you, but that's the sort of thing she'd do, really. She's a nice person."

"I must say, that was my impression. What was it you particularly disliked about Geoffrey?"

"Me?" Jeanette's fair colouring made her blush startlingly vivid. "I didn't have anything in particular against him. He just . . . I just didn't much like him. D'you want to look at my picture books or my paintings?"

"Both. But in case you're expecting an expert, I should warn you that I don't know much about art and I haven't any children."

Jeanette giggled. "That's all right. The ones that drive me up the wall are the ones who pretend to be terribly knowledgeable. Though I must say they often buy something just to prove they know what they're talking about. Then there are the people who page through the books, leaving thumbprints and bent corners, and say, 'How adorable, but you never can tell with children these days, I always give book tokens.'"

Eleanor hastily examined her hands. "No thumbprints, I promise."

Judging by Margery's comments, she had expected the picture-books to be mawkishly sentimental, but to Eleanor the puppies and kittens involved, though engaged in unrealistic pursuits, looked very realistic, and—well, adorable. She didn't like to say so, since the adjective had aroused such apparent scorn in the artist, but she did say she liked them very much. "I hope my nieces and nephews will start families soon, so that I can justify buying them. You must love animals to be able to paint them so well."

"I do. I wouldn't mind spending all my time drawing and painting them."

"Why don't you, then?"

"Oh, it's not proper art. I just do it to make some money to live on. They're sold in bookshops all over the country."

"Oh good, then I'll be able to find them when I have someone to buy them for. Let me see your 'proper art,'" Eleanor requested.

She didn't expect to understand the paintings Jeanette now turned face out from the wall. She was surprised, though, to find she actively disliked them. They were abstract, as Margery had told her, but despite the innocuous, not to say bland titles, they radiated energy. At least, that was the best way Eleanor, unfamiliar with the proper artistic vocabulary, could explain it to herself.

She suspected that the very fact that they spoke to her so strongly must mean they were "good," whatever that meant.

They reminded her of one of Nick's paintings in particular, *Storm over Rough Tor*, but that was a semi-abstract celebration of the power of natural forces. Jeanette's *ZigZag* was angry. So, less explicably, was *Grey Circle*.

How could a grey circle express anger? Was it all in Eleanor's imagination? She didn't know, but it made her uneasy. She must remember to ask Nick's opinion.

As much as anything, the contrast with the puppies and kittens was disturbing. Which was the real Jeanette? And what was she angry about?

"You don't like them," said Jeanette with a resigned sigh.

"I warned you that I'm a Philistine. I'm afraid I wouldn't choose to hang one on my wall, if I had room in my little flat, which I don't."

The young artist regarded her *Grey Circle* moodily. "No, they need plenty of space around them."

"I find them interesting, though, which is more than I can say for most abstract painting. I never realised—" She stopped as a man appeared in the doorway.

Against the light, his face was indistinguishable.

"All right, Jeanie?" he asked. To Eleanor, his voice sounded studiously casual.

"Yes! Oh Tom, Mrs Trewynn was with Nick practically all day yesterday and she's going to tell the police he couldn't possibly have killed Geoff. Isn't it wonderful?"

Eager to hear the potter's reaction, Eleanor didn't bother to dispute this misstatement of her words.

There was a distinct pause before he said, "That can't be right. Stella said Nick rang from Paddington at midday—Unless you were in London with him, Mrs Trewynn?"

Eleanor repeated her account of meeting Nick at the station and being with him thereafter.

"But—"

Jeanette broke in: "See? Mrs Trewynn's just waiting till the police come so she can tell them everything. I don't know why you're so keen to believe the worst of Nick."

"I'm not!" Tom protested. "I just don't want . . . Oh, what's the use. Mrs Trewynn, while you're waiting for the police, would you like to come and inspect my humble endeavours? I've just put some pots in the kiln and I'm about to start on a new batch."

"Yes, I'd love to."

Tom's place was next door, at the end of the row. He had an oil-fired kiln outside. The farm, he explained, had never had gas laid on, switching straight from candles and kerosene to mains electricity. Tom relied on oil because the electricity supply was liable to fail in stormy weather, which could ruin an entire kiln-ful of pots. He showed Eleanor the thermostat and made a minute adjustment to the temperature. She recalled Doug calling him a businessman. A cool head and a steady hand.

They went inside. Eleanor noticed the earthy smell of wet clay, but Teazle smelled something more interesting. She headed straight for a back corner and started to sniff suspiciously.

"Mice?" Tom said with a groan.

"Sometimes she imagines them."

"Let's hope."

Eleanor had seen primitive potteries all over the world and she was interested in the methods of a modern handcraftsman. However, Tom had lured her thither under false pretences. He wanted to talk.

"That's rubbish," he went on bluntly. "What you said about being with Nick the whole time, I mean. He had only to go into Geoff's studio a few paces ahead of you to stab him without you seeing. I understand you're a friend of Nick's and don't want to believe he could do a thing like that, but the police are never going to swallow it. Jeanette's going to be shattered when she realises he's not off the hook."

"As it happens, I was close enough to be quite certain Nick didn't stab Geoffrey. Apart from anything else, he knocked over his easel when he fell. I couldn't have helped hearing it." Eleanor was pleased to have thought of this corroborative detail. After all, she had only Nick's word for it that the flood of red was not blood, and while she believed him implicitly, others might not.

It went to show how right the police were to keep asking the same questions over and over again, however irritating it was—though it was even more irritating when they didn't ask any questions at all.

"Oh, well, if you're absolutely sure . . ." Tom picked at the ingrained clay under his fingernails. "It's just that Jeanie gets so upset . . ."

"It's a horrible business, enough to upset anyone. Geoff must have been a friend of yours." Eleanor paused, but Tom didn't comment on her assumption.

She tried to remember what, if anything, he had said about Geoffrey at breakfast. No one had expressed grief for the painter's death. Tom, she thought, had been more concerned about whether Stella would let down the employer who counted on her to turn up for the weekend nursing shift at the convalescent home. What was the doctor's name? Fenwick, that was it, like the Grand Duchy in *The Mouse that Roared*. She had forgotten the name of the home already. No doubt the police would find out soon enough if Stella did go to work and they wanted to talk to her at the weekend.

While Eleanor reflected, Tom had gone to his workbench and scraped a piece of clay off a large lump beneath a damp cloth.

"Everyone seems to know Nick, too," said Eleanor, watching him knead and mould the clay, adding a splash of water now and then from a bucket beside the bench. He had big hands, unusually well muscled from his work. If Geoff had been strangled— She suppressed a shudder.

But he hadn't, he'd been stabbed. Given a sharp dagger, even a little old lady could have done it.

"Yeah, we all know Nick." Tom sounded as if he wished he didn't. Eleanor wondered why but decided against asking. As if conscious of sounding unenthusiastic, he said, "He's a good painter. He deserves to make it in London. But after what Geoff did, it's going to be practically impossible to make people believe Nick had nothing to do with his death, even if the police let him go."

"That's exactly what I'm afraid of," said Eleanor. "Oh dear, it's not very comforting that you agree. And if the national press get hold of the story, it could ruin his career before it really gets started."

"Hell, I hope not!" Oswald was leaning against the doorjamb, a wiry, red-bearded man in a paint-daubed smock. How long had he been there? Teazle had given up all hope of mice and, snoozing in the corner, hadn't noticed his arrival. "It would mean Geoff wins, after all."

Tom disagreed. "I wouldn't worry about that. What was it that Irish bloke said? Something like: there's no such thing as bad publicity. People who don't care a hoot about art will rush to buy the work of someone suspected of murder, and pay over the odds, too. Nick'll have the last laugh, you mark my words."

Oswald nodded. "Makes sense. Jeanie told me Nick's been released already. Is it true, Mrs Trewynn?"

"I'm afraid that's wishful thinking. At least, it may be true but I haven't heard from either him or the police this morning. If not already, though, then soon, I'm sure. I hope. Or do you think they might keep him in custody until they've heard my evidence?"

"What if they don't believe you?" said Oswald.

"Don't borrow trouble," Tom advised cheerfully. Easy for him to say when he didn't seem particularly well-inclined towards Nick.

They all looked up at the sound of heels tock-tocking across the cobbles towards them. Oswald turned round.

"Good morning," said a familiar voice. "Can you tell me where to find Mrs Trewynn? Mrs Eleanor Trewynn?"

"Jocelyn!" cried Eleanor. "What on earth are you doing here?"

THIRTEEN

"So I'm free to leave?" Nick demanded.

"Yes," said DI Scumble cautiously, "but—"

"But you'll want to talk to me again and I must notify you if I'm going anywhere. Speaking of which, your colleague has stranded me here. I hope you'll at least stand me bus fare back to Padstow. Apart from anything else, Mrs Trewynn is also stranded, at Upper Trewithen Farm, I presume. I've got her car keys." He felt in his trouser pockets. "Or rather, you've got Eleanor's keys. The chap downstairs took 'em off me along with the rest."

"You'd better fetch Mr Gresham's belongings, Pencarrow."

As Megan went out, she heard Scumble continue, "Just one or two more questions, for now, sir." The *sir* came out strangulated, as if it stuck in the inspector's craw. "We'll give you a lift to Padstow later."

She hurried, hoping she wasn't missing anything vital.

There was the business of the damage to Nick's paintings. Until he talked about it, all they had was Stella's statement, since the Rosevears had merely reported what she had told them. Megan had even wondered if it was another hysterical fantasy, the invention of a mind desperately seeking a reason for the murder of her lover.

So far, it seemed to be Nick's only apparent motive for attacking Clark. Still, he would have been a fool to deny it. All they had to do was go to his gallery and look.

In spite of his strong reaction, it didn't seem like an adequate motive for murder, but in the end everything hinged on timing. Aunt Nell's evidence was essential. By not taking her statement, Pearce had really handed this one to Scumble on a plate. Whatever the inspector's opinion of Aunt Nell, and they were definitely not on the same wavelength, he would never have failed to get her side of the story last night. Let alone Nick's.

"DS Pencarrow," Megan identified herself to the uniformed desk sergeant. "DI Scumble wants Nicholas Gresham's personal possessions."

"Gresham," he said, as he spread the contents of Nick's pockets on the counter and produced a signed list. "That's the one Pearce decided isn't worth his time, right?"

"That's it. Frankly, we're puzzled. It looks like a nice, meaty case, one any good detective would like to get his teeth into."

"'S easy." He looked around with a somewhat furtive air and leant over the counter to say in a hoarse whisper, "No need to pass this on to your gov'nor, but Mr Pearce married a totty half his age a few months ago. They say she's a real termagant, gives him hell if he's out on the job too late too often. He's always looking for an excuse to dump his work on other people. The Super don't often swallow it, but looks like he did this time."

Thanks to Aunt Nell's involvement, thought Megan. "Frankly," she said in a low voice, "the gov'nor's pleased as Punch. We don't often get anything this interesting up Launceston way." If the sergeant repeated that tidbit, Pearce would be tearing his hair. Not that she had anything against him personally—except, perhaps, his marrying a totty half his age.

She checked the contents of Nick's wallet against the list, signed, and stuffed everything back into the polythene bag to take upstairs, amazed at the amount of junk men carried in their pockets. She didn't notice anything useful, though. No letters, no diary, no tube or bus tickets to prove he'd been in London.

He might have dropped the tickets in his or Aunt Nell's waste paper basket, or in a bin in the street or on the ferry. If Scumble was desperate to get hold of Stella's note, with luck he'd leave that search to the uniforms. You never could tell what you were going to find in a rubbish bin.

Megan returned to the interview room. Scumble raised his eyebrows at her and she shook her head. All the same, he watched closely as Nick took his bits and pieces out of the bag and redistributed them among his pockets. The only thing Nick really looked at was the cash in the wallet.

"Two pounds six and tenpence ha'penny," he said, and countersigned the list. "All present and correct." He was by no means as cheerful as when Megan had left the room.

"Well, Sergeant, Mr Gresham admits he could have faked the call from Paddington and reached Padstow in time to murder Clark," Scumble said blandly. He seemed intent on making Nick lose his temper, hoping, presumably, to goad him into an incriminating statement.

"Don't twist my words, Inspector! Only if I hadn't had a meeting with Mr Alarian."

"For which we have only your word."

"Ask him!"

"We will, Mr Gresham, we will." Scumble gave Megan a sidelong glance which she couldn't interpret but guessed boded no good.

"Besides," Nick went on, "why should I have wanted to kill Geoff? The only reason I was livid with him was the damage to my work, which I didn't know about till I got home."

"You admit you wanted to assault him."

"Yes, I do! As he was dead when I next saw him, I missed my chance to give him what was coming to him. Which was, I remind you, not a dagger in the back but a sock on the jaw!"

"Why was it you jumped to the conclusion that it was Geoffrey Clark who damaged your paintings?"

"I didn't . . . All right, I did jump to that conclusion. Stella had no reason to do it, and he was the obvious person for her to have told about Alarian, besides being the only person I could think of who might resent my success. Which, I must point out, I didn't know about until I met Alarian."

"So you were certain Clark was the culprit even before you found Miss Weller's note. For which we have only your word."

Nick started to search through his pockets.

"Don't bother," Scumble advised him. "There was no note among your belongings, unless you want to claim a police officer pinched it?"

"No, no. Why would anyone do that? I suppose I left it at home."

"If so, we'll find it, don't worry."

"Yes, of course."

"You're giving us permission to search your premises?"

"Certainly. But I can't see the point in answering any more questions until you've talked to Eleanor. Mrs Trewynn."

Scumble nodded. "All right, that's reasonable. Except, if, as you say, you didn't kill him, have you got any ideas about who might have? Did he have any enemies?"

"Enemies?" Nick frowned. "That's a bit strong. He wasn't too popular, but enemies . . ."

"Who wasn't he popular with?"

"The others at the commune, except Stella, of course. The fellows at the pub."

"Why?"

"He had a cutting tongue."

"As well as a cutting blade." The inspector smirked. His rare attempts at wit always pleased him, if no one else. "That's it? A nasty way with words?"

"He could be really obnoxious, even hurtful, to people he despised. Which seemed to be most people. At the pub, he was just unsociable. Up at the farm—well, there were undercurrents. I got the impression things had happened, but no one wanted to talk about it."

"Things?"

"I honestly have no idea what, Inspector. I have nothing concrete to go on. Perhaps I'm imagining it."

"Destruction of people's work, like yours?"

"Possibly, but I doubt it. He had no reason to see any of them as competition, as he apparently did me. And I see no reason why they shouldn't have discussed something like that. Unless, I suppose, some sort of loyalty to the commune?"

"Commune! Bah! Load of bollocks, if you ask me. Bunch of kids living on handouts from their parents."

"On the contrary. I've never delved into the details, but it's not a true commune, with everything held in common. I do know that many, if not all, are working artists and craftsmen who pay their own way. And none of them are kids. But you'll have to see for yourself."

"Yes," said Scumble gloomily, "we're going to have to interview the lot of them. Not till I've read the doctor's and SOC officer's reports, though. What am I going to do with you in the meantime, Mr Gresham?"

"Get a bobby to drive me to Padstow."

"Not likely. It looks like one thing that got done right last night was stopping you and Mrs Trewynn setting up an alibi between you. I'm not having you conferring with her before I get her statement."

Megan opened her mouth to protest this slander of her aunt, then closed it again and gave a minuscule shrug. Ten to one Scumble was just being deliberately irritating to see how Nick would react.

Nick's reaction had nothing to do with the slander. "You expect me to sit around in this dump for hours while you read reports?" he asked, outraged.

"I can't hold you, not on what we've got. Tell you what." He made an expansive gesture towards the window. "It's a beautiful day. Go for a walk."

"How do you know I won't telephone Eleanor?"

"I'll put someone on to tail you. No, I've got a better idea. DS Pencarrow can go with you. No one'll think anything of a couple walking around gawking at the sights, won't think you're under surveillance and draw conclusions. You can go and take a gander at the old gaol and thank your lucky star it closed down forty years ago. Just try not to break a leg climbing around the dungeons."

He waved dismissal. Somewhat to Megan's surprise, Nick took the order—or suggestion, or whatever it was from his point of view—calmly. To Megan it was an order, and not one she liked. She wanted to read the reports, not to wander purposelessly about Bodmin with Nicholas Gresham, keeping him away from telephones and buses.

Nick opened the door and held it for her in his polite way. She had never considered the matter before, but there was a touch of public school in his manners. Or perhaps he'd just gone to a private school or a good grammar. Was it relevant? In the old days, at least in books, a public schoolboy wouldn't dream of stabbing a man in the back, even a villain, whatever he might do face-to-face. But even if it had been true, few of the old myths held in modern times.

Ken, the man she had moved to Cornwall to get away from, had been a public schoolboy. The last thing she needed was another of the breed.

Megan went through the doorway and Nick followed, pulling the door shut behind him. Just before the latch clicked, he re-opened it partway and stuck his head into the room.

"By the way, Inspector, speaking of blades, I don't know if it's of interest but I recognised the hilt sticking out of Geoff's back."

"Of course it's of bloody interest!" Scumble exploded, his face turning purple. "Get back in here."

Nick opened the door wide and leant against the jamb. "Now, is that any way to speak to a cooperating witness?" he chided. "I've never actually seen it before—"

"Then what the hell do you—"

"But I have seen a design for it. Geoff wanted an old English dagger to paint. He tracked one down in some collection or other. When they wouldn't lend it to him, he took measurements and drew several views of it. That's what I saw—his sketches. Then he had a blacksmith make a copy. To give the devil his due, he was thorough. He even insisted on having it sharpened. He said otherwise it wouldn't reflect light accurately."

Scumble grunted. "You're sure he was killed with that one?"

"It's unmistakable. It's actually early mediaeval, not Arthurian, if Arthur ever existed. Viking influence in the design, I gather, but I'm no expert. It has a brass pommel and a very distinctive brass guard—I could draw that for you, but you'll see it yourself, I imagine. Even more noticeable, the handle is wrapped in red wire. And that reminds me—"

"What now? You're as bad as Mrs Trewynn, popping up with bits and pieces you should have told me long since!"

"If anyone had bothered to ask me last night," Nick responded inarguably, "doubtless I'd have remembered every detail on the spot. I just wanted to warn you not to waste time on the finger-prints your men must have found on the hilt. Stella couldn't stand the sight of Geoff's body lying there with the damn thing sticking out of his back and she grabbed it to pull it out. I tried to stop her but I was too late."

Scumble and Megan exchanged a look of disappointment. Nothing so easy as a lovers' tiff.

"Silly little git. Her prints have ruined anything else that might've been there. Got that, Pencarrow?"

"Yes, sir." Megan had whipped out her notebook the moment Nick said, "By the way . . ."

"That is," he added, "I did stop her pulling it out, but she got a good grip on it."

Scumble nodded. "Anything else?"

"Not at the moment," Nick said with a grin.

To Megan's surprise, Scumble didn't explode again. He just said sarcastically, "If you should happen to think of anything else vital, tell the sergeant. Now off you go and play, kiddies." He drew the telephone towards him and picked up the receiver.

Nick shut the door again.

"Kiddies!" Megan hissed.

" 'He only does it to annoy, because he knows it teases,' quoth the Duchess."

"I know, but it still gets my goat."

"Cultivate detachment. Let's go and get a decent cup of coffee. The stuff they serve in the cells is absolutely undrinkable."

"I don't imagine it's any worse than what they give us. Probably exactly the same."

"I dare say. Megan, I'm worried about your aunt. Knowing I didn't do the fell deed, I can't help wondering if it was someone at the farm. There she is, all alone, not knowing what's happening—"

"I rang Mrs Stearns," Megan said with what she felt was pardonable smugness.

"You what?"

"I rang up Mrs Stearns, as soon as I found out where Aunt Nell is, and asked if she could possibly go to join her and keep an eye on her. She promised she'd leave right away."

"When you went to fetch the chair?"

"That's right."

Nick burst out laughing. "And you assured Scumble you hadn't spoken to a witness!"

"I can only hope he forgets that." Megan said crossly. "How was I to know you'd rung Mrs Stearns from London?"

FOURTEEN

"What ever is going on, Eleanor?" Jocelyn enquired tartly, ignoring Teazle frisking about her feet, and regarding the potter and the painter with disfavour. They were openly listening. "Megan rang me up and claimed you desperately needed my support."

"Megan! How does she come into it?"

"I have no idea whatsoever. When I requested an explanation, she told me That Man was waiting for her and she had to go."

"Mr Scumble?" Eleanor recognised Joce's tone of voice and the epithet she had used for the inspector when last she tangled with him.

"Who else? Naturally, if Megan is involved, her superior must be involved."

"But they're not involved. A different inspector is in charge of the case."

"What case? You're waffling, Eleanor. What have you been up to? Will you please explain?"

"Of course, dear. Just let me introduce you to these gentlemen. This is . . . Oh dear, I'm afraid I don't know your surname, Tom. Nor Oswald's, come to that."

"We don't use them much," said Tom. "It's Lennox. How do you do?" He held out his hand, then glanced at it and withdrew it. "Sorry, you won't want clay all over you, Mrs . . . ?"

"Mrs Stearns," Eleanor put in hastily.

"Lennox Potteries?" Jocelyn thawed a little. "I've got a couple of your bowls. Your colours are most attractive."

"Thank you, Mrs Stearns. Always happy to hear from a satisfied customer."

A slight flush tinged her cheeks. "I bought them from the Lon-Star shop, I'm afraid."

Momentarily, Tom looked taken aback. Jocelyn's stylish clothes—also from the LonStar shop—tended to mislead people as to her means. He quickly recovered. "Too bad, but we can't all be rich connoisseurs. I'm glad they've found a second home where they're appreciated."

She gave him a nod nicely calculated to acknowledge his quick recovery while simultaneously forestalling any attempt at familiarity, then turned to Oswald. "And you are . . . ?"

He doffed an imaginary hat and swept her a low bow. "Oswald Rudd, painter."

"How do you do, Mr Rudd." This time her nod was merely dismissive. "Eleanor, is there somewhere private we can go to talk?"

"I noticed a bench in the garden behind the main house."

"That will do." Jocelyn stepped out into the courtyard and Eleanor, telling Tom she would return, followed her.

"We'll go through the house and I'll introduce—"

"Oh, Eleanor, is that necessary? I have no desire to meet these people, I just want to know what's going on!"

"But they're all part of it. Or at least, they may be. You'll understand what I have to tell you better if you know who I'm talking about."

Jocelyn sighed. "Very well, if you insist."

"Oh dear, there's Stella! I still haven't decided whether I ought to talk to her or not."

"I don't think you're going to have much choice. She's coming this way. That's the young woman who closed up Nicholas's gallery early yesterday?"

"Yes, the sculptor, but there's much more . . . Good morning, Stella." What on earth does one say to someone whose lover has just been murdered?

Stella looked magnificent, her hair flaming in the bright sunlight, flowing over her shoulders and halfway down her back. Like an avenging Fury, Eleanor thought, or did she mean a Valkyrie? No, the silky dark blue kaftan, patterned with pale stars and crescent moons, suggested a sorceress; Morgan le Fay, perhaps, in keeping with the Arthurian motif.

Before Eleanor could decide what to say to this alarming vision, Stella looked from her to Jocelyn and spoke, her voice biting. "I suppose between you you're cooking up an alibi for Nick. But it won't work, I'm telling you. I know what I saw. Give up!" She swung round, skirts swishing, and stalked away towards the farm house.

Jocelyn was far too well-bred to gape, but she stared after Stella as if she had seen an apparition. Astonishment and outrage warred on her face. "Well! What was all that about? Nicholas is in trouble with the police? That would explain why Megan phoned. Eleanor, you're not—?"

"Come along." Eleanor took Joce's arm and tugged her after Stella. "It's not a good moment to introduce you to Margery, but I think we can go round the side of the house to the garden."

"Who's Margery?"

"I'll explain, I promise. I'm so glad Stella has calmed down overnight—"

"Calmed down!"

"She was hysterical. Apparently she still has that bee in her bonnet, though. I'm afraid she'll have another shock when she realises she's mistaken about Nick. Poor girl!"

"You're sorry for that harpy?"

"She's had a terrible experience, Joce. You mustn't judge her by what she said just now. Wait till you hear what happened yesterday."

"That," said Joce pointedly, "is what I've been waiting for, for at least a quarter of an hour now."

Stella must have heard them coming along behind her, but she didn't look round. She went straight into the house.

To Eleanor's relief, between the end studio and the corner of the house was the gap she thought she had noticed. The ground was gravelled rather than paved and oil stains suggested it was the parking place for the mini-bus, presently delivering Leila to the beach and Quentin to the shop.

Eleanor and Jocelyn crunched across the gravel, avoiding the oil. In a momentary hush between crunches, Eleanor heard raised voices coming from inside the house. Then they were round the corner, between the north wall and a large metal shed. Teazle scampered ahead, hoping, perhaps, to meet the farm dogs again.

The dogs didn't appear. The garden was deserted, sunny and humming with bees. Sheltered by the house from the westerly breeze, it was surprisingly hot. They found two benches, the kind with backs, Eleanor was glad to note. They were set in a shallow V, one partially shaded by a gnarled apple tree.

Eleanor sat down in the shade and recounted everything that had happened since she met Nick at Launceston station. Jocelyn was a good listener, interrupting only twice to clarify a point. But by the end of the recital she was frowning.

"I can see why Megan was worried about you being alone

here," she said. "If Nicholas didn't kill the man, it seems probable that someone here did. I assume it couldn't have been a random robbery?"

"Joce, how clever of you! No one even mentioned the possibility last night. The policeman in charge was so blinded by Stella's certainty that she'd seen Nick that he never even considered any other possibility. That's much more likely than that one of the artists here—Oh, except that Geoffrey probably didn't have much money in his till."

"Why not?" Jocelyn was loath to see her theory shot down.

"I gather he didn't sell very many paintings. His income came mostly from doing adverts for Tintagel Brewery. You must have seen the ones for King Arthur's Stout?"

"I have not. You know Timothy and I consider it inadvisable to frequent public houses. Not that we have any desire to do so!"

"The posters are stuck up in windows, too, and I'm sure I've seen them on hoardings."

"I dare say. However, the amount of cash in his till isn't really relevant. A passing thief wouldn't know how much he had."

"True. But the police would certainly have checked right away to see if it had been emptied. If it was a random robber, Megan would know and wouldn't be worrying about me."

"You said Megan and That Man aren't involved in the case. That bit of information might not have reached her."

Eleanor conceded, though she didn't believe it. "All right, for all we know, it could have been a random robber."

"All the same, I can't help feeling it was unwise of you to tell these communists, or whatever they call themselves, that you're a witness to Nick's alibi."

"I did think twice about it," Eleanor admitted. "But, you see, they're his friends, and the longer they went on thinking he stabbed

Geoff, the harder it would be for them to believe he didn't. To really believe, in their hearts not just their heads, if you see what I mean."

"Naturally," said Jocelyn, a trifle stiffly. "Shades of belief are my business. Or Timothy's, at least."

"At any rate, that's how I saw it. If the police let him go but his friends steered clear of him, how could he be happy? I don't think any of us need have worried, not I or you or Megan. Everyone has been very friendly."

"Except the young woman who accosted us in the courtyard."

"It's only natural. He was her lover, after all. Don't bridle like that, Joce." Eleanor had seen marriage customs in various parts of the world that had shocked and distressed her. Mere cohabitation without benefit of clergy, between consenting adults, was nothing to make a fuss about. "Avoiding calling a spade a spade won't turn it into a fork. The sad thing is, Stella's the only one who's grieving for Geoffrey, as far as I can tell. He was thoroughly disliked."

"We're back to one of these communists as the murderer then?" Jocelyn said with a sniff.

Eleanor laughed. "Communists! It sounds so funny. It's not really a commune anyway. More like a sort of spread-out boarding house, with all the boarders being artists and craftsmen. Margery is a frustrated artist."

"Margery—what's her surname?"

"Rosevear. An old Cornish name. Mrs Rosevear."

"Mrs Rosevear is the landlady, I take it. She's one of those who disliked Geoffrey?"

"Yes. And from what I've been told, she had more reason than just his sharp tongue. But you won't want to know about that. I know you despise gossip."

Jocelyn looked as if she could have bitten out her tongue for ever having said such a thing. She could hardly deny it, however, after her frequent recourse to quoting the bible or the prayer book—Eleanor wasn't sure which—on the subject. Eleanor considered gossip a helpful way to get to know people. What mattered was that one should not judge anyone based on partial knowledge, however acquired, as Joce was all too liable to do.

Suppressing her pique, Jocelyn asked, "Why on earth did someone tell you Mrs Rosevear had good reason to dislike Geoffrey? I'd expect them to close ranks."

"The girl—young woman concerned is keen on Nick. That's not second-hand gossip, it's an inference from what she told me herself. Naturally she was upset because he was in trouble. When I assured her he wasn't the murderer, of course she started wondering who—"

She broke off as Teazle, sprawled in the shade beneath the other bench, raised her head and stared towards the house. The back door opened and Margery Rosevear came out. From each hand an empty metal colander dangled by the handle, glinting in the sun. She walked as heavily as if they were bags of cement.

Seeing Eleanor and Jocelyn, she frowned and came towards them.

"It's Mrs Rosevear, Joce." Eleanor stood up. "This is Mrs Stearns, a friend of mine, Margery. I'm sorry I didn't bring her into the house to meet you, but Stella went in and I didn't want to interrupt the two of you."

Margery slumped onto the second bench, acknowledging the introduction with a nod and an effortful smile. "I wish you had come in. You might have headed off the storm. I doubt it, though."

"Storm?"

"She accused me of harbouring you because I'm jealous of her and want Geoff's murderer to get away because I hate—hated him, and—Oh, what does it matter? All sorts of horrible things! The end result is that she can't stand it here another minute and

{ 131 }

she's moving out. Which leaves me with two empty places to let. Who's going to want to live here after what's happened? Especially if she starts spreading slander."

"Surely not!" said Eleanor. "I expect she'll think better of moving out when she's calmed down a bit. It only happened yesterday, after all."

"You must think I'm callous, worrying about the rent at a time like this. If you knew how hard it is to make ends meet . . ."

Eleanor saw Jocelyn open her mouth, no doubt to make some stringent comment on most people being in the same boat when it came to making ends meet. To forestall her, she said quickly, "The holiday season is upon us. I should think you could get short-term lets to tide you over till you find long-term tenants."

Jocelyn nodded. "More trouble, I expect, but higher rents."

"What I don't understand," Eleanor went on, "is how Stella, even in her present irrational state, can claim both that you're jealous and that you hated Geoffrey. It seems to me the two are incompatible."

Margery gave a bitter laugh. "There was a time . . . I can't see that it's any of your business, but everyone here knows and I suppose the police will be ferreting everything out anyway. If you really can prove Nick didn't stab Geoff?"

"I can."

"Well, it's hard to believe now, but there was a time when I found him attractive. Geoff, that is. He could be charming when he made the effort. I admired his painting—I didn't know then that all he was capable of was imitating the Pre-Raphaelites. First-rate imitation, mind you, but he hadn't got an original spark in him. He beckoned and I . . . fell for him, like a starstruck schoolgirl. Pathetic!"

"Was that before Stella came here?"

"Oh yes, as soon as she arrived he had eyes for no one else.

Youth, beauty, Pre-Raphaelite hair and a Pre-Raphaelite profile, what more could he want? But before that, he and I had . . . parted company." Margery was staring down at her hands. She seemed almost to have forgotten that she had an audience. Jocelyn was obviously shocked. Eleanor pitied Margery, and all Geoffrey's victims. She was certain she was going to hear Jeanette's story confirmed.

"Doug found out," said the farmer's wife flatly. "I would have left him. I'd have followed Geoff to the far side of the world. He'd bewitched me! But he didn't want me."

"I don't understand," said Jocelyn, more bewildered now than condemning. "Why was he still living here?"

Margery looked up with a twisted smile. "He refused to leave, Mrs Stearns. He was perfectly satisfied with his accommodation. We'd signed a long lease, so we couldn't chuck him out. As simple as that."

"Good gracious, Eleanor, while one can't, of course, condone murder, it is understandable. The young man seems to have had no sense of decency whatsoever!"

"He was a brute," Margery confirmed. "Jeanette was the one who really suffered—but that's not my story to tell. Well, sitting here's not going to get Doug's dinner on the table." She heaved herself up and collected the colanders. "Did you come to take Mrs Trewynn home, Mrs Stearns? Because the police are expecting to find her here, so maybe she shouldn't leave before they've talked to her. You're welcome to stay to dinner—lunch—if you like."

"That's very kind of you, Mrs Rosevear, but I see no reason why Eleanor should wait on their convenience while inconveniencing you. They can perfectly well come to Port Mabyn."

Recalling past battles with Scumble, Eleanor said firmly, "Margery is right, Joce. I don't want to put Mr Pearce's back up before I get a chance to tell him everything. There's no need for you to stay, though. I'm sure someone will give me a lift down to Padstow later. You must have parish business calling you, not to mention the vicar wanting his lunch."

"Are you the vicar's wife, Mrs Stearns?" Margery asked. "No wonder I felt an urge to confess to you. It's supposed to be good for the soul, isn't it?"

"The English Church does not in general practise the rites of the confessional," Jocelyn said primly, "though some High Churchmen . . . However, it's true that telling all to a sympathetic listener can often have a salutory effect. 'Getting it off one's chest,' in the common expression."

In general, Eleanor would not have described Jocelyn as a "sympathetic listener," but she had been remarkably restrained, so let her accept the kudos. Margery looked as if she were trying not to smile.

Eleanor just said, "Were you going to pick peas, Margery? We could do that, or I could, if Jocelyn has to get back. And I love shelling them, if you don't mind a few finding their way into my mouth."

"Sorry, I planted mange-tout this year. But by all means eat some uncooked, if you like them that way." She handed over the colanders. "It would be a help. Will you stay, Mrs Stearns?"

"Yes, since you've been kind enough to invite me, I wouldn't dream of deserting Eleanor to face the police on her own."

Just as well, thought Eleanor, remembering that Nick had her car keys.

Margery went back to the house, her step noticeably lighter.

"I don't know about the soul," said Eleanor, who frequently doubted the existence of such a figment, "but having told us, she'll certainly find it easier to tell the police. As she said, it's no good trying to conceal that sort of thing if a number of people already know it."

They went over to the row of peas, flourishing like everything in the garden, and picked for a few minutes in silent thought. Eleanor crunched a sweet pod or two, and offered one to Teazle, who rejected it with a disdainful sniff.

"Adultery is a sin," said Jocelyn broodingly, "and a terrible one, because it involves a breach of trust. Yet I can't help feeling sorry for the woman. Geoffrey Clark was a really nasty piece of work."

Eleanor rarely agreed with her friend on matters of theology, but on this, though she would have phrased it differently, they were at one. Unfaithfulness was not a crime, but nor was it victimless. It was a breach of trust, and Eleanor had spent most of her life as roving ambassador for LonStar working to build trust, so she felt strongly about it. She was sorry for Margery, who had believed herself in love and had been discarded like a worn-out cardigan, but she was sorrier for Doug, the victim, innocent of anything except perhaps dullness. Who could guess what he had suffered?

Who could guess what grudge he might have nursed and nourished, unable to avoid constant contact with the man who had cuckolded him?

FIFTEEN

Megan had omitted to ask Scumble how long she was expected to keep Nick occupied elsewhere. When she realised, she compounded the error by mentioning it to Nick.

"Whenever we get back, he's bound to say he's been waiting for hours," she said glumly.

"In that case, there's not much point worrying about it." Nick took a bite of the sort of gooey pastry he hadn't indulged in for years—or so he claimed—that he'd ordered after assuring himself that Megan could put it on her expense sheet. As it was a mille-feuille, cream oozed out of the other side and he had to scoop it up with his finger. The fork provided lay neglected on his plate.

Megan was too wrapped in gloom to object to his far from public-schoolboy manners. "It'll be all my fault for not asking, not his for not telling me."

"Of course." Nick licked his finger—very *Tom Jones*, Megan thought sourly. "What's the point of attaining rank if you can't blame your subordinates? He's not my boss, though. Tell him I'm responsible." He took another squishy bite.

"He won't have any difficulty believing that." She took advantage of his temporary inability to retort. "I wouldn't care to bet that he doesn't put DI Pearce's lapse down to your uncooperative behaviour last night."

Nick choked slightly and took a swig of coffee to wash down the crumbs. "I was extremely cooperative!" he said indignantly. "I walked from the gallery to the police station with Jerry Roscoe like a lamb. I was perfectly prepared to answer any questions put to me. Pearce never asked. Wilkes can tell you."

"DC Wilkes? That's right, I saw his initials on Pearce's report. He took notes. I'd forgotten you knew him."

"A good bloke. He sacrificed half a sandwich to Teazle."

"No! Tell me."

Interrupted by lengthy pauses for consumption, Nick obliged with the tale of Teazle's adventures at the Padstow police station. Megan enjoyed the story, but she listened with an ear also for any discrepancies with the reports she and Scumble had read. Everything seemed to mesh.

For a wonder, Nick used the fork to scrape up the last bit of cream. He looked ruefully at his fingers and grinned at Megan. "You'll have to excuse me for a moment. I don't dare touch anything till I've washed my hands."

Oh hell! she thought. Had he ordered the mille-feuille just to have an excuse to escape her surveillance? Surely he had too much sense to make a run for it, but what if he telephoned Aunt Nell?

His grin broadened as he read her mind. "No, that's not why I chose it. I'm not going to make a run for it and I'm not going to ring Eleanor. I'm on the side of the guys in the white hats."

"I believe you. All the same . . ." She raised her hand to summon the waitress. "Have you got a public phone, miss?"

The girl shook her head. " 'Fraid not. There's one at the post office, over in the next street." She gestured towards the kitchen in the rear.

"Is there a back door? Can we cut through?"

"No, it's a shared back wall."

"What about a Gents?" Nick asked.

She shook her head. "There's a public toilet over in the Shire Hall."

Nick raised his eyebrows at Megan.

"You're serving food," she pointed out. "You must have a staff washroom."

"Oh yes, but we're not s'posed to let people use it."

Megan was not about to let Nick disappear into the public loo. Reluctantly, she took out her identification card.

"Oooh, police! Is he under arrest?"

"Not yet."

"I shall never be able to show my face in Bodmin again!" Nick moaned.

"Go and wash your hands," Megan snapped, "before I get out the handcuffs."

He stood up. "Do you think by any chance the police will spring for another cup of coffee, Sergeant? That thing was delicious but rather sweet."

Megan rolled her eyes. "Don't push your luck, chum."

Still grinning, Nick weaved his way between the other tables, fortunately sparsely occupied as it was early for elevenses, and disappeared.

"What'd he do, Sergeant?" the waitress asked breathlessly.

"Watch the newspapers. That's all I can say. And bring two more cups of coffee, please."

When Nick returned, no longer sticky, Megan asked him, "How well do you know these people at the farm, or commune, or whatever it is? Mates of yours, are they?"

"Mates—that's exactly the right word. Birds of a feather, after all. They'd drop in if they happened to be in Port Mabyn, and I'd do the same when I was in Padstow, to the shop—they have a co-op shop—if not all the way out to the farm. Then we'd meet at darts matches. Doug is on the Gold Bezant darts team, as is Jerry Roscoe, the local copper, and I play for the Trelawny Arms."

"What about Stella Maris Weller? You had a closer relationship with her."

Nick glanced round. The tea-shop was beginning to fill up with shoppers and the odd tourist. "This isn't the place to talk. Let's go and gawk at the old gaol."

Megan paid, making sure she got a receipt, hoping she'd be reimbursed. They set out along the street, past the Shire Hall and on up St Nicholas Street.

"Well?" she said. "You show Stella's stuff in your gallery, and none of the others'. Whatever you told the gov'nor, there must be something special between you two."

He strode on faster, making her hurry to keep up. The hill was quite steep, but the side streets they passed were even steeper, leading up towards the Beacon. Nick's gaze was firmly fixed ahead so Megan couldn't see his face well, but she thought he looked embarrassed.

"As a matter of fact, when I said Stella once made googly eyes at me, I was being kind. The first time I met Stella, she offered to sleep with me if I'd sell her sculptures in my shop."

"And you didn't?" She managed to keep her voice level. "Not even once?"

"I did not! I told her if I wanted a prostitute, which I didn't, I'd go and troll the streets of Plymouth."

Megan was surprised at how relieved she felt, as well as amused. Trying not to laugh, she commented, "That must have got her goat."

"It did. She pretended I'd misunderstood her. She claimed she'd just meant that if we were to happen to get friendly, I might find a spot in my extensive premises to display her art."

"Which you did."

"For the sake of peace, I told her I'd take it if I liked it and if it didn't compete with my stuff, and if she'd run the shop occasionally to give me a day off. Luckily her seals and dolphins and such are excellent of their sort and fulfil both conditions."

"And if they hadn't?"

"I hate to contemplate the thought. She's never quite forgiven me, even though I've been selling quite nicely for her. She's got the co-op shop in Padstow as well, and I believe she has arrangements with a number of arty-crafty-gifty shops up and down the coast." He held up his hand. "Don't ask me how many of the owners she's slept with. I don't care to speculate on the subject."

"It does rather boggle the mind. What alternative inducement could she offer? A commission, I suppose."

"Yes, and Stella had much rather part with her favours than her pounds, shillings, and pence."

"Miaow. I thought it was women who are supposed to be catty."

"Come now," Nick reproved her, "that's a very sexist remark. I don't see why you should have a monopoly."

"True. She's hungry for money, is she? I shouldn't have thought she could make all that much from her sculpture."

"Just enough, at a guess, to keep her interested. She's not the sort to starve in a garret for the sake of her art, but she is genuinely talented and she enjoys it. All the same, she makes more with her nursing, and I keep expecting to hear she's thrown over the sculpture to go into that full-time."

"Nursing?"

"Oh, haven't you heard about that? I don't know why you should have. She works weekends at a convalescent home outside Wade-bridge. She's sort of half qualified, I gather. I don't know the details. She doesn't seem to like it much, but as I said, it pays much better."

"Sounds as if she's got the best of both worlds. May I ask you a question?"

"Isn't that what you've been doing for the past half hour?"

"Well, yes, but . . ." Megan desperately tried to think of the best way to word her query. "Umm . . . If you're really not gay . . ."

"I already told Scumble I'm not."

"Then why, really, did you refuse Stella's . . . offer? Not that rubbish about 'saving yourself for the right girl.' He's going to want a proper answer, sooner or later. If you'd rather talk to him—"

Nick shuddered. "Good god, no! It's simple enough. I find the use of sex as a bribe distasteful," he told her bluntly. "Gorgeous as she is, I could tell right away that Stella is not the sort of woman with whom I could contemplate a long-term relationship. Any woman who would offer a quid pro quo like that within minutes of first meeting is not for me."

"Don't tell me: 'Sugar and spice and all things nice.' That ghastly rhyme, is that your ideal?"

He burst out laughing. "Certainly not. But I really don't believe the police can have any legitimate interest in my vision of ideal womanhood. We seem to have come to the end of the town. Shall we turn back? We don't want Scumble to think I've abducted you."

They had, in fact, come to the end of the pavement, just past the barracks of the Duke of Cornwall's Light Infantry, and the top of the slope. Ahead, the road dipped beneath a railway bridge—they had passed the boarded-up central station halfway up the hill. Beyond, a wide valley spread lushly green to the next ridge.

"Yes," Megan agreed, "we'd better be getting back. I didn't

realise we'd come so far." She checked her watch. "Or been gone so long! He's going to kill me."

"I doubt it. You've extracted plenty of information to keep him happy."

Extracted? Megan wondered. She felt more as if she had been force-fed a quantity of information, most of which tended to show that Nick had no motive for being jealous of Geoffrey Clark. How much of it could she believe?

On the other hand, Nick already had a credible motive for killing Geoff in the destruction of his work. Either his alibi was valid, or he was still in big trouble. All in all, Megan realised with irritation, she had no good reason for her relief that his relationship with Stella was purely a matter of business.

They walked back into town mostly in silence. Megan was afraid it had been a mistake to ask Nick whether he'd lied to Scumble about not being a homosexual, but whether from the police or the personal point of view she couldn't decide.

Nick started whistling the tune from "Pomp and Circumstance" again.

"Can't you get that out of your head?" Megan asked. "It's so annoying when something keeps going round and round like a stuck record."

"What? Oh, no. I'm planning a painting. I don't so much hear it as see it."

"All red, white, and blue?"

"Good god no! Sorry if it's irritating."

"Could be worse. I once got caught by 'I'm 'Enery the Eighth, I am' for hours. Now that was 'orrible!"

"I hope you haven't just given it to me!"

Megan sang softly, " 'Land of Hope and Glory, Mother of the Free,' " to put him back on track. She wished she could understand just what was going on in his head.

When they reached the Bodmin nick, Scumble greeted them with the expected, "Where the bloody hell you been, Pencarrow?" but he couldn't suppress a gleeful smile. Rubbing his hands together with satisfaction, he went on, "Forensics and the medical report both agree with your version, Mr Gresham. We've got the bastard cold. Pending autopsy—these doctors are always cautious buggers—Dr Prthnavi says the deceased died before three o'clock, latest. And, as the dagger was left in the wound, there would have been next to no flow of blood."

Megan and Nick both let out long breaths.

"Then, Forensics analysed the red ink. It's the kind the deceased used for his adverts, all right, and SOC found a couple of empty bottles, or canisters, or whatchamacallems, in the waste bin under the sink. Wiped clean of prints, as you'd expect these days."

"So what's next, sir?"

The inspector's smile turned malevolent. "First things first." He glanced at the wall-clock. "I'm going to see the Bodmin Super, Egerton, in three minutes. You made it back barely in time. Want to come along and see how to demolish a colleague without saying anything actionable? No, on second thoughts, you'd better read these reports. We'll have to get going immediately after."

"Taking me home?" Nick said plaintively.

"Eh? Oh, yes, of course. Eventually." Scumble heaved himself out of his chair.

"Sir, I could read the reports in the car, couldn't I? I do think I ought to be present to witness your . . . to learn the proper way to . . . er . . ."

"Stab a colleague in the back?" Nick suggested.

"I may never have another chance," Megan said quickly.

Scumble turned on Nick and snarled, "I wouldn't talk about stabbing colleagues in the back if I were you. You're not out of the woods yet." He picked up the phone. "Scumble here. I want a detective constable up here on the double to . . . keep Mr Gresham company for a few minutes . . . No, he's not bloody under arrest! He's feeling lonesome and homesick . . . That's right, laddie, got it in one. I don't want him buzzing off, and no phone-calls." He slammed down the receiver. "Come along, then, Pencarrow, if you're coming!"

As they left the room, a hefty man came puffing up. "Sir! You want an eye kept on that artist bloke, right?"

Scumble stared at him. "Wilkes!" he said in disgust. "Think you can manage not to let him outwit you this time?"

"This time, sir? But last time it wasn't—"

Scumble didn't wait to hear his protest. Megan following, he swept on into Superintendent Egerton's office.

Egerton reminded Megan of a toad. He appeared to be wedged inextricably into his chair, as toads like to wedge themselves into a rocky niche. Doubtless he had his uses, snapping up societal pests as toads snap up horticultural pests. Megan had nothing against toads. Her mother had always been happy to find one in the garden. His appearance was unprepossessing, however, though at least he was not visibly warty.

"DI Scumble, sir," his secretary announced, "from Launceston. And . . . ?"

"DS Pencarrow, sir."

Egerton signed the paper in front of him and moved it from one neat pile to another. Raising his head, he fixed them with a cold, black, unblinking stare. "Ah yes." His voice was diconcertingly high and thin. "Scumble. Bentinck sent you down to tie up the loose ends on that case of Bixby's. You've dotted all the *i*'s and crossed the *t*'s, have you?"

"No, sir."

"What? What's that? Bixby assured me Pearce had the culprit

in custody already. Some sort of artist, wasn't it? You haven't let him slip through our fingers, I hope?"

"Certainly not, sir." Scumble sounded shocked. Megan had never guessed he could act so well. "The man is still in the building."

"I'm not talking about his physical presence, Inspector. You're not going to let him slip through some loophole in the law?"

"I hardly think he need look for loopholes, sir. As things stand, we have no case against him. There never was anything but the accusation of a hysterical woman, which is contradicted by the physical evidence. I've got the forensic and medical reports here to show you."

Superintendent Egerton waved them away. "Are you telling me DI Pearce arrested this fellow on the word of an hysterical female? Without any other evidence? The man must be stark raving mad."

"Oh no, sir, I'm sure Mr Pearce would never do anything so . . . so . . . unwise. 'Specially with a popular local artist who's an up-and-coming star on the London arts scene. Mr Gresham was never arrested, never charged, though I'm afraid he spent an uncomfortable night in the cells. But there, from what I hear you've got 'em set up all comfy-like, not like in the bad old days."

Something sly in Scumble's tone reminded Megan of hearing Egerton described as a "bring back flogging" copper. Or was it "hang, draw, and quarter 'em"?

The super's cheeks swelled. "Is he going to lodge a complaint?"

"I doubt it, sir. A very easygoing gentleman. Not the sort to hold a grudge. Nor to stab someone in the back, though it's true you never can tell."

"So you've released him?"

"Yes, sir, but kept him close, like. We still have to check his alibi for the actual time of death."

"Any chance Pearce was right to pick him up, if for the wrong reasons?"

"I rather doubt it, sir. The alibi looks good. But like I said, it's got to be checked."

"Quite right, quite right. Then I suppose you'll have to start from scratch."

"I wouldn't say that, sir. We—Sergeant Pencarrow and me—we've got a few cards up our sleeves."

"I'm glad to hear Pearce didn't completely drop the ball."

"Mr Pearce didn't pass on any names, sir. Well, you couldn't expect him to, could you, seeing he was sure he'd got the case sewn up. These are leads we've developed ourselves. Of course, Mr Pearce would soon have found 'em if he'd stayed with the case."

"Of course," said Egerton grimly. "Right, get on with it."

Megan followed Scumble out of the room. With the door firmly closed behind them, she asked, "Which leads are those, sir?"

"We'll find 'em, Pencarrow, we'll find 'em. Don't forget, we've got a nest of commies to roust out to begin with. I wonder if your auntie's managed to infiltrate," he added jocularly. He was very pleased with himself.

Though quite impressed by the way her gov'nor had handled the Super, Megan was less than thrilled at the thought of Aunt Nell, all unwary, infiltrating a bunch of possibly murderous commies, even if they weren't actually communists. Still, it wasn't Scumble who had sent her to Cold Comfort Farm, or whatever it was called. DI Pearce was to blame. Megan hoped Egerton gave him a rocket.

"What did you get from Gresham?"

"Uh . . . sir?"

"Come on, Pencarrow, I didn't send you out to babysit him. Don't tell me you spent nearly an hour discussing the flowers that bloom in the spring. Tra-la." He stopped with his hand on the door-handle of their room and gave her an enquiring look.

"He confirmed that Stella Maris Weller made a pass at him, which he rejected. In an extremely insulting manner."

"Ah, he did, did he?"

"The implication being that he had no motive of jealousy for doing in Geoffrey Clark."

"I wasn't born yesterday, Pencarrow. I can see an implication when it bites me in the arse. What I can't see—yet—is the relevance. He's already got an adequate motive. At least, I assume so. I want to see those paintings of his, and I'd really like to see the note he claims Miss Stella Weller left for him. Though unless she wrote the date and time on it, it won't be conclusive. You'll have to go and see this artsy-fartsy London dealer anyway."

"Alarian? Why me, sir?"

He gave her an evil grin. "You're the one with friends in the Met. I'm sure the boy wonder'll be happy to go with you to hold your hand."

Megan didn't bother to protest. It was true that Ken, a detective sergeant with the Metropolitan Police, would probably be helpful, and the fact that she'd prefer not to see him, let alone ask for his assistance, would not weigh with the gov'nor, even if she wanted to tell him so, which she didn't.

"But we mustn't keep Mr Gresham waiting any longer in case he decides to lodge a complaint! The victim's gallery first, I think. Let's get this show on the road."

In spite of the inspector's words, it was some time before they left Bodmin. They needed officers to go house-to-house in Padstow, and it turned out, in the face of Scumble's expressed disbelief, that the Bodmin district really was unusually busy. Egerton had instructed his flock to cooperate, but the better part of the morning was gone before the caravan of two pandas and the 1100 got under way.

In the meantime, taking advantage of the bustle and confusion, Nick had slipped out into the town, returning with a drawing pad and a box of coloured chalks. He took no further notice of proceedings.

SIXTEEN

Eleanor and Jocelyn took two colanders full of pea-pods through the back corridor to the kitchen.

"Is there anything else we can do to help?" Jocelyn enquired.

"No, thanks, Mrs Stearns. It's all under control. There's just the four of us. The ravening hordes are supposed to forage for themselves in the middle of the day. You won't mind Doug in his work-clothes, I hope? No point him changing when he'll go straight out again after."

"Of course not," Eleanor assured her, while Joce murmured something not quite appropriate about the labourer being worthy of his hire. "I'd really like to see more of the workings of Tom's pottery before the police interrupt."

They went out to the courtyard.

"What are you plotting, Eleanor?" Joce asked suspiciously.

"Plotting? What do you mean?"

"I know that look."

"Not plotting, just thinking. Wondering."

"Wondering what?"

"I can't do anything about it at present anyway. It wouldn't be fair to Margery. So you can stop worrying. Will you come with me to watch Tom Lennox make those dishes you so admire?"

"I suppose I might as well. It's very inconsiderate of the police to keep you waiting."

Tom's door still stood open. Approaching, they heard the whir of his potter's wheel. Above it rose the sound of a female voice.

"Champagne!" exclaimed Jeanette. "I want the real thing."

"Do you think that's a good idea?" Tom queried. "The fuzz are going to think it's pretty odd to celebrate the murder of a fellow-artist so . . . so blatantly."

Eleanor held Jocelyn back, too intrigued to worry about the ethics of eavesdropping.

"You can't expect me to pretend to mourn him. If you hadn't heard me scream . . . But I can wait for the Champagne till Nick's safe for sure."

"Till after the funeral. And the inquest."

"Inquest! Does there have to be an inquest when he was so obviously murdered? I mean, you can't stick a dagger in your own back, either by accident or on purpose, can you? Not that Geoff would ever have committed suicide. He had far too high an opinion of himself. An inquest! Oh, Tom, do you think we'll all have to go? As witnesses?"

"I don't know about that," the potter said grimly, "but you've got to face it, the police will be asking us all a lot of questions."

"I can't talk to them!" Jeanette sounded panic-stricken.

"You won't have any choice. None of us will. You needn't be afraid I'll tell them anything, though. You know I'd do anything—"

"Yes," said Jocelyn loudly, "I would like to see more of Mr Lennox's methods." She gave Eleanor a reproachful look, to show she felt she had been led astray, and marched into the workshop.

Eleanor sighed and followed. In theory, naturally she disapproved of eavesdropping. In general. But there were times . . .

Such as when one was attempting to track down a murderer. The trouble was, the new scrap of information that Eleanor had collected, before Joce's scruples overcame her, had made her less certain than ever that this was a murderer she wanted to see caught.

What had Geoffrey done to frighten Jeanette? she wondered, while apparently listening intently and nodding intelligently to Tom's explanation of some process or other. Perhaps the girl was oversensitive? Much as she was coming to dislike and despise Geoffrey Clark, she must try to be fair.

She couldn't speak for Jocelyn or her ethics, whether inspired by middle-class or church conventions, but to Eleanor, fairness was infinitely more important than a spot of eavesdropping.

Jeanette had slipped out. Now Oswald returned.

"No good, I can't concentrate," he grumbled. "I wish the fuzz would buck up and show up."

"Don't we all," said Tom, continuing to mould clay as he talked. "I just want to get it over, and Jeanette's having fits for fear it's Mrs Trewynn who's got hold of the wrong end of the stick, rather than Stella." He smiled at Eleanor and shrugged. "I know who I believe. Stella's always had a tendency to see what she wants to see."

"Otherwise she'd never have fallen for Geoff," Oswald agreed. "Thinks—thought, that is, the sun shone out of his . . . er, sorry."

"And vice versa. A mutual admiration society. If anything, he was nuttier about her. I'd have thought she'd be able to stop him slashing Nick's paintings."

"Maybe she didn't try too hard. She wasn't all that keen on Nick. Besides, I don't think I'd want to get in the way of Geoff with a knife in his hand."

"Sounds as if he went berserk again," Tom conceded. "He'd never concede that Nick's a better painter." He turned to Eleanor. "What's all that about, Mrs Trewynn? Stella had too much else on her mind to tell us exactly what set Geoff off."

Eleanor told them, omitting her part in connecting Nick with Alarian in the first place. She didn't want to detract from his success. Nor did she want to be besieged with requests for introductions. Not that she thought it likely. Oswald seemed to have a realistic view of his abilities as an artist, Tom regarded his work as more craft than art, and both men apparently considered Nick's luck to be deserved.

"It's not just the technique," Oswald said with a sigh, "though he's streets ahead of me there—"

"Not streets," Tom consoled him, "just a few dozen yards."

"That's as may be. But he has the imagination to go with it."

"Not to worry. When he's rich and famous we can boast that we knew him when he was just another unknown."

"Yeah, and sponge on him! That'll be the day."

They both laughed. Tom gave a twirl to the pot on his wheel, which now looked like a serving dish, and said to Jocelyn, "How does that look to you, Mrs Stearns?"

"Beautiful. An elegant shape."

"What colour, or colours, would you like it?"

"Me? Oh, but . . . I did tell you, Mr Lennox, that much as I admire them, I can't afford your wares."

"This is a gift. Or will be, assuming it comes out of the kiln in good shape. You can't always guarantee the results."

Jocelyn was rarely taken aback, and Eleanor had never before seen her so flummoxed. She was actually at a loss for words.

"But . . . but . . . why?"

Tom grinned at her. "Call it a reward for so bravely rushing to support your friend in this den of iniquity."

The vicar's wife turned bright pink, another first as far as Eleanor knew.

"I'll leave you to choose your colours," Eleanor said tactfully, or perhaps cowardly. She wasn't sure whether Joce was flattered or considered the potter grossly impertinent. "It's time I had a look at Oswald's pictures, if you'd like to show me, Oswald?"

"If you like."

"But I'd like to talk to you later, Tom, about an idea I've just had."

"Anytime. I'll be here."

She and Oswald went out into the courtyard. There they met Albert. He was coming from the mini-bus parking place, gazing past them towards the far end of the row of studios opposite Oswald's.

"What's going on?" he asked.

Eleanor and Oswald turned. Stella was lifting a box into another mini-bus, this one a blue, gleaming vehicle that looked as though it might even be comfortable and certainly didn't smell of pigs.

"It's Friday. It's just Stella going to work," Oswald said to Albert. "The home she works at send their bus to fetch her," he explained to Eleanor. "They have trouble keeping staff."

"She and the driver were loading stuff when I drove in, and they're still at it."

"Oh dear," said Eleanor, "I'm afraid it's my fault."

"Your fault?"

She reconsidered her statement as the two men stared at her in surprise. "Well, not mine, exactly. The police detective who sent me here. I heard Stella having a row with Margery, saying she was going to move out because Margery was harbouring a friend of the man who killed Geoffrey. Which he didn't, of course. Nick, that is. Didn't kill Geoffrey."

"I expect it's hard on her, too, being right here where she was with him," said Albert. "When my wife died, I just wanted to get away from everywhere we'd ever been together."

"It was just the opposite for me," Eleanor told him. "When Peter was killed, all I wanted was to retreat to Cornwall. We were both born here and always came back for our holidays. But then, we'd spent so much time abroad. But what will Stella do? Will she be able to stay temporarily at the convalescent place, do you think?"

"Oh yes," Albert assured her. "She has a room there. She always spends Friday afternoon to Monday morning there. Weekend staff's even harder to find than weekday, so she's left more or less in sole charge."

"Or so she'd like us to think," said Oswald.

"It's not as if it was a hospital, though she did once tell me that Dr Fenwick, the owner, has a flat there where he spends most weekends and he's always on call. That was quite a while ago, but I imagine it's still the case. She's not a fully qualified nurse."

"If I was old and ill," Oswald commented, "I wouldn't want Stella looking after me. Typical of her, going off like this, not thinking of anyone else. How's she going to get into Padstow? The rest of us will have to cover her days at the shop."

"She can catch a bus. There are plenty between Wadebridge and Padstow. Should we go and say good-bye, do you think?"

"Not me!"

"Someone ought to." Albert hesitated, then squared his shoulders and marched off across the courtyard.

"I'm not staying to watch the slaughter. If you'd really like to take a gander at my daubs, Mrs Trewynn . . . ?"

"Yes, of course." Eleanor went with him, but her mind was elsewhere. "Stella seems to have had three . . . well . . . places of residence," she mused aloud. "I'm sure someone said she lived with Geoffrey. As Margery was planning an artists' colony, I assume his bungalow has a studio she could use, and he has—had one behind his gallery in Padstow as well. Why on earth would she go on paying for her own studio and bedsitter?"

"Well, er, you see," Oswald mumbled, not looking at her, "they lived together in the sense that they were—um—lovers. I mean, they—um—you know, slept together as well as being in love with each other. But Stella isn't the sort to give up her freedom for love. I mean, she wasn't faithful to Geoff, or anything. He didn't own her just because she loved him. He wasn't faithful to her, either, come to that, however crazy he was about her. I mean, that's all sort of old-fashioned, if you know what I mean. People can't own each other."

"Oh," said Eleanor blankly. Though she did her best to make allowances for what some called the "generation gap," there were certain aspects of contemporary mores that she would never understand. She could tell herself that equating faithfulness with ownership was no more outré than many customs she had seen in far parts of the world, but the truth was, she hadn't expected to come home and find conventions of morality so altered.

Oswald hurriedly changed the subject. "Here they are," he said, with a gesture encompassing a covered easel and several stacks of unframed pictures leaning against one wall.

The paintings were of local landscapes, beauty spots, and landmarks such as Jamaica Inn. Though pleasant enough, they somehow lacked the vividness of Nick's work, evident even in his "tourist" paintings of similar scenes.

Eleanor would have liked to ask what made the difference, but in spite of his acknowledgement of Nick's superiority, it would hardly be kind. Besides, if he knew, presumably he'd do whatever it took to improve his.

"Very attractive," she offered.

"At least I make a living of sorts at it, which is more than most artists can say. I know I'm not brilliant," Oswald admitted bitterly, "but Geoff had no call to say they're junk."

SEVENTEEN

On arrival in Padstow, the police convoy parked in the yard of the station, now closed thanks to Dr Beeching's cuts. Scumble gathered his team around him.

They were all Bodmin officers, because strictly speaking it was Bodmin's case. Megan knew surprisingly few of them. Launceston and Bodmin were not distant geographically, but on the whole each district's CID was kept busy on its own patch. Rarely did either suffer a major crime that required collaboration. However, as the only female detective based in North Cornwall, she was recognised by all.

Detective Constables Wilkes and Polmenna she had worked with on a previous case. Wilkes had been with DI Pearce last night. No doubt he was responsible for everyone being aware of her aunt's involvement in the present case. Not that anyone mentioned it. Megan could tell from the smirks, sly glances, and covert snickers.

Obviously Scumble had noticed. His fearsome scowl quickly shut everybody up.

He sent Polmenna with two uniformed constables to go door-to-door along the street opposite and next door to Geoffrey Clark's gallery.

"Not much hope," he said, "seeing there'll have been tourists coming and going all afternoon, but maybe someone noticed something odd, or even what time the CLOSED sign went up. Make a note, by the way, that's something you'll have to ask about in Port Mabyn, too: what time Gresham's shop closed. You can find out what people thought of the dead man, too, and make a note of any strong reactions. Any questions? Right, off you go." He turned to Wilkes, who wilted a little. "You. You know Mrs Trewynn, don't you. And you renewed the acquaintance yesterday evening."

"Yes, sir."

"Good. I'm sending you straight to this communist farm place to have what you might call a preliminary chat with her. Get the straightforward questions sorted before I have to face her. You know what to ask?"

"I—I think so, sir."

"I should hope so." Scumble glared at him.

Megan was both amused and indignant at Scumble's reluctance to face Aunt Nell. Glancing at Nick, she guessed that his feelings were much the same. Anyone would think Aunt Nell was a fire-breathing dragon, not a kind, charming, inoffensive old lady. Scumble just couldn't fathom the way her mind worked, the fact that she remembered people perfectly well but was rather vague about things and events and times.

Wilkes's plump face was unhappy. "I don't know how to get there, sir," he said.

"Use your initiative, man! You know what that is? If you haven't got any, I suggest you go and ask the local man."

Wilkes scurried off. Scumble, Megan, Nick, and the remaining uniformed officer followed at a more leisurely pace.

When they reached the King Arthur Gallery, Scumble told the constable, Lubbock, to stand outside and make sure they were not disturbed. He had the key on a bunch taken from the victim's pocket by the Scene of Crime officer and sent over with his report.

He handed the clanking bunch to Megan. "Here, you sort it."

The ring held seven or eight keys, but only three were Yale. Naturally, Megan tried the wrong two first. Naturally, Scumble acted as if she were being deliberately obstructive. The lock was stiff. At last the door opened, with a jangle of its bell.

After reading Sergeant Roscoe's report of the blood-soaked crime scene, Megan was a little apprehensive when it came to entering the studio of the King Arthur Gallery. If her stomach rebelled, she would never hear the end of it from Scumble.

She reminded herself that the techs had confirmed Nick's claim that the pools of blood were nothing but red ink, but the image raised by the original description stayed with her.

Scumble had brought Nick into the gallery with them. The artist appeared not in the least apprehensive. Whatever ghost lingered here, he didn't expect it to haunt him, Megan thought, then wondered where such a fanciful notion had sprung from in her usually prosaic mind. Nick's fault, she decided resentfully. Somehow his presence made her brain stretch in directions it didn't want to go. It didn't help that the pictures in Geoffrey Clark's shop were the stuff of fantasy and legend, straight out of Tolkien, as Nick had mentioned. Or vice versa; she wasn't sure of the sequence of events.

A detective needed a certain amount of imagination, but too much could be a decided handicap.

She wondered why he had chosen to use the name Monmouth for his work. Geoffrey—or Geoffroie—Monmouth. Vaguely it rang a bell. Perhaps it had no particular meaning and anything other than Clark would have done. Clark wasn't much less common than Smith, after all.

"Stay here," Scumble ordered Nick.

"Right you are," Nick said amiably. "I shall occupy my time in studying Geoff's technique."

"If it amuses you. Come along, Pencarrow." He strode to the door at the back, opened it, and entered the studio.

Megan followed, closing the door behind her. The corpse was long gone, of course. The place where it had lain was clearly marked by the bare floor-boards between two splotches of red, bright, glossy red, the colour of fresh blood. It might fade with time, but no amount of scrubbing would get it out of the unfinished wood.

"Ink!" said Scumble explosively. "What I can't make out is why Pearce didn't at least come and have a look-see for himself. He'd only to touch it to know it's not blood."

The desk sergeant hadn't actually told Megan not to pass on the information about DI Pearce's new wife. He had just suggested there was no need to do so. She decided Scumble did need to know, if only so that he could stop wasting brainpower on wondering at his rival's strange behaviour instead of devoting it to solving the crime.

"I've heard, sir, that Mr Pearce has a new young wife who doesn't like him getting home late."

"Huh! Had to be something like that. There's no fool like a middle-aged fool. Right, get Gresham in here."

Nick came reluctantly. "Geoff had some good ideas," he admitted. "I've never really studied his painting before. It's a mistake to dismiss someone's work because you happen to dislike him intensely."

"If you're talking about DI Pearce," Scumble snarled, "I dismissed his work—if it can be called work—because the doctor and the forensic evidence refuted it. And you shouldn't be complaining, considering the result."

"You dislike Pearce, too? I must say, on the whole, I prefer your bad temper to his oily incompetence."

"Kind of you! I'm beginning to see why Pearce was only too glad to have an excuse to lock you up without taking a statement. Right, if we're done with the compliments, perhaps we can get on with the business that brought us here. Now that we're on the spot, I want you to tell me again exactly what happened and what everyone said from your arrival last night until you left this building."

Nick rolled his eyes but complied. Naturally his story varied in details from what he had said back at the Bodmin nick. As far as Megan could determine, it didn't differ in any significant way. When he finished, Scumble merely nodded, giving no indication of whether he had learnt anything new and useful or not.

He glanced at his watch. "You know a place nearby where we can get a halfway decent pasty?" he asked.

"The Chough Bakery, down by the harbour," said Nick at once. "Shouldn't we get up to the farm, though?"

Megan agreed, silently. She was hungry, but food could wait. She wasn't really worried about Aunt Nell since Mrs Stearns had promised to join her—the vicar's wife, though hide-bound and bossy to a degree, was absolutely trustworthy. Though perhaps not always in regard to cooperating with the police, Megan recalled uneasily. It had been she who came up with the plot . . . But she'd take care of Aunt Nell.

Scumble was going to be furious when he found Mrs Stearns at the farm. That would be bad enough. Megan could only hope Mrs Stearns would not have decided Aunt Nell was safer at home.

"We'll eat in the car," Scumble conceded.

So Megan would stay hungry anyway, or try to eat her pasty while driving. She looked down at the pale yellow blouse she wore under her grey terylene-cotton suit. No, not a good idea. Besides, Scumble was at best a nervous passenger. He'd have a fit if she took the wheel with a pasty in her hand. For the same reason, he wasn't likely to let the unfamiliar PC drive the 1100. After a long period of adjustment, he was used to Megan.

She locked the door of the gallery behind them, put the keys in her shoulder-bag, and hurried after the others. Scumble had stopped to have a word with Polmenna while Nick and PC Lubbock went on towards the Chough Bakery in Strand Street. Scumble gestured to Megan to follow them. If DC Polmenna kept him talking long enough, maybe Megan would manage to eat at least some of her pasty after all.

However, the inspector caught up with them just as they entered the bakery.

"Nothing doing, sir?" Megan asked.

"So far, no one's noticed a bloody thing." His gloomy face brightened as the savoury smells made his nostrils flare. Then he looked at the price-list, chalked on a board. "Highway robbery! What do they think—"

"You're looking at their specialities, Inspector," said Nick. "Chicken and mushroom, curried lamb—"

"Curried lamb! Where are we, Cornwall or Calcutta? What's wrong with plain steak and potato, I'd like to know! That's what's supposed to be in a pasty."

"We've got proper pasties," said the girl behind the counter a little nervously. "Steak and potato and a bit of turnip. That's our biggest seller."

"And the prices are just what you'd find elsewhere," Nick pointed out soothingly.

"Hnnn. Right, I'll take two." He glowered at Megan and Lubbock. "And you needn't think you can get away with curried-lamb nonsense on expenses. You." He turned to Nick. "I suppose you'll have to go on my expenses, seeing my colleague as good as kidnapped you. What'll you have?"

"The real thing, thanks." Nick was all too obviously trying—and failing—to hide his amusement, Megan saw, but Scumble didn't notice or chose to ignore it. "Just one," Nick added meekly.

Remembering the cream-filled cake he had scoffed in Bodmin, Megan wasn't surprised. She too ordered one plain, ordinary pasty. PC Lubbock, looking abashed, asked for two. He was not as bulky as Scumble nor as tall as Nick, but he was very young. Still growing, Megan thought charitably. Outwards if not upwards.

They carried their paper bags back to the car-park. By the time they reached the 1100, the bags were patched with greasy stains from the pastry crust. The smell rising from them made Megan salivate. She tried to resign herself to hers growing cold while she listened to the others eating.

Fishing in her pocket for the car keys, she hoped she wasn't getting grease stains on her suit.

"Give 'em to Lubbock," Scumble grunted. "You can sit in the back with me. We need to plan how to tackle these communists and I don't want you thinking about them while you're driving along those lanes. I suppose you can drive, Constable?"

"Oh yes, sir, of course. But . . . ?" He hefted his pasty.

"You'll just have to wait till we get there, won't you? Think a mere constable should eat before a detective sergeant?"

"No, sir." Lubbock looked mournful. "I don't know the way, sir."

"Nor does Sergeant Pencarrow. That's what Mr Gresham is for." He waited impatiently while Lubbock unlocked the rear door, then heaved himself in. "Come on, come on, what are you waiting for?"

The others piled in. Scumble was already taking his first pasty out of its bag, so Megan followed suit. The first bite, as always, was mostly pastry, but it was excellent pastry. After his second bite, Scumble said grudgingly, "Not half bad."

Nick, his mouth full, didn't respond. He just waved and pointed when Lubbock said sulkily, "Which way now?"

They took the main road south for a mile or so, then branched off, through rolling farmland. After another turn, the hedges closed in on either side, the lane barely wider than the 1100. Lubbock drove cautiously, so Scumble was able to concentrate on his food and finished his two pasties as Megan finished her one.

Too late for planning, though. The next turn was into a farm lane.

"Just a couple of hundred yards," Nick said cheerfully as they jounced over ruts and potholes.

Lubbock parked neatly beside DC Wilkes's panda, in a cobbled courtyard surrounded by gussied-up farm buildings. A horse-trough on either side overflowed with lobelia and pot-marigolds.

"You just sit here and eat your pasties, son," said Scumble. Being who he was, he managed to make the outwardly benevolent words sound vaguely menacing. "Gresham, you stay here with—I mean, please, Mr Gresham, I would appreciate you staying in the car with the constable, if you'd be so kind."

"Sit here in a car on a beautiful summer day, watching Constable Lubbock stuff his face? You must be mad!"

"For your own safety," the inspector snapped. "If these commies—"

"I've told you, they are *not* commies, for pity's sake!"

"All right, all right, keep your hair on. If these highly strung artistic types still believe you killed their chum, they may be after your blood."

"Not likely," said Nick laconically. "When you get to know them a bit, you'll find the only one who has it in for me is Stella. I assumed you needed me here for some reason, but if not, I've got work to do. I'll walk down to the road and hitch a lift or get a bus home. After I've made sure Mrs Trewynn is all right and hasn't been subjected to police brutality." He winked at Megan.

"Surely you can trust Sergeant Pencarrow for that! Now look here, Mr Gresham, let's be reasonable. I want you here because you know these people and can maybe give me a sidelight on what they say, clarify things, even suggest further questions. But for the same reason, I don't want you talking to them before we do, putting ideas into their heads."

"You've got a watchdog here." Nick gestured at the constable beside him, already engulfing his second pasty as if he'd never heard of indigestion. A pair of jackdaws, drawn by an infallible instinct, strutted across the cobbles in hopes of a bit of the crust. "Or guard dog, if you honestly think I'm in danger. He can follow me about."

Scumble regarded the back of Lubbock's head with distaste. "You listening by any chance, Constable?"

"Course I am, sir," the young man said through a mouthful of crumbs. "You want me to keep an eye on Mr Gresham and not let him talk to people."

"His suggestion, not mine. But that's the general idea. Think you can manage it?"

Lubbock drew breath to answer and a crumb went down his windpipe. He doubled up over the steering wheel, coughing and spluttering. Nick thumped him enthusiastically between the shoulderblades.

"Where do they find them?" Scumble demanded of the roof of the car. "Are they lobotomised at birth? Why me, oh—?"

"We have an audience, sir," Megan advised him.

Four people, two men and two women, had come out of the various buildings. Staring at the police cars, they were drifting together.

"Margery Rosevear," said Nick, ceasing to pound Lubbock, who seemed to be recovering. "Coming from the house. The other woman is Jeanette Jones, and that's Oswald Rudd, and the old chap is Albert Baraclough."

"Thank you. Are you with us again, Constable?"

"Yes, sir," Lubbock croaked. "It was a crumb, sir, went down the wrong—"

"We don't need the grisly details. I've changed my mind. You and Gresh—Mr Gresham can get out of the car and talk to those people. Gresham, I'm trusting you—I must be out of my ruddy mind!—not to tell them anything that's going to bollix up my investigation. In fact, don't tell them anything. I'll tell them as much as I want them to know. If you're tempted, just remind yourself one of the things I'm trying to do is clear your fair name."

"My lips are sealed."

"Lubbock, you can stroll about looking gormless—shouldn't be too difficult—and chatting people up."

"The girls, d'you mean, sir?"

"I do not! You can do that on your own time. I mean any and everyone who's not at that moment being interviewed by another officer. They just might let something drop to an innocent young lad, even if he is in police uniform, that they wouldn't mention to an experienced interrogator who's taking down their every word."

"Should I take notes, sir?"

Scumble closed his eyes. "Lord, give me patience. You will not remove your notebook from your pocket. I hope you have sufficient brain cells to remember if you hear any startling revelations."

"Oh yes, sir. I have a good memory." He started to get out of the car.

"A good memory, I'll believe when I see evidence," Scumble muttered to Megan. "Bet he wouldn't recognise a startling revelation if it walked up and introduced itself. I want you to talk to Stella Weller last, give her the sympathetic female touch. Try to pin her down to facts instead of fantasy, once you've heard what the others have to say. I'll see if Wilkes has managed to extract any useful information from your aunt."

They got out and approached the four residents, who now formed a group.

"Mrs Rosevear?" Ignoring the others, Scumble addressed the elder of the two women, fortyish, a buxom figure on the verge of becoming stout. "Detective Inspector Scumble. This is Detective Sergeant Pencarrow. We're here to ask a few questions concerning the late Geoffrey Clark, who, I understand, resided on your premises."

"That's his bungalow, there." She pointed at a low, yellow-washed building just outside the courtyard, typical of the rash of cheap holiday homes that had increasingly disfigured the countryside since the late fifties. "I've got a spare key."

"That's all right, madam, we have his keys. We'll take a look later. For the moment, perhaps you could tell me where to find Mrs Trewynn and my detective constable, and then DS Pencarrow would like a talk with you."

"Oh yes, I want to retract my statement. The one I made last night. What with Stella and Inspector Pearce, I was in such a flurry I spoke too hastily—"

"Sergeant Pencarrow will be happy to take a new statement, madam." Scumble flashed a glance of triumph at Megan. "Mrs Trewynn?"

"They're out in the garden behind the house. You can go

round that way. Will you come into the house, Sergeant? I'm just clearing the dinner things."

Megan made up her mind that no admonishment to employ womanly sympathy as an interrogation tool was going to make her help with the washing-up.

EIGHTEEN

"Well, Inspector," said Jocelyn tartly, "I suppose you were bound to turn up sooner or later, like a bad penny."

"Kind of you, Mrs Stearns."

Eleanor stood up and went to meet him. "Good afternoon, Mr Scumble. Did you bring Megan with you? DS Pencarrow, that is."

His lips twitched. "The sergeant is in the house, interviewing the residents."

"Oh, good. I can't tell you how glad I am that you've taken over from the man who wouldn't listen to me. Though I expect he had his reasons," she added, giving Pearce the benefit of the doubt.

"Don't worry, Mrs Trewynn, I'll listen. I just hope you're going to tell me absolutely everything."

"Of course. I've never deliberately held anything back from you."

"Not deliberately, no. On the whole."

He sighed, and she wondered if he was thinking of the time she had left Port Mabyn without informing him of her whereabouts. But she'd had an excellent reason . . . Better distract him. "You must admit that you sometimes rushed me and made me lose my place in what I was telling you."

Scumble's face started to turn purple.

"Eleanor, for pity's sake, let's get this over with so we can go home. I don't know what Timothy must be thinking!"

"Oh dear, the poor vicar! Do come and sit down, Mr Scumble. It's really very pleasant out here now there's a bit of a breeze come up."

"I'll just have a word with DC Wilkes first, ma'am, if you don't mind."

"Yes, of course. I'm so glad you sent him. He's an old friend. So much easier than trying to explain to a stranger."

"Wilkes!"

The detective constable was standing at near-attention—Megan had once told Eleanor that only officers in uniform were supposed to actually stand to attention—by the bench from which he had instantly raised himself on seeing the inspector.

"Sir!"

"I'll be with you in just a moment, Mrs Trewynn."

Eleanor went back to the shade of the apple tree to sit with Joce while the two detectives conferred. "I'm sorry," she said, "I'd forgotten that Timothy must be wondering where on earth you are."

"I left him a note. I told him I didn't know when I'd get home, so he won't be worried, but I must say I didn't think we'd still be here at this hour. My intention was to take you straight home."

"I couldn't possibly have left when you arrived, Joce. It was extremely kind of you to come, but you mustn't feel you need wait. Now Megan is here, I shall be perfectly all right."

"That Man!"

"Oh, come on, Joce, I'm not afraid of Mr Scumble."

"I didn't mean to suggest that you were," Jocelyn said stiffly, then said with a touch of guilt, "I meant to be perfectly polite, but the sight of him . . . I was rather rude, I'm afraid. I owe him an apology."

"I wouldn't apologise if I were you. The shock might kill him."

"Really, Eleanor! Do try to be serious."

"If you ask me, seriousness is greatly overrated." She considered her remark, remembered they were here on a matter of murder, and added an amendment: "Though undoubtedly appropriate in many situations."

"Of which this is one."

"Yes, you're quite right. Here they come."

Scumble plonked himself down on the second bench.

"I suppose you want me to leave," Jocelyn said defiantly.

"Good lord no. You're a witness, according to my information."

"A witness?"

"Unless I've been lied to. Which wouldn't surprise me. We'll get into that later."

Wilkes had taken out his notebook, but remained standing until his superior irritably gestured to him to sit. Hierarchies, Eleanor reflected, were the same practically all over the world, so they must be necessary to the functioning of society, she supposed. A depressing thought.

"Mrs Trewynn!"

"I'm listening!"

"*I'm* the one who's supposed to be listening. *You're* the one who's supposed to be telling me why I shouldn't believe your friend Gresham stabbed Geoffrey Clark."

"He was elsewhere at the time. That's what *alibi* means, isn't it?"

"You know what time the murder was committed?"

"Near enough. Stella Maris left a note to explain what Geoffrey did to poor Nick's paintings. She said he had dropped in to see her at the gallery—Nick's—shortly after she'd heard from Nick about Mr Alarian. As Nick telephoned from Paddington at midday, obviously Geoffrey was alive then. When we arrived at *his* gallery, it was after six. So he died between noon and six. And Nick was either on the train or with me the whole time," she concluded in triumph. A miracle of concise logic, she thought happily.

Scumble frowned. "You saw Miss Weller's note?"

"Miss Weller?"

"Maris. Her real name is Weller."

"Oh yes. So confusing! Yes, Nick showed me her note. I read it. Haven't you seen it yet?"

"Gresham's lost it. He doesn't know what he did with it."

"I expect it's in his waste paper basket in the gallery. Or in mine. We went straight up to tea."

"Straight?"

Eleanor thought. "Well, no, not immediately. He helped the children unload the Incorruptible, and—"

"Just for the record, Mrs Trewynn, the Incorruptible is your car, a green Morris Minor, correct?"

"That's right. It was parked in the street just outside, and I know it's a No Parking zone, but—Oh, but I remember you told me it's not your job to enforce—"

"And the children were . . . ?"

"Donna from the pub and the little Chins. Ivy and Lionel Chin, I should say. Mr Chin told me just the other day that they hate being referred to as 'the little Chins,' and who can blame them?"

With a sigh, Scumble said, "Are you confirming that Donna from the pub and Ivy and Lionel Chin are all witnesses to Gresham's presence in Port Mabyn at—what time?"

"About five. Nick's train came in at five past four, and it takes the Incorruptible about an hour to get from Launceston over Bodmin Moor to Port Mabyn."

"Yes, yes, we'll get to that in a minute."

{ 172 }

"Don't you want me to recount everything consecutively from the beginning, Inspector?"

"Since we seem to have embarked upon a discussion of where Miss Weller's note might have got to," he said, with the heavy patience that clearly expressed irritation, "let's finish that off first. Gresham helped to unload your car, taking the contents where?"

"To the stockroom, of course." Eleanor glanced at Wilkes and his notebook and, for the record, helpfully explained, "the stockroom behind the LonStar shop."

"I'm not likely to forget that bl—that stockroom! Gresham might have dropped the note there."

"Naturally a waste basket is provided," Jocelyn put in, offended at the suggestion that litter was permitted in her stockroom. "I myself emptied it into the bin when I closed and locked the shop."

"Thank you, Mrs Stearns. You didn't happen to notice a letter—What sort of paper was it written on, Mrs Trewynn?"

"The back of a blank receipt. I remember because Nick said it would upset his records. It seems they're all numbered, so—"

"Mrs Stearns?" He really did interrupt a lot, Eleanor thought. No wonder she didn't always manage to provide him with all the information he wanted. "Did you see—"

"It is not my custom to examine the rubbish, Inspector!"

"No. And which day are the dustbins emptied?"

"Friday mornings. This morning."

"I might have guessed," Scumble said gloomily.

To comfort him, Eleanor pointed out, "You know what it said, anyway. And there'll be a missing receipt number in Nick's cash register, or records, or somewhere, won't there? In any case, he could have dropped it in the shop or car."

"That's right, when he was unloading."

"Or when he drove it down to the car park by the stream."

Scumble glared at her. "He did, did he? And walked back up

the hill? I assume there's at least one council litter bin on the way. Probably emptied daily."

"Not half often enough," said Jocelyn, "at least in the tourist season."

The inspector ignored her. "This isn't getting us anywhere."

"Actually," said Eleanor, "now I come to think of it, he found the note after unloading, and we didn't go back to the shop or my flat."

"All right, Mrs Trewynn, let's try going back to the beginning." With one of his heaviest sighs, he leant forwards with his hands on his meaty thighs and appealed to her, "You know I wasn't in at the start of this investigation, and I haven't got information that ought to have been collected last night. I've got some catching up to do, so I'd very much appreciate it if you'd give me the short version. I promise you'll have a chance to fill in details you think I ought to know at a later date. Now, from the beginning."

"The beginning?" Eleanor considered. The real beginning was when she had written to Mr Alarian about Nick's paintings, but she doubted Scumble wanted to know about that. "You could say it began when Nick rang up to say he was catching the train that reaches Launceston at 4:05. He—"

"You yourself spoke to him?" Interrupting already!

"No, I was out, so he rang the LonStar shop to leave a message."

"*I* spoke to Nicholas," said Jocelyn complacently. "For once, the line was reasonably clear. I can assure you, he rang from a public telephone and it was a trunk call. What's more, I heard in the background all the sounds of a busy mainline railway station."

Eleanor gave her an indignant look. Why hadn't she said so sooner? Had she not realised how crucial her evidence was? That one little fact must clear Nick without any shadow of doubt.

"Ah, well that settles that, then, doesn't it?" The inspector seemed pleased, somewhat to Eleanor's surprise.

Now, she realised, with the red herring of Nick's possible guilt out of the way, he and Megan could concentrate on who had actually stabbed Geoffrey. Surely not Margery Rosevear, such a sympathetic, practical woman, yet seduced into unfaithfulness then dropped without a second thought when he found a new lover. Doug, the wronged husband, had an obvious motive there, too. What about Jeanette, subjected to some sort of mistreatment no one wanted to talk about? Or Tom Lennox, so obviously in love with her—had he seized a chance to avenge her? Oswald, Leila, Albert, all seemed to hate Geoffrey, though Eleanor didn't know why, apart from his generally obnoxious—

"Mrs Trewynn!"

"I can't believe any of them would have killed him. They've all been so kind and welcoming."

"Who? These communists?"

"Good heavens, Inspector, they're not communists. As I understand it, they pay rent to the Rosevears, which helps keep the farm viable. Not that I have anything against communism. I've known some admirable communists. Its fundamental creed is sound, 'From each according to his abilities, to each according to his needs.'" She cast a sidelong glance at Jocelyn. "Very like the Christian ideal. The parable of the talents, isn't it? And something on the lines of 'Inasmuch as ye do it unto the least of these.'"

"Really, Eleanor!"

"It's just that it tends to go wrong in practice, when people start imposing their ideas on others, Christianity as well as communism. It's no good scowling at me, Joce. The Inquisition, and 'holy' wars, and just look at Ireland."

"Mrs Trewynn, fascinating as this may be, I am not here to attend a debate on religion and politics. I asked you, as Mrs Stearns appears to have established Gresham's alibi—"

"Appears!" Jocelyn redirected her indignation against Scumble.

"I can imagine ways around it, and what I can imagine, another man can carry out. For a start, I've only got Mrs Trewynn's evidence that Gresham arrived at Launceston station on the 4:05. No doubt Mrs Trewynn is in general a truthful lady, but she's also a very good friend of Nicholas Gresham's. No offence meant."

"I did wonder," Eleanor confessed, "just for a moment, whether I would lie for Nick. I'm quite sure he didn't stab Geoffrey, you see, but he might not have been able to prove it, and Inspector Pearce had already decided he was guilty. I know you will find out the truth, so I don't have to decide. I'm very glad."

"That's all very well, and I'm delighted to hear you have faith in me, but it doesn't give me independent evidence that Gresham got off the 4:05."

"No, I do see your difficulty."

"Was there anyone you know at the station?"

"Oh, yes, I talked to Mr Lobcot, the porter at the station. I actually told him I was meeting Nick."

"He saw Gresham get off?"

"Oh dear, as to that I rather doubt it. He was busy with someone else. He's porter and station master and ticket collector all in one now, till they close the line."

Scumble sighed. "That's a pity."

"He might have noticed Nick, though," Eleanor said hopefully. "Nick's the sort of person people do notice, and there wasn't a vast crowd."

"Enquiries will be made. So much for Launceston. Port Mabyn, now, we seem to have covered. We'll move on to Padstow. What time—"

"Ah, there you are, Eleanor." Nick strolled round the corner of the house. Teazle bounced up and went to greet him. He stooped to scratch her head. "Doing all right, are you?" he asked, straightening. "Good afternoon, Mrs Stearns. I'm glad to see you here."

"So you should be," Scumble grunted. "Mrs Stearns just confirmed some important details of your story. But I am *not* glad to see *you* here. Go away."

"Come, come, Inspector, I'm not going to interfere with your interrogation. I came because I was being peppered with questions that you've forbidden me to answer. I'm simply avoiding temptation."

"Pull the other one. It's got bells on."

"Also," said Nick, dropping the bantering tone, "I would like to hear Eleanor's description of what happened in Padstow and I should think you must have reached that point by now. I've a feeling there's something I should have noticed, or that I did notice but have forgotten. Something significant, I mean. Something you ought to know. Going through it again, as she remembers it, just might bring it back."

"You can go through it again with me or Sergeant Pencarrow as often as you like, Mr Gresham. But all right, you can stay. Sit over there, where I can see you. One false step and you'll go back to the cells on a charge of obstruction."

"Now is that any way to treat a willing witness?" Nick complained, sitting down on the bench beside Jocelyn, as she and Eleanor moved over to make room for him. "Nonetheless, thank you, Inspector. And thank you, Mrs Stearns, for vouching for me."

"I spoke nothing more nor less than the truth, Nicholas," Jocelyn said severely.

"If you're quite finished," said Scumble, at his most sarcastic, "perhaps Mrs Trewynn would be so kind as to begin."

Eleanor had been reflecting on the best place to begin. She'd much rather not talk about the horrible experience at all. Perhaps it would be easiest to get a run at it, so to speak, like a hurdle.

"We parked the Incorruptible at the quarry in Rock," she said, "where I hope it's still sitting and hasn't been towed away."

Scumble rolled his eyes but for once let her proceed at her own pace.

NINETEEN

Meanwhile, Megan followed Mrs Rosevear into an old-fashioned, shabby, but comfortable farm kitchen, which like most of its kind obviously served as a sitting room as well. The well-scrubbed white wood table still bore the remains of a meal, with rather strange dishes. More interested in who had eaten there than what they ate off, Megan automatically counted the number of places set: five.

"Five for lunch? Sorry, dinner?"

"I don't do lunch for the whole crowd, usually just for my husband, Doug, and me. He's gone back to work. Today we had Mrs Trewynn, of course, and her friend, Mrs Stearns, and Mr Wilkes. The detective. Mrs Trewynn said he's a friend of hers, too. Does it matter?"

"Probably not." Megan grinned at her. "But it's just as well to be prepared if my gov'nor decides I ought to know."

"He won't mind the detective having eaten with us?"

"I doubt it, but if he does, he'll blame Wilkes." Or Aunt Nell. "Not you. Now, let's hear what you really saw last night."

Mrs Rosevear sat down at the table and waved Megan to a

chair. "Sorry about the mess, I'll deal with it later. I feel simply terrible about accusing Nick Gresham. It's no excuse, but Stella was so adamant . . . We were all too horrified to think straight."

"Let me briefly recap, Mrs Rosevear," Megan said, "to make sure I've got it straight. You withdraw without reservation your statement that you saw Nicholas Gresham stab Geoffrey Clark. When you entered the studio, immediately behind Stella . . . Weller, you saw—looking past her and Mrs Trewynn—Gresham standing or kneeling beside the prone body of Clark. On and around the body was a good deal of something bright red with a sheen, which you assumed to be fresh blood."

"Assumed to be? You mean it wasn't blood? Or wasn't fresh? It certainly wasn't the colour of dried blood. What was it?"

"I'm not allowed to answer that sort of question, Mrs Rosevear, but I'll remind you that Clark was a painter."

"Paint! No, more likely that ink he uses for the adverts."

"You have some technical knowledge of painting?"

"Impossible not to, with the company I keep. But actually, I wanted to go to art school. I passed my School Certificate just after D-Day, though, so I went into the Wrens, still hoping to study art after the war. That's where I met Doug. He was in the Navy. We got married as soon as we were both demobbed. I'd never had anything to do with farm life and I stupidly believed I'd have plenty of time after feeding the chickens at least to dabble in painting."

"You were always either too busy or too tired."

"Or both. Doug's mother had died several years earlier. His sister was engaged and only too anxious to escape. Everything Doug's father considered woman's work landed on my shoulders, and he was dead set against modern inventions. Doug did manage to get him to buy a tractor when the carthorses were on their last legs. But even when the mains electricity came, he swore we couldn't afford a washing machine or hoover, let alone a deep-freeze for garden stuff. He'd go on and on about not wasting the cupboard full of jars his wife had always used to preserve fruit until I could have killed him. You're not married?" She glanced at Megan's left hand.

"No."

"Well, if you ever feel the urge, make sure you meet your future in-laws before you commit yourself."

Megan wasn't learning anything about the murder, but finding out what made a suspect tick was often useful. Besides, Scumble had told her to apply a sympathetic womanly touch. Doubtless he'd expect her to offer to help with the washing-up, but she had to draw the line somewhere. "Sounds like good advice," she said.

"I wish someone had given it to me! When he died, we found out he'd made out very nicely, thank you, during the war, what with importing food being so difficult. After we'd had a bit of a spending spree with farm machinery and mod cons for the house, we had enough left, with a loan from the bank, to carry out my grand idea."

"Collecting a com—colony of artists."

"I hoped it might help me ease into the art world. All that happened is that they created enough extra work to counterbalance the mod cons. It was when that realisation struck that I went a bit off the rails." She gave Megan a slightly mocking glance. "I haven't forgotten you're a police detective, you know."

"Nor have I."

"You're not writing all this down."

"Sometimes it's better just to listen and remember. I'll start taking notes again when we get back to your revised statement."

Margery Rosevear's lips tightened. "I'm not just rambling, you know. I'm telling you all this for a reason."

"So I assumed."

"I know sooner or later you're going to ask me my opinion of Geoff, and it's no good lying about it, because everyone here knows. So I was just sort of preparing the ground, so to speak."

"Very understandable," Megan said soothingly, "and commoner than you may imagine. Would you like to go ahead and tell me why going 'off the rails' made you hate Clark enough to make us suspect you of murdering him? Or shall we polish off your revised statement first?"

"For heaven's sake, let's finish it! I don't know how we got off the subject in the first place."

"It doesn't matter. You saw Clark's body and heard Miss Weller cry out—" Megan consulted her notes. " 'My God, Nick, you've stabbed him.' "

"Or words to that effect."

"Then you realised Mrs Trewynn was faint and you turned away to deal with that. Can you give us any explanation of why you said you had seen Nick—Gresham—in the actual act of stabbing?"

Mrs Rosevear hesitated. "All I can say is, I still have a vivid mental image of the act. If I can't possibly have seen it, then it must be my imagination. Don't you ever form a picture in your mind of something that isn't actually in front of you?"

"Not so vividly I'd confuse it with reality. Perhaps that's why I've never had the least artistic ability."

"Perhaps I haven't either," she said bitterly, "only a vivid visual imagination and vain pretensions. I don't suppose I'll ever find out."

Megan had no comfort to offer. Fortunately, it wasn't her job to offer comfort. She went on briskly—she hoped not brusquely—to cover the rest of the amended statement, which from that point on didn't differ significantly from the original. Then she requested, "Tell me about Geoffrey Clark."

It was a sorry little story. The artist came out of it revealed as what Megan's father would call a rotter, bounder, or cad, or even all three. Not that it came as a surprise, given what he'd done to Nick's paintings.

Margery Rosevear had been badly treated, though, admittedly, she had treated her husband badly. However, Megan couldn't help wondering whether she herself would have behaved any better had she been married when Ken turned up in her life—always supposing he would have pursued her. To give Ken his due, fickle as he was, she had never known him to chase after married women.

But her infatuation with Ken was over and done with, and she bore him no ill will. Not much, anyway. Margery Rosevear obviously still hated Clark's guts, hardly surprising when he had flaunted his new lover under her eyes.

"How long ago did this happen?" Megan asked.

"Nearly two years. His lease is almost up, thank heaven. Oh, but that doesn't matter anymore, of course. It's almost a pity. I was looking forward to throwing him out."

Two years. Megan didn't see her as someone who would wait, brooding, until her anger reached murderous proportions. She might have lashed out when Clark first dropped her, but she didn't seem the kind of person who nursed a grudge, feeding it with bitter memories and storing up new slights. Still, you never could tell. All Megan could do was report her impressions to the gov'nor.

She was eager now to meet Douglas Rosevear. It was pure stereotyping—where did the image come from of the slow-moving, slow-thinking, stolid farmer? *Cold Comfort Farm*, perhaps, or that wireless show with the character whose inevitable line was "Oi think the answer loies in the soil." *Beyond Our Ken*, that was it. Arthur Fallowfield.

Whatever the truth or fallacy of the stereotype, surely driving a tractor round and round a field allowed considerable scope for brooding. Where Mrs Rosevear saw the end of the lease as good riddance to bad rubbish, perhaps Rosevear saw it as Clark escaping his clutches before he had got round to wreaking vengeance.

While Megan thought, her abstracted gaze had rested on the other woman. Mrs Rosevear was beginning to get a little twitchy. She jumped visibly when Megan asked, "Where were you yesterday afternoon?"

She wet her lips. "What—what time?"

"Let's say between midday and four."

"Is that when Geoff was killed? Sorry, silly question, of course it must be. I gave Doug his dinner at noon, as usual. He gets up early at this time of year. We were late today, what with everything . . . Afterwards, about half twelve, I suppose, I washed up. Then I worked in the garden. There's always something, weeding, staking, deadheading, what-have-you. I was there till Tom came and said he was ready to go."

"Go where?"

"He had crates of dishes to deliver in Wadebridge—he's a potter. I'd told him earlier I had shopping to do in Padstow."

"What time was this?"

"It must have been about twenty to two. He'd already loaded his crates, and it takes ten or fifteen minutes to drive down to the village. A bit more, perhaps, when I'm at the wheel. I'm a cautious driver. The shops were just beginning to open when we got there."

"If Tom was going onwards, why did you drive?"

She laughed. "He always sits on the floor bracing his boxes against the jolts. You came up our lane, you know its condition, and besides, the bus's springs aren't much to write home about. On a properly made road, it's not a problem."

"All right, you drove to the village with Tom—"

"And Jeanette. She had to post off some sketches to her publisher. Leila said she had an errand in Padstow but she'd walk down—it's about a half-hour walk by the footpaths—and meet us for a lift back."

"So who was left here?"

Mrs Rosevear thought for a minute. "Just Quentin and Albert. And Leila."

"And your husband."

"Doug wasn't *here*. He was out in the fields, haymaking. The forecast was for rain last night—not that Doug needs the forecast on the wireless. He's a farmer, and was a seaman. He reads the sky and the wind. He couldn't leave the haying, risk not finishing it, to go to Padstow on the off-chance Geoff might be alone in his studio."

A good point, Megan thought, but all she said was, "We'll be talking to Mr Rosevear in due course. You drove to Padstow, and then?"

"I stopped outside the shop, in Duke Street."

"The shop? Nick—Gresham mentioned a co-op shop."

"That's it, a real cooperative. They sell everyone's creations and take it in turns to staff it. Even Quentin does his day—he's there now—though it'll be a miracle if he has anything to sell in this century."

Megan raised her eyebrows.

"He's working on a massive granite sculpture, 'working' being a euphemism to keep the allowance coming from his rich aunt. Even if he ever finishes it, which I doubt, he'll have a hell of a time moving it, and it couldn't possibly fit into the shop."

"Is Miss Weller part of the cooperative?"

"Yes. Geoff isn't—wasn't."

"He didn't help with the co-op, and he had the bungalow and his own gallery."

"His own car, too."

"Did people resent it?"

"Envy, certainly. Not resent. He earned them by his own efforts. Advertising pays well. He was clever enough to make sure he kept all the rights, too, so when the brewery came up with the contest idea, they had to pay him to make the changes."

"Rights? Contest? You've lost me."

"Sorry. You can't be interested in all this."

"I am. One of my instructors at the Detective Training School was very keen on 'Know your victim.'" Megan had been lucky to get into the training, as officially there was no such thing as a woman detective in the Metropolitan Police. Come to that, she had been lucky to be one of the few WPCs seconded to the CID in the first place, even if it had led to her meeting Ken.

She was lucky that CaRaDoC was not so hidebound, but CaRaDoC was also lucky to have her. Never in a million years would Scumble have drawn so much information from Mrs Rosevear as had the "sympathetic womanly touch."

Mrs Rosevear explained about the rights of an artist in his own work. "As for the contest, it's informal word-of-mouth, not advertised, but every time Geoff comes—came up with a slightly altered picture, the brewery gave a prize to whoever found the most differences. Like one of those puzzles for children."

"Clever! A crate of beer, I expect. Let's see, you, Jeanette Jones, and Tom Lennox—Who was on duty at the co-op shop yesterday?"

"Oswald."

"Did Leila meet you?"

"Yes, she was at the shop at about quarter past four when Tom came back to pick us all up. I don't know what time she reached Padstow, though."

"You arrived before two and didn't leave till four fifteen. That's quite a long time for shopping in a village the size of Padstow."

"I like to walk along the quays and watch the boats and the people, especially the children. We've never had any. Perhaps that's another reason why I had my fling—out of frustration, that is, not hoping to get pregnant with another man's child! I suppose when I started gathering artists, I had a subconscious idea they might take the place of children, as well as inspire me. But though they're childish at times, they're no substitute, as I should have known." She sighed. "But you don't want to listen to me psychoanalysing myself. Where were we?"

"Let's go back to when you stopped the mini-bus outside the shop."

"Jeanette and I got out and Tom moved into the driving-seat."

"He drove on? And Jeanette?"

"The post office is just opposite the shop, but she needed something at the stationer's before she could post her pictures. I assume that's where she went. I walked down to the quay and sat down on a bench to people-watch, as they call it, and to finish a library book that was due back, just a few pages. Then I went to the library to drop off my books and choose two more."

"Before shopping?"

"Yes, I did that first because it's uphill and I didn't want to carry my shopping up. Then I went to the chemist's, the grocer's, a fishmonger, and the ironmonger. Not the greengrocer, because we grow most of our own. The shops were quite busy. Wednesday's early closing, so people who usually shop in the afternoon were out in force. By the time you've stood in a few queues, a couple of hours isn't all that long."

Even if any of the shop assistants remembered her coming in, they weren't likely to have noted the time or how long she was there. The librarian was a better bet. She, or he, would have to be questioned, but Mrs Rosevear was unlikely to have stayed at the library till after three, the latest time for the murder, according to Dr Prthnavi. In any case, she could have dropped in at Clark's gallery before going there, or even before sitting on the quay. Megan wished she knew the layout of the village better.

"Did you pass by King Arthur's Gallery?" Megan asked.

Mrs Rosevear hesitated before answering reluctantly, "Yes. In a place that size, you can hardly help it."

"Was it open, did you notice?"

"The CLOSED sign was up. I'm sure of it, because a couple were looking at the pictures in the window and I wondered if Geoff was missing a possible sale."

"You don't happen to know what time that was?"

"Haven't a clue. If I put my mind to it, I could probably work out which shops I was walking between."

"Leave it for now, but you might give it some thought later. Do you know the names of any of the shopkeepers who served you?"

She knew them all. They, as well as the librarian, might be able to say whether she had seemed flustered or disturbed.

"Did you see any of your friends, or meet anyone else you know?"

"Only Jeanette, crossing the Market Square, but it was just after four by then, because I'd heard St Petroc's clock strike. We went back to the shop—the co-op—together, and Oswald made us a quick cuppa before Tom came to pick us up. Otherwise, no one but shopkeepers. And swarms of emmets, of course. The tourists seem to arrive earlier every year. Perhaps I'll turn the bungalow into a holiday let-by-the-week after all. Do you know, after using the word ever since I came to live in Cornwall, I've just discovered *emmet* is an old English word for ant, not real Cornish at all."

Megan ignored the digression. Margery Rosevear had regained her composure now, but judging by her emotion when speaking of a two-year-old slight, if she had killed Geoffrey Clark, it had not been a cool, calm, cold-blooded murder.

TWENTY

Eleanor finished her recital of the events of the previous evening (omitting Teazle's adventures) with a warm encomium for Margery's calm, practical kindness.

Scumble had listened with remarkably few interruptions. Now he bestirred himself, glared at Nick, who was whistling "Land of Hope and Glory" again, and said, "Calm, was she? As if she wasn't shocked, or even surprised, to find Clark apparently weltering in his own blood?"

"I wouldn't say that," Eleanor protested. "Dealing with my stupid faintness distracted her from taking in the murder properly." Doubt crept in. After the treatment Margery had received at Geoffrey's hands, one couldn't expect her to be overcome with grief—and one could only thank heaven she hadn't succumbed to hysteria, like Stella. But her voice had been so very cool and unmoved when she told Doug to ring the police.

Still, Eleanor had been in no condition to detect the surprise that surely must have been there. She pointed this out to Scumble.

He made a sceptical noise. "Douglas Rosevear didn't come into the studio till after he'd phoned the local copper. He knew Clark was dead before he saw the body. Yet he seemed shocked and horrified, you say."

"I don't think anything can prepare you for a sight like that. It really did look like blood, you know. I'm sure he wasn't pretending."

"I agree," said Nick. "I rather doubt Doug is capable of pretence, certainly not convincing pretence. He's a very straightforward sort of bloke. He'd had a few beers, too, which doesn't make it any easier to put on an act."

Scumble nodded, not, for once, blasting Nick for speaking out of turn. "Heavy drinker, is he?"

"Not at all. But he works damn hard, begging your pardon, Mrs Stearns, and when he manages to get to a pub, he likes a few beers. He wasn't drunk, just a bit fuzzy."

Eleanor guessed Scumble already knew Doug had been at a pub. For the first time, she wondered just what had brought the Rosevears and Stella to King Arthur's Gallery at precisely the moment when she and Nick discovered the body.

They had probably told DI Pearce last night, so Scumble must know, but it was useless for Eleanor to ask him. He would just say it was his business to ask the questions and hers to answer them. She didn't like to ask Margery, either. It would really be nosy-parkering. Megan might tell her, but she didn't want to get her niece into trouble—

"Mrs Trewynn!"

"Sorry! I was thinking."

"Mr Scumble asked you," Jocelyn began, "to—"

"Thank you, Mrs Stearns, I'm quite capable of repeating my own question, if I now have Mrs Trewynn's attention. What were you thinking, Mrs Trewynn?"

"Nothing I need trouble you with, Inspector."

"Something entirely unrelated to my investigation?"

"Not entirely, but—"

"Never mind. I want you to go over again exactly what you heard from the moment you and Mr Gresham entered King Arthur's Gallery."

"I'm not a parrot, Inspector. I can't promise to repeat it exactly."

"To the best of your recollection," he clarified through gritted teeth. "Concentrate on the words and don't worry about people's movements, or the tone of voice—"

"But I remember the words much better if I think about the tone of voice."

"All right, all right! Think about it as much as you like. I said don't . . . Never mind. Just get on with it. Please."

Eleanor complied. With each repetition, she found, the horror faded a little and her memory grew clearer. Perhaps there was some sense in Scumble's requests for the same information over and over again. Otherwise, of course, he wouldn't waste time on it just to be irritating.

She reached the point where Stella had burst into tears.

"She hadn't cried up till then?" Scumble asked.

"Not that I noticed. She may have had tears in her eyes. I wasn't observing very clearly. But I would have heard if she'd been sobbing, I'm sure."

"Grief and hysteria take many forms," Jocelyn put in.

"I'm well aware of that, madam. Miss Weller seems to have gone through most of them, though not the maniacal laughter."

"Thank heaven!" Eleanor exclaimed.

"What was said next?"

"That was when the local sergeant came in," she said doubtfully. Hadn't there been something in between? If so, it was gone. Scumble's interruption had made her lose the thread. He really ought to know better by now.

"That'll do—"

"Good," said Jocelyn. "I'm taking Eleanor home."

"—For now," the inspector continued irritably. "If you have any reason, Mrs Trewynn, to leave North Cornwall, or to leave Port Mabyn for more than a few hours, I am here and now giving you specific instructions to inform me in advance of where you're going. Make a note, Wilkes."

"I will," Eleanor promised guiltily. Not that she felt terribly guilty for the time she had evaded him—and DC Wilkes, she remembered, shooting him a look of apology. He grinned. "But Joce, my car's in Rock."

"I'll take it home for you," said Nick. "I've absolutely got to get to work."

Eleanor felt in the pocket of her skirt for the keys. "Oh dear, here are the keys to the flat, but I wonder where—"

"I've got 'em." Taking the car keys from his pocket, Nick tossed them jingling in the air and caught them.

"Oh good." A folded piece of paper had come out of her pocket with the keys and fluttered to the ground, unfolding on the way down. Wilkes reached for it, but his figure was not conducive to bending in the middle. Eleanor got there first. "What on earth is this?"

The upper side was a blank receipt form, printed in blue, numbered in red, with Nick's gallery's name, address, and telephone number stamped blurrily at the top. With a sinking feeling, Eleanor turned it over.

"Here you are, Mr Scumble," she said, as brightly as she could manage, handing it to him. "It's Stella's note."

Scumble turned a curious shade of purple. Letting out his breath with a whoosh, he said in his most sarcastic voice, "I suppose I should be grateful you found it before my men had to search through every rubbish bin in Port Mabyn. You don't by any chance have Mr Gresham's train ticket stub or a London bus ticket concealed somewhere about your person?"

"Certainly not." All the same, Eleanor emptied her pockets: a clean (luckily) handkerchief, a small comb, nothing else. "No, I haven't."

With a sigh, Scumble said, "You and Mr Gresham had better each make a formal statement that this is the note you found in Mr Gresham's shop."

"Why?" Nick demanded. "I already told you exactly what it said. What do you need another statement for?"

"You leave that to me, sir."

"Don't argue, Nick. Let's get it over with." Solemnly Eleanor took the note back from Scumble and stated to Wilkes when and where she had last seen it.

While Nick was following suit, Jocelyn said, "Eleanor, I've just remembered, one of Timothy's parishioners who's been ill is staying not too far away from here. It wouldn't be far out of our way, if you don't mind my dropping by to see how she's doing." Her tone challenging, she added, "And if Mr Scumble doesn't mind, of course."

He shot her a suspicious look. Obviously he had not forgotten that she had once aided Eleanor in eluding the police. "As long as you go straight back to Port Mabyn afterwards," he said grudgingly.

"Naturally. I hope you don't insist on my giving you the name of the person concerned and the address. It would be a gross breach of privacy."

"That won't be necessary. Mr Gresham, did Mrs Trewynn's statement by any chance remind you of something you'd forgotten?"

"No, 'fraid not."

"Well, keep thinking, will you? All right, you're free to leave. I'll find you in your studio when I need you, I take it."

"When, not if? Yes, I'll be there."

"Come along, Nicholas, I'll give you a lift into Padstow."

"Thank you, Mrs Stearns," Nick said meekly.

"Are you ready to go, Eleanor?"

"I didn't bring a bag, not expecting to be away overnight. But I must say good-bye and thank you to Mrs Rosevear."

"Not if Pencarrow is still interviewing her!"

"In the circumstances," said Jocelyn dryly, "I feel sure a bread-and-butter letter will suffice."

Eleanor didn't feel it was appropriate any longer simply to walk in through the back door. When they reached the courtyard, Teazle trotting patiently at their heels, the front door of the house was open. She couldn't tell whether Megan was still there, though, without interrupting if she was, so she decided a letter would indeed have to do.

A uniformed constable was leaning against the doorpost of the pottery, chatting to someone—presumably Tom—inside. He made no move to stop them.

They took Nick down to the quay in Padstow, where the ferry was about to cast off. Eager to get back to work, he jumped out of the car with a quick word of thanks and ran to catch it.

Jocelyn drove out of the village back along the Wadebridge road, green, well-wooded country with an occasional glimpse of the River Camel on their left. Something about the sight jogged Eleanor's memory.

"The place where Stella works must be somewhere along here," she said. "Near Wadebridge, they said."

"What? What place? I thought she was an artist."

"And a nurse, in a convalescent hospital. It's just dawned on me: I wonder if that's where your parishioner is staying, the one you want to visit. Old Mrs Batchelor, is it? She fell and broke a couple of ribs, I remember."

"Yes, she's in a convalescent home near here."

"I definitely think you ought to pop in and see her while we're nearby. What's the name of the place? I'm sure I'd recognise it."

"Riverview."

"That's it. Riverview Convalescent Home."

"A very nice private hospital, I believe. Not National Health, I mean. Her son's paying for it because there really isn't room for a private nurse in her cottage, besides the stairs to worry about, and she didn't want to go and stay with him in London. Doesn't get on with her daughter-in-law."

"Then I'm sure she'd appreciate a visit."

"What have you got up your sleeve, Eleanor? That Man would be furious if he found out."

"Not if we go before he does, and he doesn't know we know Stella's there. He did say you could call on your parishioner."

"If he asks whether I knew beforehand about Stella, I'll have to tell him."

"I doubt he'll ask. In any case, he can hardly say a vicar's wife is not to visit a sick parishioner, wherever she may be. Don't you want to see if we can find out a bit about Stella's other life?"

"Really, Eleanor!"

"I don't like the way she accused Nicholas of murder," Eleanor said stubbornly. "If you're afraid of Inspector Scumble, you can wait in the car, or go for a walk."

"No, I'll come with you. You're right, it's my duty to call on Mrs Batchelor, come what may."

"I call that sophistry. If not downright Jesuitical!"

"Nonsense." Jocelyn was silent, negotiating a tricky blind S-bend. As the road straightened, a discreet sign on the north side indicated a gravel drive, leading down the hillside, to the RIVERVIEW CONVALESCENT HOME (PRIVATE). Jocelyn braked and turned in. Continuing without hesitation down the slope, she said forebodingly, "But if you ask me, it won't make the slightest difference to That Man that I'm a vicar's wife, or whether we visit the place before or after him. Either way, when he finds out, he's going to throw forty fits."

TWENTY-ONE

Megan emerged from the cool dimness of the farmhouse into the hot afternoon. In the enclosed courtyard, it felt more like mid-August than June. She decided to begin with the studios on the south side, facing north.

The door of the nearest was closed. A glance at the window showed only her own reflection and that of the building opposite. The circumstances did not justify peering, so she plied the piskie-shaped door knocker.

No one within responded, but a red beard poked out of the studio at the far end. "Fuzz? We're all in here. Most of us, anyway. Did you want me in particular?"

Walking towards him, Megan decided to try to get the sympathetic female touch business over with before Scumble reappeared, except for Stella, whom he'd said to take last. "Ladies first, please, sir," she said, wondering what the whirring noise had been. She hadn't noticed it till it stopped.

He turned back to the room. "Jeanette, you're first."

"Me?" It was a wail. "Why me?"

"Because you're the only 'lady' present and the police set great store by etiquette."

"Don't worry, I'm going with you." A second male voice, determined.

A tall woman came out. Her head was turned back towards the room, so that Megan couldn't see her face, only a head of unruly, straw-coloured hair. "No, Tom," she protested.

A man burst forth after her. Seeing Megan, he looked relieved. "It's the woman cop. Okay. But call if you want me." He stood watching as Jeanette came to meet Megan.

His reaction annoyed her, though it was typical and one reason women detectives were at last making their way into progressive police forces.

"That's my place," said Jeanette, gesturing, "the door you just passed, the middle one. Do you want to go in there?"

"I expect that'd be most convenient. Who's the chap with the beard?" She ought to have had Mrs Rosevear draw her a plan with names.

"Oswald. He paints, too." She led the way into the studio, which had a draughtsman's table as well as an easel. Megan glanced at a couple of paintings leaning face out against the back wall. They were geometrical abstracts, somehow unsettling, though she couldn't have explained why. They went straight across, through another door into a pleasant, sunny bedsitter, cooled by a breeze through the wide-open window. The room featured Indian bedspreads, as, in fact, did Megan's. There was nothing to beat Indian bedspreads for cheap and cheerful decorating.

CaRaDoC was progressive enough to employ a woman detective sergeant. It was not yet sufficiently progressive to pay her as much as her male colleagues.

Jeanette sat down on the divan-bed, waving Megan to an

armchair that looked as if it could well have come from Aunt Nell's LonStar shop, in good enough condition not to need draping, but faded to an indeterminate colour. She would have chosen to sit at the small table by the open window; too formal for her present sympathetic role, she decided. Still, she had to start with the formalities. She introduced herself and took down Jeanette's full name.

She went on, "The man who wanted to come with you, he's Tom?"

"Yes. He once saved me from a dragon and for some reason he now thinks he has to protect me from the world. I expect you can guess who the dragon was, if someone hasn't already told you."

"Geoffrey Clark, I take it. Will you tell me about it?" She probably didn't need to hear the whole story, just a simple reason why Jeanette had hated Geoffrey—assuming she had. But if she had to listen to the whole story to make the woman at ease talking to her, then listen she would.

"It was all rather sordid. And very silly, really. It's just, I find it hard to look at it that way. One Saturday evening, a bunch of us were down at the Gold Bezant—that's the pub we usually go to. Doug's on the darts team. I was tired and wanted to leave, but the others wanted to stay. Geoff said he'd drive me home. I knew he'd had a few. If I'd realised how drunk he was . . ."

"You often can't tell till the person gets behind the wheel."

"I'm sure he would have failed that breathalyser thingy. The drive back here was pretty scary, but we made it in one piece. He parked by the bungalow. I got out and thanked him. He said to wait, he wanted to show me something, and he started rooting behind the seat. His car's an MG Midget, you see, so there's not much room. I told him to show me in the morning and I came back here. He followed me, calling to me to wait. I suppose I should have been scared then. I could have gone to Tom's. I saw his light was on."

"Tom hadn't gone to the pub?"

"No, he was in the middle of something he couldn't leave. Glazing, or firing, I can't remember. I came into my studio and started to shut the door. Geoff was right behind me, carrying a bundle wrapped in sacking. I told him to go away, but he pushed past me and went on in here. I still wasn't too worried. I mean, it wasn't as if he was a stranger. So I followed him, like a complete moron. He unwrapped the sacking, and there was this bloody great sword."

"A sword!"

"A broadsword. The sort King Arthur and his knights may have used, if they ever existed. He'd had it specially made so he could paint it. Pathetic! His work's so derivative, it's not much better than copying. The worst thing was that he seemed to think the sword made him irresistible. He started waving it around, sort of as if he was in a sword fight. But the way he was smirking made me think he was—I don't know if you'll under-stand this—but as if he was showing off his prick."

Somewhat startled by such frank language coming from a young woman who appeared neither sleazy nor sophisticated, Megan assumed it must be the aftermath of life-drawing classes. "When it comes to sex," she said, "people get some strange ideas."

"Maybe Stella likes that kind of thing. I just thought it was weird. And when I got it through his thick head that I wasn't going to sleep with him, he went berserk. He started slashing my cush-ions. I was petrified. For a moment I didn't believe my eyes, and then I screamed my head off. Both my window and Tom's were open, and luckily he wasn't using his wheel. He heard me and came rushing round."

"Unaware that he'd be facing a broadsword."

"Yes, of course. I heard him come in. I was glad not to be all alone with a drunk maniac, but I was terrified for him, too. I shouted something to attract Geoff's attention away from the door. He took it as an invitation! He said, 'Aha, you do want it, after all,' and he advanced on me making these sort of stabbing moves with the sword. It was utterly revolting." She shuddered.

Megan's training had equipped her to deal with a great many unlikely situations, but facing, unarmed, a maniac wielding a broadsword had not been one of them. She hoped she would rise to the occasion if she ever had to, but she couldn't imagine how. "What did Tom do?"

"He made it look so simple. He's not big but he's really strong from throwing clay around and lugging boxes of china. Muscles like a coal-heaver. He came up behind Geoff and grabbed his sword-arm in both hands and twisted, shouting, 'Drop that thing if you ever want to paint again!' Geoff yelped and dropped it. Then he spewed all over my floor." Jeanette looked at her floor, covered with sisal matting, in remembered disgust. "I had to throw out my carpet."

"Yuck!"

"Tom was wonderful. God knows what would have happened if he hadn't come. I'll always be grateful to him. The trouble is, he says he's in love with me and I just don't love him. It wouldn't be fair to either of us to go with him out of gratitude, would it?"

Megan's love life was not such a blazing success that she felt qualified to give advice. "It doesn't sound like a good idea," she agreed cautiously, while noting that Tom also had a very good reason for hating Geoffrey Clark.

"I'll tell you what made me as angry as what Geoff did. Stella said I'd made a big fuss over nothing, he wouldn't have hurt me. But how was I to know?"

"You couldn't, and it isn't necessarily true. She wasn't upset with him for making advances to another woman?"

"Not at all. She's always said she wants her freedom so it's only fair to let him have his." Jeanette shrugged. "It seems strange to me, but I'm quite sure it's what she believes. I mean, it wasn't just to save face afterwards, she'd said it before."

"When did this happen?"

"A couple of months ago. When we had that warm spell in April, remember?"

A few weeks. Just time enough for a not naturally vengeful man to come to the boil? Perhaps to feel himself inadequate because he hadn't called his beloved's assailant to account? Perhaps even to fear that was the reason she refused him. And soon he might lose his chance, when Clark was kicked out of his bungalow.

As she thought, Megan scribbled a note to herself: Tom's alibi would have to be closely checked. He was a serious contender for the person who had rid the world of an obnoxious, not to say dangerous pest. The more she heard about Geoffrey Clark, the more she felt the murderer should be given a medal, not prosecuted.

Very unprofessional, she told herself. Stella had loved him, in spite of his faults. He must have some redeeming qualities. Aunt Nell, always charitable, could probably see them.

"What did you do before going to Padstow yesterday?" she asked. "Say from noon onwards."

"Yesterday?" Jeanette sounded bewildered, as if coming back from far away. "Oh yes, yesterday, sorry. I was finishing off the work I had to send my editor. And hunting for an envelope. I usually keep a few on hand, but I'd run out. Then I had something to eat. I can't remember . . . Probably a bit of salad. That's what I usually end up with."

"Did you see or speak to anyone?"

"No. Oh, yes. Tom was outside wrestling his boxes into the bus, and I went to make sure what time he wanted to leave."

"What time did you speak to him?"

"Haven't a clue. He might know. I rather doubt it, though."

"All right, what about in Padstow? What did you do there?"

On arriving, she had gone straight to a stationer to buy a stiff envelope for her illustrations. There had been some difficulty in finding the right kind and size, necessitating a consultation between the shop assistant and the owner, followed by a lengthy search in the stock-room. Then she had gone to the post office.

"Did you stick it in the letter-box or go in?"

"I went in. I always send my work registered because if it got lost I'd have to do it over again from scratch."

"Registered post? They'll have a record then."

"Yes, of course."

With a time stamp. At last a scrap of indisputable evidence. The gov'nor would be pleased. What a pity she had obtained it by luck, not by clever questioning or brilliant deduction.

"Do you remember the time it was postmarked?"

"Four minutes to three. The post goes at ten past, so they nearly made me miss it. I've got the receipt in the studio if you want to see it. There's not much point paying extra for the service if you don't keep the proof of posting."

"True. It took the stationer's nearly an hour to find the envelope you needed?"

"It would have been quicker if they hadn't kept stopping to serve other customers, not to mention wasting time trying to persuade me to make do with something else. I've tried other kinds, and they're just not as sturdy."

The stationer and his staff shouldn't have any trouble remembering Jeanette, with her persistence and her flyaway hair. It looked as if she was out of it.

For form's sake, Megan asked about her movements after the visit to the post office and wrote down a few small purchases followed by an ice-cream cornet eaten while strolling on the quay. Jeanette hadn't at any time passed Geoffrey Clark's gallery.

"I go out of my way to avoid it if there's the slightest chance he might be there. I know it's silly, when he lives just a hundred yards from here, but . . . well, I do, that's all."

Megan noted but didn't comment on her use of the present tense. It seemed entirely unconscious, as if the reality of Clark's death hadn't sunk in yet. When it did, it could bring Jeanette nothing but relief.

"That's all," she echoed. "At least, for the present. DI Scumble may want a word with you later. I'd like to see the post office receipt. I won't take it, but please keep it safe."

"I will. I always keep them anyway. Though I can't see how it could help you catch . . ." She shivered, though the breeze had dropped and the room was growing hot. "Whoever did it."

"It's not at all likely."

"If I thought it really might," Jeanette said fiercely, "I'd tear it into little bits and burn them. I don't want him caught! You don't still think Nick did it—Nick Gresham—do you?"

"As far as I'm aware, he's out of the picture."

"I was sure Stella couldn't really have seen him stab Geoff. Why on earth did she say she did?"

"I don't know. We haven't talked to her yet. We've still got several people to interview here at the farm."

"Oh, but Stella's not here. She's packed up and gone. Didn't you know?"

"Gone?" All Megan could think of was that somehow Scumble would find a way to blame her for the disappearance of a vital witness, though it was his fault for telling her to leave Stella till last. "Are you sure? Mrs Rosevear didn't mention it when she was talking about finding a new tenant for the bungalow."

"Maybe Marge doesn't believe she's gone for good. She may well be right. If you ask me, Stella loathes that place and the job a lot more than she hates being here, surrounded by reminders of Geoff."

Megan breathed a sigh of relief. At least Stella's present whereabouts were not a complete mystery. She got the details from Jeanette and went to tell Scumble.

TWENTY-TWO

The Riverview Convalescent Home (Private) was a white two-story building, a plain rectangle with a roof of the local slate. It was smaller and less grand than Eleanor had pictured it, bigger than most farmhouses but too small to be called a manor. The drive circled a bed of roses in full, glorious bloom, their fragrance perfuming the warm air. Jocelyn stopped before the blue front door, which stood hospitably open.

"Well, here we are," she said. "What next?"

"I suppose we go in and ask for Mrs Batchelor," said Eleanor, surprised.

"You don't want to snoop round outside first?"

"Good gracious, no! Whatever for?"

"I thought you were suspicious of the Stella woman, the one who's been living under a false name."

Eleanor laughed. "Oh, Joce, there's nothing suspicious about her calling herself Stella Maris. It's like a writer's using a pen-name."

"Which I've always considered a decidedly peculiar thing to do." Jocelyn was obviously put out. "What did you want to come here for, then? When you said Stella's here, I would have dropped the idea of visiting Mrs Batchelor if you hadn't insisted."

"Nothing specific. I find Stella hard to fathom and I hoped seeing this side of her life might help me to understand her."

"What on earth do you mean?"

"Well, her sculptures are straightforward depictions of real creatures, without a trace of whimsy. Not a sign of a Cornish pisky, even, let alone the sort of high romantic fantasy Geoffrey Clark went in for. And nursing is surely a thoroughly prosaic profession. You might reasonably assume she was lacking in imagination. Yet she imagined seeing Nick stab Geoffrey vividly enough to convince not only herself but Margery Rosevear! Wouldn't you expect her to use her imagination in her art? It's an odd contradiction."

"I can't see anything odd about it. People in a state of shock imagine all sorts of things."

"I expect you're right." Eleanor sighed. "It's just *my* imagination. Let's go and see Mrs Batchelor. Is it too early to hope for a cup of tea? My throat is dry as a bone after being interrogated by Inspector Scumble. Teazle had better stay in the car. I'll ask for a bowl of water for her."

"Bring her in. I'm sure she'll cheer Mrs Batchelor up." With all the assurance of a vicar's wife bent upon doing her duty, Jocelyn led the way into the house. Eleanor half expected the usual institutional odour of cabbage and disinfectant, but the hall, floored with gleaming parquet, smelled of furniture polish and the roses that filled a vase on a half-moon table.

Beside the vase was a brass bell. Jocelyn dinged it.

In response to the sound, a woman popped out of a door to one side. In a russet-brown skirt and polka-dotted blouse she didn't look like a nurse, but she announced herself brightly as Nurse Jamieson.

"Please call me Miss Jamieson," she added in a conspiratorial tone. "And our patients are always referred to as guests. Dr Fenwick has discovered that it aids in people's recovery if they're not regarded as being ill, merely in need of a little assistance for a short while. In fact, we don't accept guests who are ill enough to need serious nursing, though we do have qualified help available for emergencies, of course. And we have a small dispensary, so we take charge of all medicines and make sure they're taken at the proper times. I do hope your loved one—"

"We're not looking for a place for a family member," said Jocelyn. "We've come to visit Mrs Batchelor. The vicar of her church, the Reverend Stearns, is my husband, and Mrs Trewynn is a friend."

"Mrs Batchelor? Such a nice lady. I expect she's outside. We encourage our guests to enjoy the fresh air on a fine day like this, and even a little exercise. Do come this way, ladies. Oh, is this dog with you?"

"Mrs Batchelor is very fond of Teazle," Jocelyn declared, with absolutely no basis for the statement. "If we're going outside, I can't see that there can be any objection."

As they followed her the length of the hall, passing a carpeted staircase leading up, Eleanor said, "Isn't it unusual for a convalescent hospital not to take in—er—guests who still require some nursing care?"

"Convalescent *home*, Mrs Trewynn," Miss Jamieson chided. "We *never* use the word hospital. Many of our guests come to us from hospitals. We want them to put the unpleasant experience and all thoughts of illness behind them and concentrate on being healthy. Dr Fenwick himself enjoys the benefit of joining his guests at the weekend and focussing his mind on good health. He has an extremely busy practice in Plymouth, you know, with many very ill patients."

She opened a door and they stepped through into a sort of enclosed cloister running round three sides of an open courtyard.

Through the wide windows, Eleanor saw that two single-story wings ran back from the main block. The paved courtyard had a couple of benches as well as wicker chairs set round small tables shaded by large, colourful umbrellas. Several people, in pairs or groups, sat chatting or playing cards or backgammon.

Beyond them, on the open side of the courtyard, a grassy slope led down to the river. A paved path looped down to the bank and back, partially shaded by a huge chestnut and several bird-cherry trees. The cherries lived up to their name, laden with dark red fruit squabbled over by noisy blackbirds and wood-pigeons.

"An idyllic place to recuperate," Jocelyn remarked as Miss Jamieson ushered them out through French doors.

And commensurately expensive, Eleanor assumed. Riverview was not somewhere she or Joce would ever be able to afford. It was more like a small but luxurious hotel, apart from an abundance of Zimmer frames. Mrs Batchelor's accountant son must be paying a fortune to keep his mother, a Cornish villager, and his wife, a London socialite, safely apart.

"We do our best," the nurse-in-disguise said, modestly complacent. "There's your Mrs Batchelor, sitting at the table over there. My goodness, it's warm out here. I'll have someone bring out something to drink."

"And a bowl of water for the dog?" Eleanor requested.

"What? Oh, I suppose so."

As she left them, Jocelyn hissed at Eleanor, "For pity's sake, don't go asking a lot of nosy questions!"

Mrs Batchelor, a heavily built old woman, was delighted to see them, though she didn't appear to notice Teazle's presence. "Set ee down, set ee down, me lovers," she said and introduced her companion, Mrs Redditch.

"How do you do," said Mrs Redditch in refined tones very far from Mrs Batchelor's slow, soft country voice. A wizened creature, she didn't look strong enough to lift her ring-laden fingers.

They were an odd couple, one in a faded cotton print dress, the other in a beautifully cut tweed skirt and a white silk blouse, pearls at her wrinkled throat. Eleanor wondered what they could possibly have in common.

She soon found out. As soon as Jocelyn commented on what a pleasant place the Riverview Home appeared to be, the two started reporting the life histories of all their fellow "guests." How much was true and how much was made up for sheer love of gossip was impossible to tell. Unlike many gossips, they didn't concentrate on the scandalous aspects, if any, of their subjects' lives. Every detail of their families, ailments, homes, and occupations was of interest to them, and they were pleased to have a new audience.

Nothing could have suited Eleanor better—how else was she to find out about Stella?—but of course Jocelyn disapproved of gossip as a matter of principle. "I really don't think it's any of our—"

"How interesting people are!" Eleanor said quickly. "Who's that tall gentleman over there, the one with the moustache?"

An exceedingly boring recital of the feats of arms of Colonel Nesbit followed, intermingled with the symptoms of his recent indisposition. He was a diabetic who had been taking too low a dose of insulin and had suffered the unpleasant consequences.

"Poor fellow," said Mrs Redditch, "he didn't like the injections."

"And who can blame him!"

"He's supposed to have two shots a day."

"Just like Dr Fenwick, Maybelle tellt us."

"But he couldn't bear to give himself more than one. Here, they're making sure he's stabilised. He had a very unpleasant stay in hospital."

"Had a nasty shock, he did and won't be such a skalliock when they let him go oome."

Eleanor had no desire to know the medical details. She was wishing she hadn't asked about him when a West Indian girl in a white cap and apron came out, pushing a tea-trolley. No institutional steel apparatus, it was of Scandinavian blond wood, heavily laden with glasses and a bedewed pitcher as well as a large tea-pot and cups and saucers, milk and sugar. She came towards their table.

"Just like the old days," said Mrs Redditch with a sigh of satisfaction. "My late husband was in the colonial service, a lieutenant governor, and we spent many years in East Africa."

"Frighted me a snippet at fust," Mrs Batchelor admitted, "seeing darkies close up, I mean. But Maybelle's a nice cheerful maid, and helpfuller nor most. What've you got there for us then, lovie?"

"Lemonade, Mrs Batchelor. Lots of vitamin C, Miss Jamieson says. She thought it'd be better than tea, seeing it's so hot today." She laughed. "Not that it's what we'd call hot at home."

"Of course, in those days it would have been gin and tonic," mourned Mrs Redditch. "The doctor says, with my condition, I mustn't touch a drop except a spot of brandy after dinner."

"But you'll have some lemonade, won't you, Mrs Redditch?" Maybelle coaxed. "Go on, it's not the kind you don't like, out of a bottle. Cook made it fresh. And you ladies?"

She served them all, including a bowl of water for Teazle, and took her tray to the next table, where they heard her laughing again.

"Proper cheers the place up," Mrs Batchelor commented.

"In those days," said Mrs Redditch severely, "the blacks knew their place."

"What I say is, 'tes better than long faces any day. 'Tes lucky you didn' come at the weekend, Mrs Trewynn. That Miss Weller wouldn've sent out lemonade, I can tell you. Let us die of thirst, first, she would."

"Oh?" Eleanor didn't see how Jocelyn could possibly object to a simple monosyllable.

Mrs Redditch nodded agreement. "Too busy making up to Dr Fenwick."

"She's a purty maid. Clean-off slocked, he is, the poor gaupus."

"Pretty, I dare say. Maid, I doubt. Slocked and gaupus, I haven't the faintest notion."

"Pisky-led. Bewitched, you'd say, likely. A bewitched fool."

"Ah, yes. He does appear to be somewhat susceptible, though one would expect a doctor to have more sense. Still, there's no fool like an old fool."

"Dr Fenwick is elderly, is he?" Eleanor asked.

"I wouldn't call him elderly, would you, Mrs Batchelor?"

"Not if us be elderly." Mrs Batchelor cackled. "Some'eres betwix fifty and sixty, wouldn' ee say, Mrs Redditch?"

Mrs Redditch would. "But well-preserved," she added. "What's more, Miss Weller's no chicken. She must be thirty, if she's a day."

"Twenty-five years or more atween 'em. 'Tes not what I hold with."

Returning, Maybelle set down the lemonade jug, still a third full. "Here you are, ladies. Help yourselves. Most people seem to want tea, even though they're complaining about the heat." She rolled her eyes expressively and went off.

"Maybelle, now, she has a swettard in Plymouth," said Mrs Batchelor.

"A black sailor." Mrs Redditch was disapproving, but no doubt she'd have disapproved of a white sailor as much, or more. "She takes the bus all the way to the city whenever he has weekend leave."

The two old ladies continued to chatter about Maybelle's

sweetheart. She had told them all about him, so it was a fruitful topic, but not one in which Eleanor had much interest. She failed to steer them back to Stella before Jocelyn said firmly that she really must be getting home.

In the face of their disappointment, it was easy for Eleanor to promise to visit again soon.

"It's a pity their relatives don't come to see them," she said to Jocelyn as they got into the car, Teazle hopping over onto the back seat.

"You're only going again because you're curious about the Stella woman."

"Not 'only.' Are you saying that I shouldn't visit because my motive isn't entirely disinterested?"

Jocelyn started the car and started off round the rose-bed before she answered. "No, of course not. I suppose you could argue that *I* have an ulterior motive when I call on parishioners."

"Joce, I didn't mean to suggest anything of the sort! What do you mean?"

"Just that I do it because I consider it my duty, not—or not only—because I care for their welfare."

"What nonsense!" Eleanor was alarmed by her friend's unwontedly introspective mood. "I'm just being nosy, whereas yours are both admirable motives."

"Those two bored and irritated me," Jocelyn confessed, combining guilt and gloom. "Not exactly admirable."

"Joce, remember what you said about Anglicans not going in for confession!"

"Not practising the rites of the confessional," the vicar's wife corrected, with some of her usual asperity.

"Besides, you didn't let them see you were bored and irritated. You can't help how you feel."

Though Jocelyn gave a dissmissive snort, she didn't argue, to

Eleanor's relief. She had no desire to find herself wrestling with someone else's conscience.

Having negotiated the awkward turn onto the Wadebridge road, Jocelyn said, "I don't believe you were entirely motivated by inquisitiveness. You're still worried about Nick, aren't you?"

"A bit. Not so much that he might be arrested, but I can't credit that Stella would have jumped to the conclusion he was guilty if she didn't hate him. And why did she tell Geoffrey about Nick's success in London? She can hardly have been unaware that he was jealous. It's almost as if she was bent on stirring up trouble."

"You're afraid she'll be looking for a new way to harass him?"

"Exactly. Have I taken leave of my senses?"

After a moment's consideration, Jocelyn said judiciously, "No. It seems all too likely. We must hope she'll be too busy trying to hook the doctor."

"Dr Fenwick? You think she wants to marry him?"

"He must be coining money with the Riverview Home."

"It's a beautiful place. I expect he has a waiting list."

"More to the point, compared to similar places, his overhead is much lower because he doesn't have to pay qualified nurses. Only one, anyway, since he takes charge himself at the weekend."

"Overhead?" Eleanor ventured to enquire. She had a feeling she'd heard the word in connection with the LonStar shop, but she'd either forgotten what it meant or never properly understood in the first place.

"His fixed costs." Correctly interpreting her blank look, Jocelyn patiently explained. "The amount of money he pays out every week or month. Wages, electricity, rates, possibly rent or mortgage payments, that sort of thing. Bills that have to be paid whatever your income. The lower those are, the more of your income you keep. Which is why the LonStar shop is a success, because you let us use your ground floor free."

"I'm sure it's more because you're such a good organiser."

"Yes, well, never mind that. The point is, Dr Fenwick is probably a wealthy man even though, come to think of it, he may have to employ two or three nurses to work in shifts during the week. It's still cheaper than a whole medical crew on duty. You know Stella better than I do. Would she marry an older man for his money?"

"I don't *know* her, Joce. But I have to say, from what I've heard of her, I shouldn't be in the least surprised. Oh dear, ought we to warn him of the sort of person she is?"

"Good gracious, no! I'm sure it would be slander. It's not really any of our business. He's old enough to take care of himself."

TWENTY-THREE

"What's that, Pencarrow?" The inspector didn't invite her to sit down on the second bench. "You let our most important witness hop it?"

"Most important?"

"First on the scene."

"Third, surely, sir. After Gresham and Aunt—Mrs Trewynn. As a matter of fact, it seems she'd already left before we got here."

"Hnnn. You say you know where she's gone?"

"Yes, sir. Apparently she works weekends at a nursing home near Wadebridge. She has a room there."

"Oh, so she's just gone off to work as usual."

"Well, not exactly."

"Yes or no, Sergeant!"

"No, sir. She packed up bag and baggage and shook the dust—"

"Don't get fanciful on me!"

"She's taken all her belongings with her. She's never coming back. She can't bear to stay here where she was so happy with Geoff. That's what she said, sir. Or rather, what I've been told she said."

Scumble nodded approval of the emendation, for once without adding that he might make a detective of her yet. "Who told you? The landlady?"

"No, Mrs Rosevear didn't mention it." She frowned. "It's a bit odd, really. She was talking about renting out Clark's bungalow. I'd have expected her to be planning for Stella's studio, too."

"Never try to fathom the mind of a witness."

Megan thought that was pretty much what her job consisted of, but she didn't contradict him. *Never try to fathom the mind of your gov'nor*, she told herself. "Shall I go and look in the studio to see if her stuff is gone?"

"No hurry. Why would anyone tell you she's gone if she hasn't?"

Gritting her teeth, Megan managed not to shout, *Never try to fathom the mind of a witness!* The fact that she couldn't imagine any reason why Jeanette should have misled her didn't mean there wasn't one. "Shall I go after her right away?"

"No, I still want to leave her till last. Let's get on with the ones you haven't let get away."

He was definitely being more awkward than even his usual high standard. Megan hoped he wasn't having second thoughts about his ability to beat DI Pearce at his own game.

"Do you want a report on what I've already got, sir? It would help if I knew what Aunt—Mrs Trewynn's told you. I'd have a better idea of what to ask."

Grudgingly Scumble agreed that it might conceivably be useful to exchange information. He handed her Wilkes's notebook, which he'd been conning, and took hers in exchange. After one glance at the shorthand, he closed it again and said, "Tell me in your own words. Briefly. I'll read the reports when they've been typed up."

She gave him a précis of her interviews with Margery Rosevear and Jeanette Jones.

In return, he told her little more than that her aunt and Mrs Stearns between them had confirmed Gresham's story. "I sent Wilkes to radio Launceston to send someone to the station to talk to the ticket collector." He glanced at his watch. "Where the devil has the lazy sod got to? I wonder if he can be trusted to take himself down to Padstow to talk to the bloke who's at their shop today. Quentin something?"

"I don't know his surname, sir."

"Why not? What do we know about him?"

"I haven't heard anything to suggest that he had any particular quarrel with Clark. DC Wilkes could probably cope, at least with the initial interview."

"Good. Oh, there you are, Wilkes. Where the hell have you been?"

The detective constable came out of the back door of the farmhouse, bearing a tray. "Mrs Rosevear called me into the house, sir, and asked me to bring this out. Homemade clotted cream, homemade raspberry jam, homemade splits, and a nice pot of tea." He set the tray on the bench beside Scumble.

"Very nice, too. Pity you're off to Padstow but maybe the chap at the artists' shop down there'll give you a cuppa."

"Sir!"

The heartfelt protest failed to induce Scumble to relent. "I want to know what he was doing yesterday afternoon. Also, try to get him talking about Clark, find out what he thought of him. Off you go, and don't be all day about it."

Wilkes gave the tray a last wistful look. "Yes, sir," he said gloomily and trudged away round the corner of the house.

"Who's left?" asked Scumble, his mouth already full.

"Douglas Rosevear." Megan poured two cups of tea. "Albert Baraclough. Oswald Rudd. Tom Lennox."

"He's the one who's sweet on Miss Jones?"

"Yes, sir. Very protective."

"Supposed to have driven to Wadebridge yesterday. That the lot?"

"One more, Leila—again, I don't know her surname, I'm afraid. They don't seem to go in for surnames much here. All I know about her is that she walked to Padstow yesterday afternoon, leaving here after the mini-bus, and came back in the bus with the others. I haven't seen her about."

"Not another one gone!"

"I'll go and ask Mrs Rosevear." Megan hoped there would be some splits and cream left when she returned. Cornish cream teas were an indulgence she usually managed to resist, but home-made, and free . . .

Margery Rosevear was sitting at the kitchen table, head in hands, staring into the depths of a mug of tea. She turned, startled, when Megan knocked on the open door.

"Thanks for the tea," said Megan.

"You can't have finished already!"

"No, I just have a quick question for you."

A wary look crossed Mrs Rosevear's face. "Yes?"

"Two questions, actually. What is Leila's surname, and where is she?"

"Arden. She went to Trevone Bay to collect shells for her work. Albert gave her a lift when he took Quentin to the shop."

"When do you expect her back?"

She shrugged. "By suppertime, I imagine. More likely earlier. She goes her own way. She may phone for someone to pick her up, but quite likely she'll walk home. She likes walking. It's not that far cross-country."

"Thank you. One more question while I'm here: Where can we find your husband this afternoon?"

"He said he was going to muck out the pigs. Go through the yard and the pens are just over the brow of the hill."

Guess who's going to get that job, Megan thought sourly. With that prospect before her, clotted cream didn't sound like such a wonderful idea after all. What a pity Wilkes had already left for Padstow!

Would it be worth suggesting that the farmer would probably respond better to a male questioner? It might even be true, but no, she had worked long and hard to convince the gov'nor she could do the job as well as any man. She wasn't going to jeopardise her progress just to get out of a nasty job.

When she told him, Scumble said, "Well, now, sounds as if both of 'em are trying to avoid us. They must have guessed we'd turn up. I'll send that oaf Lubbock to fetch the farmer." He gave Megan a knowing look as she swallowed a sigh of relief. "If I can find him. Where the hell has he got to? Then we'll deal with the others and see if the shell woman turns up by the time we're done. As you know all about what happened between Clark and Jeanette Jones, you can take Lennox."

Quickly, before she could be sent off without her tea like Wilkes, she sat down, picked up her cup, and took a swig of the lukewarm liquid. After all, rank had its privileges, and she was a DS, not a mere DC. She cut open a split, spread jam, and slathered it with what was left of the cream.

He eyed her irritably. "I hope *he's* not going to disappear before you finish eating."

"I doubt it. He'd surely be gone by now. I heard his potter's wheel whirring as I came away from Miss Jones's studio."

"He rescued her from Clark's unwanted advances, you said."

"Worse than advances. It was pretty nasty." Megan hoped he wouldn't ask for details. She would have to put it all in her report, but she wasn't sure she would be able to bring herself to pass on Jeanette's description verbally, face to face with the inspector.

"I suppose you'd better use a bit of tact with the fellow."

"Of course, sir." No wonder he had given Lennox to her. His own make-up included not an atom of tact, and to do him justice, he knew it.

"That leaves me with Oswald Rudd and Albert . . . What was his name?"

"Baraclough, sir."

"What a mouthful! What do you know about them?"

"Not much, sir. I saw Rudd briefly. Jeanette Jones said he's a painter. He was in charge at their shop yesterday. Mrs Rosevear, Jeanette Jones, and Leila Arden met at the shop and Lennox picked them up there on his way back from Wadebridge, but that was after four. I haven't heard anything about his relationship with Clark."

"Which probably means he had no major quarrel with him," Scumble grumbled. "Waste of my time."

"Perhaps he's really good at hiding his feelings, behind his red beard. Regard it as a challenge, sir."

He groaned. "Not a beardy-weirdy!"

"They are artists, after all. You have to expect a bit of excess hair."

"At least Gresham wears his behind where you don't have to stare at it. What about Baraclough?"

"I don't know about his facial hair situation, sir. Only that he's supposed to have stayed here yesterday afternoon. This morning he drove Leila Arden to the cove and the sculptor, Quentin, to their shop, then came back."

"Right. If you've quite finished eating, let's get going."

She had finished, if only because there was no food left. "I'll just take the tray back to Mrs Rosevear."

"Leave it. I'll take it in. I want a word with her and your next job'll probably take longer than mine, 'challenge' or not."

Megan found both Jeanette and Oswald Rudd in Lennox's pottery, as well as an elderly, clean-shaven man—wearing a suit!—whom they introduced as Albert Baraclough. The potter's wheel was silent. Lennox was incising swirling marks on a row of reddish-brown bowls with what looked like an ice-lolly stick.

"Mr Rudd, Mr Baraclough, Detective Inspector Scumble will be coming to talk to you in a few minutes. Mr Lennox, I'd like a word with you now."

"I've got to get this done before the clay dries."

"That's all right, sir. Judging by your company, you can talk and work at the same time."

"I suppose so," he said grudgingly. Then he gave her an unexpected grin. "Yes, of course I can. Ask away."

Rudd and Baraclough had departed but Jeanette Jones still lingered, perched on the seat by the wheel.

"Miss Jones, if you wouldn't mind . . . ?"

"I know you're going to be talking about me. Can't I stay?"

"No."

"Off you go, Jeanie."

"Oh, all right." She left, pouting.

"She's a bit young for her age," said Lennox, excusing her. "Not stupid, just . . ." He shrugged.

"Unsophisticated?"

"Yes, that's it," he agreed, a bit too eagerly.

What was it he shied away from saying? Immature, perhaps? Emotionally immature?

Why didn't he want to come out with it? Perhaps he was afraid that Jeanette, with little control over her emotions, had stabbed Clark in a fit of retrospective rage.

Megan could obey the injunction not to "try to fathom the mind of a witness," or she could go with her instinct. "Tell me about her paintings," she requested.

"Jeanette's paintings?" he asked, startled.

Obviously the last subject he had expected, and it was never a bad thing to have a witness off balance. "Yes. I caught a glimpse of a couple. They didn't seem to me unsophisticated."

"I don't pretend to understand art. I'm a craftsman, and a good one, and that's all I aspire to."

Properly put in her place! And stymied. Oh well, it had been nothing more than the vaguest of hunches that Jeanette's work might have some significance. All the same, Megan wondered whether Nick Gresham might have something to say on the subject.

Changing gears, she asked about his movements the previous afternoon.

"I made a delivery to a shop in Wadebridge, as I'm sure you've been told."

"Where to? What time? Details, please."

Leaving Padstow at two, he had taken a good half an hour to drive to Wadebridge, going carefully with due regard to the twisting road, his fragile cargo, and the vagaries of the mini-bus. By the time he had found a parking spot, unloaded his crates, and trucked them to the shop on his handcart, it was past three. The shopkeeper had revived him with a cold drink, then insisted on opening all the crates and checking the contents for breakages. He had barely made it back to Padstow to pick up Margery, Jeanette, and Leila at half past four.

"Thank you. And before you left here?"

"Before? I was packing up the crates and loading them into the bus. Just out there, in the courtyard. Quentin gave me a hand and two or three people came over for one reason or another."

"Who?"

"Let me see. Jeanie—Jeanette wanted to be sure I'd get her to the village in time to catch the afternoon post. Leila told me she

{ 224 }

was going to walk down and would like a lift back. I think that's the lot."

"Can you give me times?"

He shrugged. "Not a chance. I suppose Quentin might know, but I can't see why he should. He had no reason to look at his watch, and Upper Trewithen Farm never ran to a stable clock."

Everything would have to be checked, but at first sight Lennox's alibi looked pretty solid. Megan wondered whether she really needed to delve into the embarrassing business of his rescue of Jeanette from Geoffrey Clark. More to the point, would Scumble consider it necessary?

She compromised. "Tell me about Clark."

"I'm sure you've already heard it all."

"Probably. But I'd like your perspective."

"He was an arrogant, malicious bastard who enjoyed making people squirm."

"Completely insensitive to other people's feelings?"

"On the contrary. He had an instinct for the weak spot. When the mood took him, which was all too often, he could be not only offensive but hurtful."

"Did he pick on anyone in particular?"

"Like all bullies, he didn't bother those who could defend themselves. Or, more accurately, those he couldn't get a rise out of. Albert, Quentin, and I were more or less immune. We've all got thick hides. Stella wouldn't put up with any nonsense from him, either. Perhaps that's why he fell for her. I may be risking my life saying this to a female police officer, but on the whole women are comparatively thin-skinned."

Megan wasn't about to let him get a rise out of her. "You're saying on the whole he despised women?"

Lennox hesitated. "Yes, I suppose I am. Plenty of women seem to like it. He was always surrounded by hopeful hordes."

"We've been told he was a womaniser."

"Until he met Stella. Not that she seemed to care one way or the other, but I got the impression he was pretty much faithful to her, though you'll hear plenty of talk to the contrary, I expect."

"'Pretty much.' I gather it was quite recently that he attacked Jeanette Jones."

"He was sozzled, and Stella had been giving him a hard time. He suspected she'd taken up with someone else. Knowing her, probably just a one-night fling. But she was definitely the one who held the whip hand. He was pissed as a newt, if you'll excuse the expression, and after that disgusting display he got disgustingly weepy."

"Drunkenness is no excuse in the law." Megan decided Scumble would expect her to concentrate on the assault. "Why wasn't the attack reported to the police?"

"No point. I got there in time to stop him hurting her. When I disarmed him, I . . . uh, *he* somehow wrenched his shoulder badly enough that he couldn't paint for a fortnight. I made him pay to replace everything he'd dirtied, damaged, or destroyed. What would have been the point of dragging the whole thing into court, making Jeanie describe in public just what she went through? You know what some people say about women who are assaulted. No, reporting it just wasn't on."

Privately Megan agreed. She spared him the requisite lecture on taking the law into one's own hands. Lennox apparently considered Clark had got what was coming to him for his drunken shenanigans, and as far as he was concerned, the incident was over and done with. He seemed a pretty straightforward character. Megan tended to believe him.

Which left open the question of whether Jeanette had been equally able to put the whole thing behind her. No, Megan thought, for Jeanette it was still a gaping wound.

TWENTY-FOUR

"Drop me at the butcher's, Joce, please," said Eleanor as they started down the hill into Port Mabyn. "I haven't got anything for supper."

"Come and eat with us."

"Oh no, dear, the vicar will want you to himself after you've been gone all day."

Jocelyn examined this dubious proposition—Timothy Stearns was quite likely to have assumed he was supposed to know about her absence—but she decided not to dispute it. "All right. I'll see you at the shop in the morning." She drew up outside Dinmont's Fine Meats. "I hope That Man is not going to be bothering us any more."

"We can but hope." Eleanor climbed out, a trifle wearily, and Teazle bounced after her. "Bother! I still don't have her lead and I've lost the bit of string."

Ever efficient, Jocelyn provided a ball of twine from the glove compartment—as well as scissors to cut off a length. She drove off up the opposite hill towards the vicarage.

Eleanor tied Teazle to a convenient pipe and went into the

shop. She asked Mrs Dinmont for half a pound of chipolatas, then decided she'd better invite Nick in case he didn't make it to the shops before they closed, as they would in a few minutes.

"Make that three quarters, please, Mrs Dinmont." She felt in her pocket for her purse. "Oh dear, I forgot, I haven't got any money on me."

"That's all right, dearie," said Mrs Dinmont, wrapping the sausages in wax paper. "You can bring it in tomorrow, unless you'd like to start an account? Lots of ladies do."

"No, no, I'll pay you tomorrow." Eleanor didn't like to run monthly accounts. Somehow she always ended up short of money at the end of the month. "Thank you."

Mrs Dinmont placed the packet on the counter but kept her hand on it. Leaning forward, her blood-smeared apron pressed against the edge of the counter, she asked, "Is it true Mr Gresham's girlfriend wrecked his shop?"

"No, it's not!" Who—? Oh, Donna, of course. And there would be worse rumours flying once the police came to ask the girl to confirm Nick's presence in Port Mabyn at five o'clock yesterday. "Stella isn't his girlfriend. She's a colleague who took care of the shop while he was in London."

"Not his girlfriend, that's as may be. But take care of the shop, she didn't, Mrs Trewynn, mark my words. Never opened after lunchtime closing yesterday, and if they've changed early closing to Thursday, it's more than anyone's told me or Mr Dinmont. Not that I'd put it past the gov'mint, mind."

"There's no accounting for the whims of the government," Eleanor agreed with a bright smile, managing to ease her sausages from Mrs Dinmont's slackened grasp. "Thank you, and I'll be sure to come in and pay first thing tomorrow. Good-bye."

Flurried, she almost left Teazle behind. An anxious yip reminded her. She fumbled with the knotted string and for a moment was afraid she'd have to go back into the shop to borrow scissors, but at last it came loose. They went on down the hill to the old stone bridge over the stream. To Eleanor's relief, the parapets were unadorned by the customary selection of retired fishermen. Only a couple of herring gulls perched there, eyeing her small parcel hungrily as she passed. One took off with a raucous cry and flapped up to join its fellows circling above.

Down in the harbour, the stream carved a shallow channel through the sandy mud, where three small boats lay tilted on their sides. The tide was out again. Eleanor remembered Leila, at breakfast, in a hurry to get to the sea while the tide was low, to collect her shells. Or had that been no more than an excuse to get away from the farm?

From what Eleanor remembered of the conversation at breakfast, Leila had certainly disliked Geoff, even hated him. Wasn't it she who had called him an arrogant pig? And surely Jeanette had hinted at something between the two.

Suppose Leila had killed Geoff. Why would she have waited until this morning to decamp? The only reason Eleanor could think of was that she wouldn't be missed for twelve hours or so. No one would realise till suppertime that she wasn't coming home, giving her plenty of time to disappear to . . . To where? Perhaps she had spent the intervening hours wondering where to go, where she might find refuge.

But would anyone have noticed if she hadn't returned to the farm last night? Margery had said it was difficult for her to cater to her lodgers because people were pretty casual about turning up for meals.

Trying to remember just what Leila had said at breakfast-time, Eleanor had walked on up the hill, oblivious of passers-by. She found herself outside Nick's shop. The CLOSED sign was up and her knock brought no response. A push on the door proved it locked.

He was probably in the studio working on *Land of Hope and Glory*. The best way to get his attention was to go through the passage beside the shop and round by the back path to knock on his window. Besides inviting him to supper, she was now eager to find out if he knew what the trouble was between Leila and Geoff. An affair followed by rejection, like Margery Rosevear, or had Geoff pressed his unwanted attentions on Leila as he had on poor Jeanette? Or had he simply made unbearably derogatory remarks about the artistic merit of her shell-work?

Eleanor found it nearly impossible to comprehend that anyone could consider an insult an adequate reason for murder, but she had a feeling history proved the point, if only she could remember her history. Though she had forgotten why Cain slew Abel, surely Romulus had killed Remus because the latter had laughed at the wall built by the former and jumped over it . . . Or was it the other way round? No, Romulus had survived because Rome must have been named after him. What should have been a mere tiff, and a brotherly tiff at that, had escalated to murder. Admittedly the two were brought up by a wolf, yet she rather thought she read somewhere—probably in *National Geographic*—that wolves led lives of domestic felicity.

These reflections had taken her round to Nick's window, open a few inches at the top to let in air but not the brisk breeze off the sea. There he was, scowling ferociously at the painting on his easel.

Not wanting to startle him, she tapped softly on the pane.

He swung round, snarling, "What the hell do you—Oh, it's you, Eleanor. Sorry. I opened the shop and had swarms of people dropping in to find out if Stella had really wrecked the place.

{ 230 }

That wretched child, I suppose! I thought someone had decided to attack from the rear. Come in." He threw a cloth over the easel and wiped his hands on a turps-soaked rag.

"I don't want to interrupt, dear. I just wanted to ask if you'd like to come over for supper, about seven? Sausages, baked potatoes in their jackets, French beans, and there are some strawberries if they've survived my absence."

"What's this, bribery and corruption?"

"Well, I do want to talk about . . . well, everything. But I promise not to ask if Stella wrecked the shop! Can you spare the time? Is that *Land of Hope and Glory*? How is it going?"

"I haven't got much further than the background, thanks to all the busybodies. It's all planned, though. There's not much to be said for spending a night in a cell, but it does give one time to think. Yes, please, I'd love sausages. What time?" As he spoke, he absently pulled the cloth off the canvas and started painting furiously.

"Seven o'clock," Eleanor told him again. If he wasn't listening and didn't turn up on time, she could always pop down and fetch him.

She called Teazle from her investigation of a rabbit hole under the blackthorn bushes, loaded now with small green sloes. Teazle scampered up the stairs to the flat, obviously as happy as Eleanor to be home at last. Eleanor toiled after her, feeling her age.

While the oven was preheating, she scrubbed a couple of large King Edwards, then added a couple more. Nick had a big appetite; he probably hadn't been fed well in the lock-up and she didn't know if he'd had any lunch. Any leftovers could be turned into rösti tomorrow. As long as she was careful not to let it burn, she was quite good at rösti, the greatest invention to come out of Switzerland since cuckoo clocks. She dried the potatoes with a tea-towel, the only way, according to Jocelyn, to ensure the crispness of the jackets, though Eleanor couldn't help thinking that the hot oven alone must dry them pretty quickly.

The rest wouldn't take long. She fed Teazle, topped and tailed the beans, and went to sit down for a few minutes in her chair by the window. The sun was peeking in . . .

The next thing she knew was Teazle's *wuff-wuff*, the smell of baking potatoes, and Nick coming through the door.

"Oh, Nick! I fell asleep." Blinking, she started to get up.

"Stay there." He glanced at the table. "You've got everything ready to go. Believe it or not, I can fry sausages and cook beans."

"Thank you, dear. I don't usually take a nap. I don't know why I'm so tired. I haven't done much all day except sit and talk."

"That's exhausting enough, when it's DI Scumble you're talking to. Are you sure you wouldn't prefer to drop the subject now?"

"No!" Eleanor was wide awake now. "I want to hear all about your side of the story, how you convinced Scumble that Stella was talking through her hat, everything." She moved over to sit at the table.

"That was the easy part. He knew Geoff died hours before we got there. He didn't seem convinced that I hadn't managed somehow to sneak back from London to do it earlier."

"I'm sure he doesn't really believe you did, Nick. How could you, between talking to Jocelyn from Paddington at midday and arriving at Launceston by train at four?"

"I could have faked the phone call, with a tape-recorder."

"Could you? How clever! Only wouldn't that mean you'd have had to plan long in advance? And you didn't know Mr Alarian was going to accept your paintings or that Geoff would react so violently. I know the inspector doesn't count me as a reliable witness, but he has only to talk to Mr Alarian, and Lobcot at Launceston station, and Donna—"

"Donna! Don't talk to me about Donna! Little witch! I swear

I'm never going near the Trelawny Arms again. Having got hold of the wrong end of the stick, she seems to have nattered to everyone in Port Mabyn."

"It only takes one. I expect she told one of her friends, in confidence." Eleanor sniffed. "Are those sausages burning?"

"Oops!" he swung round and turned down the heat. "I hope you like them well-browned."

"Luckily, yes. I prefer my beans green, though. You'd better concentrate."

For a few minutes the only sounds were the sizzle of the sausages, the bubbling of boiling water, and an occasional hopeful whine as Teazle stared up at the frying pan.

Even if the sausages were burnt, Eleanor was very glad to be at home, rather than at Upper Trewithen Farm surrounded by possible murderers. Which of them had done it? Or could it have been someone not connected with the artists' colony, someone nobody had yet considered?

Nick dished up. "They're a bit crispy but only one's actually got a black streak. Teazle probably wouldn't mind."

"I'm sure she'll be more than happy to dispose of it. Leave it to cool for her. These look perfectly all right to me. Nick, I just thought, what if it wasn't one of the artists who killed Geoff? Who else could it have been?"

His mouth full, Nick shrugged, swallowed, and said, "I don't know all the people he associated with. There's the brewery, of course. He's been working for them for several years. As far as I know, a purely business relationship, and he's been good for their business. The smith who made his sword and the deadly dagger. Perhaps Geoff took it without paying, the smith went to the gallery to demand payment, and they quarrelled."

"Was Geoff bad about paying bills?"

"Not that I've heard. I don't know the smith, either, so it's fruitless wondering. I expect Scumble will get after the also-rans, if it turns out not to be anyone at the farm."

"But you think it *was* someone at the farm?"

"They knew him best and had most reason to dislike him. Reasons, plural."

"Yes, it's very sad. Do you know Leila's reason?"

"What makes you think Leila had a particular reason?" Nick asked cautiously.

"When I had breakfast with them all, hints were flying thick and fast." Should she mention that Leila had accused Jeanette of being in love with Nick? Better not. He might be unaware of that complication. Jeanette's solicitude for him, her certainty that he was not guilty, suggested there was something in it—unless Jeanette had been pretending in order to divert suspicion from herself? Another possibility that Eleanor would have to consider.

"They were accusing each other?" Nick's patient tone reminded her of Scumble. He must have already posed the question once, while her mind was elsewhere.

"Nothing so blatant. It was more as if they were sort of reminding each other of why they weren't mourning Geoff."

"It sounds very odd."

"It was. I'm wondering about Leila because she went off alone this morning and hadn't returned by the time I left."

"You think she's done a bunk?"

"Well, it seems possible. Jeanette implied—I can't remember her exact words—that Leila was, or had been, keen on Geoff. Is it true?"

"I believe so. Some women do seem to fall for the 'mad, bad, and dangerous to know' type."

"When was this?"

Nick sighed. "I've always tried not to get too involved in their family squabbles—they're like a big, unruly family—but I can't help hearing things. How long Leila had nursed her passion I don't know. Apparently, after Geoff assaulted Jeanette, Stella was so angry with him that Leila thought she had a chance. Needless to say, Geoff turned her down flat. I hate to repeat this, but I gathered he called her an old bag. Or possibly hag; there seemed to be some uncertainty."

"What a brute! So it was quite recent," Eleanor mused, "and you know what they say about 'a woman scorned.'"

TWENTY-FIVE

Leaving the pottery, Megan saw the police 1100, with Wilkes leaning against it, chatting to Albert Baraclough. There was no sign of Scumble, so she went over to them.

Wilkes straightened as she approached. "What gives, Sarge? I couldn't see you or the gov'nor and I didn't want to interrupt anything, so I was just sitting here minding my own beeswax when this kind gentleman brought me a glass of water."

"The inspector came to see me just a while past Miss . . . er, Sergeant, as you said he would. He's with Oswald now, Oswald Rudd." He pointed at Redbeard's studio. Megan wondered how Scumble was getting on with the beardy-weirdy. "It's a warm day," Baraclough went on, "and I thought, best not offer a beer to a policeman on duty but there could be no harm in a glass of water."

"None at all, sir, it's very thoughtful of you."

"Would you like a glass, too?"

"I'm all right, thanks."

"I suppose you can't tell me whether you've found any clues to this horrible crime?"

"Afraid not, sir."

"It's very difficult not knowing if one of the people you've re-garded as friends is a murderer." His tone was querulous. "Can't you at least tell me whether you suspect anyone else, any outsider? He probably had enemies all over Cornwall."

"I'm sorry, sir, I'm not allowed to discuss the case."

"Oh. Well, never mind." Disconsolate, he went off towards the house.

Wilkes and Megan watched him go.

"Don't you think it's a bit fishy, Sarge, him being so keen to know what we've found out? Like he's afraid we're on his trail."

"It's perfectly natural. The one I find a bit fishy is the one who seems to have vanished off the face of the earth before we came on the scene."

"Uh . . . ?"

"Miss Leila Arden. Or Mrs, for all I know."

Wilkes snapped his fingers. "Right. The one who went collect-ing shells. That's a likely story, for a start. What's a grown-up woman want with a pocketful of shells? Kid stuff!"

"She's an artist, remember. She works with them. All the same, I'd like to know where she's got to. You'd better ask around, see if she came back while we weren't looking. She might have phoned Mrs Rosevear. But first, tell me what you got out of the bloke at the shop."

"Not much." He flipped open his notebook. "Quentin Durward—you'd think his parents named him after that Kay Kendall flick that came out in the fifties, but he's too old."

"It was a book before it was a film. Scott, I think."

"French it was, not Scottish. King Louis the something. That was Robert Morley. I remember I saw it—"

"For pity's sake, Wilkes, forget about the film. What was Mr Durward doing yesterday afternoon?"

"Went for a *constitutional*—what you and me'd call a walk. Up

Bear Downs, he says." Wilkes gestured vaguely in no particular direction. "Looking for—nah, *seeking* inspiration." He rolled his eyes.

Megan wondered if Quentin Durward always spoke that way or if he'd been taking the mickey. "I suppose it's too much to hope you got any times out of him?"

"Much too much. He left sometime after lunch and got home sometime before supper. Before their usual suppertime, that is. It didn't—um, *materialise* yesterday, because of Mrs Rosevear being *unavoidably detained*. So I asked, what did they all do when their meal didn't turn up?"

"That's a point. What did they do?"

"*Pooled* their *resources*. Shared what they'd got."

They had missed a trick there, Megan realised. They should be asking everyone whether they'd noticed any of the others behaving in an abnormal manner last night. Or perhaps—awful thought!—Scumble was asking and assumed she would do likewise on her own initiative.

"So then I asked," Wilkes continued, "was anyone acting peculiar. And he said, no, just annoyed, because they pay Mrs Rosevear for the *evening meal*. But it seems to me, Sarge, you can hide a whole lot of peculiar behind a little bit of annoyed."

"Yes, I expect so. Did he meet anyone on his hike?"

"Not that he remembers. But—get this, Sarge!—he reckons he was too busy seeking inspiration to notice."

"He wasn't exactly feeling helpful, was he! What did he have to say about the victim?"

"He said he was a bit of a bastard but easy to avoid and not worth the trouble of bumping off—*eliminating*'s what he said. I don't think he was kidding, either, apart from the fancy language. He just put that on to get up my nose. I mean, nobody could spout like that all the time or they'd be spending half their time explaining what they were talking about. But if you ask me, he meant what he said about Clark: He just didn't give a damn."

Megan nodded. "Could be. I haven't heard anything to suggest he had any particular quarrel with Clark. That's it?"

"Pretty much."

"All right, go and see if Leila Arden's back or if anyone's heard from her. I'm just going to have another word with Jeanette Jones."

As Megan approached Jeanette's studio, she heard the raised voices of Scumble and Oswald Rudd from the next studio. She was very tempted to stop and listen, but through Jeanette's open door she could see her standing at an easel. The canvas on it appeared to be blank, and Jeanette was making no move to paint. Perhaps she was seething with ideas, occupied in deciding where to start, but judging by the droop of her shoulders Megan suspected she was simply staring at it, her mind as blank as the canvas.

Not wanting to startle her, Megan knocked softly.

Jeanette swung round. "Oh, it's you. You made me jump. Is there something else?"

"Just a couple more things that have come up. Sorry to interrupt."

"You're not interrupting. I don't seem to be able to think."

"I'd be more surprised if you could, with all that's been going on. This shouldn't take a moment, but shall we sit down?"

"Yes. Yes, all right. Come through." She shivered, and hugged herself as she entered the bedsitter. "It's suddenly cooled off, hasn't it? I'm chilly now." She crossed the room to close the windows. "Would you like a cup of tea?"

Megan didn't really, but she thought tea would be good for

Jeanette, who probably wouldn't make it for herself alone, so she accepted. Jeanette switched on an electric kettle.

"Typhoo or Typhoo," she said.

"I'll have Typhoo, thanks."

"Oh, and there's some camomile Marge gave me for my nerves, home-grown, but it tastes like straw to me."

"If you mix it with the Typhoo, you might not be able to taste it."

"You think I need it?" Jeanette demanded.

"I think it can't hurt. I'm no doctor, but I think you've been living on your nerves since Clark attacked you."

"I haven't been able to put it out of my mind, not even when I'm painting. Only when I'm working on the children's books . . ." Abandoning the tea-making, she slumped down on the divan. "I thought it would go away now he's dead, but if anything it's worse."

Megan didn't like the sound of this. Was it time to start considering mitigating circumstances? It might turn out to be a great pity that the assault hadn't been reported to the police at the time. Jeanette hadn't quite confessed to stabbing Geoffrey Clark, but she seemed to be approaching that point.

It was one of those moments when Megan wondered why on earth she had chosen to be a detective. She would have preferred to turn things over to the gov'nor at this point. However, a delay, let alone Scumble's manner, was almost certain to dry up the source. Pressing for a confession wouldn't work. Keeping Jeanette talking was all-important.

"Darkest before the dawn, let's hope," she said, getting up as the kettle clicked off and going to make the tea. Her back to Jeanette, she went on, "Is there somewhere you can go to get away for a bit, after this is all over, after we've made an arrest?"

Too much to hope that she would admit to not expecting to be at liberty at that point.

"I suppose I could go home. To my parents, that is. They were upset when I came here to live and paint, but they didn't cut me off without a shilling, or anything. They even buy my books for my nieces and nephews. Only, if I go home because things have gone wrong, Mum will say she knew it would end in tears, or something equally humiliating."

Megan wasn't sure this was the right moment for empathy. On the other hand, none other than the gov'nor had told her to employ the "sympathetic female touch," so what had she got to lose? "I know what you mean," she said, pouring tea into crooked mugs—the camomile was not immediately in evidence, so she skipped it. "My parents had fits when I went to London and joined the police. I was supposed to marry a lawyer or doctor or someone like that and settle down to be a housewife. I see them regularly, but now, when things get tough, I just remind myself of the flak I'd get if I resigned. Here, drink this. Where do your parents live?"

"Gerrards Cross," said Jeanette in tones of deepest gloom, sipping the hot tea. "Dad's a stockbroker."

Gerrards Cross, in southern Bucks, the heart of the stockbroker belt—Megan would know where to start looking for her if she went missing. Speed might prove important should her wealthy father try to smuggle her out of the country. Megan had to recognise that Jeanette was no longer on the point of confessing to stabbing Clark, if she ever had been. So far, the sympathetic female touch had not been a wild success.

Time to get back to business. "I'm sorry to drag you back to an unpleasant subject, but after talking to Mr Lennox, I've come up with, as I said, a couple more questions."

"I suppose you have to."

"First, was it your idea or his not to report the incident to the police?"

Jeanette looked surprised. She thought for a moment, then said, "Neither of us, as a matter of fact. I don't remember too clearly, but I'm pretty sure Stella and Marge cooked it up between them. Stella didn't want Geoff getting into trouble, of course, and Marge was afraid it would reflect badly on the farm. The colony, whatever you want to call us. I went along with it, of course, because the last thing I wanted was for Tom to be had up for injuring Geoff. He said he didn't care, but he agreed with Stella that Geoff had been punished enough for a drunken spree. Spree! I told you, Stella calling it that made me almost more angry than what Geoff did! And then she had the nerve to say I was blowing it up out of all proportion!"

"Not exactly the soul of tact. How did Mrs Rosevear and Miss . . . Stella come into the picture?"

"Oh, Tom went to fetch Marge to take care of me and Stella to take Geoff away. Which she did eventually, though Tom had to help her. He was too pissed to walk. Ugh!"

"Right, let's move ahead to yesterday." Megan assumed, for the moment, that both Jeanette's and Tom's alibis for the time of death would hold up. "Last night, Mrs Rosevear wasn't here to cook for you. How did you find out?"

"Quentin came round to tell us all. He got to the house first. A bit early, actually. He said he was starving after a long hike. When we found out she really wasn't there, we all put our bits and pieces together and had a picnic. In here, actually."

"Who was there?"

"Well, Quentin. Tom, Albert, Oswald, Leila. Not Doug, of course, nor Stella. She often didn't join us, anyway, so we didn't think anything of that."

"Did anyone seem out of sorts? Nervous? Upset? In a state of shock?"

Jeanette frowned. "Everyone was upset to some degree, wondering where Marge was—she's usually very reliable—and grumbling about no proper supper. Nothing more than that."

"That's all for now, then, thanks."

Dissatisfied, Megan went out through the studio. Outside in the courtyard, a disgusting sight awaited her. A disgusting smell, too.

After a shocked moment, she recognised PC Lubbock, or rather, deciphered his identity from what was visible of his uniform through the muck.

"Ye gods!"

"I couldn't help it, Sergeant, honest," the large young man said miserably. "The inspector, he said I'd got to bring in Mr Rosevear, so I went out to the pig pens, like he said, and told him he was wanted at the house and he said he wasn't coming till he finished the job. So I put my hand on his shoulder, like, not violent, just to show him it was serious business, and he went and knocked me down in the muck. And somehow we got into a bit of a wrestle and then he said since I was all mucky already, I might as well help with the job and it'd be done sooner and then he'd go peaceable. Which I did and he did. I couldn't see no help for it!"

"I'b sure you did your best, Codstable." Holding her nose, Megan tried to keep a straight face. "Where is Mr Rosevear now?"

"Taking a bath, Sergeant."

"Well, you'd better throw yourself od Mrs Rosevear's bercy and ask if you cad do likewise."

"But my uniform . . ."

"We'll have to see if someone will give you a polythene bag and lend you something to wear."

By this time, Baraclough, Jeanette, and Lennox had come out. They stood at a safe distance, all grinning.

"I can let you have a bag," said Lennox. "A bit of clay dust isn't going to make much difference to that lot. But only Quentin's big enough to rig you out. He should be home soon."

"I'll get you something," Jeanette offered. "Quent won't have locked up. His work dungarees, I should think. The amount of work he does, he won't miss them for weeks. And a pair of sandals. I'll bring them to the house." She crossed the courtyard to Quentin's studio.

"Let this teach you, young man," said Baraclough, "never to tangle with a pig farmer. You won't want to go to the front door of the house in that condition. I'll show you round the back, if you like, and go in to warn Marge."

"Sergeant?" Lubbock appealed.

"Aren't you supposed to report to DI Scumble?"

"Not like this! Please, Sarge . . ."

"Oh, all right." The artsy types had rallied round, the least Megan could do was follow suit. "I'll tell him you had an altercation with a pig, and you'll just have to hope Mr Rosevear won't accuse you of assault and battery."

As Megan turned towards Oswald Rudd's studio, Baraclough and the unhappy constable headed for the house. Hearing raucous laughter, Megan looked round. They had met DC Wilkes coming away, and Wilkes was having a hearty laugh at his colleague's expense.

"Wilkes!"

"Coming, Sarge. What happened to sonny-boy?"

"I'm sure you'll hear the whole story sooner rather than later. What about Leila Arden?"

"She hasn't come back and no one's heard from her. Course, the only phone's in the house and Mrs Rosevear was back in the garden some of the time. She said she's prob'ly stopped in to see a friend, but I could tell she's dead worried. You reckon the Arden woman did it and she's scarpered, Sarge?"

"I have no idea," Megan told him. "What I do know is that the gov'nor is not going to be happy."

"Never is, is he?" Wilkes retorted, as she turned back to Rudd's open door.

TWENTY-SIX

DI Scumble was anything but happy when he emerged from Oswald Rudd's lair a couple of minutes later.

After one glance at his face, Megan said, "No luck, sir?"

"The stupid bugger!" he snarled. "Says he didn't kill Clark but he'd like to buy a beer for whoever did, and he's not going to answer questions without a lawyer present and he hasn't got a lawyer and hasn't the money to pay one."

"We could take him in for obstruction," Megan suggested dubiously. It was a tactic Superintendent Bentinck frowned on—though perhaps they were now under the jurisdiction of Egerton, whose views on the subject were unknown.

"I did just happen to think of that, Pencarrow." Scumble's voice dripped with sarcasm. "I warned him, and he said if Gresham can survive a night in the cells, so can he. Snarky sod! We'll hold that option in reserve. Waste of time right now."

"You don't think he did it, then."

"Who knows? He was in Padstow all day. He had the opportunity and the victim provided the means, but unless you've dug up a respectable motive . . . ?"

"Only that Clark told Rudd his paintings were third rate. Given the artistic temperament—"

"Don't give me the artistic temperament! I've had it up to here with the artistic temperament."

"Right, sir. What about Baraclough?"

"No arty nonsense about him," Scumble said with something approaching enthusiasm. "He's a businessman. Calls himself a designer. I might," he added casually, "take the wife to their shop in Padstow to pick out one of his cardies for her birthday. Just the sort of thing she likes."

Flabbergasted by this sign of humanity, Megan merely murmured, "Yes, sir."

He reverted quickly to normal. "I know what you're thinking, Pencarrow. No, he did not offer me a discount!"

The gov'nor might be a pain in the arse, but he was an honest pain in the arse, Megan knew. "No, sir," she murmured, and added, "Lennox said he has a thick skin."

"What did he mean by that?"

"Just that Clark had insulted Baraclough as he insulted everyone, apparently, but it rolled off Baraclough's back. Or so I imagine. I didn't pursue the matter."

"Why the hell not?"

"Because there were more useful lines to follow, sir. In my opinion."

"All right, tell me about it, but make it quick. That oaf Lubbock must have brought Rosevear in by now."

Megan told him about Lubbock's misadventures. A snicker behind her added to the difficulty of keeping a straight face, as well as informing her that Wilkes had joined them at some point, presumably after the business about Mrs Scumble's cardigan, or the gov'nor would never have mentioned it.

Scumble glared at Wilkes. "Well?"

Wilkes hastened to report on his interview with Quentin Durward, skipping the fancy language and not adding significantly to what he'd told Megan. Leila Arden still hadn't come home or phoned.

"We'll give her a bit longer. Pencarrow?"

She gave a recap of her interview with Lennox.

The response was a grunt. "Let's go see Rosevear."

"You want me along, sir?" Wilkes asked.

"The more the merrier," Scumble said sourly. "Yes, you'd better come, in case he has to be hauled out of his bath. There's still an occasional job a woman officer's no use for." He swung round and headed for the farmhouse.

As they followed, Wilkes raised enquiring eyebrows at Megan. She shrugged. It was awfully hard to tell the difference between the gov'nor's everyday manner and his bad moods. If he was suffering the latter, once again she fervently hoped it was not because his plan to show up DI Pearce was unravelling.

A man who was obviously Douglas Rosevear was seated at the kitchen table putting away a hunk of brown bread and yellow cheese and a mug of beer. He looked spotless, in a check shirt and jeans, the fringe of greying hair round his sun-freckled pate still damp from the bath. Nevertheless, a porcine odour hung in the air.

He glanced up when Scumble knocked on the open door. Gesturing to come in, he went on chewing.

Scumble introduced himself and Megan.

Rosevear nodded, swallowed, and said with a straight face and a slight Cornish accent, "Not a bad worker, your lad, once he got *into* it."

"Glad to hear he's good for something." Refusing the bait, Scumble sat down uninvited at the table. Megan followed his example, taking out her notebook, while Wilkes discreetly disappeared before some other task could be assigned to him. "Have any help haying yesterday?"

"Naw. The machine does it all."

"Did you speak to anyone? See anyone?"

"I saw Durward, heading off to the southeast. Hiking to the Nine Maidens, likely. He goes up there a lot. Got nothing better to do than look at a row of stone pillars."

"Did he see you?"

"Couldn't hardly have helped it, could he. Hearing the tractor, leastways. No matter, he waved."

Quentin Durward had told Wilkes he saw no one on his hike. No, Megan recalled, he'd said he didn't *speak* to anyone—and at the time he'd been teasing the detective constable with his choice of words. Wilkes had reported to Megan pretty much verbatim, she was fairly sure, whereas he greatly abbreviated what he told Scumble. Hadn't he said Durward didn't *meet* anyone?

Scumble would not have forgotten, but he rolled on without a blink. "Can you put a time to it, Mr Rosevear?"

"Well, now, let's see. Clock-time, naw. Panch-time, it'd be maybe an hour and some after dinner." Was he being deliberately difficult with his use of the dialect word for stomach, or was it just the word he usually employed? If he was trying to irritate the inspector, he failed to evoke any visible reaction. "Sun-time," he went on, "half twelve or thereabouts. Mebbe quarter to one. That's sun-time, mind, not government time."

Not summer-time, still much resented by farmers because their animals, particularly cows waiting to be milked, refused to conform to the government's edict. Megan tried to work it out and got confused, as always, but if it was after his dinner it must be quarter to two, not quarter to twelve.

While wrestling with the concept of summer-time, Megan had missed a couple of questions. At least, her conscious mind had missed them, but a different brain circuit, going straight from her ears to her fingers, had taken them down in shorthand. She could read it later.

Scumble had moved on to the events of the previous evening. He took Rosevear's typed statement to Pearce from his pocket and proceeded to go through it thoroughly.

And he found discrepancies. Rosevear had said he had time for a pint at the pub because he had finished haying.

"So you decided to go down to the village?" Scumble pointed to the tankard at Rosevear's elbow, now empty, its sides coated with drying foam. "Even though you keep beer in the house and you'd had a hard day?"

Rosevear was disconcerted. After a moment's thought, he said, "Naw, it was Marge said we'd go, right when I came in from the field. Stella was worried about Nick giving Clark a basting, and Marge said we ought to go to support her. I said it was rubbish, Nick wasn't the sort to pick a fight. Then they told me what Clark had done. I reckoned he deserved whatever he got, but it wasn't worth arguing, so I went along."

This answer appeared to please Scumble, though Megan wasn't sure why. Margery Rosevear had told them much the same.

"Did you happen to notice the time?"

"I looked at the clock to see was the pub open. Just on quarter past five it was, so by the time we got down to the village, it'd be opening. Just gave me time to get out of my work clothes, they did, and off we went. I don't know why you're asking all these questions. Marge says you know Nick didn't kill him."

Rosevear was a slow thinker, but by no means thick, Megan decided.

"Just making sure we've got it all straight, sir. Suppose we hadn't bothered to check on Miss . . . Weller's statement that she saw Mr Gresham stab the victim? Very unfortunate, that would've been. Now, you say here," he tapped the statement, "you were hungry for your supper. You telephoned the local police at six twenty-five—it's in the police log—and we've been told Mrs Rosevear usually serves supper at seven o'clock."

"She allis gives me a bite to eat to-wance when I come in." He pushed aside his plate, now holding nothing but a few crumbs. "Yesterday, with Stella chivvying, they rushed me off without."

Scumble crossed off a question mark he'd written in the margin of the statement. Megan had done the same on her carbon copy, and scribbled a few questions she couldn't now remember. Nor had she thought to bring it with her. In fact, once Stella's all-important statement had proved false, Megan had more or less dismissed her statement and both the Rosevears' from her mind as being next to useless.

"As we now know, Clark had by then been dead for some time." Scumble straightened the papers, folded them, and stuck them back in his pocket. "Do you—"

"Doug, I'm worried about Leila." Margery Rosevear came in from the courtyard. As her eyes adjusted to the dimness, she saw the detectives. "Oh, I didn't know you were still here."

"Still here," said Scumble. "Why are you worried about Miss Arden, Mrs Rosevear?"

"She should have been back long ago. She went to collect shells and the tide's come in and gone out again since she left."

"Ivers, Margie, she's a grown-up! She can take care of herself, and she won't thank you for keeping an eye on her comings and goings."

"She always lets me know if she's not going to be in for supper. They're all supposed to," she explained to Scumble, "though some of them are pretty erratic. Leila's usually pretty reliable."

"But not always," Rosevear muttered.

"What happened to Geoff has made me nervous," Mrs Rosevear went on, ignoring him. "Is it possible—You'll probably think I'm crazy—I was wondering if he could have been killed by some maniac who has it in for artists? Or even for those of us who live here. We're not really a commune, but that's what people call us, and people get funny ideas about communes."

"That's an interesting theory," said Scumble, "and theoretically possible, of course. Be that as it may, I'd like to know where Miss Arden's got to. I think it's about time we did something about finding out. I'll just have a word with DS Pencarrow, and then you can maybe give me some tips about where to start looking."

He went over to the door and stepped out, Megan following.

"Do you really think Arden killed him?" she asked.

"Could be. There's another possibility."

"That she saw or heard something—"

"Or someone thinks she saw or heard something. If the murderer got to her before I did, it's going to make that bastard very happy."

"DI Pearce?"

"DI Pearce. But you let me worry about Pearce. We still haven't talked to Stella Whatsit. You get over to the hospital right away and see what she has to say for herself. There's no need to let on we're perfectly happy that she misled Pearce."

"You don't think she might be in danger, too, sir?"

"In danger? She's in a bloody nursing home, not wandering about the countryside all on her lonesome. I need Wilkes. Somehow I've got to fit in finding out whether Polmenna's come up with anything useful in the village. You can take Lubbock, though he won't be much help for anything but driving. Don't come back here. Radio the Bodmin nick. I'll probably be there."

"Yes, sir."

"Off you go, now. If you happen to come across that lazy bugger Wilkes, send him here."

Wilkes and Lubbock, a strange sight in dungarees and sandals, were leaning against the 1100, chatting. Lubbock saw Megan first. He straightened and saluted. Wilkes turned.

"We were just discussing the case, Sarge," he said, glibly but unconvincingly. Either cars or cricket, she guessed, or perhaps even hurling, an ancient Cornish sport recently making something of a comeback.

"You can go and discuss it with the gov'nor in the house. Constable, you'll be driving me."

"Yes, ma'am." Lubbock reached to open the door of the 1100.

"In the panda. Mr Scumble will be needing his car."

Obviously disappointed, he went to the black-and-white Mini and opened the passenger door for her.

As they bumped down the track, she asked, "Did you come to any conclusions about the case?"

"Uh?"

"You were discussing the case with DC Wilkes."

"I . . . um . . . we . . . No, um, not exactly."

Which was a touch of revenge for all the male conversations she'd been shut out of because she had little knowledge and less interest in cars and sports. It was a bit unfair to take it out on the boy, though.

Boy? When had she started seeing new-fledged police officers as boys? What an alarming thought!

"What I wondered," Lubbock said eagerly, "is, could they all be in it together? I mean, I don't know much about it, but from what I've heard, they none of 'em's sorry he's dead."

"That's an interesting theory." And not only highly unlikely, given the variety of personalities involved, but unnecessary. A single hand had sufficed to stick the dagger into Clark's back.

An uncertain method of dealing death, now she came to think of it. A knife thrust in the back was liable to glance off a rib or two. Dr Prthnavi had said Clark died virtually instantly. Did that indicate luck or anatomical knowledge? Not that the latter would narrow the field of suspects much. Megan didn't know much more about art than she did about cars and sport, but she did know art students usually, if not always, studied anatomy.

She had no time to follow the idea. She had to concentrate on remembering exactly what Stella had said in her statement.

When she had first read it, she had known very little about the case, only what was in Douglas Rosevear's statement. In hindsight, she realised how little Stella had added to his story. Pearce hadn't bothered to ask her a single question about the earlier part of the day, the incident in Nick Gresham's shop that had set in motion the whole chain of events. He must have been in an almighty hurry to get home to his impatient totty.

On the other hand, she had to sympathise a little. According to a note added by the ubiquitous Wilkes, the witness had cried throughout the interview.

Still, even if Stella had been in no state to provide useful answers, Wilkes would have recorded everything Pearce said. The inspector, after swallowing whole her mistaken impression of what she'd observed without even taking a look at the scene, had simply failed to ask almost all of the obvious questions. There could be no excuse for such sloppy work.

It left Megan a clear field. Anything she found out would be fresh information, and she had the advantage that Stella had had time to get over her hysterics. Hadn't she?

Perhaps not. Maybe that was why Scumble had sent Megan to talk to Stella instead of organising the search for Leila Arden, which she was perfectly capable of doing. Or maybe he just didn't expect Stella to have anything useful to say.

TWENTY-SEVEN

"This looks like the place, Sarge." Lubbock swung the panda left into a drive leading downwards. "Riverview Convalescent Home."

"That's right." She was being ridiculously paranoid, she told herself. If the gov'nor had an ulterior motive for sending her, it was just the old "sympathetic female touch" nonsense. Stella was an important witness, the third on the scene, and there was a good chance she would have noticed something Gresham had not. With any luck, she'd have calmed down enough to remember.

The car pulled up in front of a largish, well-kept house. The grounds were well-kept, too. Obviously plenty of money here.

"Move the car to a less conspicuous place, will you? Then you can wait in it."

Lubbock's face fell. Another disappointment: no 1100 to drive, no helping with questioning a suspect. "Yes, ma'am."

"Come on, in that get-up, you've got to stay out of sight." Megan looked at the large young man squeezed in behind the wheel and took pity on him to the extent of saying, "You can get out to stretch your legs. Don't go farther than you can hear our call signal on the radio."

The door of the house stood open to the still-warm evening air. She stepped inside and looked around. Gleaming parquet, a big bowl of roses, delicious food smells emanating from somewhere beyond, all confirmed that there was no dearth of funds. There was, however, a dearth of people. Megan rang the bell on the table.

Nothing happened. She waited a couple of minutes and rang again.

A woman came out of a room to the left and asked impatiently, "Yes? What is it?"

Megan didn't answer for a moment, studying her. She had red hair, the kind that might lead to the nickname "copper-knob" but couldn't possibly be called carroty, done up in a careless-seeming chignon. She wore a no-nonsense white blouse with a paisley print ankle-length skirt in greens and blues and high-heeled sandals over nylon tights. Her face was striking—and vaguely familiar.

Holding out her warrant card for inspection, Megan introduced herself: "Detective Sergeant Pencarrow. I'd like to—"

"Oh!" She clapped a hand to her mouth and shook her head. "I can't talk to you here," she whispered. "I'm trying so hard not to let the guests—our patients—see how upset I am. And my employer . . ."

"Of course. I can see it might set the cat among the pigeons. We'll go over to the Wadebridge police station."

"I can't leave. I'm on duty."

"You must want us to find your . . . friend's murderer as quickly as possible, I'm sure." Megan kept her voice calm and friendly. The last thing she wanted was more hysterics, for her own sake, regardless of the patients. "You have a private room here, don't you? We can go there, no problem. You'll be close enough if you're needed. Ought you to tell someone where you'll be?"

"No. No, if they want me they'll ring through."

They went upstairs. Several doors led off the landing. One was a solid affair of polished oak, more like a front door than an interior door.

Stella noticed Megan looking at it. "That's Dr Fenwick's flat. The owner. He's downstairs chatting with the guests before dinner. This is my room." She unlocked a door.

No Indian bedspreads and cushions on the floor here. The bedsitter was very comfortably, even luxuriously furnished in the blues and greens that a redhead would naturally favour. Megan remembered Margery telling her that Stella was well paid because of the difficulty of getting weekend staff.

A couple of fashion magazines lay on a table, a third on the floor, half covering a pair of flat sandals, but no books were visible. Nor was either a wireless or a record-player, an odd omission in these days of ubiquitous music. What was it Shakespeare said about people who didn't like music? Megan couldn't remember.

On the wall hung a portrait in oils of the occupant. That was why she seemed familiar, Megan realised. At the scene of the crime, her image was everywhere. Megan glanced back at the subject of the painting. It was a good likeness, the colour looking somehow more natural than the touch of lipstick and dusting of rouge that Stella was now wearing.

Stella turned away, head bowed. Her voice trembled. "He'll never paint me again."

"I'm sorry. Let's get this over with." They sat down. Megan's chair was almost too soft, like the Mama Bear's, wonderful for lounging, but all wrong for conducting an interview. Taking notes was going to be difficult. She did her best to sit upright. "We'll go back to yesterday morning."

"Morning? But Geoff was killed in the evening!"

"I'm afraid I have to fill in all sorts of nit-picking details for my report. You were in Padstow, you told DI Pearce? How did you get there, and what time did you arrive?"

"I don't know the time. A bit late for opening the gallery, if you want to know the truth, but it's no good trying to hurry Geoff. He took me in his MG, because he was going to Tintagel to pick up that horrible, horrible dagger from the ironsmith. How I wish he'd never had the idea of getting the damn thing made! Just because he thought the light would reflect differently than from the sword."

"You disagreed?"

"About the light? I expect he's . . . oh, he *was* right. But who cares? A waste of money, if you ask me. And effort."

"Did you go to art school?"

"What's that got to do with anything?"

"I'm just trying to understand," Megan said soothingly. She wasn't quite sure why she had asked, but it linked somehow with something in the back of her mind.

"I took a few classes. Painting bored me, but sculpture was more fun." Once she got going, she talked readily. "I love the feel of the stone when I've polished it really smooth. I see people in the shops fondling my seals and porpoises. They sell quite well. In fact, I sold one yesterday morning, at Nick's shop."

"That was before Geoffrey Clark returned?"

"Yes. He got there just before Nick phoned from London. I wasn't expecting him so early. Usually when he goes to Tintagel he moons about the castle for ages, 'catching the vibes,' he says. Used to say. But he wanted to show me that damn dagger. He was unwrapping it when Nick rang. Of course I told him Nick's news. He started spouting about how unfair it was, so I told him not to get his knickers in a twist. I guessed he was probably hungry—he wouldn't answer when I asked but he tends to skip breakfast—and it was making him irritable. So I went across the street to pick up a couple of pasties. When I came back . . . Well, I'm sure you know by now what he'd done."

"He wrecked several of Mr Gresham's paintings."

"I was horrified. I decided we'd better make ourselves scarce. I wrote a note to Nick and cleared out my stuff while Geoff fetched his car from the car park. Then I closed the shop and we drove to Padstow. The bastard was in such a hurry to have a go at painting the dagger, he wouldn't drive me up to the farm, so I hitchhiked."

"Why did you clear out your sculptures?"

"Well, obviously, Nick was going to be so furious he wouldn't let me go on selling there. It wasn't till later I started worrying that he'd be mad enough to beat up—"

Megan held up a hand to stop her. "We'll get to that in a minute. Where did Clark park in Padstow?"

"The Strand. Hell, I suppose it's still there!"

"Did you go to his gallery with him?"

"Yes. It wasn't far out of the way to get to the Wadebridge Road to thumb a lift or catch a bus. I still hoped to talk him into taking me."

"What time did you get there?"

Stella shrugged. "No idea."

"Did you go in?"

"Just for a minute. I wanted to take off my tights for hitching. I wear them for work—here and in the shops, not for sculpting—but I hate them, hate nylon on my feet. And I got a drink of water."

"Presumably the CLOSED sign was up when you arrived. Did Clark flip it to OPEN?"

"I . . . I don't remember."

"Never mind. Why did you hitch a lift, rather than phoning for someone at the farm to pick you up?"

"I couldn't do that. Doug lets us have the bus if it's arranged in advance, but he uses it on the farm, too, and he gets shirty if you push it. Besides, I like hitching. You meet some interesting people, though sometimes hereabouts you're on the back of a haycart.

Yesterday I was picked up by an Aussie tourist who took me all the way to the beginning of the track. He had a hired car and he wouldn't risk it on the potholes. Luckily I was wearing flats."

"Did he tell you his name?"

"Bert? Pete? Mike? Something utterly unmemorable."

She hadn't noticed the make or colour of the car, hadn't really listened when Bert or Pete or Mike had talked about his plans.

"To tell the truth," she admitted, "I was still a bit rattled by what Geoff had done. I was thinking about what on earth I was going to say to the others."

"What *did* you say?"

"Nothing, not then. I chickened out. My studio is at the end so I just sneaked in and got to work."

"You didn't speak to anyone. Did you see anyone, or might anyone have seen you? Or heard you working?"

"Someone might have looked through a window, I suppose. I wasn't chipping or grinding, just polishing, so I wasn't making any noise. But like I told you, I started worrying about just how mad Nick would be. I worked out that if he arrived in Launceston at about four, then went home and discovered the damage, he wasn't likely to get to Padstow before half five. So I went and told Marge and we talked Doug into going with us to the pub, so I could keep an eye on Geoff without him knowing."

"And in fact, you saw Nick Gresham arrive at Clark's gallery, though some time later."

"If only we'd got across the street quicker! Doug had gone off to the gents and Marge wanted to wait for him. I had to haul her along and by the time we got there—"

"It wouldn't have made the slightest difference. I'm sure you must know by now that Gresham did not stab Clark just as you arrived in the studio. Whatever you saw, it was not that. The medical evidence shows he died long before."

"Oh, medical evidence!" Stella said scornfully. "You forget, I've worked with doctors. I know they'll give a wrong diagnosis rather than admit they don't know the answer."

"I assure you, there is absolutely no question that Clark died before four o'clock, and probably before three. No one is blaming you for jumping to conclusions when you saw him lying dead with Gresham beside him. You were in a perfectly understandable nervous state. But I would advise you not to go on claiming that Gresham killed Clark. In fact, I'd like you to think back to that moment which you misinterpreted and try to tell me what you actually observed, rather than what you imagined."

That was too much for Stella's composure. "I can't, I can't," she wailed. "I don't want to think about it." She buried her face in her hands and started to sob. "It was horrible. Horrible!"

Megan had overestimated the woman's sangfroid. Once she had pulled herself together, she had seemed so cool and calm! The ever-unsympathetic Scumble might just as well have come himself, she thought, for all the good she'd done.

"I realise it's difficult to think about it so soon after it happened," she said. "I won't press you now, but we'd appreciate it if you'd really try to picture the scene, as soon as you feel up to it. You'd be surprised how much detail people remember when they put their minds to it. I'm sure you must be eager to see the murderer brought to justice."

"What difference will it make?" Stella moaned. "It won't bring him back."

This response was not uncommon and it always irritated Megan. She suppressed her irritation. "All the same, we'll be back. Either I or Detective Inspector Scumble. We have to make quite sure to get every scrap of information you can possibly provide. I'm sorry, that's just the way it is. Don't move, I'll let myself out now."

Head still bowed, Stella didn't stir as she left.

She was about to start down the stairs when a tall, lean man appeared at the foot, about to come up. He stood aside with a smile and a slight bow, gesturing for her to go first. He was in his late fifties at a guess, very well dressed in a formal style, with silver hair still thick. He gave an impression of being well pleased with life.

As Megan neared the bottom, he said in a friendly way, "You must be a friend of Miss Weller?"

She smiled at him. "Not exactly. I dropped in on a matter of business. You must be Dr Fenwick? My name's Pencarrow. I hope you don't mind my coming here." Because if he did, next time it would be the Wadebridge nick for Stella.

"Not at all—" He glanced at her left hand. "—Miss Pencarrow. Miss Weller is bound to have a few matters to be cleared up at such a time. I trust she's not in any difficulties?"

An odd way of putting it when Stella had just lost her lover in grim circumstances! But she didn't want her employer to know she was upset. Megan quite understood. She herself wouldn't want Scumble to know if she was upset over a personal matter; it was bad enough that he guessed something of her former relationship with Ken Faraday, alias the boy wonder. Fenwick might not even know about Clark's place in Stella's life. "Living in sin," as he'd no doubt call it, wasn't exactly a recommendation for a responsible job.

As Megan wasn't about to arrest her, she said, "Not that I'm aware of. I may have to come by again, but I'll do my best not to disrupt things. You have a beautiful place here."

"Thank you. I'd give you a tour, but as you say, we don't want to disrupt things. My guests are assembling for dinner. I dine with them on Fridays so I must be down again in a few minutes. I find it the best way to discover if there are any little, niggling discontents to be remedied. Good evening, Miss Pencarrow." With a nod of farewell, he went upstairs, a surprisingly youthful spring in his step.

Megan went out to the car. PC Lubbock had parked it to one side under a tree, where Dr Fenwick, even if he had happened to look out, might well have overlooked it and so not known of the police presence. The constable was leaning against the far side of it, whistling softly and tunelessly.

Lubbock straightened not quite to attention and gave a sort of sloppy salute. "Message from the inspector, ma'am. He won't need you again this evening. I'm to take you to Launceston so you can type up your reports and statements ready for a meeting with Superintendent Egerton in Bodmin at eight ack emma. You're to pick him up at home at seven."

With a groan, Megan got into the panda. She'd be lucky to get five hours' sleep.

The radio went on muttering to itself. They were nearly in Launceston when their call signal was heard and Lubbock turned up the volume.

It was Wilkes, announcing that Leila Arden had been found. She had sprained her ankle on her walk home from Trevone Cove, naturally on a rarely frequented stretch of footpath overlooked by no houses and no farmer's fields.

"Damn," said Megan. Yet another lead had evaporated.

TWENTY-EIGHT

Eleanor's telephone rang at five past ten the next morning. As usual on a summer Saturday, she was not planning one of her donation-collecting drives in the countryside. The roads were too busy with tourists arriving and leaving. She had just finished a shopping list and was about to go out. Teazle was waiting at the door with her lead already clipped on.

"Eleanor, it's Nick. I need help!" He sounded desperate.

"What on earth's wrong?"

"The press. I've got reporters coming out me ear 'oles."

"Oh dear! It must have been in this morning's papers."

"It was. With a picture of yours truly, and one of Geoff's shop with King Arthur's glower glimmering through the glass. I haven't got time to deal with them, and I can't afford to shut up shop—"

"Didn't you say you have nothing left to sell?"

"I was exaggerating a bit in the heat of the moment. Eleanor, dear Eleanor, please pretty please could you come over and sit in the shop so that I can lock my studio door?"

"Nick, you know cash registers don't like me!"

"If things go as far as actually making a sale, you can call me in."

"But I don't understand your *good* paintings. I can't possibly explain them. I take it you've found enough of them undamaged in the studio to move to the shop."

"Just tell people I have similar work hanging in a major London gallery. That should bring in the punters."

"I'd hate to lose you any sales."

"I'm going to lose all sales—or my mind—if you won't come."

"And you expect me to deal with hordes of reporters, too?"

"I'm pretty sure they don't know you're involved. You just have to play ignorant."

"Oh, all right. But—"

"But me no buts. If you don't come quickly they'll be bashing down my door."

"I'm on my way," Eleanor said valiantly.

As Nick had said, hordes of reporters were ravening at the door or champing at the bit, or both. Eleanor had scarcely stepped inside Nick's shop when several recognised her from her previous brief notoriety. Protected by the police, she had then managed to avoid all but one, David Skan, a nice young man from the *North Cornwall Times*. She had given him an exclusive comment, if no information, more or less in exchange for his promise to press his editor to let him write an article about the LonStar shop and LonStar's good work.

He had succeeded, though the article had focussed more on the "Little Old Lady Saves Starving Billions" angle than Eleanor would have preferred. Still, the embarrassment was mitigated by the rush of business to the Port Mabyn LonStar shop. Though the rush had soon abated, Eleanor had noticed an increase in donations of goods to sell and Jocelyn said visitors, receipts, and monetary donations were still higher than before, as was the number of volunteers.

The moment Eleanor appeared on the threshold of Nick's gallery, David Skan took her under his wing. A local reporter among the London crowd, he had only what authority his height and a voice as yet unmarred by cigarette smoking gave him, but it was enough to clear a path to the counter. He helped her up on the high stool behind the terrifying cash register.

She found herself faced with seven or eight men and a couple of women, all peppering her with questions.

"Why did the police release Gresham after arresting him for murder?"

"What did Gresham have to do with Geoffrey Clark's murder?"

"Can't you persuade him to give us a statement?"

"Was Gresham jealous of Clark's commercial success?"

"Why won't he give us a statement?"

That she could answer, and was happy to do so. "Mr Gresham is extremely busy because . . ." she started. They were too busy shouting out more questions to listen. She had always found a soft voice ultimately more persuasive than a loud one, but obviously that tactic didn't work when confronting a pack of newshounds on the scent of a crime story.

"Shut up, you lot!" yelled Skan. "Let the lady get a word in edgeways!"

Silence fell.

"Mr Gresham is extremely busy," Eleanor began again, "because he's working on an important commission from America and has a deadline to meet. Now that the merit of his work is recognised in London . . ." She continued to tout the importance of Nick's work, even bringing in his contribution to the Export Drive (hadn't she heard something about an Export Drive recently? There usually seemed to be one on).

The national reporters turned away, disappointed. One muttered something about notifying the Arts Page people, another mentioned his paper's financial editor, and a third glanced for the first time towards the paintings, apparently calculating the odds of picking up something cheap before everyone caught on. Three local people, Skan, an elderly chap from southern Cornwall, and a woman from Plymouth, clustered round Eleanor. A couple who had hovered in the background, actually examining Nick's work, drifted closer.

"'Local Artist Makes Good,'" said the woman reporter, scribbling in her notebook. "Can you give us some details, dear?"

"'—Hits the Big Time,'" the elderly man preferred.

"'—Fame Spreads Worldwide,'" Skan said enthusiastically.

Eleanor told them about Alarian's illustrious art gallery in Albemarle Street, and surprised herself by finding words to describe Nick's serious work that seemed to be intelligible to her listeners. Either that, or they were as ignorant as she was and pretending to understand.

She was about to run out of things to say—and three of the national reporters still lingered hopefully—when the couple interrupted.

"We'd like to buy a painting," the woman said hesitantly.

"Oh, good!" said Eleanor, then stared in dismay at the lurking cash register. If she called Nick to come and deal with it, the reporters would nab him. But who could tell what sort of a mess she'd make of things if she tried to tackle it.

"What's the matter?" Skan whispered.

Eleanor, feeling silly, whispered back an explanation.

"Never fear, Gallant Reporter Rushes to Rescue. My dad's a greengrocer. Let me at it."

In the meantime the other two locals left. The woman's husband, a military-looking man, short but very upright, with a bristling grey moustache, had put his arm round her shoulders. Eleanor saw that her eyes were filling with tears.

"Not if it's going to make you cry," he said firmly.

"Oh no, it'll be a comfort. Please, George." She turned away to stare at the folding screen hung with wildflower miniatures and a fresh set of landscapes.

In a low voice, George said to Eleanor, "Sorry. The one we want is *Slow Movement, Shostakovich Second Piano Concerto*. We're both rather keen on Shostakovich. My wife feels a special connection with the second piano concerto—he wrote it for his son's nineteenth birthday, you know. Maxim, the pianist. Our son was killed in the war when he was just nineteen. Shostakovich expresses the grief of war like nobody else. And Gresham's painting . . . She sees something in it. I don't know if it's what he intended, and it doesn't really matter, but it seems to Jessie to show the composer's wife—a woman, anyway—standing at a window with a baby in her arms. Goodness only knows whether that's what was going on in the composer's mind. If she thinks it'll bring her comfort, I'll take it."

David Skan was scribbling madly in his notebook. "Sir," he said, "I don't want to intrude, but I'm going to be writing an article—I'm a reporter for the *North Cornwall Times*—about Mr Gresham's work. I would really appreciate your permission to mention what this particular painting means to you, and if you wouldn't mind giving me your name . . . ?"

"No names. But otherwise go ahead, if you can make it anonymous."

"Sure. May I photograph the painting before you go off with it?"

George havered. "I'll ask Jess if she'd mind," he said in the end.

His wife gave her permission. Skan was obviously disappointed when he saw the painting, a nebulous affair with a square of dazzling white that could be a window looking onto the endless snows of Russia and beside it what could, indeed, be the figure of a woman cradling a child in her arms. As a newspaper photograph, it would probably come out as nothing but a blur. He took a couple of shots anyway—the *North Cornwall Times* didn't run to photographers, even for what was supposed to be a sensational local murder story.

Wrapping the picture in endless quantities of white paper from the roll she found under the counter, Eleanor marvelled at the emotion both the music and the art could evoke. She'd have to listen to Nick's record of the concerto sometime.

Not till he was finished with *Land of Hope and Glory*, though.

True to his offer, Skan dealt with the couple's receipt and deposited a very nice, fat cheque in the drawer of the till. Then he helped George carry the painting to their car.

"I'll be back," he said to Eleanor as he left. "You owe me!"

The woman turned to Eleanor before following them. She had mastered her tears. "Please thank Mr Gresham for me," she said softly, holding out her hand. "I'll . . . I'll try to write to him."

Eleanor pressed her hand. "I'll tell him," she promised.

The other reporters had given up and gone off, so Eleanor went and knocked on Nick's studio door. There was no response.

"Nick, it's me! I've sold a painting."

"Are they gone?"

She didn't need to ask who. "Yes. At least, for now. Have you got another picture to hang in the space?" She was quite proud of herself for thinking of that practical detail.

He opened the door, turning the knob with a cleanish rag. "Good work. What did you sell?"

"The Shostakovich concerto."

"Good heavens! Really? What did they pay?"

"The price on the back. Isn't that right?"

"Without haggling? Good heavens, I regard that more as a pious hope than bearing any relationship to reality. Must be my new notoriety—or your salesmanship. Can I employ you?"

"Of course not, Nick. It was very touching." She told him the couple's story. "And she said to thank you."

He nodded. "As a matter of fact, that is pretty much what it was supposed to be. There's a sort of tenderness about the music . . . How gratifying that someone else would hear and see it just the same way. You managed to work the till all right?"

"Actually," Eleanor said guiltily, "Mr Skan did it for me. The *North Cornwall Times* reporter."

"Hell! What's he going to expect in exchange?"

"Just a nice little exclusive," said a cheerful voice from the doorway. "I won't keep you from your work for long, Gresham, but there must be *something* you can tell me without bringing down the wrath of CaRaDoC on our heads."

A look of fiendish glee crossed Nick's face. "Yes, indeed. Might even do us some good in certain quarters. You can say that I was arrested on false charges by a—let's see, I think overzealous is the word I want—yes, by an overzealous detective. I won't tell you his name, but he's based in Bodmin and I'm sure a shrewd chap like you can find out. And you can say that I have every confidence that the murderer will soon be collared, now that Detective Inspector Scumble, ably assisted by Detective Sergeant Pencarrow, is in charge. That should make Scumble mind his manners next time he grills me."

"I wouldn't count on it," said Eleanor.

"No, you're probably right. Anyway, that's all I have to say, except thanks for helping Mrs Trewynn to sell my picture, so be a good fellow and hop it."

"Okay. It's not much but it's more than anyone else has got out of you. They'll be back, though, so you'd better lock your door again."

"I shall." Nick grinned. "Don't worry, I'm not going to spoil your exclusive."

"Ta muchly. And by the way, congrats on achieving an international reputation!" He disappeared.

Nick turned to Eleanor. "A *what?*"

"I had to tell them something. They were besieging me. It's true, after all. *Land of Hope and Glory* isn't the first American commission you've had."

"The last one was enlarging a landscape to match a sofa!"

"But still, it's true. And I can't see why you should object."

"I don't. I'm just a bit stunned. It was the national dailies you told?"

"Yes. And I told them about Alarian's Gallery, too," Eleanor confessed.

"Ye gods!"

"They went off muttering about Arts Page editors."

"Ye gods! You know, I think Alarian had better be warned, just in case someone actually goes to talk to him, or writes about it without talking to him. Would you mind ringing him up for me?"

"No, of course not."

"And now I come to think of it, it might be just as well to warn him that he'll probably be asked to give me an alibi."

"Don't you think you ought to do that yourself?"

"No," Nick said firmly. "It's a perfect mission for your diplomatic skills. Besides, I have a painting to finish."

"And there goes the bell. I'd better get back to the shop."

"Sell a few more three-figure pictures for me, will you? Let me know when the place is empty again and I'll hang a replacement."

So Eleanor returned to the shop. The locals were beginning to filter in now, most having read about the murder and Nick's arrest in the morning papers or heard it on the wireless news, but not yet aware of his release. A few pretended to look at pictures, but most were simply avid for information. Eleanor fed them a selection from what she had told the national reporters and what Nick had said to David Skan.

Most went away empty-handed, tut-tutting about false arrest and police misconduct. However, three bought paintings, two from sympathy and one shamefaced at being one of the inquisitive masses.

Two miniatures—the cheapest things in the gallery—and one landscape: Eleanor was quite pleased with herself. It wasn't till she put up the CLOSED sign at lunchtime that she realised she hadn't done her weekend shopping and now the shops were shut till Monday. Oh well, she had leftover sausages and several tins at home, and there was always bread and cheese, or fish and chips if she felt extravagant. However, she had also forgotten to telephone Alarian to warn him of the impending visit of the police—which very likely was no longer impending.

TWENTY-NINE

In the meantime, Megan had risen at an ungodly hour, picked up the 1100 without falling into any verbal traps set by the sergeant—if she dodged often enough the sneaky bastard just might give up trying someday—and picked up Scumble as instructed.

The previous evening he had stayed late in Bodmin and been driven straight home from there, so she hadn't seen him. He had not read her reports and she hadn't heard the results of the various house-to-house enquiries. The first thing he wanted was an oral report on her meeting with Stella Weller. He listened with his eyes closed. He looked tired, Megan noticed, taking her eyes from the road for long enough to glance at his face. Again she wondered whether he had bitten off more than he could chew.

But when she finished, he said, "Not bad, Pencarrow. You're learning. We've a long way to go yet, but things are beginning to come together."

They were? Megan was surprised enough almost to voice her surprise. She managed to stop herself in time to say instead, "Did the children in Port Mabyn confirm Aunt—Nick Gresham's story."

"Yes, of course," he said impatiently. "Your aunt may forget to tell me things, but when she remembers, I believe her. Usually. All the same, there are ways Gresham could have faked the Paddington phone call. We should be able to get phone records from the GPO, but we still need a signed statement from the art bigwig in London that he was there that morning. We have to dot all our *i*'s and cross all our *t*'s on this one."

Megan's heart sank. "You want me to go up to London, sir?"

"No, no, I can't spare you just now. You're the one with the contact at the Yard, though. You'll have to ring the boy wonder and talk him into doing it for us."

Not good, but a big improvement on having to see Ken face-to-face. And nice to know the gov'nor couldn't spare her, although she wondered what exactly he needed her for.

"Yes, sir." Her concentration split between driving and thinking out what she needed to know, she had no attention to spare for the moorland scenery she usually enjoyed. "Have Jeanette Jones and Tom Lennox's alibis been checked?"

"Not yet. There's still plenty of work to be done on the statements we took yesterday."

"What about Leila Arden? I heard she was found."

"Yeah. Pity she hadn't made a run for it. We'd have known who we were looking for at least. She claims she stayed at the farm working till three. She didn't see or talk to anyone. Not the sociable kind, if you ask me. Then she walked down to Padstow to buy glue and varnish."

"Couldn't one of the others have picked them up for her?"

"She says she's tried that before and they've bought the wrong kind."

"If she's so particular, the shop people might remember her. But that's too late, anyway, and she could have gone down earlier."

"Top marks, Pencarrow."

Megan had long ago stopped wincing at his sarcasm. "Any suggestion of a motive, sir?"

"She hated his guts, that much was obvious if unstated, but I didn't find out why. That's one of your jobs."

"Yes, sir. Did anything useful come out of the house-to-house in Padstow?"

"Not much. A couple of local people think King Arthur's Gallery had the CLOSED sign up all day, but couldn't swear to it. One got sarky"—Scumble was a fine one to talk!—"about having better things to do than stare at his neighbour's door all day, as reported verbatim by some idiot constable. No one noticed anyone going in or out."

"There must have been a lot of tourists passing."

"Yes, the place is swamped with holiday people already. Must be sheer hell in August. But I'm not ready to put out a call in the press for casual passers-by who might have seen one of our suspects going in, not until we've got it narrowed down."

Requests for assistance from the general public tended to bring a response from countless cranks, would-be detectives, and other equally imaginative citizens. In most circumstances, winnowing the few grains of wheat (some of which would prove to be weed seeds) from vast quantities of chaff was apt to absorb more police time than it was worth.

Megan pulled out to overtake a lorry loaded with bales of hay. The inspector closed his eyes tight and went on talking, rather fast, as if to take his mind off the manoeuvre. "We do know the artists' co-op shop was open all day except for the lunch hour. That doesn't help much, though, as Clark may well have been killed between one and two. I had another word with Rudd, who now claims he stayed inside, ate a sandwich, and sketched out some new pictures. He's got the sketches to show for it, which proves nothing, of course."

"And Port Mabyn's house-to-house?" Megan asked.

"Now there's a proper village, where people mind each other's business! Not just a tourist trap. Gresham's place was open until shortly after noon. Then an 'artistic-looking bloke' walked down the hill from the north and went into the gallery. The way Clark dressed left little doubt of his profession! A few minutes later, the sign was turned to CLOSED. Shortly after that, he came out again and walked back up the hill. After he'd gone—How long after is anyone's guess; we don't have actual times for most of this—the woman came out and went over to the bakery to buy a couple of pasties. She didn't go back to the gallery but waited a couple of minutes outside the bakery till Clark came down in his MG and picked her up."

"It all fits in with what she told me, sir."

"That's my impression from what you've told me. Surprisingly accurate recall for someone who imagined she saw Gresham stab Clark."

"Very different circumstances, sir!" Megan protested. "It must have been a nasty shock seeing Clark destroy Gresham's paintings, but nothing compared to seeing her lover lying dead with a dagger in his back."

"Very true," Scumble conceded. "Now, if you've got any more questions, save 'em till you've read the reports. Concentrate on your driving!"

The advice was quite unnecessary. It was still early enough for little traffic to be about, and once Megan had turned right off the A30, they went straight down the Launceston Road towards Bodmin town centre. She didn't even have to negotiate the centre itself as the police station was on the side of their approach. She drove round behind the building and parked.

As they walked back to the steps, the inspector glanced at his watch. "All right, you can read the reports while I tackle the Super."

"You don't want me to go with you, sir?"

"Not this time. Egerton's going to start out unhappy about us having proved his man doesn't know his arse from his elbow, so I've got to make him happy about the progress we've made."

Megan's mind boggled at the very notion of Scumble smoothing ruffled feathers. "Yes, sir," she said doubtfully.

Halfway up the steps, he turned and glared at her. "I know tact's not my strong suit, but I managed him before, when we had practically nothing to go on, didn't I? We're a lot further on now. In fact, if you ask me, we've done bloody well for just one day. It's just a matter of maybe smoothing the edges of a few speculations to make them look more like facts. I don't need you standing there looking as if I've gone out of my mind. I do need you to bring yourself up to date on everything we've got so far."

"Yes, sir." Megan decided to seize the opportunity to talk to Ken without the gov'nor listening in. The chance of catching him actually in the office at the Yard at any given moment was pretty slim, but eight o'clock in the morning was as likely a time as any, and she could make a case for having tried before he went out on some job.

The stacks of folders on the battered desk in their borrowed office had grown to impressive proportions. The two wooden chairs had reproduced—there were now half a dozen—and a long metal table as battered as the desk stood against one wall. On another wall were drawing-pinned a street plan of Padstow, with coloured pins marking various spots, and a map of the area, including Padstow, Trevone Bay, and Upper Trewithen Farm. The latter showed public footpaths as well as roads and farm tracks. A second telephone had been added to the one on the desk, and two more stood on the table. The ancient biscuit tin was gone; in its place were boxes of brand-new pencils, biros, and varicoloured drawing-pins.

"It looks as if you've already made quite an impression, sir."

"Oh, the Super's got them cooperating, I won't say he hasn't."

Scumble went off to work his flim-flam on Egerton. Megan sat down in the swivel chair behind the desk and pulled a telephone towards her.

"This is DS Pencarrow. Get me Scotland Yard, please. I want to speak to DS Faraday if possible."

Waiting for the connection, she turned the chair to look out of the window. She hadn't had time to even glance that way before. Now she realised that the lucky coppers who had a window on this side of the building had a view over the town, across the valley to the obelisk on top of Beacon Hill. Perhaps the unlucky souls on the other side got new desks to compensate.

"DS Pencarrow? I have DS Faraday on the line. I'm putting you through."

Taken by surprise—she hadn't really expected to get straight through to him—Megan hadn't worked out what she was going to say. Ken beat her to the draw.

"Meggie! Sorry, *Megan*. What a pleasant surprise. I hope this means you're coming up to town. We must make a date for dinner."

The public-school accent was more pronounced on the phone, the charm slightly diminished but still there. Megan wondered what his current leggy blonde model would think if she could hear him turning it on for a fellow police officer. She was glad Scumble didn't expect her to go to London herself. As long as she could win Ken's cooperation . . .

"'Fraid not. Strictly business. The gov'nor's hoping you can check an alibi for us."

"I expect so. We've just wrapped up a big job. If it'll give me an excuse to postpone writing up reports, I'll do my best to talk my gov'nor into it."

"Yes, we'd like you to call in person, or we could have phoned ourselves."

"Where is it? Whitechapel or Wimbledon?"

"Oh, a cut above Wimbledon. Much posher. At least, that's my impression. It's an art gallery in Albemarle Street."

Ken whistled. "Alarian's."

"I knew it was right up your street."

"Caters to the cognoscenti. The rich cognoscenti. He's a cagey bloke, and the art business is rife with fraud, but as far as I know we've never had any hint—"

"We're not suggesting he's not on the up and up. We just need to make sure our man was there on Thursday morning and what time he left." She gave him the details. "Be tactful. Alarian's taken a couple of Gresham's pictures to sell, which I gather is a big deal. We don't want to give the impression he's in trouble with the law when we're ninety-nine percent certain he's not. But we've got a delicate situation here and we need a hundred percent, including a signed statement."

"Nicholas Gresham. Wasn't he involved in that jewelry business?" What a memory! No one could say Ken wasn't a good detective.

"Peripherally, as a next-door neighbour."

"What's he mixed up in now?"

"Ken, I haven't got time to tell you any more now. I've got a stack of reports to read and you have some to write. Will you do it?"

"I'll put it up to the gov'nor—he should be in any minute now—and ring you back. I imagine the gallery doesn't open till ten but I might be able to knock Alarian up earlier."

"Thanks a lot, Ken. I'm sure Nick will be very grateful."

"Nick? Hey—"

Megan hung up. She had no intention of letting him interrogate her about her use of Nick's nickname and the degree of familiarity involved. She mustn't let him revert to the subject when he rang back. Not that there was anything to tell, she thought gloomily. Perhaps she ought to take a serious look at the worthies her mother regularly produced on her monthly visits home, hope springing eternal in the parental breast. But she thought of them collectively as "worthies," not a good sign.

With a sigh, she turned to the reports.

Like any detective with the ambition to rise through the ranks, she had developed the technique of skimming to a high art. She went rapidly through the stack, pausing now and then to read something in depth, making notes as she went and occasionally scribbling a question mark in the margins. When Scumble returned, she was two thirds of the way to the bottom.

He was grinning. "The Super is delighted with our progress."

"Well done, sir."

The grin faded. "Of course, you realise what this means, Pencarrow."

"Sir?"

"The inquest's on Monday. The verdict can hardly come in as anything other than murder. Mr Egerton sincerely hopes that it won't be 'by person or persons unknown.' In other words, from now on he expects miracles. So we'd better get down to it and see if we can at least produce a rabbit from a hat."

THIRTY

At one o'clock, after thankfully turning the sign to CLOSED and locking the street door, Eleanor had great difficulty persuading Nick to stop painting for long enough to eat lunch. He was in the throes of inspiration, but she was tired and hungry.

"Don't be silly. You have to eat sometime, and it might as well be now, while you've got me to get it for you. Have you got anything edible upstairs?"

"Not a crumb. I was away for three nights, remember, four including my time in clink, and you fed me last night."

"Well, I didn't have a chance to shop this morning," Eleanor said crossly.

"Sorry!" Contrite, he plunged his hand into his pocket, smearing yellow paint on his brown trousers, and pulled out a ten-shilling note. "I hadn't thought. Here, I'll spring for pasties. If you don't mind getting them. I just want to . . ." He turned back to his easel, already reaching out with his paintbrush.

Eleanor told Teazle to stay, unlocked the door again, and crossed the street, glad that the bakery stayed open at lunchtime once the tourist season had begun. Returning a few minutes later with the fragrant paper bag in her hand, she heard the telephone on the counter ringing before she pushed open the door. She fancied it sounded impatient, no doubt because she suspected it could have been ringing the entire time she'd been gone without Nick taking the slightest notice.

Lifting the receiver, she gave Nick's number.

"Aunt Nell?" came Megan's incredulous voice. "What on earth are you doing there? Where have you been? I was about to radio for your local bobby to check—"

"For pity's sake, Megan, why shouldn't I be here? Nick's my next-door neighbour. As it happens, I've been taking care of the shop for him so he could paint. I've sold several pictures and the cash register has survived intact. I just popped out to buy pasties for our lunch."

"Nick's there? Why didn't he answer the phone?"

"Did you ring just to scold us?"

"No, of course not. Sorry, I've been worried. Remember, there's a murderer out there who might well think you or Nick is a danger to him. After all, you both know all the people involved."

"Him or her."

"Or her. I rang to tell you that the inquest will be on Monday afternoon, two o'clock at the village school in Padstow. You and Nick have to be there."

"Oh dear, I won't have to give evidence, will I?"

"I very much doubt it, unless we've arrested someone by then."

"Not Nick!"

"Not Nick what?"

"You're not going to arrest him?"

"No. Actually that's the other thing I was ringing him for. Mr Alarian's given us a statement that clears Nick completely. The inspector can't think of any way he could have been in Albemarle Street at eleven and King Arthur's Gallery by three."

"Thank heaven! I'll tell him. And I'll get him there on Monday even if he hasn't finished his blasted *Land of Hope and Glory*."

"Thanks, Aunt Nell. I'll see you then. 'Bye."

"Good-bye, dear."

Eleanor replaced the receiver in a thoughtful mood. She had forgotten about the inevitable coroner's inquest. She and Nick had to attend. Who else? Certainly Marge and Doug Rosevear and Stella. Could she use the occasion to reconcile Nick and Stella? It was a pity to break up a useful working relationship—she wasn't sure it could be called friendship—over a misunderstanding. Not to mention the added advantage that restoring amity would give Nick someone other than Eleanor herself to mind the shop should he receive any more urgent commissions.

Suppose she phoned the Riverview Home and offered to pick Stella up on the way to the inquest in Padstow. The worst that could happen would be that she'd say no. Eleanor would have to be honest and tell her Nick would be a fellow-passenger. She must warn Nick, too. You couldn't expect cooperation if you sprang unpleasant surprises on people.

Besides, Nick would smell a rat as soon as she told him they were driving by way of Wadebridge instead of parking in Rock and taking the ferry across the Camel.

No harm in trying, she decided. She picked up the pasty bag and was turning to go through to the studio when the phone rang again.

"Eleanor?"

"Yes. How on earth did you know I was here, Joce?"

"Megan just told me. She rang to invite me to the inquest. She said you'll be going."

"I don't think it's an invitation, more of a . . . a summons. Like when you break the speed limit."

"I do not break the speed limit," Jocelyn said severely.

"Well, nor do I. The Incorruptible's practically incapable of it, like the vicar's putt-putt. Those motor scooters don't go over thirty, do they?"

"I have no idea, but I'm quite sure Timothy never breaks the speed limit. Knowingly." The vicar was the vaguest of men, as his wife admitted only to very close friends. "What has this to do with anything?"

"I think that's what they call it, a summons. I suppose it's a kind of legal invitation but you're not allowed to send your regrets."

"Megan said it's most unlikely I'd be called to give evidence, but I suppose we'll have to go. Nicholas, too, she said. We might as well all drive together."

For a moment, Eleanor was afraid she'd have to abandon her plan for rapprochement. But Jocelyn should understand. Christianity was supposed to be about forgiveness, after all, though Eleanor had met a few Christians who were among the most unforgiving people she knew.

She explained her hopes of bringing Nick and Stella back together.

"That hussy? Do you think it's wise? She's so very volatile. Eleanor, you're still investigating her, aren't you?"

"I don't know what you mean!" Eleanor was indignant, but a brief survey of her motives revealed to her that she was indeed still curious about what made Stella tick.

"We'll take my car, of course," Jocelyn said decisively. "You'll sit beside me, so they'll have to share the back seat. That's if they're both willing. We can drop in to call on Mrs Batchelor on the way back."

"I don't know if Nick will agree to that part. Entertaining elderly ladies—"

"Why not? He entertains you frequently."

"Jocelyn, that's thoroughly disingenuous! Still, I can but put it to him."

"Come to supper tonight and tell me all about it. Timothy will be worrying over his sermon and won't disturb us."

Eleanor accepted as gracefully as possible under the circumstances. Not that she minded singing for her supper. At least the problem of what to have was solved, and Jocelyn was an excellent cook.

She took Nick his pasty and, as he wolfed it down, sitting on a stool and staring at his picture, she laid her proposal before him.

"What's that? Meet Stella? If you and Mrs Stearns think it's a good idea, it's all right with me." He tossed a last morsel to the dog and reached for his paintbrush.

Hoping the paint Teazle ingested with the scrap of pastry wouldn't poison her, Eleanor finished her pasty at a more leisurely pace. Assuming Nick didn't expect her to reopen the shop for the afternoon—he was too absorbed to notice her departure—she then went home via the back doors, so that Teazle could have a run in the bushes.

She wondered whether to ask for Miss Weller or Miss Maris. Weller, she decided. Even in these enlightened—*enlightened?* Well, interesting—times, Star of the Sea didn't seem an appropriate name for a nurse.

She guessed right. Miss Weller was called to the phone. To Eleanor's considerable surprise, she accepted the offer of a lift to the inquest. Still more surprising, she said, rather grudgingly, "I suppose I owe Nick an apology. The police say he didn't kill Geoff. I honestly thought I saw . . ."

"The eyes play tricks when one's in a state of shock. Or is it the brain?"

"What does it matter! I've got to go, I'm working. What time will you pick me up on Monday?"

Eleanor hadn't settled a time with Jocelyn, but she could always telephone if Joce disagreed. "Half past one should be time enough," she said.

"Okay. I'll be ready. Oh, thanks." The click of her receiver followed.

Eleanor hung up.

"No good-bye," she reported to Jocelyn later. "And the thanks were very much an afterthought."

Jocelyn pursed her lips. "Modern manners. Or rather, lack thereof. You say Nicholas wasn't really listening when you asked him? I'm still not at all convinced it's a good idea to reintroduce her into his life."

"It's too late now. Even if she hadn't said 'thank you' at all, I could hardly withdraw the offer. And she does realise she ought to apologise."

"She's up to something," Jocelyn said darkly, "you mark my words."

Monday started wet and windy, with squalls blowing in off the sea.

"Perfect weather," Eleanor said to Nick as they stood with Teazle, sheltering in the doorway of his shop, waiting for Jocelyn to pick them up.

"What! It's foul."

"Exactly. Beastly for catching buses. Stella should be extremely grateful for a lift."

Nick laughed. He was in a cheerful mood, his painting finished but for a few final touches. "On the other hand, we wouldn't want to cross the estuary in an open boat in this weather, so we'd probably go round by Wadebridge anyway, so we're not going out of our way, so she has less to be grateful for!"

The first thing Jocelyn said when they scurried across the street and jumped into her car was, "You know what this dreadful weather means, don't you? Every holiday-maker in Padstow is going to be looking for somewhere to get out of it, and the most interesting prospect will be the inquest. We'll never manage to get seats."

"I'm pretty sure they'll save us seats, Mrs Stearns. The police, or the coroner's officers, or whoever's in charge. We're not the general public, we're witnesses."

"Oh, that's all right then. But I sincerely hope I shan't be called to give evidence."

Eleanor suspected Jocelyn was regretting having agreed to aid the reconciliation. Luckily the cheerful whistle—something other than "Hope and Glory" at long last—emanating from the back seat suggested Nick was not subject to last-minute qualms.

They reached the convalescent home a little early. There was no sign of Stella. Nick hopped out and dashed through the rain to ring the door-bell. After a short wait, the door opened. He went in and several minutes passed before he emerged with Stella. She was a striking figure even dressed for the weather in sombre hues suitable for the inquest, a navy-blue mac over a trouser suit patterned in dark blues and greys. Eleanor wondered if Nick had been making up with her inside or just waited for her and then brought her straight out.

The latter, she hoped. She wanted to hear what was said, to judge for herself how sincere Stella managed to be in person.

Nick opened the back door for Stella, stood dripping while she got in, and closed it again before circling the car to get in himself, with Teazle sandwiched between them. As Jocelyn started the car, he introduced Stella to her, by her artistic pseudonym.

"How do you do, Miss Maris," Jocelyn said stiffly.

Stella thanked her for the lift. She was very subdued. Eleanor felt sorry for her. However little commitment she had felt towards her lover during his life, having to attend an inquest on his murder must be a nightmare.

"You've met Mrs Trewynn, of course," Nick went on. "We've sorted it out, Eleanor. I'm hoping Stella will bring her sculptures back to the shop."

"I can't do that, Nick. I'm going to be moving away."

"You are? Where to?"

"Not far enough. Everywhere reminds me of Geoff." She started quietly sniffling.

Eleanor glanced back and surprised a look of cynicism on Nick's face. Facing forward again, she wondered what had prompted it. For some reason it brought to mind something that had happened in King Arthur's Gallery, but she couldn't recall quite what.

No one spoke as they drove on to Padstow.

In the two-room school, the juniors' classroom had been appropriated for the inquest. It was crammed with press and public, but as Nick had prophesied, chairs at the front were reserved for prospective witnesses. The Rosevears were already there.

Anyone expecting to learn how the police investigation was progressing was doomed to disappointment. First, Douglas Rosevear identified the deceased as Geoffrey Clark, known also, for artistic purposes, as Geoffroie Monmouth. Dr Prthnavi's evidence, first in incomprehensible medical terminology and then briefly in layman's terms, produced nothing new: The victim had died of a stab in the back by a sharp instrument consistent with a weapon now in the possession of the police; in his view, the wound could not have been inflicted by the victim himself, nor could he conceive of any possible accident that would produce such a result.

He was the only witness called. The coroner asked the jury whether they wanted to retire to consider the verdict. After a brief consultation, the foreman announced that they were already agreed on "murder by person or persons unknown."

Detective Inspector Scumble requested an adjournment to allow the police to proceed with their enquiries. The cooperative coroner granted a week and, on the advice of the police, signed a burial order. The proceedings closed.

"Well, that was a waste of time!" said Jocelyn.

THIRTY-ONE

Stella was obviously dismayed when Jocelyn announced, on arrival back at the Riverview Home, that she intended to call on her husband's parishioner.

"Have you any objection?" Jocelyn's voice was chilly.

"No, of course not. I'm not even on duty. It's just—I don't use the name Maris here. Miss Weller, if you don't mind."

"Certainly." Jocelyn could be gracious, too. "If I should have reason to refer to you."

The weather had ameliorated by that time. Gusts of wind still made the new-leaved trees sway, and an occasional spatter of raindrops had flung itself at the rear window of the car as they drove eastward. But there was enough blue sky in the west to make several sailors a pair of trousers each, and Nick said firmly, "I think I'll go for a walk. How long, Mrs Stearns?"

"Half an hour? Forty minutes? We shan't leave without you."

"If you go down through the garden," said Stella, "there's a footpath along the river bank."

"Thanks." Nick went off around the side of the house.

The others went in. Stella actually said good-bye and repeated her thanks before disappearing up the stairs. Miss Jamieson popped out of her office.

"To see Mrs Batchelor?" she enquired brightly. "She may be in her room, but I expect she's in the lounge. One of our most sociable guests, I'm happy to say."

She showed them to a large room with windows facing south, to the drive and the circular bed of roses, and west over a long bed of bearded irises, somewhat bedraggled after the heavy rains, and a wooded hillside. Mrs Batchelor was again sitting with Mrs Redditch. They were both delighted to see Jocelyn and Eleanor.

"Ever so kind!" Mrs Batchelor beamed.

"I shall mention it to the bishop," said Mrs Redditch regally.

"Please don't." Jocelyn looked thoroughly disconcerted, as well she might, Eleanor thought, considering her mixed motives for the visit. "We just happened to be passing. I didn't know you were acquainted with the bishop, Mrs Redditch."

"I live in Truro, and my late husband was the Dean of the Chapter. I must say life in the cathedral close is much less interesting than here."

"Such goings-on," put in Mrs Batchelor. "Ought to know better at his age, he did."

"Who is that?" Eleanor asked hopefully.

"The doctor, Mrs Trewynn. Dr Fenwick."

"What Maybelle tellt us is, he's to wed Miss Weller. Well! Nurse or no, she's a giglet if ever I saw un. A flighty piece," she translated.

"Good gracious!" exclaimed Jocelyn. "How would Maybelle know such a thing?"

"She tidies up Dr Fenwick's flat and Miss Weller's room. She doesn't do the heavy cleaning—charwomen come in from Wadebridge for that, early in the mornings."

"Clains the dispensary, she does." Mrs Batchelor pronounced

the difficult word with care and some pride. "That's where they keep everybody's pills and tonics and such. It has to be done over special. Disinfected, like, with Dettol."

"Maybelle's more of a parlourmaid than a housemaid. She hears things."

The two old ladies nodded at each other, in perfect agreement though one might conceivably have been a parlourmaid in her heyday and the other had certainly employed one or more.

"And I don't mean spirits," Mrs Redditch added. "In my young day we all went in for a bit of table-turning and ouija boards. Before I married the Dean, of course. Though he was only a canon then."

"Like my Joe started a deck hand and ended up master of his own boat."

Reminiscences of deceased husbands, now sainted whatever their flaws in life, are hard to stop. Eleanor and Jocelyn heard no more about Stella and the doctor.

As they left half an hour later, Jocelyn whispered crossly to Eleanor, "Tittle-tattle about the clergy and Port Mabyn, where I've spent half my life! I wish you'd told some stories of your husband's adventures, and yours."

"They wanted to talk, not to listen. If I reach my eighties, you shall hear everything, over and over, until you're heartily sick of it."

"You should write a book." They stepped into the hall, Teazle pattering close at their heels. "Ah, Miss Jamieson, we're just leaving."

"Already?" said the nurse in a perfunctory tone. She looked upset. "I was just going to invite you to stay for tea. I'm sorry, I should have sent Maybelle sooner, but I have a good deal on my mind."

"Is something wrong?" Eleanor asked.

"Yes, there is!" At this small sign of sympathy, grievance and worry burst forth. "Stella—Miss Weller—has just informed me that neither she nor Dr Fenwick will be here for the next two weekends! She asked if I would come and stay here for the whole time. I can have her room, if you please, because she's never coming back! And it's true I could do with the extra money—who couldn't?—but I have other obligations, and so I told her."

"It's a lot to ask," Eleanor agreed warmly.

"She said both the others—we do eight-hour shifts during the week, so as to always have an RN on the premises—both Gloria and Mrs Hendred refused, too, so the doctor will have to get someone from an agency. Which is all very well, but some of our older guests get very anxious when there's any change in our routine. A new nurse in sole charge is going to set them all in a flutter. They all have their little ways, you know, their preferences, and she won't have time to get to know them all. She won't understand about calling them guests instead of patients. The whole atmosphere we've worked so hard for will be ruined! It makes me feel terribly guilty, but I simply can't!"

"My dear Miss Jamieson," said Jocelyn, "your concern for your patients—guests—is admirable. You have no cause for guilt. I'm sure Dr Fenwick will make adequate arrangements for his absence and your guests will survive the experience. It seems very short notice, however. I'd have expected the doctor to plan for his absence well in advance."

"They're getting married! Can you believe it? I'm not supposed to tell anyone, but I didn't promise, and you're a vicar's wife, after all. They've been planning it for some time, apparently! No one knew a thing! Then Stella suddenly had to leave the place she was living. A row with her landlady, she said. So they're getting married at the Plymouth registry office on Saturday and going off to Greece for their honeymoon. Talk about luck! She is very pretty, of course. Still . . . She's going to stay at a hotel in Plymouth till Saturday, then move into his flat when they come back.

All super de luxe, of course. She's gone up to finish her packing now."

Maybelle came into the hall with her tea-trolley. "You was busy, Miss Jamieson, and it's getting late, so I thought I'd better go ahead with tea."

"Yes, yes," Miss Jamieson said distractedly. "You're a dear good girl, Maybelle."

Maybelle looked astonished, then grinned and said, "I does my best, Miss Jamieson." She trundled onwards.

"You appreciate loyalty," said the nurse with considerable bitterness, "when you don't get it where you ought to be able to rely on it. I'm sorry, I oughtn't to unload my troubles on you. I hope you won't tell Stella I told you—you know what. It's very kind of you to visit Mrs Batchelor and I know it cheers her up no end. Do come again. Good-bye."

She marched off towards the rear of the house.

Thus dismissed, Eleanor and Jocelyn went out to the car. There was no sign of Nick.

"Bother him," said Jocelyn. "It's been quite three quarters of an hour."

"Let's go and look round the corner of the house to see if he's in sight."

They walked over to the southeast corner, which had the advantage of being out of sight of the guests' lounge. Nick was just starting up the slope from the river. He saw them and waved. Teazle gave a little yelp of recognition and dashed to meet him, short legs covering the distance at an amazing speed.

"Hmph," Jocelyn snorted. "He's in no hurry! He'll be another five minutes. You can't believe anything anyone says these days. By the way, didn't Mrs Redditch tell us before that her husband was a colonial governor?"

Eleanor smiled. "Yes, I wondered whether you'd remember.

She's a romancer. I expect he was something very ordinary and dull like a schoolmaster. She's obviously 'gently bred,' as we used to say, and I dare say she lives in Truro—"

"She certainly knows a lot about the cathedral clergy!"

"—But we'd better not take anything she's told us too seriously."

"Miss Jamieson confirmed Stella's engagement to the doctor. So that's why she's moving away, as she told Nicholas. I wonder why she didn't tell him about the marriage."

"Oh Joce, I'm sure she wants to keep her past and present as separate as possible. You can't blame her, if half what we've heard about her is true."

"I would hope she'd have confessed to the doctor when he asked her to marry him!"

"Well . . . perhaps. It would still be most uncomfortable to keep up an acquaintance with people who knew her before she reformed."

"What makes you think she's reformed?"

"At her age, surely she's ready to settle down," Eleanor said charitably. "She's leaving her job. I expect she wants children. That's something you can't put off indefinitely." She sighed. She and Peter had been too busy, and frequently in such inhospitable places, that they had never seriously considered starting a family until it was too late.

"The question is, should we tell the police?"

"Tell the police what?" Nick's long legs had brought him up faster than Jocelyn had reckoned. "I've discovered a very pretty spot to do some painting. What have you discovered that the police ought or ought not to be told?"

Eleanor and Jocelyn exchanged a glance.

Jocelyn started walking towards the car. "Sorry, Nicholas. We were told partly as a rumour and partly in confidence."

Eleanor wasn't sure she would have been so scrupulous had Jocelyn not been there to keep her on the straight and narrow. They had not, after all, actually promised Miss Jamieson not to tell, but she supposed silence signified consent. Jocelyn apparently didn't extend this protection to the extent of keeping the information from the police.

Did Eleanor's silence now lend her consent to not telling Nick? She knew him much better than Jocelyn did and trusted him absolutely not to pass it on. She decided that if they told the police, she would tell Nick, too.

She did understand Jocelyn's point: Once you started choosing whom it was safe to tell, you started on a slippery slope.

Nick opened the back door of the car for Teazle and the passenger door for Eleanor. As he got into the back with the dog, he said in a somewhat piqued voice, "Then I hope you don't expect to hear from me what I've remembered."

"What, Nick?"

"Oh, just a question I wanted to ask Scumble. A point that's been nagging at me in a vague sort of way, but I've been too busy with *Hope and Glory* to track it down."

Ignoring this, Jocelyn drove round the rose-bed and up the drive, and turned onto the Wadebridge road before she said, "Eleanor, I think you'd better tell Megan. She's the best person to decide whether That Man needs to know. I can't see that it has anything to do with the murder, though. Geoffrey Clark seems to have let Stella . . . um . . . disport herself with other men. He wasn't the jealous sort, and, of course, they were not husband and wife."

"That's a good idea. I'd much rather talk to Megan." She would wait to call her when she got home from work, to avoid the risk of finding Mr Scumble on the other end of the line.

And she could invite Nick to ask his question on her phone at the same time. Thus each would hear the other's story. An admirable—though admittedly sneaky—solution, in Eleanor's view. If Jocelyn asked whether she had told Nick about Stella's marriage, she could honestly deny it. Well, fairly honestly.

Wilkes drove Megan and DI Scumble back to the Bodmin nick after the inquest. In the back seat of the 1100, Scumble said, "That went nicely. Some coroners are too thick-headed or bloody-minded to accept any suggestions. I've got to report to the Super when we get back, so you needn't drive too fast, Wilkes."

"Right, sir."

"Pencarrow, I want you to give me a summary of where we've got to. You never know, it's just barely conceivable that you may have picked up something I didn't. Wilkes, are you listening?"

"I . . . uh . . ." He obviously wasn't sure whether he was supposed to be listening or not. "I'm concentrating on the driving, sir."

"I'm glad to hear it. But if you can spare us a modicum of your attention, and use whatever brains you happen to have concealed about you, if any, you can put your oar in if you think the sergeant has missed something important. Or if there's any details you haven't got round yet to reporting properly. I don't want constant interruptions, mind you. And keep concentrating on the driving."

"Uh . . . yes, sir."

Scumble rolled his eyes. "Go ahead, Pencarrow."

Megan was also uncertain of exactly what he wanted. She plunged in.

"For a start, sir, we've shortened the period when Clark could have died from the doctor's three hours. He left Port Mabyn after noon so couldn't have been killed in Padstow before half past at the earliest. We've also narrowed the list of suspects a lot. Tom Lennox and Jeanette Jones's alibis are solid. Douglas Rosevear and Quentin Durward give each other an alibi smack-bang in the middle. Either could conceivably have made it down to Padstow before three, but neither had any reason to suppose that Clark would be alone in his studio. Durward has no apparent motive. I'd knock him out, and I'd say Rosevear is pretty unlikely though his motive is strong."

She paused. Scumble grunted.

"Of the others at the colony, Leila Arden is still a possibility. She hated Clark, though we still don't know why."

"There she is, stuck in the middle of nowhere, unable to walk, and we come along and rescue her, but will she tell you? That's gratitude for you. I wonder if Gresham knows. He might give us a hint."

"I doubt it, sir, but you could try him."

"I'll leave that to you, Pencarrow. Not that we absolutely have to know. Go on."

"Oswald Rudd: He has no proof he stayed in the co-op shop during the lunch hour. On the other hand, there's no rear access, so he'd have had to come out through the shop door at the front, and he's quite noticeable with that red beard. The risk of someone having spotted him out and about would be pretty high. Motive not strong, unless you put it down to the artistic—"

"Temperament!" snarled Scumble. "Didn't I say I didn't want to hear those words again?"

"Sorry, sir. Albert Baraclough," she went on quickly.

"No artistic temperament there!"

"No, sir. No alibi, either. There could be some motive we don't know about."

"What, Clark seduced his daughter and abandoned her pregnant? Ran over his grandchild while driving drunk? You're romancing."

Megan thought it wisest not to point out that the gov'nor was the one doing the romancing. Still, he was the one who had talked to Baraclough, and if he considered him an unlikely murderer, she was willing to accept his judgement. For the present.

"Yes, sir. That leaves the two women, Weller and Mrs Rosevear. Weller had all the opportunity in the world, but I can't see that she had much of a motive. It would have been embarrassing having everyone know her boyfriend destroyed Nick Gresham's pictures, but hardly a motive for murder. She'd already shrugged off the far worse embarrassment of his attack on Jeanette Jones. I suppose they could have argued about it and she picked up the dagger in a fit of rage." Megan frowned. "I can't see it somehow."

"Not in character?"

"Exactly, sir. If she gave him a dressing-down, I think he'd have stood there like a whipped dog. Lennox seems to think she definitely held the whip hand. If she was tired of him, all she had to do was tell him to shove off. She had no visible financial motive. They weren't married and we haven't been able to trace a will. In any case, though his income was adequate, he didn't put anything aside and his belongings aren't worth offering to the LonStar shop, apart from the dagger and the sword and, I suppose, the paintings. Mrs Stearns would turn most of the stuff down flat."

"Any relatives?" Wilkes enquired from behind the wheel.

"None in his life. Mrs Rosevear says he told her they belonged to some peculiar sect. They cast him off when he started to take an interest in the arts, and he was happy to be cast. We haven't had time to run a thorough trace. Clark's not exactly an uncommon surname. It could even be as phony as Monmouth. There's nothing for relatives to covet, in any case."

"And Mrs Rosevear?" Scumble said. "What d'you make of her?"

"She could have done it. She had a strong motive. She was in Padstow and we can't account for all her time."

"Seems to me," said Wilkes, growing bolder since his first

attempt had not been derided, "what we need is to narrow down the time a bit more. Most of 'em's got alibis for part of the time."

"A good point," Scumble agreed. Wilkes's ears and the back of his neck turned red. "I've got a notion something in the gallery could help, but I can't say what. We'll have to go back there tomorrow, Pencarrow. Go on."

Megan was annoyed. He hadn't mentioned his notion to her. Suddenly, instead of fearing he was out of his depth, she was sure he had a theory, and he bloody well ought to share it with her, however nebulous it was.

She tried to keep the annoyance out of her voice. "Then there are all the people he came into contact with regularly, other than those at the farm. All we've been told about, at least. The only one who liked him is the Tintagel blacksmith. They have a common interest in ancient weapons. The brewery people appreciate his work but refused to commit themselves to any comment on his character. The rest, local tradesmen and frequenters of the Bezant Inn bar for the most part, mostly admitted to disliking him, but there was no hint of any more . . . specific ill-feeling."

"According to the uniformed blokes who did house-to-house."

"Well, yes, sir. But anyone they had the slightest doubt about, DC Polmenna had a go at them."

"You may yet have to talk to those, Pencarrow. We'll have to see how it goes." He brooded in silence till the car stopped behind the police station building.

THIRTY-TWO

Jocelyn dropped Eleanor, Teazle, and Nick outside the LonStar shop and drove off up the hill towards the vicarage.

"Are you going to ring Megan right away?" Nick asked.

"No, I thought I'd wait till later, till she gets home, to avoid the risk of getting Scumble by accident. They may be working late, so I was going to try at eight o'clock."

He grinned. "Great minds think alike."

"Why don't you come round and talk to her at the same time. That way, she won't have to keep answering the phone."

"You're a wily woman, Eleanor Trewynn! I'll be there. Now I'm going to put those finishing touches to *Hope and Glory*. My kind patroness said she'd drop in sometime this week to see how it's going. She should be pleased to find it done. See you later."

Eleanor went up to her flat for the cup of tea that hadn't materialised at Riverview. Then, feeling herself and Teazle very much in need of exercise, she walked up the path behind the shops and out onto the cliffs. The sky was now blue and quite a few walkers were taking advantage of the sunshine and the glorious view from the heights of the ruffled sea crashing on the rocks below.

However, only a few dedicated hikers ventured more than a mile or so from the village. Soon Eleanor found a spot sufficiently isolated to practise Aikido without attracting too much attention.

She had visited her *sensei* in London for a lesson just a couple of weeks ago. Breathing deeply, she emptied her mind of all but his advice on her weaknesses. The rest of the world vanished from her consciousness and slowly she began to bend and stretch, warming up. Swifter and swifter she moved, whirling, carving space with sweeping gestures.

If hikers stopped to stare at the small woman with snow-white curls spinning like a dervish, patiently watched by a small, snow-white dog, they forbore to intrude. Eleanor completed her practice in peace and went home, much refreshed.

Nick appeared promptly at eight, just as Eleanor finished washing up. She made each of them a cup of coffee—she'd never progressed beyond Nescaff, so it was quick and easy. They sat down and she dialled Megan's number.

"Megan? It's Aunt Nell, dear. There's something I ought to tell you. Are you on your own?"

"Yes." The single syllable sounded tired. "I just got home. What is it, Aunt Nell? Something to do with the case?"

"Yes, dear. Perhaps I should ring back when you've had something to eat."

"That's all right, I had a sandwich at the canteen. It was pretty grim, but filling. Tell me."

"After the inquest," Eleanor said tentatively, glad she didn't have to confess to Scumble—at least, not yet—"Jocelyn and I went to visit old Mrs Batchelor at the Riverview Convalescent Home."

"Where Stella works? Oh, Aunt Nell, that was not a good idea."

"She's a parishioner. One of the vicar's flock."

"I dare say, but all the same . . . What did you find out?"

"Well, you may know already. Or it may not be of interest, but we decided we ought to tell you." She started to report what Mrs Batchelor and Mrs Redditch had told them.

"Hold on a mo, let me get my notebook."

Eleanor covered the mouthpiece with her hand, gave Nick a thumbs up, and whispered, "She wants to write it down."

Looking rather stunned, he exclaimed, "I should think so! Eleanor, is this true?"

"Of course it is, Nick, or I wouldn't be telling the police. To be accurate, it's truly what we were told, though of course—" She held up her hand.

"The maid's name is Mabel?"

"No, dear, not Mabel, Maybelle, with a y, two lls and an e, I believe. West Indian. A nice girl, if rather given to gossiping, but the police can't possibly object to that."

"So it's just gossip," Megan said gloomily.

"What I've told you so far, but from the horse's mouth. No, strictly speaking I suppose it's at second hand."

"But it's just gossip."

"Just wait, dear. We heard the same story and more from the day nurse in charge, and she got it directly from Stella." Eleanor relayed Miss Jamieson's story. "That's everything, I think."

"Do you know which hotel she's gone to?"

"No, Miss Jamieson just said 'super de luxe.' There can't be many super de luxe hotels in Plymouth, surely."

"We'll find her. Thanks, Aunt Nell."

"But now I've told you, I can't see that it helps. It would make more sense if Geoffrey had killed Stella, like Othello. Only the other way round, sort of, because Othello was married to Desdemona and Geoff and Stella weren't. Only he doesn't seem to have been jealous of her . . . um . . . escapades. Everyone said he accepted that she insisted on her freedom."

"Let us worry about that. Thanks for passing on the information. Good night and sweet—"

"Don't hang up, Megan. Nick wants a word with you."

"Nick's there? What does he want?"

"To ask you a question."

"What about?"

"I don't know, dear." But she was dying to find out. "Here he is. Night-night."

Eleanor handed over the receiver and sipped her cooling coffee while listening to Nick's end of the conversation.

"Good evening, Sergeant . . . Because this is an official call. Is your pencil at the ready, well-sharpened . . . I dare say. Here we go, then. For all I know, you may already know the answer and have factored it in, but the question's been nagging at me when I haven't been otherwise occupied . . . All right, keep your hair on! Geoff was standing in front of his easel when he was so rudely interrupted. What I've been wondering is, had he started painting? If so, how far had he got? We know he'd just acquired a prop . . . Property. Stage-talk, but we use it, too. The dagger. He was eager to try his hand at painting it and he was an impatient sort of fella. I can't imagine him hanging about, not starting in on it as soon as he got to the studio . . . Yes, exactly . . . I agree, it's the sort of thing the SOC boys wouldn't pay much attention to, so I hope they still . . . Good. Will you let me know? . . . Silly of me, of course he won't. But you will tell him right away? . . . Good girl, you're a pleasure to work with . . . All right, all right, I beg your pardon, we are not working together and I won't call you a good girl! Good night, Miss Pencarrow." He dropped the receiver on the cradle. "Whew!"

"I do wish you wouldn't deliberately provoke her, Nick."

"I started out as good as gold," Nick protested. "Even called her 'Sergeant' rather than Megan, as it was official business."

"Tell it to the Marines! What is all this about Geoffrey's painting?"

"Probably nothing. Just that if he got a fair amount done, it would suggest that he'd been there for quite a while before he was killed. At best, it'll narrow the time frame for them."

"Oh dear, I don't think we've been very helpful after all. I hope Megan will let us know."

But all day Tuesday they didn't hear from the police. Eleanor didn't exactly forget about the murder—that would be impossible—but it was no longer on her mind constantly. She went out on her collecting round, took Teazle for a long walk, shopped, made spaghetti bolognese, and decided she'd better practise a bit more before she invited anyone to share it.

On Wednesday, at two minutes past eleven, a succession of thuds on the stairs, suggesting someone bounding up, set Teazle barking in her gruff little voice. After a perfunctory knock, Nick burst into the flat.

"Eleanor, I'm so glad you're here. I thought you might have left the doors unlocked. They came, they saw, and she liked it!"

"Who? What?"

"The Harrisons. Mrs Harrison. Janice Hazard Harrison, the American I met in St James's Park."

"*Land of Hope and Glory?*"

"Exactly. I'm not sure that he was equally keen, but they're honeymooners, you know, still at the 'deny her nothing' stage." He waved a cheque. "Payment on the nail! I wrapped it, they put it in the 'trunk' of their American whale, and off they went. I've closed the shop for the rest of the day to celebrate. Now I can start thinking of something else. I suppose you haven't heard from Megan about Geoff's canvas?"

"Not a murmur."

"Oh. Well, either Scumble dismissed it as insignificant, or it was so significant he's keeping it under wraps." He stared hungrily at the packet of digestives she was about to open.

"Elevenses?" she offered.

"Yes, please. I'll take you out for a slap-up meal tonight. How about the Indian in Camelford? I'm feeling rich!"

The phone rang. "You make the coffee," said Eleanor.

Jocelyn didn't even wait for her to give her number before she started talking. "Eleanor, I've just had a most odd telephone call from Mrs Redditch."

"Mrs . . . ? Oh, Mrs Batchelor's friend? How odd!"

"That's what I just said. Do concentrate, Eleanor."

Eleanor muttered slightly rebelliously that she had meant it was odd that Mrs Redditch should ring up Joce, whereas Joce had implied the content of the call was odd. Quite different, but not worth quibbling over, she decided, especially as Jocelyn was in a most unusual tizzy.

"What was that?"

"Nothing. What did she say?"

Nick, spooning coffee powder into mugs, mouthed, "Who?" and Eleanor mouthed back, "Jocelyn." This bit of by-play made her uncertain that she'd heard correctly. "What?" she asked. "She told you what?"

"Do listen!"

"I am listening. I just can't believe my ears."

"Nor could I," Jocelyn admitted grudgingly. "She said Dr Fenwick was found dead in his bed—"

"At the home? I thought he was only there at weekends."

"As far as I could gather, they had some sort of emergency last night and the nurse on duty called him in. After escorting the patient to Bodmin Hospital in an ambulance, he went back to Riverview and stayed in his flat upstairs rather than drive all the way back to Plymouth. And there he was found this morning dead in his bed, by that nice little maid, Maybelle."

"Poor child! Very sad, but why on earth did Mrs Redditch ring you? Even if there was anything you could do about it, she's not a parishioner. Nor was he, come to that."

"She kindly rang on behalf of Mrs Batchelor. You know how it is, some elderly people still think of the telephone as a brand-new invention and don't want anything to do with it. That's one reason Mrs Batchelor's son put her in the home in the first place—she doesn't have a phone and doesn't want one and wouldn't use it if she had one, so she couldn't call for help."

"But what does Mrs Batchelor think you can do about the doctor's death?"

"She's in a state and wants to come home. Apparently, after the body was found, someone overheard one of the staff saying they'd all be out of a job. Talk about setting the cat among the pigeons! Most of the residents seem to have jumped to the conclusion that the home will suddenly close without warning any moment. And to add to the flap, the police have turned up at Riverview."

"The police? Dr Fenwick didn't die naturally?"

"Of course he did. They have to be called in to any unexpected death."

"Oh dear! I don't suppose you know the name of the police officer who—"

"Someone called Pearce, I think. The name sounds vaguely familiar. At least they don't have to contend with That Man. The trouble is, Mrs Batchelor's son has gone off to Majorca or the Riviera or somewhere and can't be reached, and of course she doesn't have the funds to go to a hotel, or even to pay for a taxi home. Naturally we'll advance whatever it costs to get her home, if necessary, but she's still in need of help . . . Eleanor, what she really needs right now is reassurance. I ought to go over there, but I simply *can't* get away this afternoon. I've got a Mothers' Union meeting and they'll tear each other apart if I'm not there to keep the peace. You've no idea what they're like."

Though Eleanor had never attended a meeting, she was acquainted with some of the 'Mothers' and she was prepared to believe it. "Don't worry, dear, I'll go," she said resignedly.

"Will you really? You're an angel! They can't—surely!—expect the patients to leave today. Oh dear, there's a parish council meeting this evening as well, and Timothy simply can't cope on his own. Tell her I'll get it all sorted out in the morning. LonStar's not likely to be so busy I won't be able to make a few phone calls. I've got to run now. Ring when you get back, will you?"

"I will. I hope you survive your meeting, Joce. 'Bye." She hung up with a sigh.

Nick was all agog. "Go where?"

"Riverview." Eleanor explained. When she got to the bit about DI Pearce arriving on the scene, Nick groaned.

"What's he doing there? He'll probably arrest the maid. Perhaps we'd better alert Freeth and Bulwer as a precaution." The Port Mabyn solicitors didn't handle criminal cases, but they could recommend, someone who did.

"Oh, rubbish, Nick! There's probably nothing fishy about Dr Fenwick's death anyway. But I do think Mr Scumble should be in charge, given the connection with Stella."

"Indubitably. I wonder if anyone's even bothered to inform him? Perhaps he's the one we ought to alert. How can we get hold of him?"

"We could try ringing the police station in Launceston," Eleanor said doubtfully.

"It's worth a try. Want me to do it?"

"No, dear, I'd better. At worst they'll just write me off as a meddlesome old lady, whereas they might—oh, I don't know—think you have it in for Pearce?"

"I do."

"Exactly."

To Eleanor's astonishment, she was put through very quickly to Superintendent Bentinck. He assured her that Mr Scumble was keeping him up to date on the murder investigation, had, in fact, reported the latest progress only that morning. He hadn't heard about the death at the Riverview Convalescent Home, and he had no idea whether Scumble was aware of it. Grasping the significance at once, he promised to have the information radioed to the detective inspector immediately.

"And I'd better have a little chat with Mr Egerton," he mused aloud. "Thank you very much for notifying us, Mrs Trewynn. How on earth did you find out so soon?"

"It's a long story, Mr Bentinck, and I don't want to delay you. Thank you for listening. Good-bye."

"Well done!" said Nick, applauding. "I was sure he'd make you promise not to go there, but you rang off pretty smartly."

"I don't imagine it crossed his mind that I might. But I promised Jocelyn I would."

"I'm going with you. You'll need someone to protect you from Pearce."

"Oh, nonsense, Nick. I'd be glad if you'll drive, as it looks as if it's going to rain, but you needn't think Pearce can intimidate me."

"I don't really," Nick assured her. "I just don't want to miss the Battle of the Titans."

THIRTY-THREE

"The bastard!" snarled Scumble.

"It's possible Mr Egerton really didn't see how Stella Weller could be involved, sir," Megan pointed out without much conviction. "He must have heard about the doctor's death just after you told him we'd traced her hotel in Plymouth."

"Bollocks! No, I do not want siren and lights!" he snapped at Wilkes, who had just executed a hair-raising U-turn on the busy A38. "Just get us there. Alive. I'd told him the Weller woman is a person of interest and we've been told she's engaged to this doctor. The first thing he should have done when he heard the doctor died was notify us, not leave us rolling to our rendezvous with the Plymouth force and send that cretin Pearce to balls up the scene. You didn't hear that, Wilkes."

"No, sir."

"I suppose he wanted to give his own man a chance to redeem himself," Megan guessed. "I wonder how the Super—ours, Mr Bentinck—found out?"

"We'll never know, nor how he forced the bastard to acknowledge that it's our case. Alive, I said!" he yelled as the 1100 zipped through the streets of Bodmin's town centre, busy with last-minute early-closing-day shoppers.

As much to distract him as in hope of any answers, Megan said, "Sir, I don't see why she would kill the doctor before they were married, let alone how she did it, when he was at the convalescent home and she was in Plymouth."

"Nor do I, Pencarrow, nor do I. Maybe she didn't. Maybe she didn't kill Clark, and we're on the wrong track altogether. But I'll be damned if I'll let any idiot go messing about with what could turn out to be evidence in *my* case."

"I don't believe we're on the wrong track."

"All right." Scumble leant back and closed his eyes, only his white-knuckle grip on the edge of the seat indicating his dislike of the way Wilkes was taking the curves on the winding road to Wadebridge. "Convince me."

Megan took a moment to marshal the mixture of facts and speculations that had put them on Stella's trail.

"Never mind getting things in the right order. Get on with it."

"Sir. First, Weller's engagement gave her a motive for wanting to be rid of Clark. As suggested by Lennox's statement, Clark was in fact, jealous of her casual liaisons. Several of the others at the farm agreed when pressed that the only reason he didn't kick up a fuss was that he was afraid of driving her away if he tried to curtail her freedom. If she married, he'd lose her altogether, reason enough for threatening to spill the beans to her fiancé about her promiscuity. A middle-aged man, he's—he was unlikely to take a lenient view."

"Luckily we don't have to prove motive. If she'd told Clark she was going to get married, why didn't he tell anyone else?"

"Um . . . He found it humiliating? That she'd drop him for a much older man?"

"I'm getting a very confused picture of Clark's character."

"I know what you mean, sir. It could be that all the braggadocio was cover for a fundamental insecurity. An inferiority complex. Or perhaps he really was full of himself until he took up with Stella and she put him in his place."

"Reasonable," Scumble grudgingly agreed. He didn't approve of what he had been known to call psycho-drivel.

"Then we've got the evidence that the whole business was planned: The blacksmith in Tintagel says Clark told him Weller had asked him to pick her up in Port Mabyn at midday. He's prepared to swear that Clark said 'pick up,' not 'drop in on.' Weller told us he arrived earlier than expected and she left Gresham's shop early, in spite of having promised to stay till closing time, only because of the damage Clark did to Gresham's work. It was a stroke of luck for her that Gresham rang from London with his good news. Although, if he hadn't, she could doubtless have found some other way to work on Clark's jealousy of Gresham, possibly sexual as well as professional. She may even have done the damage herself, while he fetched his car from the car park. It wouldn't take more than a few seconds." Megan paused for comment.

"Go on."

"The evidence of the SOCO and the pathologist is that Geoffrey Clark had not started painting when he was killed. Given his eagerness, affirmed by several people, to get to grips with—uh—" Not a felicitous choice of words.

"'Get to grips' will do," Scumble said impatiently.

"Given his eagerness to try his hand at painting his new dagger, this suggests that he died shortly after arriving at his studio. Weller admitted to going there with him. It wouldn't have taken more than a moment to stab him, less time than to get a drink of water and take off her nylon tights, which is what she claims to have gone in for. The pathologist says the dagger is hard and sharp enough to notch bone, and she has at least some anatomical knowledge, partial training in both nursing and art, so she'd have a good idea where to aim a lethal blow."

"Yes, this anatomical knowledge, it's going to be a problem. How could even a half-trained nurse possibly delude herself that we'd mistake dried ink for fresh blood?"

"Double bluff," Megan said promptly. "She knew it wouldn't fool anyone for long—"

"Long enough to cook Pearce's goose."

"Yes, sir. She expected us to reason that a nurse would know she couldn't hope to fool us, so we'd see it as a point in her favour. What's more, together with her subsequent actions, the instant impression of floods of freshly spilled blood had the additional advantage of throwing immediate suspicion on Nick Gresham."

"Why would she want to do that?"

"She had a grudge against him, probably related to his having turned down her offer of . . . er, sexual favours, though we have only his word for that. I don't see why we should disbelieve him, though, do you, sir?"

"Who knows? Weller was obviously happy to throw him to the wolves, whatever the reason. If Pearce can be described as a wolf. Go on to her subsequent actions."

"Later that afternoon, after allowing time for Gresham to reach Port Mabyn and discover the wreckage, she told the Rosevears her story and insisted on their going with her to protect Clark against Gresham's vengeance. Her note to Gresham practically assured that he would come. She wanted witnesses when she followed him into the studio and accused him of stabbing Clark. She made sure she was first in. Mrs Rosevear, who is not only imaginative but impressionable—in my opinion that's proved by her infatuation with Clark, the fact she took him at his own value—Mrs Rosevear was convinced she also had seen the actual stabbing. That was a real bonus for Weller."

"What do you make of her hysterical grief."

"Fake," Megan said promptly. "On further questioning, Douglas Rosevear remembered that after Weller burst into tears on his wife's shoulder, she was sufficiently compos mentis to remind him not to let Gresham escape. What's more, not a tear was shed until the local copper was almost on the scene. And Mrs Rosevear told us that among the training courses Weller started and didn't finish was acting! I still wonder what she expected to gain from casting suspicion on Gresham, apart from working off her grudge by giving him a hard time. She must have known he'd soon be cleared."

"Save your wondering for how we're going to prove—" He cut off abruptly as the car swerved across the road. "What the hell?"

"Nearly missed the sign, sir," Wilkes explained cheerfully, slowing as they continued down the winding drive. "Here we are."

In front of the house stood several cars. Among them was an aged pea-green Morris Minor.

"Noooo!" moaned the inspector, his face apoplectic. "Tell me I'm seeing things!"

Megan was unable to oblige, and Wilkes rubbed salt in the wound by observing quite unnecessarily, "That's Mrs Trewynn's car. I'd know it anywhere."

They went into the house. To Megan's relief, Aunt Nell was not immediately visible. Nor was Detective Inspector Pearce. Only PC Lubbock stood in lonely vigil at the foot of the stairs.

As he came forward eagerly, saluting, Megan could have sworn she still detected a slight odour of pig.

"Sir! DC Polmenna told me to stop anyone going upstairs. That's where the deceased died."

"Not DI Pearce?"

"No, sir. When he heard you were going to be in charge, sir, he went back to Bodmin and left DC Polmenna in charge. He said it's obviously an accident anyway, seeing the doctor said the deceased was a dire-betic and—"

"Where's Polmenna?"

"Over there, sir, in the office. I'll show you the way."

"You stay here and guard the stairs."

"Yes, sir! No one's tried to go up," Lubbock added sadly.

"The body's still there, I take it."

"Yes, sir."

"Wilkes, have a chat with the constable and find out if he knows anything," ordered Scumble, turning away.

They crossed the hall. From outside the open office door, they heard Polmenna's pleading voice. "Please, sir, just another five minutes. I'm sure he'll be here by then and he's bound to want to talk to you."

"And here I am," Scumble announced. "It's very good of you to wait, Doctor. I'm sorry you've been inconvenienced."

Dr Prthnavi was usually the most equable of men, but now he spoke quite sharply, his English more clipped than ever. "Your colleague suddenly dashed off without an explanation, Inspector. I am not—Well, that is water over the bridge." Even his usually perfect grasp of English idiom had slipped. "You wish for a report on the deceased and I will not waste more time."

"Thank you, Doctor," Scumble said meekly.

"He is Dr Frederick Fenwick. I was acquainted with him as a colleague, though I did not know him well. I was not aware that he suffered from diabetes, but I found insulin in the refrigerator in his flat on the first floor. According to the label on the bottle, he prescribed for himself. Possibly he wished to conceal the illness, fearful that it might harm his practice. He was on a low dosage—"

"Could he have taken the wrong dose accidentally?"

"That is highly unlikely. He was a medical professional."

"Could he have been given the wrong dose intentionally?"

"It is possible, of course, but it would take a certain amount of medical knowledge. The contents would have to be removed with a hypodermic needle through the cap, and a substitute inserted in the same way."

"Suppose it done. What would happen?"

"Too little, he would notice the symptoms and have plenty of time to correct the deficiency. Too much, a very large dose, would act much more quickly. Still, normally, as a medical man, he would notice the symptoms and have time to take glucose and call for help."

Scumble pounced. "Normally?"

"He appears to have taken a sleeping pill, Inspector. Asleep, he would be unaware of the symptoms of overdose. He would slip into a coma and die within a few hours."

According to Polmenna, the bottle of insulin had been finger-printed and only the doctor's dabs found on it. After a few more questions, Dr Prthnavi left with it, promising to have the contents analysed immediately. The answer to whether Fenwick had died of an insulin overdose would have to wait for the autopsy, but if the bottle had been tampered with, it would be fair to assume the probability.

"What I don't get, sir," said Megan, "is why? She's all but bagged her sugar-daddy, why kill him before they're even married?"

"We'll worry about that later. First things first. Polmenna, give me a report on what was done before Mr Pearce departed. And make it quick. Just the highlights."

"Well, sir, for a start," Polmenna said portentously, "I oughta warn you, the victim's solicitor's likely to turn up any minute."

"His solicitor? Why the hell—?"

"There's a desk in the flat, sir. Mr Pearce looked through it, looking for next-of-kin and such, and he found a recent receipted bill for drawing up a will. So he phoned him—office in Plymouth—and turns out he was a personal friend of the deceased and he said he was coming over right away."

"A recent will," Scumble said thoughtfully. "Makes sense, what with him getting married soon. What else?"

"We found out Dr Fenwick shouldn't've been here at all."

"What? What do you mean?"

"Oh, didn't you know?" Aunt Nell appeared in the doorway. "Dr Fenwick spent his weekends here and worked in Plymouth during the week."

"No, I did not know! No one happened to mention it to me."

"You wouldn't have been interested before he died, would you?" Aunt Nell retorted with spirit. "Hello, Megan dear. I'm so glad you've come."

Megan smiled at her. One might as well try to stop the wind blowing as expect Aunt Nell to remember to treat her differently because she was on duty.

"And what exactly, may I ask, are you doing here, Mrs Trewynn?"

Nick Gresham loomed behind her. "She's on an errand of mercy, Inspector, because Mrs Stearns couldn't come."

"You, too! And the dog, of course."

Teazle greeted Megan rapturously.

"I was talking to Mrs Batchelor and Mrs Redditch," said Eleanor. "Rajendra—Dr Prthnavi—came to say good-bye and told me you'd arrived, so I thought I ought to come and tell you what I've found out. Just in case Mr Pearce didn't bother."

"Either to find out," Nick put in, "or to tell you."

Scumble visibly mellowed. "Well, you'd better both come in and we'll all make ourselves comfy and you can tell me everything I don't know yet. Have a seat, Mrs Trewynn."

Polmenna had to go and find another chair because Nick wouldn't take the third unless Megan also was seated, to Scumble's irritation. Less a matter of chivalry this time, Megan suspected, than, in his own words, "he only does it to annoy because he knows it teases."

Before Polmenna returned, Aunt Nell leant forward and said earnestly to the inspector, "You must realise, Mr Scumble, that all I know is what I've been told by two gossipy old ladies. So it doesn't count as evidence, does it?"

"You're quite right, Mrs Trewynn, but I hope it'll point us in the right direction. You'd better take notes, Pencarrow. First, did you find out why the doctor was here last night?"

"Oh yes, there's no secret about that. The nurse on duty was worried about one of the guests—patients—and phoned him. He drove over from Plymouth straight away, took one look at the colonel, and sent for an ambulance. By the time it came from Bodmin and took the poor man away, it was late. Dr Fenwick decided he was too tired to drive safely back to Plymouth."

"I don't suppose you know what was wrong with the patient?" Scumble asked idly, not particularly interested.

"I don't know what *went* wrong, Inspector. That is, what caused the emergency. But I do know that Colonel Nesbit was a diabetic."

THIRTY-FOUR

Scumble's reaction to Eleanor's words startled her. His mouth dropped open and he was rendered momentarily speechless.

"Sensation in Court," said Nick sardonically.

At that moment, Polmenna came in carrying a chair.

"Has Dr Prthnavi left?" Scumble snapped at him.

"Sir, you didn't say to stop him!"

"Go and find out and if you catch him, stop him—that is, ask him to kindly step back in for a moment."

Polmenna set down the chair and disappeared again at a run.

"I'm sure Miss Jamieson can help with medical questions," Eleanor suggested.

"Miss Jamieson?"

"The nurse in charge. She's an RN. She wasn't here last night but I expect the nurse who was told the night nurse everything and she—"

"Yes, yes, very likely. Pencarrow, go and find—"

Polmenna reappeared. "He's gone, sir, and this gentleman—"

"The name's Meadowes." A short, balding man in a pinstripe

suit pushed past the detective constable and addressed Scumble. "You must be Inspector Pearce."

"Detective Inspector Scumble, sir. I'm in charge here now. And you're . . . ?"

"Poor Fenwick's solicitor. I can hardly believe he's gone." He sank into the chair Nick graciously vacated and blotted his forehead with a large linen handkerchief. "Why, I was talking to him only on Monday and he was in very good form, looking forward to his marriage. You're aware that he was about to be married?"

"We are, sir."

"Dear, dear, a heart attack, I suppose. Overwork. It takes all the best men."

"As far as you know, he wasn't ill?"

"No. But he never talked about his health."

"You don't happen to know the name of his doctor?"

"He didn't have one. He wouldn't go on the National Health and he used to say he'd be damned—begging your pardon, ladies . . ." Mr Meadowes looked at Megan, busy taking notes, with a puzzled frown. "He'd be—ah—he wouldn't pay someone for advice when he knew as much as any of them. The old saying's true, I'm afraid: 'The doctor who treats himself has a fool for a patient.'" He sighed.

"Very true, sir. You mentioned his coming marriage. When you heard of his death, did you notify his . . . er . . . bride-to-be?"

"I fear I was unable to do so, though such was undoubtedly my duty. Fenwick had mentioned that she was staying in an hotel in Plymouth until the ceremony, but unfortunately he neglected to tell me which. I find it extremely difficult to know what to do. But perhaps you can help me, Inspector?" The solicitor seemed suddenly to realise that he was talking about his deceased client's affairs in the presence of an interested audience. "Er . . . May I ask, Inspector, who these people are?"

Scumble waved a hand at Megan. "My assistant, Detective Sergeant Pencarrow."

"Dear me, dear me, a lady detective! How . . . how forward-looking. And—surely not a police dog?"

Recognising the word *dog*, Teazle wagged her tail.

Scumble did not introduce her. "These are Mrs Trewynn and Mr Gresham, who are helping us with our enquiries."

"How do you do, madam. Enquiries, dear me. Does this mean there is some cause for doubt about the cause of poor Fenwick's demise?"

"I'm afraid so, Mr Meadowes. You'll understand that I can't discuss—"

"What do you mean no one can go up?" Stella's voice rang loud and clear from the front hall. "I'm not just anyone, I'm Dr Fenwick's fiancée."

Wilkes's voice was equally loud and clear. "No one means no one, miss. If you'll just step this way, the inspector will explain."

"Inspector! Oh lord, something's happened to him! I knew it. What's wrong?"

Eleanor suddenly wondered how much Scumble knew. She and Nick hadn't had a chance yet to tell him everything. Was he flying in the dark?

A glance at his face reassured her. He looked interested but not in the least puzzled. He probably understood better than she did. At least he wasn't going to be easily taken in by Stella's acting ability, as Pearce had been.

He stood up as Stella swept in. "Miss Weller?"

"Tell me what's happened to Freddy! A car smash? Is he badly hurt?"

"My dear Miss Weller," Meadowes began, only to be silenced by Scumble's glare.

"Do sit down, Miss Weller."

"I don't want to sit down," she stormed. "I just want to know—"

"I think you'd better." He waited till she subsided unwillingly onto the chair Megan placed facing the desk for her. "What makes you think Dr Fenwick was here? I gather he normally came only at weekends."

"He left me a message at my hotel. You see, we were going to be married on Saturday and Freddy wouldn't let me stay at his flat in case people jumped to conclusions. He was very old- . . . very considerate that way."

She was giving herself away with every word, Eleanor thought. Quite apart from the past tense, if she were truly worried about the doctor, she wouldn't be intent on her explanation.

"He left a message when he was called away last night?" Scumble asked. "I assume you expected to spend the evening with him?"

"No, actually. He had a lot of work to do, preparing his patient notes for his locum. We were going away, you see, for our honeymoon. A fortnight's cruise in the Greek islands."

"Ah, I see." Scumble looked as if the last piece of the jigsaw had neatly fitted into place. "But he considerately let you know he was coming over here."

"Yes, there was an emergency. I have the receptionist's note here." She handed over a slip of green paper. "But the stupid things didn't give it to me till this morning."

"Not right away, when the doctor telephoned?"

"I wasn't in. I went out to dinner with a woman I met at the hotel, and the night receptionist came on duty while I was gone. At least that's what they told me this morning. I was furious, of course."

"So as soon as you received the message, you came rushing here."

"Rushing! I didn't have enough money for a taxi so I bused it. Two buses! It took forever."

"And why exactly did you feel it necessary to come after Dr Fenwick?"

Stella's expression went blank. Then she cried out, "I was worried about him!" and burst into noisy sobs, burying her face in her hands. "I know something dreadful's happened. Why won't you tell me?"

"Really, Inspector!" Meadowes protested, patting her shoulder. "Is this absolutely necessary? And in front of . . . all these people?"

Raising her head, Stella glowered at Eleanor, who noted uneasily that she had tears in her eyes. Was she a good enough actress to cry on demand? But her weeping had cut off rather abruptly. She had switched it on and switched it off, just as she had in King Arthur's Gallery, Eleanor remembered. That was what had been niggling at the back of her mind. One minute Stella had been weeping in Margery's arms, the next warning Doug not to let Nick escape.

Thank heaven she had done it again in Scumble's presence so that Eleanor would not have to confess to having forgotten.

Meanwhile Stella had tranferred her glare to Nick, standing with his hands on the back of Eleanor's chair. "Yes, what are you doing here?" she demanded. "Come to gloat, have you?"

"What do I have to gloat about?" Nick asked blandly.

Scumble frowned at him.

"I know something's happened to Freddy!" Stella wailed. "I rang his flat this morning and his daily said his bed hadn't been slept in."

"My dear, I'm afraid I have bad news for you." This time Meadowes would not be stopped, and Scumble seemed willing to let him continue. "Dr Fenwick died in the night. I'm told a maid found him this morning, in his bed upstairs."

"No! I don't believe it. He can't have died before we were even married! I must see him!" She jumped up. "I must see for myself."

"By all means," said Scumble with suspect benevolence. "Pencarrow, escort Miss Weller upstairs. No hurry. You'd better take Wilkes with you, just in case she's . . . overcome by the sight." Sotto voce, he added, "Again."

Wilkes and Polmenna had been standing on either side of the door since Stella came in. They stood aside, and Wilkes followed the women out.

"A very unconvincing display," Scumble said acidly. "I can't think how you came to be taken in the first time, Mrs Trewynn."

Eleanor was indignant. "I was in shock, just as she pretended to be. I bet you knew it was ink, not blood, when you first saw it."

"True. And the body had been removed."

"There you are, then. It really was a horrible sight. I nearly fainted, even though I didn't know the man and I'm not unused to death. It didn't seem at all unlikely that his lover should have hysterics."

"I don't know what you're talking about," said Meadowes a trifle querulously.

"All will be explained in due course, sir. That's the easy part. I know how, and why, and what went wrong. Miss Weller is clever enough, but she doesn't think things through. No stick-to-itiveness, as the Yanks say. Just look at all the training courses she started and never finished—art, drama, nursing—and it sticks out like a sore thumb. It's proving it to the satisfaction of a jury that's going to be the hard part. Tell me, Mr Meadowes, what provision was made for Miss Weller in Dr Fenwick's will?"

"I suppose it's proper for me to tell you, since there seems to be some suspicion about his death. Fenwick left everything to her, apart from a few minor bequests. The terrible thing, and I dread having to break it to her, is that the will very definitely specifies 'to my wife, Stella Fenwick.' As Stella Weller, she inherits nothing."

Nick straightened with a look of enlightenment. "Ah, now I

understand. The question is, did she realise that? If he told her he had made and signed a new will in her favour, she quite likely assumed it went into effect immediately. All the same, she didn't want him to die too soon, leaving her a rich widow only a few days after the murder of her lover. It was supposed to happen after the honeymoon, wasn't it, Inspector?"

"That's my guess, Mr Gresham."

"And you know what went wrong, you say?"

"I'm fairly certain it was entirely her own fault, her lack of thorough forethought. I need more information about the medical side of things. Polmenna, fetch the nurse. Miss Jamieson, did you say, Mrs Trewynn?"

"Yes, Inspector. I do hope you won't have to bother my old ladies. They're already upset."

"*Your* old ladies? I thought they were Mrs Stearns's."

Before Eleanor started an explanation that at best Scumble wouldn't really want to hear, and that at worst would make him accuse her of interference, Nick interrupted.

"If I'm not putting two and two together to make five, I think you'd better talk to the maid, Maybelle, too. I was chatting to her—"

"Flirting," Eleanor muttered to herself.

Nick heard and winked at her. "A bright girl, but she obviously had something on her mind. I coaxed it out of her. Definitely a story you need to hear, though I doubt if it provides quite the proof you're looking for."

"Well, what is it?"

"You should hear it direct from her, Inspector."

"All right, Polmenna can get her after the nurse."

"It would be better if I went. She's a black immigrant and a bit skittish where the police are concerned. They don't have the best of reputations in that community."

"You don't need to tell me. You can fetch her, but if I find you've been coaching her to get your own back at Weller—"

"*Miss* Weller," Meadowes objected. He still looked thoroughly bewildered.

"I might be tempted," Nick said at the same time, grinning, "but that it would get Maybelle into trouble, too. If you're so suspicious of my motives, I wonder that you let me sit in on all this."

"For one thing, you do provide an occasional snippet of useful information," Scumble retorted. "We might not have got round to the maid for some time. More to the point, I want as many witnesses to *Miss* Weller's behaviour as I can get. If I can't find proof positive, you and Mrs Trewynn may be essential to the case."

Eleanor sighed. She didn't really want to be an essential witness, no matter what Stella had done. And though it was now perfectly obvious that she had stabbed Geoffrey, what hand she had had in Dr Fenwick's death was still not entirely clear.

THIRTY-FIVE

DC Polmenna ushered in Miss Jamieson. The poor woman was obviously both upset and nervous. Eleanor jumped up and went to meet her.

"It's all right, Miss Jamieson. The inspector just wants to ask you a few questions."

"I don't know anything!"

"Yes you do, dear. You're a Registered Nurse, which means you have specialised knowledge that the rest of us lack, and you're also trained to be observant."

"Oh, well, if that's all . . ." She stood in front of the desk with her hands folded in front of her, as apprehensive as if she faced an unpredictable consultant doing his hospital rounds.

"Do sit down, Miss Jamieson."

"I'd rather stand, sir, if you don't mind."

Scumble rolled his eyes. Megan would undoubtedly be better at handling her, Eleanor thought. It was a pity she wasn't here—but she'd be better at handling Stella, too. "No hurry," Scumble had told her, so she was probably keeping Stella out of the way till summoned. Eleanor hoped she wasn't having too difficult a time of it. Or perhaps she was deliberately encouraging hysteria, real or not, both to delay their return to the office and in hope of an inadvertent admission.

"Polmenna, take notes. Miss Jamieson, tell me about this emergency you had last night."

"I wasn't here, sir. I have the nine-to-five shift."

"But you know about it."

"Well, then, I do. Mrs Hendred, that's on one to nine in the morning, told me what Gloria—Miss Flitch—who works five till one told her. I did notice Colonel Nesbit didn't have much appetite for his lunch and he drank several cups of tea at tea-time. I mentioned it to Gloria—and she said she'd keep an eye on him."

"What do these symptoms signify?"

"He's diabetic, you see. It could be just a temporary quirk but both together could mean his insulin dose needed upping. By dinner-time he had other symptoms that made it obvious he was suffering from hyperglycemia—that's high blood sugar. Gloria did a test but she didn't like to give him more insulin on her own initiative, because he was already on a very high dose, so she rang Dr Fenwick. He came at once. He was a very good doctor. I can't believe he's dead." Her already reddened eyes filled with tears.

"That's enough for now," Scumble said hurriedly. "We'll have to talk to you again later, and to Miss Flitch, of course. Thank you."

Nick was obviously dying to speak, like a schoolboy waving his hand for his teacher's attention. He restrained himself until the nurse was well out of the room, then said, "One is sickened by too little insulin, the other dies of too much. As you said, Inspector, she just didn't think it through. You really ought to talk to Maybelle now."

"Go see if you can persuade her I don't bite!"

"What, never?" Nick skedaddled before Scumble could respond.

"I don't understand," Meadowes said plaintively. "Surely, Inspector, you're not accusing—"

"I'm not ready to make any accusations in front of a lawyer, sir." As he spoke, he took out a notebook and started jotting down what Eleanor assumed were notes to himself, perhaps reminders of questions he wanted to ask. Without looking up, he continued, "I'm afraid you'll have to wait a little longer, unless Mrs Trewynn would care to explain to you."

"Mrs Trewynn?" the solicitor appealed.

"Oh dear, I think I've got it all worked out, but whether I can keep it straight is another matter. First, I'm sure you can't be aware that Stella was leading a double life."

Scumble raised his head and looked at her in surprise.

"Well, what would you call it?" she asked defensively.

"No, no, you're quite right. I just hadn't looked at it in quite that way before. Go on."

Put off her stride by the knowledge that he was listening to her, Eleanor bravely went on. "Here, she was a respectable nurse, Miss Weller, and as such Dr Fenwick employed her. In Padstow she was a sculptress, known as Stella Maris, and she lived what I'm afraid I can only call a rather irregular life, even by today's standards."

"Good heavens!" Meadowes wiped his forehead.

"Or perhaps not. I'm not entirely certain what today's standards are. If any. To put it bluntly, she lived with a fellow-artist, a painter, and it seems she was not faithful even to him." Eleanor felt a need to wipe her own forehead. It was very difficult talking about such a subject to an old-fashioned gentleman who was so obviously deeply shocked.

The most he could summon up was a weak "tut-tut."

"Dr Fenwick fell for Stella and proposed to her. I didn't know him, so I can't say whether she might have been in love with him."

"A very personable chap," Meadowes uttered, "but considerably older."

"And richer," Eleanor said dryly. "It seems probable, judging by her subsequent actions, that she told her lover and he threatened to tell the doctor of her liaison. Perhaps she didn't realise how jealous he would be. At any rate, it would appear that she stabbed him to death, previously arranging matters so that suspicion would fall on someone else, someone against whom she had a grudge."

"Dear me, dear me!"

"It seems possible, as Mr Scumble suggested, that she didn't consider what would happen when the scapegoat was released. I tend to think she knew she would come under suspicion but she expected the process to take long enough for her to escape into her other life. She was the respectable Nurse Weller. She was to become the even more respectable Mrs Fenwick, whereupon she'd be off to Greece for a couple of weeks. By the time she returned, the hue and cry should have died down."

"Most unlikely. Most improvident," Meadowes asserted, as if a client had gone against his advice in the matter of some investment.

"She didn't think ahead. Or no further than to decide she'd rather be a rich widow than a rich wife. Again she prepared a clever snare, this time one that would kill her husband in her absence and after the passage of a period of time such that his death would not, she hoped, be connected with that of her lover. But again, she didn't think far enough ahead, didn't work out all the consequences of her actions."

"Spot on, Mrs Trewynn," Scumble congratulated her. "At least, that's pretty much how I see it. But you're out of time."

Nick ushered in Maybelle, who looked even more nervous and upset than had Miss Jamieson.

Scumble bared his teeth in what he probably thought was a friendly smile and made his best effort at geniality. "Come in, come in, Miss Maybelle. I'm hoping you can tidy up a few loose ends for me."

She turned scared eyes to Nick. "Loose ends? I don't know nuthin' about loose ends. You said—"

"It's just a fancy way of saying 'things he doesn't know,'" Nick reassured her.

Reluctantly, Maybelle sat down and gave her full name. Once she got started, however, her story was clearly and smoothly told. One of her duties was to disinfect the dispensary—she pointed at a door that Eleanor hadn't noticed before, on the far side of the office, first thing every morning. On Monday, she had gone in and found Miss Weller there. Miss Weller, who seemed flustered, had explained that she had neglected a couple of tasks she should have seen to on Sunday evening. She told Maybelle to come back in a few minutes.

"But I seen what she was doing, sir. She thinks I'm stupid, but I learn what I can. I want to be a nurse someday. She was messin' with hyperdermies, them needles you use for injections, takin' stuff outa one bottle and squirting it into another one. I didn't think nuthin' of it then, but when I come in this morning and they tole me the colonel'd been took ill 'cause of not gettin' enough insulin, I guessed that was what she been messin' with. Only I didn't say nuthin' 'cause they might've said I shoulda tole right away."

And then she had gone upstairs to tidy the doctor's flat and found him dead in his bed. Small wonder she was scared to death.

"Thank you, Maybelle, you've been very helpful," Scumble said triumphantly. "I hope, later on, you'll be able to show us exactly what Miss Weller was doing, since you're obviously an excellent observer. We'll take a formal statement then, for you to sign, but for now that will be all."

"You mean I can go?"

"You can." The inspector bared his fearsome grin again. "And once more, thank you for your cooperation."

"That weren't so bad," Maybelle said to Nick as she passed him on the way to the door.

"Didn't I tell you he's almost human at times?" said Nick.

This time Scumble's teeth were bared in a snarl, but as Nick had successfully persuaded the girl to talk to him, he could hardly complain.

"Polmenna, fetch Miss Weller," he growled.

"Am I to understand, Inspector," ventured Meadowes, looking as if the world had crashed about his ears, "that Miss Weller deliberately switched Dr Fenwick's insulin with that of this colonel?"

"She might have given the colonel plain water," said Scumble, "being hurried because of Maybelle's interrupting. That would hasten his collapse, if I'm not mistaken. She doesn't seem to have considered the effect of her plan on the colonel. That, of course, was what brought Dr Fenwick here three weeks before . . . Hush, here she comes."

Stella made a magnificent entrance, supported by Megan. She should have been wearing Victorian widow's weeds, with a black veil, Eleanor thought. She sank weakly into a chair.

"The one thing that makes it endurable," she announced in a throbbing voice, "is that Freddy went to meet his maker knowing he had provided for me. If he was conscious at the last, it must have been a great consolation to him."

Scumble, Nick, and Eleanor looked at Meadowes.

"Er." The solicitor tugged at his tie, suddenly too tight. "Er, I'm afraid not, Miss Weller."

"What?" she screeched, turning on him. "What the hell are you talking about? He told me he signed his new will, leaving everything to me. Don't tell me the old coot was lying!"

"No indeed, no indeed. He did sign the will and it does indeed name you as chief beneficiary, but you in—as it were—your future role as Mrs Fenwick. As Stella Weller, you have no claim whatsoever upon his estate."

Now Stella rounded on Eleanor. "This is all your fault, you meddlesome old bitch. If you hadn't given Nick an alibi—" She rushed forward, outstretched hands ready to claw.

Rising swiftly from her seat, Eleanor raised her arms between Stella's. Stepping diagonally forwards and to her right, with her right arm she knocked Stella's left arm down. Stella's chin collided with Eleanor's left forearm and she staggered backwards. Before Eleanor had to take any further measures to protect herself, Megan and Polmenna grabbed Stella by the arms and pulled her away.

Nick sprang to steady Eleanor—not that she needed it. Teazle stopped barking and tried frantically to climb up her. Eleanor picked her up and had her face thoroughly licked.

"Aunt Nell, are you all right?" Megan shouted over Stella's vituperation.

"Quite all right, dear." Rather shakily, Eleanor dusted herself down. She never expected to actually have to use her Aikido in peaceful old England. How lucky she kept in practice! And the whole thing had happened quickly enough, she hoped, that everyone would assume she'd escaped the attack by sheer luck. She had no desire to be known as a martial arts aficionado.

"Stella Weller," Scumble's cold voice cut through the din, "you're under arrest for attempted assault. Further charges may follow. You have the right to remain silent but anything you choose to say will be taken down and may be used in evidence. Polmenna, Wilkes, take her out."

Eleanor sat down. "Good gracious," she said, "if that's how she behaves when she's really in a passion, I'm not surprised poor Geoffrey always gave in to her. She's certainly showed her true colours."

Megan surprised herself by saying, "'The man who has no music in him . . . is fit for treasons, stratagems, and spoils.' And woman, too. I noticed, in her room, she doesn't even have a transistor radio."

"Well I never," said Meadowes. "Well I never."

"Well I never," said Jocelyn. "And I thought a Mothers' Union meeting was hazardous. My dear Eleanor, I never would have asked you to go if I'd dreamt—"

"Of course you wouldn't, Joce."

"Eleanor, would you like this last bit of chicken dopiaza?" asked Nick.

"No, dear, you eat it. I'm FTB and TTT."

"Eleanor, really!"

"Come on, Mrs Stearns, she didn't say 'full to bursting' or 'tummy touching table.' Surely the acronyms are acceptable?"

"From children."

"I must say," Eleanor quickly intervened, "these take-away meals are a wonderful value. Much cheaper than eating in the restaurant. Oh, there goes the phone. I hope the reporters haven't caught up with us yet."

"Don't answer," Nick advised.

"It's probably Timothy, wondering if I'm going to get back in time for the parish council. I'll get it."

Jocelyn went to the phone. "Oh, hello, Mr Alarian. No, this is Eleanor's friend, Mrs Stearns . . . No, we haven't had the pleasure . . . Yes, she's right here . . . Nicholas Gresham? Yes, as a matter of fact he's here, too . . . Nicholas?"

Nick was already at her side, reaching for the receiver. "Mr Alarian, Gresham here."

Eleanor waited in an agony of anticipation while he listened to the art dealer talking, his face a study in incredulity. She couldn't be sure whether he was delighted or horrified. What if some disaster had overtaken another two of his best paintings?

At last he said, "A conductor, sir? No, I've never heard of him . . . Oh, I see. Thank you, sir. And thank you for letting me know so promptly . . . Yes, of course, I'll ship another two to you tomorrow . . . Yes, insured . . . Yes, here she is. And thank you, sir. Good-bye."

Eleanor was forced to listen to several minutes of rhapsody in Alarian's eclectic accents before she was able to hang up, turn to Nick, and exchange big hugs. He started to waltz her about the room but it really was too small for such activity.

"Both of them!" he crowed.

"Congratulations, Nicholas. I couldn't help overhearing—to a conductor?"

"A wealthy amateur patron of the arts who supports a local orchestra in exchange for being permitted to conduct it. Not Giulini, perhaps, but he paid the full price without argument." Nick sat down rather suddenly. "I can hardly believe it!"

The phone rang again. Eleanor answered it.

"Aunt Nell, I've been worrying about you."

"Megan dear, I'm perfectly all right, truly. I've just overeaten enormously."

"Did you go to the Indian?"

"Yes, we got take-away in the end. Such a pity you couldn't join us."

"I'm still writing reports. But the gov'nor's so pleased to have put one over on DI Pearce that he's actually gone to the length of giving me tomorrow off. I'll come over and see you."

"That would be lovely, dear. Come to lunch. I'll get something special that doesn't require complicated cooking."

"Lovely. And we'll take Teazle for a walk afterwards if it's fine?"

"If that's what you'd like. Or you can put your feet up and relax. You've been working awfully hard for the past week. We'll decide when you get here."

"Right. Good night, Aunt Nell. Sweet dreams. Don't think about you know who."

"I'll try, dear. Good night."

Eleanor hung up and turned to find that Jocelyn had dashed off to her parish council meeting. Nick was clearing up the mess of boxes and papers and foil.

"Nothing left but half a paratha," he said. "I've given a bit to Teazle."

Teazle sat at his feet, tail wagging, gazing up at him hopefully.

"No more," Eleanor said severely. "It's hard to believe I'll ever want to eat again, but Megan's coming to lunch tomorrow. I'm hoping she'll fill in the gaps, because I don't feel I've quite got a grasp yet of exactly what Stella did. Do say you'll join us? I thought you'd want to give her the news from London yourself."

"Do you think she'd be interested?" Nick asked doubtfully.

"It's part of the case, after all, your visit to Mr Alarian."

Eleanor thought of Jeanette, a painter like Nick, with similar interests, who fancied herself in love with him. Would she suit him better than Megan? She was so angry at the world, but in time that would fade now that Geoffrey Clark was dead. Perhaps her infatuation with Nick would fade, too, and with a new perspective on life, she might turn to poor Tom Lennox.

Tom Lennox: Eleanor had plans for him. She must go back to

the farm and talk to him about sharing his skills with the primitive potters of Africa.

"Well, if you think it won't bore her, I'll be happy to come and do a little boasting about my national and international triumphs." Nick grinned. "I'll try to get hold of some Champagne at last, the real thing!"

Policewoman and artist—an odd couple, perhaps, but Eleanor still had hopes . . .

Manna from Hades

by Carola Dunn

The first in the charming crime series set in 1960's Cornwall featuring
amateur sleuth and charity shop worker, Eleanor Trewynn and
her westie Teazle.

After a lifetime of travel and experiences, widow Eleanor Trewynn is more
than happy to retire to the sleepy village of Port Mabyn in Cornwall - but
unfortunately, excitement seems to follow her around!

Her friend and neighbour, artist Nick Gresham, discovers several of his
paintings in his shop have been slashed and destroyed. The finger of
suspicion rests on rival local artist Geoffrey Monmouth but when
Nick and Eleanor go to have it out with him, they find Monmouth's
stabbed body in his studio – and Nick is immediately flagged
up as most likely suspect. But is he the only candidate
with a compelling motive for murder...

'*Manna from Hades* is the modern-day version of the
classic English village mystery.' *Kirkus Reviews*

Valley of the Shadow

by Carola Dunn

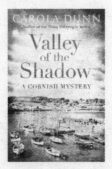

The third in the charming crime series set in 1960's Cornwall featuring amateur sleuth and charity shop worker, Eleanor Trewynn and her westie Teazle.

A cryptic message spurs Eleanor on a frantic search for a refugee's missing family.

While walking her dog with friends, Eleanor rescues a young half-drowned Asian man out the water. Delerious and concussed, he talks about his family being trapped in a cave. While the young man, unconscious by this stage, is whisked away to a hospital, a desperate effort is mounted to find the family of which he spoke.

The local police inspector presumes they are refugees from East Africa, abandoned by the traffickers who brought them in, so while the countryside is being scoured for the family, Eleanor herself descends into a dangerous den of smugglers in a desperate search to find the man responsible while there is still time.

Damsel in Distress

by Carola Dunn

Simply mad about the girl...

In spring a young man's fancy will turn to love and the Honourable
Phillip Petrie is no exception. Daisy's chum is totally smitten with
Miss Gloria Arbuckle, daughter of a millionaire Yank. But before the
enthusiastic suitor can pop the question, his beloved is abducted
by kidnappers. As a distraught Mr Arbuckle begins assembling the
ransom, Phillip enlists Daisy to help him recover his missing sweetheart.
Strictly forbidden to contact Scotland Yard, Daisy must resist the
temptation to bring dashing Detective Inspector Alec Fletcher onto
the case. But as she closes in on the abductors' rural hideway, she
begins to suspect that Gloria isn't the only fair damsel whose life
hangs in the balance...

The fifth book in the Daisy Dalrymple series

'Engaging...Dunn's style gives an entertaining spark.'
Publishers Weekly

Dead in the Water

by Carola Dunn

May the best man die!

July, 1923, and Daisy has been invited by an American magazine to
cover the Henley Regatta. But unknown to her, she steps right into a
class war between two members of the Oxford rowing team. Cox
Horace Bott – a shopkeeper's son and scholar student – has always
hated rower Basil DeLancy – younger son of an earl and all-round
cad and bully. And after a particularly brutal public humiliation by
DeLancy, Bott swears revenge – so when DeLancy keels over and
dies mid-race, it would seem he's made good on his promise.
Yet Daisy isn't convinced, and with the help of her fiancé Detective
Inspector Alec Fletcher of Scotland Yard, she dives into a tangled
web of jealousies and secrets, where appearances are everything and
good breeding may just be a cover for a killer intent on keeping
Daisy mum forever…

The sixth book in the Daisy Dalrymple series

'A dauntless Daisy and good-natured fun.' *Kirkus Reviews*